Raven

by

Charmaine Mainwaring

For James Edward Round & Evelyn Round

Cherry Haycock & James Haycock

Richard Mainwaring

*In a violent age of warrior kings, Raven tells a tale
of bloody rivalry and undeniable love.*

Contents

Title Page

Copyright

Dedication

Epigraph

Part 1   1

1.1   2

Part 2   17

2.1   18

2.2   26

2.3   33

2.4   38

2.5   43

2.6   52

Part 3   64

3.1   65

3.2   70

3.3   87

3.4   92

3.5   104

3.6   118

3.7	128
Part 4	134
4.1	135
4.2	153
4.3	169
4.4	175
4.5	185
4.6	200
Part 5	207
5.1	208
5.2	225
5.3	232
Part 6	237
6.1	238
6.2	256
6.3	263
6.4	275
6.5	280
6.6	291
6.7	297
6.8	308
Part 7	324
7.1	325
7.2	328
7.3	340
7.4	356
7.5	361
7.6	369

Part 8   380
8.1   381
About The Author   399
Books In This Series   401

Place Names

10th Century

Jorvic
Alba
Ath Cliath
Cenheardsburg
Folesfight
Isle of Clouds
Brunnanburg
Gailgedhael
Galwensis
Ivarr's Green   Hingars Green
Earlsness
Poclinton
Richalle
Birca
Hesslport
Anlafsburgh
Blacarscroft
Cymru, Walensis
Isle of Mona
Trevf

21st Century

York
Scotland
Dublin
Knaresborough
Folifoot
Isle of Skye

Nunburnholm
Norse Galloway
Alban Galloway
Hoggen Green
Holderness
Pocklington
Riccal
Birka, Bjorko
Hessle
Anlaby
Blacktoft
Wales
Anglesey
Threave

Part 1

The Archbishop

1.1

Cenheardsburg
Summer 934AD

Entering her father's meeting hall, known by the locals as the Doomhalla, Lady Rafyn instinctively placed her hands on her two sword pommels. Her pale blue gown swished against her slender legs as she walked, past her eight older brothers, towards the raised dais.

Her father Earl Cenheard, sat at the far end of the hall with his guests.

The archbishop's voice tinged with tedium, "Incredible engineering, very impressive defences, your fortress is magnificent my dear Earl Cenheard. May I take a walk around the palisade later?"

Beaming as she approached, Cenheard enjoyed the flattery, "Archbishop, may I introduce my daughter, Lady Rafyn of Cenheardsburg?"

She smiled as she gracefully walked up to her father and curtseyed elegantly.

Proudly, Cenheard continued, "Lady Rafyn, may I present the new Archbishop of Jorvic. His Grace, Wulfstan."

Casting an inquisitive glance at him, she hid her surprise. He was not at all what she had expected. He was perhaps, in his early thirties and quite robust for a man of the cloth. He dressed in black battle leathers. She noticed, slightly hidden by his long green cape, a well maintained sword and dagger hanging from his belt.

His black shoulder length hair hung limply about his dour face. He looked back at her with dark emotionless eyes.

Cenheard beamed, "Daughter, you remember Jarl Orm and his son Gamel?"

"Of course father." Curtseying deeply she looked up into the Jarl's smiling blue eyes, "I hope this day finds you both well my lords."

The archbishop's eyes glinted wearisomely.

Beaming, Cenheard turned to the archbishop, "What do you think of my daughter Your Grace? Does she equal the ladies at court?"

Looking over Lady Rafyn as if she was a horse, his dark eyes glinted coldly, tedium hung on every word, "A good height for a woman, I suppose. Shining hair, good teeth and unblemished skin. Remarkably handsome eyes. Her weapons are a status symbol I presume?" Not waiting for an answer, waving his hand dismissively. His eyes met hers. He paused for a moment as his heart rate quickened. Desire filled his eyes as he took in a deep breath through open lips. He conceded gruffly, "Quite lovely."

Surprised to see such changing emotions in a man of the cloth, she demurely lowered her eyes.

Cenheard smiled, "May I introduce my sons, Archbishop?"

Whilst Lord Cenheard introduced him to a never ending supply of battle dressed sons, Archbishop Wulfstan looked jaded. He felt sick of the incessant but necessary travelling, to every hamlet and burgh in Northumbria, to drum up support for his great ambition. Finally, the youngest son stepped back and he turned to Earl Cenheard. He almost snarled, "I have news. The English Prince Edwin, King Athelstan's half-brother, has been drowned at sea."

A surprised look flashed over Lord Cenheard's face, broodingly, "Some say that Prince Edwin was the rightful King of England."

Wulfstan nodded, "Indeed they do Lord Cenheard. Prince Edwin attempted to seize the throne from his brother." His black eyes hardened, "Treason is punishable by death and this time King Athelstan showed no mercy."

Listening to them, Lady Rafyn stepped forward. Her pale blue gown brushed against her legs. Adjusting the two short swords that hung on her sword belt, confident in her standing to question the men, she spoke up clearly, "I had heard that King Athelstan is illegitimate. I have never understood how he could have united the southern lands."

Wulfstan eyed her sharply, "How dare you even attempt join in a conversation about politics! Be quiet woman!

Her dark eyes smouldered with antagonism, "Archbishop! I am an unmarried land owner and it is my judicial right to be treated as Lord of my domain. I have every right to speak at my own pleasure, just as my father does!"

Spittle flew from Wulfstan's lips, "Do not quote judicial law to me woman!"

Jumping to his daughter's defence, Lord Cenheard thumped his fist onto the arm rest of his high backed chair, menacingly, "Archbishop Wulfstan, my daughter is a woman of status. As Earl of her own land, she out ranks all of her brothers." Loudly, "If my daughter wishes to speak about politics then she will do so!"

Unmoved, Wulfstan's dark eyes glanced at Cenheard's sons. The eight men each looked like a younger dark haired version of Lord Cenheard.

They looked back at him impassively.

Silence hung in the dimly lit room. Only a few black wrought iron candelabras helped to light the hall.

Knowing he was beaten his eyebrows lifted condescendingly. He would never have allowed a woman in his family to surpass his power. A snarl formed on his top lip, as he eyed her slight figure and the two swords on her sword belt. He thought furiously to himself, women are only fit to breed!

Ignoring the tension on the room, Rafyn continued evenly, as if nothing had happened, "How can Athelstan be High King of Britain?"

Jarl Orm pushed back his white blonde hair, "My Lady, it is a story which commenced in the southern lands many years ago, in the reign of King Alfred the Great of Wessex." He paused a moment to take a sip of fragrant berry wine, "When King Alfred's son, Prince Edward, came of age he took to his bed a concubine of inferior Kentish nobility. Her name was Ecgwina and by all accounts, she was exquisitely beautiful."

His voice tinged with tedium, Wulfstan interjected sullenly, "Some say he had a handfast marriage with her but it was not proven. In any case, it was apparent to all that Edward loved her deeply and he soon begot a son on her."

Cenheard inclined his head, "My father once told me that it was well known that King Alfred adored his first grandchild. The boy favoured him in golden haired looks."

Orm smiled too, "King Alfred himself chose the baby's name. The name Athelstan means 'noble stone.'"

Irritably, Wulfstan glanced sideways at the Jarl, "Soon after, Prince Edward fathered another child on Ecgwina. The baby girl was called Eadgytha."

Jarl Orm continued, "King Alfred was ageing and riddled with disease. He felt the need to secure his dynasty. You see, he was the youngest of four brothers, each of whom had been king before him."

Glaring more pointedly at the interruption, Wulfstan continued wearisomely, "Alfred's elder brother's sons, Aethelwold and Aethelhelm, were children when he first became king. Now grown up, they gazed at the throne of Wessex coveting their lost inheritance."

Cenheard nodded, "King Alfred wanted the throne for his own son and dynasty. Athelstan was only five years old when King Alfred bequeathed to him the royal purple cloak and a small sword of state."

Looking at him perplexed, Rafyn asked softly, "Is this a ceremony of some sort?"

Archbishop Wulfstan's black eyes gazed at her as she took a seat. It was obvious that beneath her pale blue gown her young lithe body was lovely. Watching her with a predatory gaze, he nodded, "Yes it is my Lady. It is a very important ritual of the

Wessex royal family, to distinguish the potential heirs of the throne."

Interjecting bluntly, Cenheard stated, "More importantly to King Alfred, the nobles of the court clearly understood his message with that act. Athelstan may not be born in purple. He may even be illegitimate. However, his eldest grandson carried his blue blood and would have the status of a prince."

Continuing tersely, Wulfstan added, "It was not long after the ceremony, Lady Ecgwina and her two children were sent away from court."

Lifting her head in surprise, Rafyn turned to him confidently addressing him, "Archbishop, where were they sent to?"

He uttered broodingly, "They were sent to the protection of King Alfred's daughter, Princess Aethelflaed, the Lady of Mercia." Wafting his jewelled hand in a circular movement, he elaborated, "Lady Aethelflaed was married young to her cousin, Lord Aethelred, the last of the line of the old Kings of Mercia. Lady Aethelflaed had given him a healthy daughter but her labour had left her barren. There would be no sons."

His dark eyes glinting, Cenheard looked at his daughter, "King Alfred decreed that as a 'Prince of the Realm', Athelstan was to be groomed by his aunt and uncle in all kingly ways. One day Mercia would be his to govern."

Coldly, Wulfstan continued, "As much as she privately cried for her loss, Ecgwina could do nothing. King Alfred had convinced his son to cast her aside and marry a young noble woman called Aelfflaed."

Speaking softly, she looked at her father, "Why would King Alfred separate the lovers?"

Looking at her gently, he answered, "Aelfflaed was a royal Atheling princess. She was Prince Aethelhelm's thirteen year old daughter."

She frowned, "Father, do you mean King Alfred's nephew Aethelhelm?"

"Yes. By marrying his son Edward to Aelfflaed, King Alfred secured his nephew Aethelhelm's support."

Looking shocked, she blinked, "This marriage was a strategic move to secure the throne for his son?"

"Yes Rafyn."

Disbelief shone in her eyes as she looked at her father.

Jarl Orm smiled roguishly, "Don't look so surprised my dear. It happens all the time in affairs of state." Turning to Cenheard he stated, "You have sheltered your daughter from the strategies of courtly marriages."

Ignoring the remark, Cenheard continued the tale, "Edward's new wife was soon pregnant. Queen Aelfflaed made no secret of her jealous hate for her rival Ecgwina and her children."

Jarl Orm nodded, "Aelfflaed relentlessly referred to Ecgwina as 'the shepherdess' claiming that she was little more than a peasant."

Waving his hand dismissively, Wulfstan cut in, "This was untrue of course. Ecgwina was a noble, the daughter an Ealdorman, a descendant of the Kings of Kent."

Interjecting, Orm added, "She was not however, an Atheling. So to Aelfflaed, Ecgwina was inferior in status."

Eyeing Jarl Orm coldly, Wulfstan continued, "The Lady of Mercia adopted Prince Athelstan and he was schooled with her daughter. She paraded the two children together at every chance. The Mercian people and their nobles adored them."

Picking up his goblet of wine, Cenheard pondered, "A few months later, King Alfred died too. As the old king had wisely predicted his other nephew, Aethelwold, raised an army. Aethelwold attempted to overthrow the newly crowned King Edward. He even called upon the support of his brother." He inclined his head, "Aethelhelm unsurprisingly supported his daughter Queen Aelfflaed. Aethelhelm knew, he would never have the crown but at least his grandson would be king. Aethelwold's rebellion failed and he was put to death for his treachery."

Wulfstan sipped his gloriously tasting berry wine, "Then of course, the Lady of Mercia died. Her husband had died years before. Her daughter, the heiress of Mercia, tried to fill her mother's shoes but she was weak. King Edward did not stand for his niece's ambition to rule Mercia. He captured her and had her locked away in a nunnery."

Pursing her lips, Rafyn eyed him.

Sweeping back his lank dark hair, he unflinchingly locked eyes with her.

Cenheard inclined his head, "Over the years, Queen Aelfflaed delivered many more children to King Edward. Later, after her death, Edward married again. His new queen was named Aelgifu and King Edward fathered two more sons on her."

Carefully placing his wine onto the side table, Wulfstan held up his hand signalling the importance of his next statement, "Yes, King Edward reigned for twenty five years. On his deathbed in the year 924AD, King Edward bequeathed his kingdom of Wessex to his eldest legitimate son. Born of Queen Aelfflaed, Prince Aethelweard was anointed King of Wessex."

Interrupting him, Cenheard did not notice the exasperated look on Wulfstan's face, "Most of the nobles of the court believed that old King Edward would leave the sub-kingdom of Mercia to Queen Aelfflaed's second son Prince Edwin."

Cutting in, Jarl Orm stated quickly, "King Edward knew that the people of Mercia would never accept Prince Edwin, a noble of Wessex, as their overlord." His eyebrows rose up, "There would be war. With his last breath, King Edward was true to his first love Ecgwina. He gave the sub-kingdom of Mercia to Prince Athelstan."

Softly, Cenheard added, "Unfortunately, only a few weeks into his reign, King Aethelweard died. Aethelweard's fourteen year old brother Prince Edwin, hastily attempted to seize the throne."

His eyes slanting, the archbishop jumped in, "But the powerful bishops refused to crown him." Looking at Lady Rafyn, he watched her reaction as he spoke, "Certain evidence pointed to Edwin as King Aethelweard's murderer."

Taking in a deep appalled breath, she whispered, "He killed his own brother?"

Wulfstan's cold eyes narrowed wickedly, "King Edward's other legitimate sons, the princes Edmund and Edred, by Queen Aelgifu were still infants." He paused, "But there was another. Even though he was not born to an anointed queen, Prince Athelstan was acknowledged as King Edward's firstborn son. He was also recognised as the eldest grandson of King Alfred the Great."

A smile played on Jarl Orm's lips, he nodded, "And, he had been given the royal purple cloak, by King Alfred himself. So it was possible that he could be ordained king."

His eyes glinting, Cenheard continued, "In 925AD the bishops met to choose their king. Many of the younger nobles of Wessex supported Prince Edwin. He held the majority vote of Wessex. But at fourteen years of age, he already had a reputation for being malicious, violent and depraved. He was already called, by some, the murderer of his brother. He was however born to an anointed queen."

Glaring at him, Wulfstan added tersely, "He was reckless and sinful!" Tediously, "Because he had been born in Wessex, and favoured by King Alfred, many of the older Wessex noblemen gave their allegiance to Prince Athelstan."

Orm stretched his muscular leather clad legs out. He casually crossed his leather booted feet and relaxed back into his chair, "The powerful Mercian contingent backed Athelstan of course. But the vote was still tight."

Wulfstan sucked in a deep breath, "Born of the Lady of Kent, Prince Athelstan also had the backing of the less powerful Kent nobles. He represented all three factions of the southern land." Calculatingly, "Most important to the bishops though, Athelstan is a devout and pious Christian. The final vote fell to the bishops. They anointed Athelstan as king and succeeded in uniting the royal houses of Wessex, Mercia and Kent."

Pushing back his white blond hair again, Jarl Orm looked up, "King Athelstan named his united land England. He chose his colours, a white dragon on a crimson field."

His brown eyes twinkling, Cenheard took up the account again, "A few months later King Athelstan was attacked and his bodyguard killed. He escaped though, narrowly avoiding the serious attempt on his life."

Orm added softly, "It was proven that his half-brother, Edwin, had instigated the attack."

Nodding, Cenheard continued, "King Athelstan was merciful and he forgave his young half-brother but he realised that he needed to quickly fortify his position. Word reached him that the Norse King of Northumbria was raising an army against him. Athelstan realised that he must ensure an unchallenged rule in England. Therefore, he needed the support of the Northumbrian Vikings."

Orm looked uneasy, "To this end King Athelstan offered his blood sister, Princess Eadgytha, in marriage to Sihtric, the Viking King of Jorvic and Northumbria."

Surprised, Rafyn's dark arching eyebrows rose up.

Lifting his goblet of wine, Wulfstan shook his head wearily. He eyed Lady Rafyn, "She was the start of all our troubles. I warned him against marrying her but he would not hear me."

Watching the archbishop intently as he took another sip of his wine.

He looked back at her thoughtfully. His mouth opened as he felt the quickened heartbeat of attraction. He attempted a smile of sorts.

Looking away quickly, she sipped her wine.

Misconstruing her aversion for feminine coyness, he gazed lingeringly at her for a moment longer, "King Sihtric had been widowed for five years when news came of Athelstan's surprising offer. A prestigious marriage to a princess of the southern lands, illegitimate or not, was more than any Norse King could hope for. His advisors talked excessively of Lady Eadgytha's great loveliness and grace. And of course, she carried the blue blood of King Alfred the Great. A great asset for any future sons." His eyes narrowing, Wulfstan continued coldly, "King

Sihtric was intrigued and against my advice, he agreed to meet the princess at the Mercian capital Tamworth. The first time he set eyes on Eadgytha, she delighted him with her refinement and beauty. He fell passionately in love with her."

Jarl Orm smiled, "I knew him well. He was a rough and coarse follower of Odin and Thor, but he would do anything to possess her, even convert to the Christian faith."

Glaring at him for the interruption, Wulfstan grunted, "However, within one year of their marriage, King Sihtric had turned back to his old pagan ways. Pious Eadgytha refused to have him near her and he angrily abandoned her. A short time later, King Sihtric was found dead." Shrewdly, he eyed them, "I am convinced, poisoned by her hand but I could not prove it."

They all looked back at him silently contemplating that.

"By 926AD, Athelstan's fortunes had changed and he was in a much stronger position in his united England. Receiving word from his sister of the events in Northumbria, he seized his chance. He marched his army north to rescue her." Wulfstan eyed them belligerently, "Sihtric had a five year old son Prince Olaf, begot on his first wife. I quickly crowned Prince Olaf as Jorvic's king. I had hoped that upon seeing the child king, pious King Athelstan would not have him killed." He shook his head tediously, "I also sent word to Sihtric's brother requesting aid. Hearing of his brother Sihtric's death, King Guthrith of Ath Cliath immediately sailed for Jorvic. King Guthrith arrived the day King Athelstan attacked." Wulfstan's dark eyes glazed darkly as he remembered that long ago day.

Lady Rafyn watched the archbishop's changing emotions.

Wulfstan frowned, "My great city did not last long under siege. King Athelstan crushed Jorvic. The boy, King Olaf went into hiding. Athelstan was now the undisputed King of England and Northumbria."

Jarl Orm eyed them, "With subterfuge, King Olaf and the boy's faithful bodyguard Jarl Canute escaped. Under cover of darkness they boarded a ship and fled by sea."

Wulfstan glared, "Meanwhile, King Guthrith was forced to

kneel before King Athelstan. Eventually, Guthrith converted to the one true faith and after signing a treaty, he was released to go back to Ireland." He added bitterly, "And we were left with an English King!" He flicked his lank hair away from his face, "King Athelstan was thirty one years old and in his prime. To him, taking Northumbria had been too easy. He saw his chance to rule Britain as Emperor. Rich on Jorvic gold, he continued travelling north, attacking each kingdom in turn. Ealdred King of the Tees was the first to submit. Then Owain of the Cumbrians knelt before King Athelstan. Mailcoluim of Alban Galwensis yielded next."

Nonchalantly, Orm added, "Athelstan did not venture into the dark hills of Norse Gailgedhael but turned instead to Alba."

Frowning at him, Wulfstan continued, "After Constantine the King of Alba had laid down his arms, Athelstan turned back south west. Next, he took the four Welsh kingdoms ruled by Hywel Dda, Idwal Foel, Twdyrr and Wurgeat. Each king had a choice, kneel and pledge their allegiance to Athelstan or suffer his wrath."

Animated from the story, Lord Gamel interrupted excitedly, "Hearing of Athelstan's mighty victory, the western Cornwall Celts knelt to his power without even a battle! Athelstan is the first High King of Anglo-Saxon Britain!"

In unison, Wulfstan and Cenheard swung round and scowled at Gamel.

Surprised at Gamel's enthusiastic interruption, a smile played on Rafyn's lips.

Blinking with awkwardness, flushing deep red, he sheepishly looked at her, then his father.

She glanced at Jarl Orm to see is reaction. He shook his head feigning fatherly embarrassment. Her lips twitched as she forced back a giggle.

Turning away from Gamel with a disgusted expression, Wulfstan quietly predicted, "But it will not end there. We Northerners cannot stomach a southern king for long."

All of the men in the room murmured in agreement.

Coldly, Orm stated, "And now Prince Edwin is dead. He made another attempt on King Athelstan's life and paid the ultimate price for his treachery."

Thoughtfully, Cenheard looked up, "So, both of Aethelhelm's grandsons are dead. At least his blood line will continue through his many daughters' marriages to the European Kings."

Lifting his goblet of wine confidently, Wulfstan continued, "There is serious news hailing from Ath Cliath." The room was silent, "King Guthrith of the Norse is dying. They say from a horrible illness of the stomach."

Listening in the shadows, Cenheard's brother-in-law Ragenhare, walked forward, "I know King Guthrith's sons, Anlaf and Black Arailt. I met them when I travelled to the Isle of the Clouds. They were studying the art of long sword fighting."

Surprised, Wulfstan lifted his dark eyebrows as he cast his eyes over the man, "You have travelled to the mystical Isle of the Clouds?"

Jarl Orm sat up straight as a maid filled his goblet, then moved on to serve his son, "You have met the Viking Masters, Thord and Grani?"

Waving the maid away impatiently, Gamel looked at his father with a big awed grin on his face.

Smiling, Cenheard beckoned him forward, "Archbishop, may I introduce my brother-in-law, Earl Ragenhare of Hammerton. My brother-in-law travelled widely in his youth, studying martial arts and honing his battle skills."

Looking over Earl Ragenhare, noting his exceptional height, weapons and obvious alertness, he immediately recognised the stance of the warrior, "Very remarkable. You have met Prince Anlaf?" The archbishop gestured for Ragenhare to come closer.

Standing still, Ragenhare eyed him obstinately. He silently rested his hands on the hilts of his two swords.

Regaining his imperious expression, showing no reaction to Earl Ragenhare's disobedience, Wulfstan murmured,

"Prince Anlaf is likely to be elected the next chief of the Clan Ivarr. That will make him ruler of the Norse of Britain and Ireland."

"There is no treaty between Anlaf and the English." Speculating, Cenheard added, "He may try to take Jorvic and Northumbria back from King Athelstan."

His dark eyes glinting, Wulfstan lifted his chin. They were starting to see his point without him committing treason by spelling it out.

Ragenhare was not surprised. He jutted his chin out confidently, "Black Arailt is King of the Isles of Man and Colonsay. He is also King of Norse Gaelgedhail. If Anlaf becomes King of Ath Cliath, he may give Northumbria to his youngest brother Prince Ragnal to rule. I for one would prefer a Norse King in Northumbria."

A muscle flickered in Jarl Orm's jaw, impulsively, "Earl Cenheard, I have known you for a long time. I know that you are also being hounded by the English nobility for outrageously high taxes. Earl Cenheard, the archbishop and I have come to Cenheardsburg to find out two things. One, can this fortified burgh really defend itself? The answer to this question had been a resounding yes. Two, does the burgh favour the English or Norse?"

Looking surprised at Jarl Orm's outspoken statement, Wulfstan shifted uncomfortably in his high backed chair. He kept to himself his burning ambition to see a Norse king rule Northumbria.

Thoughtfully, Cenheard spoke up, "King Guthrith's sons are ruthless but fiercely loyal to each other and their clan. And, let us not forget Prince Olaf Curan Sihtricsson. Old King Sihtric's son would now be fourteen years of age. He may make a bid for the Norse throne."

Sweeping back his unruly lank black hair, the archbishop stated knowingly, "King Sihtric's son is a contender but Prince Olaf has no kingdom or fortune, and he is still unproven in battle. I have heard though that he is very ambitious. He craves his lost inheritance." Taking in a deep breath, his dark eyes slanted. What he was about to confide could see him hung, "The Northumbrian Witan will back the Norse. They are even considering one the Norwegian King Fairhair's sons." He took in a short breath.

As unease filled him, Cenheard spoke carefully, "This would mean war with the English."

"Yes I agree," Wulfstan continued gravely, "so we must be careful. If you are called to a Witan election of a Norse king, Earl Cenheard, will you back the Witan?"

"Your Grace, the Witan has my backing."

Grudgingly, Wulfstan turned to Lady Rafyn, "As an earl of your own lands my Lady, you will be called to the Witan to vote. Does the Witan have your backing Lady Rafyn?"

Lifting her chin, she spoke clearly, "I will decide that when I meet your chosen man."

A smile played on Cenheard's lips. He knew that his daughter would always follow her own path.

Frustrated, Wulfstan eyed her belligerently for a moment. Sweeping back his lank hair, he huffed loudly. Turning to Ragenhare, "Earl Ragenhare, will you back the Witan?"

"Yes."

"Good." Looking over at the tall warrior thoughtfully, "Earl Ragenhare, we must talk more. Your knowledge may be of much use to our cause. May I meet with you later?"

Ragenhare thoughtfully eyed him.

"In point of fact," Wulfstan added quickly, "I may in the future call upon you to accompany me on my travels."

Hiding his surprise, Ragenhare nodded. He had been feeling restless lately and the thought of travelling again excited him. His green eyes glinted.

"There is more." Orm's eyes travelled the room as they all looked at him, "News has reached High King Athelstan, that King Constantine of Alba has refused to pay tribute. Obviously, King Athelstan must punish this transgression. It is an insult to his absolute power and a blatant break of their treaty. He has called his armies to his white dragon banner and ordered them north. Athelstan's armies include the forces of Walensis and the might of the Scandinavian settlers from the Five Boroughs. It is a massive show of strength."

Ragenhare looked at Cenheard. Both of their faces were stony with concern.

Grimly, Cenheard asked, "Which way do they travel?"

Drearily, Wulfstan eyed him, "They used Ermine Street and passed through Jorvic weeks ago to Dere Street."

Visibly relieved, Cenheard raised his goblet, "Thank all the Gods, they did not pass through here. Marching armies of men steal, ravage and rape!"

Lady Rafyn placed a hand on her sword pommel.

Brushing back his white blonde hair, Jarl Orm continued gravely, "We have heard that King Constantine marched two thousand men south to meet the English. The Albanacs fought well but they were no match against King Athelstan's army. They have been forced to retreat. I heard, only days ago, that Constantine has fled back to the east coast of Alba. He is now besieged at his great fortress, Dunnotter."

Part 2

The King of Alba

2.1

Dunnotter, Alba,
June 934AD

Towering high above the deep green crashing sea, the majestic craggy fortress of Dunnotter, stood unscathed and darkly dramatic. Floating on air currents, seagulls screeched as they circled above. Built on the peninsula's flat summit of the naturally defensive cliff, surrounded on three sides by ocean, only a sheer deep chasm of land bridged, what was almost an island, to the mainland of Alba. Natural rock earthworks and sheer faces of stone supported the massive timber castle.

Stood high in the wooden parapets, King Constantine regally surveyed the scene before him. Dressed in dark brown leather battle gear, his hard muscular body oozed leadership. His shoulder length, auburn hair, now showed more white hairs than red. Twinkling with intellect, his light topaz coloured eyes were still as piercingly sharp as ever. A man of true presence, he stood quietly, watching his men in the courtyard below. Most the men were young and dressed in full leather battle gear. A few of the more wealthy men wore fine chain mail tunics. Some were tending to their horses, or sharpening their weapons on whetstones. Dropping his head and closing his eyes, he took in a deep breath. He realised wearily for the first time that he was probably one of the oldest warriors still fighting.

A grizzled bear of a man stood next to him. Concern flickered into his blue eyes, "Are you well my King?"

With a sudden feeling of profound sadness, "Doungallus my friend, only a few of us old comrades from the early days are still alive."

Nodding his head understandingly, Doungallus looked over the parapet. He could see his two sons, Dubdon and Duncan, chatting together, happily working on repairing their shields. He smiled fondly, his voice deep, "Yes, the years have passed swiftly. Now our sons fight with us. We are getting old."

Taking in a deep breath, gathering an intense strength from within himself, he lifted his head proudly. His chin jutted out strongly again, "Yet, I am Constantine, King of Alba, son of King Aedh, grandson of King Kenneth Mac Alpin. I have paid for my crown with my own blood and the blood of my ancestors. I am not yet ready to pass it over, especially not to an Englishman!" He ducked instinctively when he heard the sudden whizzing sound of an arrow. His eyes widened with horror. The flaming fire cage arrow that pierced straight through Doungallus' neck, left a gaping red hole, and stifled any reply before it was uttered. Immediately, a second burning arrow fell from the sky, plunging into Doungallus' chest as he collapsed. Instinctively reaching out his arms, Constantine caught his old friend before he dropped to the dirty wooden floor.

Doungallus' wide open glazed eyes reflected the barrage of hundreds of blazing arrows, whizzing through the sky. They hung on the last apex of their flight, sinisterly in the air for a moment, like a huge red flaming cloud.

Constantine bellowed, "Arrow wall!" Grabbing his shield, he scrambled to cover them both. The arrows dropped like stones, thudding into his shield. Hunkering down, he heard his men's shouts, as burning arrows clattered into the courtyard below. Quickly pulling the arrows out of Doungallus' bleeding body, he threw them into a large bucket of water. The arrows hissed out the last of the flames life, and smoke turned to steam. As the light went out in his old friend's eyes, Constantine's fists clenched. He roared out a bellow of grief. Then he heard more shouts from the men below. Taking in one deep controlling breath, he quickly stood up against the wooden parapets. Using his shield to cover his head and back, he leaned as far forward as he dared. Where had the deadly had arrows fallen? Several of his men screamed in agony. Burning arrows had sunk deep into blistering flesh, spewing out rancid black smoke. Others had managed to cover themselves with their shields. They quickly pulled the arrows out of their shields before the scorching beeswax cloth, secured in the small arrow cages, set the wood on fire. Several of the dry wooden out buildings suddenly burst into orange and red flames, casting dark grey whirling smoke high into the sky. Several horses shied and reared as they shrieked with alarm.

Someone shouted deeply, "Arrow wall!"

This time men huddled together and locked their shields together, in front of their bodies and over their heads. As a second wave of flaming arrows came in, the projectiles hissed through the air, many of them thudding into the shields.

Ducking under his shield, Constantine got to the other side of the parapet. Peering down, his eyes hardened angrily. The enemy arrows were a distraction to the main attack. More than one hundred English foot soldiers were crossing the causeway. Some carrying ladders, others weapons and shields. Turning back to the courtyard, he bellowed ferociously, "Cellach! Protect the main gate!"

Suddenly, Cellach appeared running through the smoke. His broad shoulders pulling against his woad blue shirt. The wide sword belt at his waist accentuated his lean strong stomach. The fire did not touch his leather breeches and boots as he leapt over a burning mound of straw. His war cry, "Albanich!" echoed in the air. Racing through the black rancid smoke, his distinctive auburn hair shone like a beacon for his men.

That now familiar shiver of dread and fear for Cellach's safety went through his body. Ignoring it, Constantine shouted fiercely, "Attack, my son! Attack!"

As he ran, his strong young muscular body pumped blood and adrenalin to his brain. Behind him, he could hear the roar of his men's war cries.

"Albanich! Albanich!" They raced through the smoke to

catch up with him.

His blazing topaz eyes glinting, he reached the wall. The first to pick up a boulder, he threw down the missile crushing in an Englishman's head. Barely breathless as his men reached him, he grinned at the closest man, "What kept you Ruardri?"

His hair, light auburn and his face smudged with soot, Ruardri grinned back cheekily, "Your sister!" Picking up a massive bolder, he hurled it over the rampart.

Guffawing back a laugh, Cellach picked up another rock and tossed it over the side, "Over my dead body!"

Up in the parapet, Constantine bellowed, "Murdock of Lochaber! Send your archers to the main gate!"

Hearing his father's shout, Cellach frowned as he hurled another boulder over the parapet.

Pulling an arrow from their quivers as they ran, Thane Murdoch of Lochaber and thirty of his men in their mid-twenties, immediately sprinted to the walled gate.

Dropping to his knees, Cellach ducked behind his shield yelling, "Cover your backs men!"

Crouching down low, they all covered their bodies as best they could.

Murdoch's archers let loose five sets of arrows high over the main gate. They dropped at amazing speed, killing at least another forty attacking English soldiers.

One arrow misfired. Whizzing through the air it pierced Cellach's shield with a quivering loud thud, he grunted, "Shit that was close!"

Chuckling, his young teeth white against his sooted face, Ruardri crouched much lower behind his shield.

"King Suibne of the Isles," Constantine yelled, "send your javelin throwers to the main gate!"

Blonde haired Suibne immediately threw down his arrow studded shield. He roared deeply, "Men of the Isles!" He picked up his javelin, his arm muscles bulging, "Attack!"

Fifteen wide shouldered blonde haired Norse men, jogged fearlessly towards the wall. Their nine foot long javelins held strongly in their right hands above their shoulders.

Hunkering down, Cellach shouted, "Stay down lads!" Glaring at Ruardri, he gulped, "I think my Da is trying to kill me."

Ruardri smiled, his blue eyes twinkling, "If you die this day rest assured my friend, I will take care of all of your sisters."

Shaking his head, Cellach retorted as he raised his eyebrow mockingly, "And if you die today, rest assured, I will continue to take care of your mother."

Shocked, Ruardri spluttered, "Not me Ma," he pleaded over dramatically, "that's just wrong."

A mischievous twinkle glinted in his topaz eyes as he winked, "Have you ever wondered why your youngest brother has the same colour hair as mine?"

Exaggerating his horrified expression, Ruardri shook his head repeating dimly, "That's just wrong."

Cellach chuckled as he hunkered down lower.

King Suibne and each of his men increased their running speed. At the last possible moment, they twisted their bodies back, their left arms outstretched for balance. Every muscle in their thick lithe bodies was taut. In an explosive movement, they grunted out their loud war cries as they hurled their spears over the side of the wall.

With amazing accuracy, Suibne's spear cut through three Englishmen's bodies. Their simultaneous death screams cut through the air like a knife.

The war hardened English soldiers were undeterred. Clambering over their dead, manhandling huge wooden scaling ladders, they pushed the ladders up against the high wall.

Looking down over the parapet, Cellach saw the first English climbers were over half way up their ladders. His topaz eyes flashing with concentration, he yelled, "Dubdon and Duncan of Atoll, fetch Greek Fire!"

Dubdon and Duncan and the men of Atoll heaved up several large wooden barrels of natural oil and tar. Grunting out their exertion, they tipped the dark tarry liquid over the side of the wall. Then they tossed down the empty barrels.

Soaked to the skin in highly combustible oil, the English soldiers still at the bottom of the ladders started to run. Fear contorted their faces into terror masks.

Suibne walked up to Cellach, carrying a flaming torch.

Taking it, Cellach hurled it over the wall and then ducked down covering his body with his shield. He yelled at the top of his voice, "Incoming!"

Suibne and the men close by crouched under their shields.

Constantine watched from the high parapet. The English men high up on the ladders immediately burst into flames. They fell like screaming fiery comets to the ground igniting everything in their path. Drenched in the oil and tar, the wooden barrels immediately caught fire. Suddenly exploding upwards, the barrels blasted vicious thick splinters of flaming wood through the air. Hit in the face, neck and chest with shards of burning barrel wood, the English soldiers ran, screaming and stumbling in agony, back along the causeway. A few men dropped to the ground and tried to crawl away. The deep blue and orange flame travelled slowly, like a predatory snake along the ground, eating their fallen screaming bodies. Hungrily the flames followed the trail of tar and oil that the retreating English men left. The still running English men did not get far. From where he stood, Constantine watched coldly impassive as their writhing bodies exploded into infernos.

His young topaz eyes glinting, Cellach hunkered down, as the sky reigned down smouldering wooden splinters onto his shield.

A short time later, filthy with soot and coughing from inhaled smoke, Cellach bounded up the wooden steps of the keep. Behind him, Ruardri of Moray, Dubdon and Duncan of Atoll, Murdoch of Lochaber and Suibne of the Isles, jogged up the steps.

His topaz eyes piercing, Constantine stood waiting, "Well Lad?"

"About eighty of the English are dead. The rest have retreated, but," Cellach added with sincere and profound sorrow, his topaz eyes bright against the dark soot on his face, "we lost another six brave men and several more are mortally wounded."

Shaking his head, Constantine sadly glanced down at Doungallus' still body, "We lost seven good warriors son." He paused as two of the young warriors behind Cellach gasped in unison.

Seeing his father lying dead on the wooden floor, Dubdon felt complete desolation, he could only utter, "Da?"

Duncan stood staring at his father, his eyes unbelieving.

Taking control, Constantine ordered calmly, "Dubdon and Duncan of Athol, your father, Moramer Doungallus of Dunkeld, Strathclyde and Dule," he paused as his own pain filled his eyes, "is dead."

The two lads stared back at him, ashen faced in shock.

"Take his body and revere him, as a true warrior of Alba deserves."

His face downcast, Ruardri stepped forward with Murdoch. Taking the large shield, Suibne laid it down as Dubdon and Duncan gently lifted their father on to the shield. The five men then lifted the shield high with their strong young powerful arms and they carried the body reverently down the steps.

Watching them respectfully, Cellach whispered, "Da, what are we going to do?" We lost our last grain store to the fire. We are already starving."

"Of the two thousand men that I marched against King Athelstan, only four hundred and seven men are left." The nagging disappointment of defeat and hunger was beginning to depress him. "It has been nearly eight weeks since we said goodbye to your sisters." His deep voice softened to almost a whisper, "Maelmare and Bethoc will be safe in hiding."

Cellach nodded quietly.

Wearily looking around at his bedraggled and hungry army of warriors, he sighed. There was filth everywhere. Men lay battered and bleeding. Some still had smoking arrows in their flesh. Others ran to and from the well carrying buckets of slopping water, frantically trying to douse out the buildings that had caught fire. Their situation was desperate. As the northerly wind buffeted salty air and wisps of smoke against his body, Constantine looked out of the wooden fortress, past the deep chasm, to the camp of the English. He could see Athelstan's army, huge and bustling with men and horses. Gruffly, "Athelstan has at least five thousand men." White tents, colourful flags and battle regalia, stood out against the dirt and filth of the soldiers and horses. Everywhere he looked, he could see Athelstan's white dragon banner. Small fires blazed and dark smoke rose out of the foul-smelling camp. Constantine shook his exhausted head again, "We have been trapped here for nearly a month. Our supplies are almost exhausted. Food is now down to minimum rations."

He hated saying it to his own father but he knew that he must, "We have lost Da."

The words tore at his heart but he knew that it was true. Turning to Cellach, his topaz eyes glinting with pain, "Son, I have two choices, watch my men die slowly of starvation, or submit and try to save them. Call a war council son. I need to take advice from my Moramers."

2.2

On the other side of the treacherous chasm, King Athelstan stood tall. His deep blue eyes glittering with frustration as he intensely surveyed the imposing smoking fortress. The shimmering grey green ocean expanse stretched as far as the eye could see. Gulls floated on thermals above the fortress, screeching like banshees. Salty cold air buffeted his body. Dressed in dark battle leathers and a pure white tunic trimmed with gold, he stood out from the other men in the camp. With both hands, he brushed his shoulder length light golden brown hair back from his handsome face. Through his nostrils, he took in a deep smell of the briny ocean. So sweet, compared to the putrid smelling camp behind him.

Alfbert stood close by to attention. Older now, his dark wiry hair was almost completely grey. His light brown battle leathers felt a little snug lately. Uncomfortable around his bulging mid-drift, his dark eyes glinted as he tried to loosen off his sword belt.

Frowning at him, Athelstan suddenly roared, "Fetch me Cardinal Dunstan!"

Stumbling with surprise at the ferocity of his king, he ran as fast as he could towards a large dark red pavilion tent.

The soldiers bustling around the filthy camp ignored Alfbert as he dashed past them. Some of the soldiers chatted together whilst they tended horses. Others sat quietly cleaning their weapons.

He skirted a pack of eight large hounds, all savagely snarling as they tore into the remnants of a large oxen carcass. Reaching the royal pavilion, he darted through the canopy draped doorway into the interior.

Moments later, dressed in dark grey battle leathers and a flowing dark grey cape, the twenty five year old cardinal walked quickly towards his king. Carrying a large sword and dagger on his waist belt, he could easily have been mistaken for a high born warrior. Only the large gold cross, hanging on a thick gold chain from his neck, distinguished him from the other soldiers in the camp. Reaching the agitated king, he bowed deeply.

Shuffling back out of the pavilion, Alfbert leaned against the tough canopy and sucked in deep gasps of air, trying to get his breath back.

A few of the younger teenage soldiers sat around a fire eating gruel. They chuckled at him, until he eyed them ferociously. They quickly looked away sheepishly. He was well known as the king's fearless shield bearer. Very few shield bearers had lived to his age. They knew better than to antagonise him.

His dark eyes glinted intensely as he angrily raged inside. He knew that he was losing his edge. He hated it. He felt shamed by it. Coughing, he spat thick curd phlegm on to the churned up muddy ground close to the lads.

One of them pulled a face and shifted slightly away from it.

Standing up straight, Alfbert sucked in his stomach and pushed out his renowned thick barrel chest. He would not lose his pride in front of the youngsters. Holding his head high he strode off.

Away from the bustle of the camp, still gazing at the castle, Athelstan spoke softly, "Dunstan, these last few years I have grown accustomed to confiding in you cousin."

Smiling, eye to eye with the king, he inclined his head, "I am proud to serve you Majesty. You know that I keep your confidences."

Turning away from the men, tents and horses, Athelstan demanded tersely, "Walk with me cousin."

Following him, adopting a saintly expression, with one

hand, Dunstan made the sign of the cross across his chest. Then he put the palms of his hands together, as if in prayer. Even to himself, his voice sounded deep and melodic, "My King, how may I be of service to your Majesty?"

Irritably, "I need God's grace." The sea breeze ruffled his golden brown hair, "I am worried, very worried. When I first arrived at this fortress I was struck, to my very soul Cardinal, by her dark dramatic beauty. Now," he spat out, "I loathe the sight of it!" He took in a deep breath, "The traitor Constantine has been barricaded up in there for over a month!"

Surprised by the venom in the king's voice, Dunston raised his dark eyebrows. His hazel eyes glinted as he consciously steadied his voice, "I understand that the fortress has proven to be impregnable to all attacks."

"I have tried everything to breach Dunnotter's walls. See here." Placing his large tanned hand on Dunstan's wide shoulder, the pale light of the day cast glimmering multicolour rays on each of his jewelled finger rings, "The fortress is protected on three sides by sheer cliffs that plummet into the sea."

Looking up at the formidable dark fortress, Dunstan raised his eyebrows and breathed out slowly. He had no idea how they could defeat Constantine's army. To him, the fortress looked utterly impenetrable.

"The only way across to the peninsular is by that narrow causeway."

His eyes followed the line of the causeway. Smoke still rose up from the blackened twisted corpses of English soldiers. He crossed himself, as long tufts of grass swayed in the sea breeze, helping to shield his troubled gaze.

Pointing with his right hand, to a dark area in the left side of the cliff, Athelstan's deep blue eyes glittered intensely, "The great main gate of the stockade is built into that cleft in the cliff. However, this route can be easily be defended by just a handful of men up above. The second gate is accessible of course. However, the climb to the gate, up a rocky creek is exhausting. The creek leads to a cave. From there, a path leads up the steep face of the cliff to another highly defended gate." Shaking his head, "Day after day, my men fight hard to gain access to both gates, but each day I have suffered heavy losses."

Grimly, "I understand that your army has already run out of supplies and has been forced to ravage the local countryside. I heard that the closest village, Stonehaven, has been all but destroyed."

"To my great sorrow it is true cousin. This land barely supports the local inhabitants. Food is in short supply. Disease is now taking hold in my camp and each day I lose as many men to the flux, as are slain by Constantine's men!" Harshly, "I cannot sustain this siege for much longer but I dare not back down either. To do so would invite rebellion and attack from every sub-kingdom in Britain."

Adopting a saintly expression, he rolled his eyes piously to the heavens. Making the sign of the cross across his chest, "Your Majesty, God is with you and will deliver you. I will pray for your deliverance."

Athelstan's eyes burned fervently, "From the moment that I took Northumbria, all those years ago, I knew God's path for me. I have waged war on the sub-kingdoms of this island in obedience to God's divine command. My cause is just. It is to protect the people of this great island from evil and to create one great nation, ruled by God, through me!" Turning, he looked towards his huge regal pavilion.

Softly, "Your Majesty."

Turning, Athelstan eyed him thoughtfully, "Speak cousin."

Carefully considering his words, "You are well aware that your half-brothers are coming of age."

Raising his eyebrow quizzically, Athelstan nodded.

"Prince Edmund is now twelve years old. Prince Edred is still young at ten years old. However, they each covet your throne."

"I am fully aware that my half-brothers and my uncle's progeny regard my Royal Person as a bastard usurper."

"Prince Edmund respects you and learns from your wise rule daily but the young prince's supporters are looking for any sign of weakness to undermine you."

"Cardinal," ominously, "last year my own half-brother Edwin, foolishly tried to have me assassinated again. I was merciful the first time he attacked me. This time I had that reckless fool drowned at sea."

Taking in deep breath, feigning shock, Dunstan made the sign of a cross across his chest.

His face hard as he remembered his brother's insults, forcibly lowering his voice Athelstan spat out, "That son of a whore had the impudence to tell me, to my face, that my blood was inferior to his! He called my mother a shepherdess," his deep blue eyes glistened intently, "to my face!" Clenching his fists, "He demanded that I hand my throne to him. To that weak fool! My kingdom would be ruined in less than a year!"

Eyeing his cousin warily, Dunstan felt his heart pumping the blood through his body. He forced his voice to remain steady, "Queen Aelfflaed brought up her children to hate you, as much as she hated your mother. She always knew that your father had deeply loved your mother."

"I was ordained to be king by my grandfather, King Alfred the Great! I was brought up to rule Mercia! When faced with the possibility of her evil son Edwin as king, the bishops begged me to rule. They told me Edwin was as self-indulgent and malicious as his mother!" He looked at Dunstan earnestly, "Have I not proven my royal blood runs strong? Have I not conquered every sub kingdom of this realm? Am I not High King of Britain?" Shaking his head, "Edwin had no idea what I have given up for my sovereignty." Breathing out a deep breath, he sighed, "After my father died and my brother became king, I had thoughts of a life devoted to my faith and to Mercia. I even hoped to take a wife one day."

Dunstan eyed him, "Then Edwin murdered your half-brother."

Shrugging his shoulders, "He murdered his own blood brother for a crown. When that failed and the bishops chose me to be king, he tried to murder me." A hint of a smile played on his lips, softly, "Aelfflaed's sons are dead now and her daughters are married off abroad. I have secured my crown and the allegiance of Europe."

Dunstan took a deep breath before continuing, "May I speak frankly my King?"

Calming now, he looked at Dunstan. His intelligent eyes glinted. He had always liked his cousin's grit, tenacity and honesty, "Always my friend. I trust your counsel more than any man in my kingdom."

Eyeing him intently, he whispered guardedly, "Do not disclose your thoughts to anyone else. More importantly my king, do not disclose your thoughts to the Atheling's. Each of whom truly do have a stronger claim to the crown than you, as they were born of truly ordained queens." His heart thumped in his chest. He knew he had spoken dangerous words. Silence hung on the air.

Carefully regarding Dunstan, an amused smile suddenly twitched his lips. A laugh bubbled up from his core, "Cardinal, I am very much aware that my mother was nothing more than a beautiful concubine of low noble birth."

Bluntly contradicting him, "Your mother was my aunt, and she carried the bloodline of the Kings of Kent. She was your father's first wife."

Firmly, "She was not an anointed queen."

"No she was not. However, your mother was more of a queen in her heart and in her dignified presence, than either of those other two selfish bitches!"

Surprised at his cousin's venom, Athelstan lifted his eyebrows, "It makes no difference Dunstan. Even though I am the eldest of my father's sons, I will always be a bastard in the eyes of the aristocracy."

"You are the anointed King of Wessex, Mercia and Kent. The Bishops chose well, nearly ten years ago, when they chose you to govern the southern lands. You have united your England and you now hold sway over Northumbria. You are the wisest and the most proven of kings."

His deep blue eyes glinted intently, "Thank you Dunstan. Your support and friendship is appreciated."

His confidence fuelled, his eyes locked with Athelstan's, "Be ever on your guard my king. Your half-brothers and their supporters lurk in the shadows around you, waiting for any sign of weakness. Do not give them the satisfaction of bringing you down. I send a prayer to God for your victory." Looking down, he closed his eyes, as he sincerely uttered a prayer, "Lord God, bless King Athelstan. Make him steadfast and resolute against our enemies. Grant him a great victory over the traitor Constantine. Let the gates of Dunnotter open. Let the Albans submit and beg for mercy. Bless us holy father." Making the sign of the cross, he whispered, "Amen." Looking up towards the tents, he hesitated as the camp seemed to come alive with noisy commotion.

Alfbert ran towards them. Flushed and sweating profusely, he skidded in the dirt, ungainly falling to his knees in front of his king. His barrel chest heaved as he breathed heavily, "Majesty, a rider has come out of the castle gate bearing a white flag!"

Raising his eyebrows, Athelstan eyed Dunstan curiously, "It would appear Cardinal, that our Lord heard your prayer." Ignoring Alfbert, his voice calmly regal, "Dunstan, arrange for the envoy to be conveyed, unharmed, to my royal tent."

Bowing respectfully, Dunstan hid his own surprise, "Yes Majesty."

2.3

Decorated with golden furniture, opulent colourful silks and luxuriously sheer rainbow voiles, the vast royal pavilion looked a Mercian palace.

The commanders' of his great army stood together. Dressed in battle leathers, their faces looked grim. Their eyes glinted with curiosity as they waited.

He strode in to the tent confidently. Now wearing his crown and a red flowing cloak, King Athelstan looked imposing. In every corner there was a tapestry image of the white dragon on a blood red field, his chosen emblem. Sitting down on his imperial purple cushioned throne, he felt his heart beating incredibly fast. He knew each one of his commanders personally. They were each a member of his noble family. Allowing only Cardinal Dunstan to stand near him, to the right of his shoulder, with a consummate performance, he managed to muster a look of jaded boredom. Constantine would have no idea just how close he had come to winning.

Watching their king with glittering envious eyes, the Athelings saw him as always, in complete and absolute control. Turning their resentful eyes to the king's favourite, Cardinal Dunstan, they scowled.

Ignoring the Athelings, Dunstan lifted his chin confidently.

A servant shuffled up and bowed. He offered his king a goblet of wine.

Barely acknowledged the man, Athelstan took the chalice shaped goblet. With imperious tedium, he sipped the aromatic crimson wine.

Alfbert escorted the unarmed Alban messenger into the pavilion. Eyeing the Alban with distrust, Alfbert stood rigidly on guard, his barrel chest puffed up. One false move and the stranger would feel the sharp end of his sword.

The messenger introduced himself proudly, "I am Murdock McDoir, MacAedh, McAlpin, Thane of Lochaber and nephew to King Constantine II of Alba." About thirty five years of age, pale and gaunt looking, his proud bearing and manner, proved his noble line better than the words he spoke. Strongly, "King Constantine has come to realise, that your Majesty has God's divine blessing as High King of Britain."

Flicking an imaginary spec of fluff from his red cape, Athelstan wearisomely eyed the Alban noble.

"My King acknowledges that he was wrong to challenge your Grace. However, in his defence, he felt that he needed proof of our Divine God's intent before he could truly, humbly, acknowledge you as overlord. King Constantine attests that he has been shown by the one and true God, that our Divine Lord wishes your Highness to be his king. He is ready to accept this fate. We will surrender, if King Constantine has your exulted Majesty's word of honour, that his son Prince Cellach and his men will have safe passage to their homes. If your Mercifulness agrees to this small request, King Constantine will willingly leave the fortress of Dunnotter and recognise your Exulted Person as Emperor."

Smiling, stretching his hand out like a lion flexes a paw, Athelstan looked at the heavy gold jewelled rings on his fingers. He hid the relief that coursed through his body.

The tantalising smell of roasted meat filled his nostrils. Murdock could not stop his eyes flicking to the long table laden with food. He felt sick with hunger.

Watching him closely, Athelstan's deep blue eyes thoughtfully narrowed for moment, impassively, "Would you care for some wine and food ambassador?"

Hating himself for not having control, Murdoch grabbed a whole cooked goose and tore into it with his bare teeth. Ripping the breast meat from the bone, he hardly chewed it before swallowing. Instructed by Constantine to assess the English force of arms and their resources, his eyes darted about the pavilion, he felt shocked by the opulence in the king's tent. The table contents alone would feed forty of his men for a day. His eyes betrayed him.

Beckoning the cardinal closer, Athelstan's eyes glinted. He whispered smugly, "So, they are already starving." He turned to the young noble of Alba, loudly commanding, "Take this message back to your King. I agree to his terms, except," softly menacing, "I require the eldest son of King Constantine, to reside with me as hostage."

Inwardly squirming at Athelstan's demand, Murdock stated frankly, "Emperor, since my eldest son Ferguard was born to me five years ago, I understand the love that a father has for his eldest born child. Will you guarantee the safety of Prince Cellach?"

Feigning a look of abject boredom, Athelstan nodded imperiously. He motioned with a sweep of his hand for Murdoch to leave his presence.

"I will advise my King of your demands." Feeling fuelled by the sudden rush of protein in his blood, Murdock boldly added, "King Constantine wishes to continue to act as a sub-king in Alba, ensuring that your Excellency's tribute and taxes are paid."

Raising his eyebrows in surprise, Athelstan eyed the ambassador. Turning to Dunstan, he lowered his voice, "I like this man's audacity and bravery in, what is after all, the enemy's camp. What think you to his request to keep Constantine as sub-king?"

Dunstan looked momentarily thoughtful, then he smiled, "Better a conquered man as king, than a new untested king who may rally the Albans to war again."

Turning back to Murdock, Athelstan spoke confidently, "Murdock of Lochaber, if your king proves his allegiance to me, I will allow him to continue to rule as sub-king of Alba." He added thoughtfully, "I will require the presence of King Constantine and Prince Cellach as I travel south back to Wessex. A public display of their loyalty to me will be necessary. If your master accepts my terms, I will give him his men's freedom."

"I require one day Emperor, to confer with King Constantine. Would your advocate draw up an accord in writing?"

Nodding, Athelstan eyed Dunstan, "Draw up the treaty."

Walking to a nearby table, Dunstan sat down. Picking up a white feathered quill, he dipped the quill nib into the clay ink pot. Tapping the nib against the rim of the pot, he watched the excess black ink dribble back into the pot. He began writing. Moments later it was finished. Carrying the treaty and his quill to the king, he bowed as he offered the document and quill to Athelstan.

Quickly reading the document he signed it, 'Athelstan Rex'.

Carefully carrying the treaty back to the table, rolling up the document, Cardinal Dunstan walked up to the emissary and handed it over.

Taking the document, bowing curtly to King Athelstan, Murdock strode out of the tent. He still had the fat goose under his arm. The cool evening breeze swept his lank hair against his face. His bony horse stood with his head in a bucket of maze. He was hungry too.

Alfbert silently followed him out.

The bridle was held by an English stableman, who kept his eyes averted. The horse snorted with annoyance when the bucket of maze was removed.

Pulling himself up onto his saddle, looking up to the pale grey hazy sky, Murdock shook his head. He could just see the outline of the silvery moon and a few stars beginning to glimmer in the heavens. The war was lost. Crestfallen, he rode off through the camp towards the causeway of Dunnotter.

RAVEN

2.4

Dunnotter Fortress

In the centre of the dimly lit room, the picked white bones of the goose lay on a platter.

Constantine sat stony faced in a huge chair, his topaz eyes glinting intelligently.

The sparsely furnished room was crowded with noblemen waiting to hear the news from Murdock. The place stank of sweat, filth and rotting food.

"Furthermore my King, King Athelstan requires the presence of yourself and your son on a progress into the heart of England. I can confirm that I have secured a guarantee for Prince Cellach's safety."

The nobles around the room bellowed, "No!"

Clenching his teeth, Murdoch impatiently waited until the room quietened enough for his voice to be audibly heard. "Finally my King, I have an agreement that you will remain King of Alba."

The room erupted again with angry cries, "No, you cannot trust the English king!"

Cellach, Suibne and Ruardri watched silently by the door.

Slamming the large manuscript document on the table, Murdoch shouted above the din, "I have it in writing! This treaty is signed by the King of England himself!"

Standing up, Constantine bellowed, "Silence!"

The king's heated demand was immediately obeyed.

Fuming inside, Murdock waited.

Looking around, Constantine raised his head proudly.

Watching his father command the room, Cellach glanced at

Ruardri.

Ruardri noticed how many of the men in the room physically shrank and bowed their heads in subconscious respectful deference. That was the power of their king.

Constantine strode slowly, purposely across the room to where Murdock stood. Placing his large hand on Murdock's shoulder, he stated loudly so that everyone could hear, "This brave man volunteered to go unarmed to the enemy camp. They could have sent his head back to me on a platter, instead of the goose!" Eyeing the crowd of men fiercely, "I trust Murdock with my life!"

Feeling the warmth of his king's hand on his shoulder, he stood proudly, "Thank you Majesty."

Loudly, "You have done well nephew and once again proved your loyalty to me." Steering Murdock towards a side annexed room, Constantine bellowed, "Cellach, come with us! I will take counsel privately with my son and my nephew, away from the stench in this room!"

Instantly obeying his father, Cellach strode after them.

By the door, Ruardri lifted his muscular arm and sniffed loudly under his armpit.

Suibne watched at him quizzically.

His face inane, Ruardri drawled, "He definitely means you."

Shaking his blonde head, Suibne chuckled.

Well lit by candles the smaller room felt cooler. Walking over to the huge fireplace, Murdock knelt down. Picking up a metal poker, he stirred up the embers in the hearth until they glowed red. Carefully, he placed a couple of small old dry logs on the smouldering cinders. He blew gently through his mouth until small flames licked at the logs. They suddenly crackled into burning life. His eyes reflected the glow of the flames as they threw light and warmth into the room.

Wasting no time, Constantine sat down on a wooden high backed chair, "Son, we will take seven noblemen with us on this progress to England. I need to pick them well. I also need an acting sub-king who I can trust."

Pulling up a chair, Cellach inclined is head, "I recommend we take with us Mailcoluim MacDovenald, King of Alban Galwensis. He is your heir designate under Tanist law. I am sure, if Mailcoluim was left behind, he would rally his brother and make a challenge for your throne."

"Agreed son, I need to take Mailcoluim with us. He is too powerful to leave behind."

Still holding the poker, Murdock pulled up a small wooden three legged stool and sat down close to the fire, "Dubachan Moramer of Caithness is the son of MacIndrechtach of Iona, a descendant of Fergus II of the Picts. He is a powerful warrior too but unquestionably loyal to you. I think a good man to take with you as body guard. You never know what dangers this progress to England will bring."

"Aye," Cellach agreed, "Dubachan is devoted to you. He gave you Iona, I believe?"

Constantine nodded.

"He also has a good alliance with the Viking Kings of the North. He married his daughter Grelod off to the Norse King of the Orkneys," Cellach emphasised the nickname with relish, "Thorfin 'Skullsplitter' Einarsson."

Smiling, Murdock raised an eyebrow, "King Thorfin wants Caithness but Dubachan keeps his son-in-law in check. Dubachan would be an asset to us. If King Athelstan tries any tricks, he would risk an uprising from the Orkney Jarls."

His voice deep, Constantine nodded, "Agreed, Dubachan has always served me well, he travels with us."

Thoughtfully, Cellach looked up, "Suibne, King of the Western Isles, has proven himself to be a reliable supporter to you Da."

Moving the glowing embers again with the metal poker, Murdock threw another small log onto the crackling fire, "He is a good man."

"Yes he is." Constantine nodded thoughtfully as he watched red sparks fly upwards into the chimney. Rubbing his hands, he held them up to the fire to warm them, "Suibne commands a navy of two hundred and thirty Norse warships."

Nodding thoughtfully, Murdoch's eyes glistened, "King Athelstan would risk a fleet of Viking ships invading his shores if the King of the Isles was taken."

"Agreed, Suibne of the Isles goes with us."

"Domhnall MacMorgan, MacDonall, the Moramer of Moray," Cellach pondered, "is also descended from the Royal Picts."

"All of the royals of Alba are. We had to marry into the Pict dynasty to secure the throne of Alba."

The muscles in his jaw flexed, "I know Da, but Domhnall is far enough removed from the royal line of Alba, not to be a threat to us on our return. He also commands the immense force of the House of Moray. He is clever, fair and fiercely loyal to you."

"Yes, he is a good man."

"He would be my choice to leave behind as acting king."

Smiling proudly, "Good choice son but you must never forget the allure of a throne. It corrupts the best of men. As added insurance we will take Domhnall's son Ruardri of Moray with us to England. I will honour him by making him my standard bearer. Domhnall will be proud of that, and he will not forget that I have his son."

His young topaz eyes lit up, "Good. Ruardri is also a good man, a little younger than me but already a great warrior. I like him. He will be good company."

"Well that is the acting king decided." Constantine added, "I also want Doungallus' sons, Dubdon of Athol and Duncan of Dunkeld & Dule to come with us. They have suffered a great loss with their father's death and will benefit from a distraction."

Counting out on his fingers, Murdock named them, "That is Mailcoluim MacDovenald of Alban Galwensis, Dubachan Moramer of Caithness, Suibne MacNialgussa King of the Western Isles, Ruardri MacDomhnall of Moray, Dubdon of Athol and Duncan of Dunkeld and Dule, makes six. Who will be the seventh man?"

Both Cellach and Constantine eyed him incredulously.

Grinning with anticipation, Murdock chuckled, "I take it that'll be me then?"

The next day, freshly bathed and dressed in clean clothes, riding his white horse at the head of what remained of his army, King Constantine of Alba led his few hundred men out of the castle. Seagulls' squawked as they landed on the battle scarred ramparts, once again claiming the coastal fortress for themselves.

Sat on his favourite black stallion, watching them from the other side of the causeway, King Athelstan waited. His generals were all dressed in full battle gear and mounted on their finest horses close to him. The whole of his army stood darkly behind him to watch his moment of triumph. His deep blue eyes glittered with exhilaration. Victory had never tasted so sweet!

Crossing the causeway, his back straight, Constantine's topaz eyes took in everything. His men still carried the banners of Alba as they left the darkly beautiful fortress but they looked sullen, weak and beaten. Reaching the grassy mainland, he slowly walked his white horse up to the English king's retinue. Grimacing with humiliation, he dismounted in front of Athelstan and sank to his knees in submission.

Watching his father, Cellach lifted his chin. He felt nothing but deep pride. He knew his father would do anything to save what was left of Alba.

The cheers from the English army could be heard for miles, drowning out the screeches from the gulls.

25

**England, summer
934AD**

Patting his white horse's muscular neck, wisps of long shimmering white mane tickled Constantine's wrist. His right hand expertly held the beautifully worked leather reins. They felt soft and pliable in his hand. "Easy." He soothed his skittish horse as he watched a small but heavy firewood cart get stuck in a rut. The donkey pulling the cart started honking loudly in annoyance but the cart refused to budge.

Two young soldiers wearing King Athelstan's colours ran up.

One of them looked up at the dignified man sat on the magnificent white stallion. He noticed his fine clothes made of exquisite purple silk and velvet. He recognised him and doffed his cap, "Begging your pardon, your Majesty."

The second soldier dragged his scruffy cap from his head and half bowed.

His hair clipped neatly and his beard trimmed, Constantine nodded to them. He sat tall, his back straight in his saddle. His voice naturally commanding, "Put your backs into it lads."

They immediately obeyed. They grunted as they heaved the cart out of the rocky dry rut.

Still honking with immense annoyance, the grizzled donkey walked on. The cart trundled by.

Impressed, Constantine grinned at the lads, "Well done men, good work."

The two lads doffed their caps again.

"Walk on." He gently dug his heals into his mount's twitching white flank.

"You know who that was?" the eldest lad looked in awe, "That was King Constantine of Alba." He smiled proudly, "He noticed us."

Taking his time, he let his horse walk at its own gentle gait. The stallion was special to him. He was the purist white horse he had ever seen. When the sun shone, his long mane and tail took on a heavenly ethereal glow. He had been a gift from Cellach. Constantine took a deep breath. Watching the entourage with a hooded gaze, he hid the raw humiliation that he felt from the core of his being. As they travelled south, they had been paraded from town to town at the conquering King of England's pleasure. Holding his head high, he regally surveyed the land, less hilly than Northumbria and much warmer. Bird song filled the air. He conceding to himself grudgingly, "England is a beautiful land."

They passed huge beautiful oak trees lining the dirt road. Either side of the road lush meadow fields full of pink clover, white daisies, big yellow buttercups, and all manner of grasses swayed gently in the warm breeze. Bees and other flying insects buzzed from flower to sweet smelling flower. The sky was as blue as the wild cornflower growing in clumps at the edge of the road. There was not a cloud to be seen.

The retinue of riders sat on huge war horses and trudged along, two abreast. Soldiers buoyant from their victory wore their lord's uniform, or town's heraldic colours. Flag bearers carried the vibrant colours of all of the main dynastic families of the now united England. Their grand progress was deliberately ostentatious and deliberately slow.

Travelling up a gently sloping hill, Constantine's topaz eyes glittered. He smiled. Proudly held higher than all of the other banners, he saw his colours. The Saltire of Saint Andrew, a white saltire cross on woad blue field. He could just see young Ruardri MacDomhnall, sat on his chestnut brown stallion, holding the lofty flag. It was easier to see Cellach's fiery auburn head riding alongside him. Murdock, Mailcoluim, Dubachan, Suibne, Dubdon and Duncan rode at the back of them. Constantine suddenly frowned with concern as Ethelwine, a grandnephew of old King Alfred the Great of Wessex, purposely nudged his horse into Cellach's stallion, spooking him. The hackles on his neck rose up. Immediately turning his horse into the field, breaking into a gallop, he rode to catch up to them.

Cellach's horse shied and nervously neighed.

Laughing maliciously, Earl Ethelwine loudly berated, "You Albans have no control over your horses! You would do better riding in the wagons with the washer women!"

Close by, a few of the English nobles sneered as they laughed.

Murdock's horse twitched uneasily, snorting, her nostrils flared as she shook her head.

Feeling the hot red mist of aggression rising in him, Cellach suddenly pulled his dagger. Pointing it at Ethelwine's crotch, he growled menacingly, "You come near my horse again Atheling and I will turn you into a woman! It will be you riding in the wagons!"

Their faces hostile, the English nobles immediately urged their snorting horses forward.

Frowning, Murdock and Ruardri turned their horses to block their path.

Their way obstructed, the nobles tried to turn their huge horses.

Mailcoluim, Suibne and Dubachan blocked them in, causing havoc in the retinue.

Murdock watched the chaos. His right hand rested menacingly on his sword pommel.

Circling the mayhem at a gallop, Constantine reached the two princes just as they squared up to each other. Expertly using his reins to spur his horse on in between them, he eyed Ethelwine with the full extent of regal Alban contempt, "Get back to your men Lord Ethelwine."

Laughing sarcastically, Ethelwine's nostrils flared aggressively. His hazel eyes flashed as he flicked his dark golden hair back.

Eyeing him scornfully, his topaz eyes murderously cold, Constantine leaned in towards him. Forcefully he bellowed, "Now!"

Visibly flushing, he tried to cover his apprehension with a sneering laugh. Blinking agitatedly, Ethelwine skilfully backed his horse away.

Murdoch and Ruardri nudged their horses apart to let him pass.

Posturing like a boy full of bravado, Ethelwine turned his mount and trotted back to his chaotic entourage.

Cart horses were now bumping into each other and rearing up. The men driving the wagons shouted out warnings as they tried to back them up. Some of the washer women cried out in alarm but the procession behind them noisily pushed forward.

Riding a short distance ahead, King Athelstan turned to see what the commotion was. His deep blue eyes widened as Ethelwine's horse collided with a wagon. The agitated pony pulling the wagon reared up almost turning it over. Women screamed and hung onto the sides of the cart. The soldier driving the wagon did well to stay on the seat but he still shouted loudly for help as he lost the bridles. The pony reared again, screeching out a whinny.

As men ran to the horse to try to calm him and get him under control, Constantine turned quickly to Cellach. His eyes filled with concern as he lowered his voice, "Listen to me my boy."

Cellach's chest heaved as he furiously eyed Ethelwine.

Glaring at his son, his voice rasped, "Cellach, look at me!"

Angrily obeying his father, his topaz eyes flashed at him.

"Do not let the English Princes antagonise you." He eyed the English nobles around him, hoarsely, "I saw Lord Ethelwine try to bate you. You handled it badly my son. Pulling a knife on him was stupid. It could have got you killed. Remember, you are a Prince of my Realm. You have far more chance of ever seeing your throne, than that upstart Ethelwine, or any of the other Athelings for that matter." He lowered his voice still further, his eyes shimmered as they bored into his son's eyes, "For the moment, we must survive."

Drawing in a deep breath, Cellach blinked. Feeling his anger abating, he nodded his head sharply to his father.

"We must submit to King Athelstan. Once we are free and back in Alba we can regroup. I have a plan that will knock Athelstan from his throne."

His deep blue eyes glistening with suspicion, Athelstan eyed Constantine. He edged his horse nearer trying to hear them above the commotion. His horse snorted excitedly.

Seeing Athelstan from the corner of his eye, Constantine suddenly raised his voice, deeply, "Listen to your Emperor," He winked at Cellach, "the Father of Kings. Listen to our, Emperor Athelstan. He is chosen by God and you would learn much from him my son."

Nodding imperiously to Constantine, smiling at the compliment, Athelstan reached them.

Cellach cheekily winked back. Calmly turning his horse towards King Athelstan, he bowed his head graciously, "I was just saying, to Earl Ethelwine, that I was very impressed with your sermon this morning your Grace. I felt," Cellach paused theatrically for a moment, gazing upwards to the heavens, as if trying to find the right words to express himself, "a kind of a calling."

For a moment, Constantine looked with incredulous amusement at Ruardri and Murdock. They could not have looked more stunned, if all of the angels in heaven had decided to fly down to earth at that precise moment. Gathering his wits quickly, he composed himself.

Cellach continued gravely, "Your nephew found this mightily amusing, Majesty. He laughed so hard, he spooked the horses."

Eyeing Ethelwine with displeasure, Athelstan loudly berated, "Lord Ethelwine is young, impatient, and has much to learn!"

Embarrassed in front of his men, Ethelwine looked at his king, hatred contorted his young face.

Staring him down with his deep blue eyes, Athelstan growled, "When you become a king, God invests His divine power and His divine blessing in you. You would do well to respect that power, Earl Ethelwine."

Submissively dropping his gaze, Ethelwine mumbled, "My deepest apologies Majesty."

Turning his back on his nephew, his eyes softened as he turned to Cellach, "I am pleased that my sermon affected you. I will instruct that you and your father sit at my side tonight, so that we can discuss your thoughts."

Bowing his head graciously, "I look forward to that, your Grace."

As Athelstan cantered back to the cardinal, he did not see Constantine fix his cheekily smiling son with a stern look, rasping a whisper, "Thanks son, now I've got to sit through another evening of his ranting!"

Serious for a moment, "Da, you are right. Our only chance for survival is convincing him we think he is God's chosen Emperor of Britain. I am going to put on the most convincing show of allegiance. He will want to give me the throne of England!"

Reaching the cardinal, Athelstan smiled with satisfaction, "Dunstan, I am certain that through Prince Cellach, we can convert the whole race of Alba to Roman Christianity. As soon as we reach Winchester, I will send messengers to Rome detailing my methods and sermons."

Dunstan gazed up at the heavens, "God indeed works in mysterious ways. The Pope cannot fail to send word, to all of the kingdoms of the known world, that High King Athelstan, the wise ruler of Britain, is a devout Christian leader of kings and men."

The next day, Dunstan's dark eyebrows rose up when auburn

haired Prince Cellach, strode into the king's makeshift church. The tent was sparsely furnished, with just a table and wooden cross. Most of the Athelings were there, on their knees, their faces sullen with barely hidden boredom. His topaz eyes glinting, the Alban prince strode past them and dropped to his knees next to the king. This act shouted out that his status was higher than any of theirs. Prince Cellach was immensely confident, that he would one day rule Alba. A smile played on Dunstan's lips when he saw the king's expression. It was pure gratification. Dunstan watched the Alban prince, as he clasped his hands together and listened intently to the ceremony. After the service, Prince Cellach silently stood and left. The next day, and every day after, Cellach joined the congregation. This act of pious devotion to religious learning greatly impressed him. Dunstan's one concern was Lord Ethelwine. Continuing his vendetta against the prince, Lord Ethelwine had tried numerous times to publicly antagonise him. Witnessing the raging turmoil in the Alban prince's topaz eyes, realising that Cellach was barely keeping control of his temper, Dunstan stepped in and spoke to the king. He advised Athelstan, that the prince's conversion would be jeopardised if Prince Cellach called Lord Ethelwine out. A common duel could not be looked on favourably by the church. Enraged, Athelstan had furiously and publicly put down Lord Ethelwine, threatening him with banishment from his court. After that, Lord Ethelwine kept his distance but it was obvious that his jealous hatred for the Alban grew daily.

By late August, the progress reached the hill fortress at Buckingham. Athelstan's father had built the castle in 914AD, to defend against the Vikings. Overlooking the small ramshackle town by the river, the stone fortress looked formidable. There, in the small dark priory, Cellach devoutly accepted the Roman baptism performed by King Athelstan himself.

As the sun began to set, nobles congregated in the great hall. Sitting on a throne next to King Athelstan, Cellach took great pleasure in the fact that his arch enemy, Lord Ethelwine, was required to bow low to him.

Sitting to the left of the king, Cardinal Dunstan saw the clawing hate in Ethelwine's eyes. He shifted uncomfortably when Ethelwine's scowling face turned to him. Looking around at the factions of nobles, all eyeing him hostilely, Dunstan felt the tension in the room. His quickening heart rate told him to be wary. He was making enemies at court.

Sat next to his son, Constantine looked jaded. He felt sick of being traipsed around the country and paraded to, what felt like, every noble house in the country. It was deeply humiliating. He felt weary of the constant threat to his son's life. But most of all he missed home, he missed Alba and his family.

Stomping away to his seat, Lord Ethelwine frowned at the muscular Albans sat at a table close by. Glaring at them, he did not notice the two guards escorting a barefoot monk to King Athelstan.

Travelling his pilgrimage in bare feet, the monk brought news from Ireland. Clasping his thin dirty fingers together, the monk stated loudly, "King Guthrith of Ath Cliath died weeks ago, your Grace. His son, Anlaf, has been elected King of the Norse in his place."

Looking up with interest, Constantine eyebrows furrowed broodingly.

Assessing the changing dynamics of Britain, King Athelstan stated politely, "I am deeply saddened to hear of King Guthrith's death. He was my guest years ago. He will be a great loss to his people." At the back of his mind, he pondered if this new king would try to take back Northumbria. It was possible that King Anlaf might try to invade at some point in the future but he was convinced not yet. King Anlaf would need to stamp his power in Ireland. Looking back at the monk, Athelstan noticed his habit was soiled and frayed. His bare filthy feet were encrusted with dried blood. Turning to Dunstan, he ordered, "Cardinal, see that this monk is tended to."

Shaking his head, the monk spoke clearly, "My pilgrimage to Canterbury is a devotion to God that must be taken unaided."

As he turned and limped from the court, the scabs on his feet pulled and tore leaving a trail of bloody footprints.

Clearly moved, Cellach crossed himself and whispered, "May God go with you."

A hint of a smile flickered on Athelstan's lips. That small gently spoken sentence convinced him. Prince Cellach was truly converted. From his own neck, he took a beautiful garnet jewelled cross on a heavy gold chain. Holding the necklace with both hands, he placed it over Cellach's head. His deep blue eyes glittered, "Prince Cellach, it is now the time for you to return to Alba. Your father has proven his allegiance to me. Pray, take the word of God with you."

Hardly daring to believe what he was hearing, Cellach's topaz eyes glistened.

Constantine looked up sharply as relief flooded through his being. Cellach had done it! They were going to go home. It took every ounce of control not to show emotion.

Athelstan smiled confidently at Cellach, "Cardinal Dunstan has advised me that you already show great wisdom and faith beyond your years. One day in the future, God willing, you will lead your people to the true faith."

Hearing his king's words, Ethelwine's scowl deepened. The loathing he felt for Prince Cellach crawled through is soul. Eyeing the cardinal with murderous eyes, he clenched his fists. He hated the cardinal almost as much as the Alban.

2.6

Cenheardsburgh
Autumn 934AD

Mid-September still felt warm but the V-shaped flocks of birds, flying south over amber tipped trees, foretold that winter would soon be upon them. Scores of early evening starlings took flight, making entrancing swirling displays in the air. Watching them was mesmerizing.

Riding his white stallion, Constantine led his small procession on horseback, up the dry mud high street, towards the castle. Looking up, the wrinkles around his eyes crinkled as he noticed the sun just starting to drop in the perfect blue sky. Either side of the road, small wattle and daub thatched hovels spewed smoke from chimneys. An old abandoned cart stood empty, propped up against a wall. Inside a wattle pen, several chickens clucked, as they pecked at the ground. Stacks of logs and an old wooden wheel lay in a heap, under a thatched roof lean-to shed.

As the strangers passed, a woman sweeping out her home quickly dropped her broom and dragged her children indoors.

A man with a shaggy beard, wearing baggy dirty leggings and a ripped tunic, passed them. He carried a large bale of kindling sticks on his back. His face stony, he eyed them warily.

Noticing a man with a score or more of arrows in a quiver on his back and a long bow in his hand, Constantine nodded to him. Dressed in dark brown leathers and wearing finely decorated wrist guards, the man looked wealthier than the other folk. His topaz eyes glinted as he addressed him, "What is your Lord's name?"

Stood confidently, the archer answered loudly, "Earl Cenheard, milord."

"Where can I find him?"

"Earl Cenheard will be overseeing building work at the fortress milord." He pointed towards the castle.

Nodding, he urged his white stallion on.

As soon as they had gone past him, the archer jogged down a side street to the back of the castle heading towards a small hidden doorway.

Stood in the valley below the castle by a mass of hazelnut shrubbery, Lady Rafyn's nephew Samwulf, her youngest brother Badwulf, and the burgh's priest, brother Ordberht waited.

About the same age as them, the young monk could not have looked more different. Their tanned, muscular bodies were dressed in dark battle leathers and weapons. His pale plump frame was dressed in nothing more than a very itchy long habit, tied at the waist by a rope belt. His poor skin had dried and crusty pink scabs had formed on his arms and legs. Irritated by them, he scratched his arm, then his thigh, then his backside.

Eyeing the monk with amusement, Samwulf chuckled, "Have you got fleas' brother?"

A little embarrassed, he flushed as he scratched his arm vigorously, "My habit is so coarse lord Samwulf, it's itching me something terrible."

Shrugging his wide shoulders, Badwulf grinned mischievously, "Have you tried a petticoat under your dress, brother Ordberht?"

With a mock look of perplexed tedium, much like the look that the archbishop used to give him, he shook his head wearily, "Lord Badwulf, I wear a habit, not a dress!"

A chuckle bubbled up from Samwulf's core.

Ordberht rolled his eyes, but in reality he liked their banter with him. He had to admit that after Archbishop Wulfstan had abandoned him in this heathen burgh, he had been terrified. That first day, after taking him into her home, Lady Rafyn had stood in front of him and formidably stated her house rules. He was under no illusion that if he broke any of them, his life would be in serious danger, man of God or not. A smile drifted across his face. His wattle and daub cottage was finished now. Although still meagrely furnished, he was warm and well fed. He even had shelves for his parchment and ink. He was experimenting with the local minerals that he could turn into paints. Stood at his easel, he loved working on beautifully painted manuscripts in the evening. Lady Rafyn's men were now building his wooden church close to the main road. Each day, the building grew bigger, and each day, he thanked God that He had sent him here. He looked up when he heard the clatter of hooves.

Cenheard, his sons and Lady Rafyn, galloped up the winding path covered by a canopy of trees. Reining in their horses, they quickly dismounted.

Cenheard looked tense as he eyed the monk with glittering dark brown eyes, "Thank you for coming brother."

Samwulf and Badwulf quickly moved aside the branches of the two hazelnut bushes, revealing a concealed tunnel entrance.

His wide eyes blinking with surprise, Ordberht gazed at the tunnel. He had no idea that it was there.

A thin lad appeared, from what looked like a hovel, slightly downhill from the tunnel. His dirty apron covered his leggings and tunic.

Impatiently, Cenheard ordered, "Look after the horses' lad."

Doffing his greasy head cap, the lad took the horses' bridles, "Yes milord."

Her dark eyes flashing, Rafyn followed her father into the tunnel, "Who recognised him Da?"

Gruffly, "Old man Ewan fought for him twenty years ago against the Norse. He insists that he is not mistaken."

"My archer Coluim, is looking out for them on the High

Street" Lifting her long mulberry coloured skirt higher, she strongly climbed the steps into the pitch black tunnel. The unnerving scream that suddenly filled the tunnel nearly made her stumble. She could hear Samwulf chuckling in the darkness. Brother Ordberht was squealing like a girl for some reason. Moments later, she saw the distant shaft of light from the castle courtyard. Picking up her pace on the stone steps to keep up with her father, she reached the warm sunlit courtyard. Looking around herself, she saw many a man working on building the new castle keep. The sound of hammers and sawing filled the air. Samwulf and her brothers trooped out of the tunnel looking very amused. Lastly, still screeching, poor brother Ordberht, emerged covered in cobwebs and very large spiders. He wailed in short high pitched successions as he brushed them off him. Finally, he frantically rubbed his tonsured head, leaving what hair he had sticking out at all angles. She looked at him with amazement.

Barely winded, Cenheard ignored the monk. He crossed the cobbles and strode into the Doomhalla.

They all quickly followed him.

Cenheard marched up to his great high backed seat. Sitting down, he looked relieved as he eyed Ragenhare, "We made it before the king's arrival?" Perspiration hung in glistening droplets on his brow.

Bobbing a curtsey, a maid handed Lord Cenheard a goblet of wine and a clean white cloth.

Jogging into the judgement hall, Coluim grinned with excitement. He forgot to bow to Lord Cenheard but no one noticed, "The Albans are crossing the market!"

Brother Ordberht quickly moved to stand to the right of Lord Cenheard.

As Rafyn and his boys quickly took their places, Cenheard drank a mouthful of the cool wine.

Outside, Cellach and Suibne trotted their mounts beside King Constantine. Behind them, Mailcoluim and Dubachan rode alongside each other. At the rear, Ruardri carried the Alban standard.

Crossing the empty market towards the impressive castle, their horse's hooves clip clopped on the densely packed well-trodden dirt.

Passing a large beerhalla with rustic tables and benches, he turned to his son, "As soon as we are back home son we will call a council of war."

Clenching his fist around his horse reins, Cellach looked up pessimistically, "It will take years to recover from this war." Shaking his head, "Da, King Athelstan is too powerful. We will need more men and provisions."

"Thank you for your honest advice son." He inclined his head, "I take your point. Alba is weak from war. But as I said before, I have a plan."

Suibne pushed his blonde hair back from his face, "It goes without saying that my navy is at your disposal."

Smiling, Constantine breathed deeply, "Thank you King Suibne. I will need many battle ships." Grimly, "But your ships alone will not be enough. I need to form an alliance."

Moving his brown horse closer, Mailcoluim looked at him, "You can rely on an alliance with Galwensis, Majesty."

"Your loyalty to Alba is greatly respected King Mailcoluim. However, all our armies are depleted. I need a greater alliance."

Several large chained hounds barked at them as they approached the castle gateway.

Ignoring the castle guards, frowning as he walked their horses through the immense metal studded castle gates, Cellach pushed his thick auburn hair back from his eyes. The inner castle keep was still being built by the many stone and wood cutters on the site. All around the courtyard was the sound of hammers banging and axes chopping. Looking around he saw there was already a sizeable stone building in the centre of the courtyard. Smoke drifted out of a chimney. Gently pulling the bridle, his horse's hooves clip clopped, as he headed towards it, "A greater alliance Da? What do you mean?"

Looking confident, Constantine smiled, "Alone, we cannot defeat King Athelstan. We need to form a coalition," taking in a deep breath, he hesitated for moment, "with all of the sub-kings of Britain."

Raising his eyebrows in surprise, Cellach shook his head, "How Da? All of the sub-kingdoms are constantly at war with each other."

"We can guarantee the support of King Suibne of the Isles and, of course, King Mailcoluim of Galwensis. I know our cousin, King Owain of Strathclyde will pledge to us." He flicked his bridle as they headed towards the halla, "But the four Kings of Walensis and the King of Cornwall will need convincing. Then there is the power of Northumbria."

Broodingly, Cellach nodded as he looked at his father, "Athelstan diverts their riches to England. With the promise of a new king, the people of Northumbria may be convinced to raise an army against King Athelstan."

Shaking his blonde head, Suibne cut in, "Majesty, with all of our combined ships our forces are still too small to take England in battle."

Frowning, Constantine turned to him, "Then what do you suggest, King Suibne?"

Confidently, "Secure the Norse as allies. I know King Anlaf Guthrithsson personally. He owns over two hundred war vessels. He also commands the allegiance of his brothers. King Black Arailt Guthrithsson owns at least one hundred ships. Prince Ragnal Guthrithsson has sixty ships. Then there are their Jarls, mostly kin, who have their own ships. All together, I calculate, King Anlaf has over five hundred ships at his disposal."

Constantine's eyebrows rose up in surprise. He muttered, "I have underestimated his force."

Cellach's frown deepened, "King Anlaf has a legendary reputation as a warrior and he is also well known for good judgement and leadership. If he refuses to join us, he will influence the other kings. What can we offer him to join us? We cannot risk his refusal."

"Good point son." Questioning himself, his brow furrowed, "What is in my power to give him?" Breathing deeply, he reined in his snorting white stallion. Swinging his leg over the saddle he dismounted, "It is well known that King Anlaf wants Jorvic back under the control of the Clan Ivarr. The Northumbrian bishops want a Norse king." Thoughtfully, "If we win, Anlaf will get Jorvic. He will protect our borders."

"Or, he will attack our borders Da. In any case, will the promise of Jorvic, if we win, be enough to entice him to join us?" Cellach shook his head as he easily alighted from his horse. His stallion nudged him with his head and his ears pricked up. Stroking his stallion's sleek neck a smile played on his lips. He had developed a real bond with this horse. Lifting the bridle over his horse's head, he threaded the reins through an iron ring embedded in the brick mortar and tied them off quickly, "The Clan Ivarr has long been our enemy. Their attacks on our lands have been recorded by the monks for over two hundred years. I tell you now," his topaz eyes flashed with concern, "being allied with the Vikings does not sit well with me."

Looking down at him from his horse, Suibne spoke evenly, "My Prince, I am part Viking and I am your ally. My Norse ancestors married into your family. They settled in the Isles and govern them well."

He blinked as embarrassment flushed his cheeks, "Forgive my bluntness King Suibne. Your great Norse heritage is a gift from your illustrious and famous ancestors. I am also aware that our blood carries the same great Pict line of the Kings of Alba. However, Anlaf's line does not carry our blood."

A hint of smile played on Suibne's lips as he strongly dismounted and tied the reins to the iron ring. His horse stood docilely next to the others, "My sister Tasha, may the Gods protect her soul, married Anlaf's brother Black Arailt. His family and friends call him Blacarri. My nephews will one day rule Norse Gailgedhael, Man and Colonsay. It would seem that our blood lines grow ever closer."

Smiling affably, Cellach chuckled, "Suibne I apologise. You speak the truth. Our blood lines do grow closer."

"Well said King Suibne." Constantine raised his head, "Do you think you could convince the Clan Ivarr to join us?"

Suibne looked at him, "No. My brother in law respects me and he will listen to me but he will not follow me." A strong breeze rolled over the long grass at the edges of the courtyard like a wave. The trees in the distant forest rustled as amber and red leaves brushed against each other. His white blonde hair blew onto his shoulder. "In any case, it is Anlaf who you need to convince."

Turning to his father, Cellach suggested, "Da, maybe he would join us if you do offer him Jorvic."

Interrupting, Suibne smiled, "No. Anlaf would say he can take Jorvic back on his own."

Constantine frowned, "What can we offer him to join us?" Shaking his head, he walked towards the open halla door.

Eyeing each other curiously they followed him into the halla. As soon as they entered the shady long hall, their eyes suddenly glinted with concentration. Each of them noted where the burgh's men stood, and the fact that most of them carried two swords.

As he strode past them, Constantine's left eyebrow lifted when he recognised the man with the bow from the high street. He was obviously a lookout guard.

Coluim looked steadily back at him.

Looking up sharply, Cenheard stood to his feet, "Welcome to my burgh, King Constantine."

Astonished to be stood before a king, brother Ordberht's eyes widened with wonder.

Surprised that he had been recognised in these parts, Constantine strode up to the earl. Stood tall, eye to eye with him, he smiled, "Lord Cenheard, thank you for receiving us. May I introduce King Maelcoluim of Galwensis and King Suibne of the Many Isles?"

Brother Ordberht's eyes widened further. He forgot all

about his itching skin.

His expression remained impassive but Cenheard's dark brown eyes glinted as his heart raced with excitement. Every muscle in his body felt taut.

As the King of Alba introduced his son and the other nobles, Rafyn glanced at her father with concern. He looked very tense.

Cenheard eyed them sternly, "What is your business here my Lords?"

His topaz eyes glinted, "Lord Cenheard, we have travelled many leagues and our horses are tired and in need of attention. We are hungry and in dire need of hospitium."

"Hospitium?" Relief filled him, "Of course you are welcome to stay here tonight." He opened his arms welcomingly, "Whilst you are in my domain you will have my protection."

Constantine inclined his head respectfully at the very old fashioned pledge of safety to guests and travellers. He still used the words himself on occasion.

"Come, we will feast and when you are rested the Masters of Morrigu will entertain you." He eyed his youngest son, "Badwulf, arrange for our guest's horses to be taken to the stables. Ensure that they are well fed and watered. Ask the smithy to look over their hooves and replace any worn horseshoes."

Flicking her eyes to the door, Rafyn whispered to the maid, "Go to the kitchens Hanora, and tell my mother and the cooks, that we have royal guests. Thankfully it's a feast day and we have meat ready."

Much later, the Albans picked the last of the meat off the bones. Drinking very agreeable ale, they watched Lord Ragenhare and Lord Cenheard's sons perform in synchronisation, the incredible martial stances of the dance of the Goddess Morrigu.

Sat close to her grandfather and mother, Rafyn delicately drank her wine. Their guests and even brother Ordberht looked very entertained.

Leaning in close to her, Cellach smiled, his topaz eyes flashing with attraction, "This must be very boring for a pretty little thing like you?"

A smile played on her lips. Subtly, she lowered her eyes. Her long dark lashes fluttered against her cheeks. She hated playing the fragile lady, especially in front of her brothers. It almost felt demeaning. Standing up, she eyed him with a deep confident glance and walked slowly over to her brothers and uncle. Her long dark hair shimmered in the light from the many candles in the long hall.

Watching her with an unsure look on his handsome tanned face, he wondered if he had offended her. When she joined in, lithely and expertly moving into all of the stances of the martial art, Cellach grinned. Her moves and balances were so graceful and seamless, so perfect in fact, it was like watching a flawless dance. He could barely take his eyes off her when she led the astounding two sword martial dance.

For Brother Ordberht, it was the first time that he had seen the Dance of Morrigu and he found it incredible to behold. The speed of the dance, the flash of the swords, the absolute danger of just one mistake made him hold his breath. And Lady Rafyn was leading it! When the dance ended with a score of swords hurtling into the air and descending pommels first, only to be caught expertly by each of them, everyone in the room stood and clapped. Grinning from ear to ear, no one clapped more effusively than him.

The next morning, each of them nursed a slight hangover as they climbed on their refreshed horses.

Glancing up, Cellach felt disappointed not to have got to know Lady Rafyn better. He had found her fascinating, and elusive. Last night, at a very respectable time, she had left with her mother and the other maids, and that had been the last time he had seen her. The men, including the monk had stayed, drinking until the candles burnt out. Finally, one by one, they had fallen asleep. Only he and the monk had remained awake. Sat by the light of the fire, he had talked with brother Ordberht about the way of God. The monk had gently answered all of his searching questions and he felt as if all of the stars had aligned. He understood now, why he had not removed King Athelstan's gold cross from his neck. He truly felt God's presence in his life and it gave him immense peace to know this.

Stood next to Lord Cenheard, brother Ordberht called loudly, "Go with God."

Nodding to him, Cellach turned and cantered his horse to keep up with his father.

Cenheard breathed a sigh of relief as he watched them ride out of the fortress, he grunted with irritation, "Thank the Gods they have gone. I have no time for strangers in my burgh!"

Watching them leave, brother Ordberht smiled. He had rather enjoyed himself. The meal and the ale had been delicious. And, even though he knew that the thought was verging on sacrilege, he knew that he would never forget the dance of the Goddess Morrigu. But more than that, he felt he had helped Prince Cellach come to terms with his new found religion. That meant more to him than anything. In this pleasant Celtic burgh, his tiny congregation had grown to six already and he did not even have a fully built church yet. Away from the domineering archbishop, he was starting to truly believe in himself.

As they left the burgh, gazing north at the hills in the distance, Constantine's thoughts drifted to home. He missed his family so much. His thoughts turned to his youngest son and his girls.

Next to him, Cellach's brow furrowed as he contemplated, "What are we going to do about the Norse Da? How will we entice them to join our alliance?"

Suddenly lifting his chin, he frowned as his heartbeat raced. He knew what he must do. His eyes glistened as he turned to Cellach, "Son, I know what I must give King Anlaf to join our alliance. I will need to offer him a treasure so precious, so exquisite, that he could not conceivably refuse."

He looked quizzically at his father.

The strengthening breeze rolled over the green meadow grasses ominously. The long grasses reeled and rolled, like sea waves. Constantine turned away, his topaz eyes glazed desolately, "But it will break my heart to give it."

Part 3

The Princess

3.1

Ath Cliath, Ireland
April 935AD

The purple sail appeared in the distance just as the sun began to drop in the sky. The river Liffey shimmered, reflecting every shade of the auburn and golden yellow sunset that gloriously lit up the heavens above.

Sat on a barrel, his young bright hazel eyes keen, one of the scruffy lookouts glimpsed the purple sail through a myriad of red square sailed ships. The others had missed it. He said nothing. Watching intently, he saw the ship turn rudder and rigging. The veer was only slight, the vessel was a long way off, but he knew it was heading towards Wood Quay. He suddenly jumped off the barrel and raced past the fishermen mending their nets.

The other lookouts stood up on the barrels and craned their thin necks, trying to see what could have made him react so quickly.

Dodging rickety wagons, pushed by well-built men, he sprinted through the colourful noisy streets at break neck speed. He knew that if he could get to the castle first with the news, he might earn himself a meal or even a piece of silver. Turning uphill towards the fortress, he ducked past noisy merchants carrying baskets full of their wares. Some carried flat bread, others carried fur pelts. One man carried a mass of dried fire wood strung to his back with rope. People dressed in shabby clothes strolled around lean to shops and loudly bartered for goods. The huge fortress stood proudly golden, reflecting the glorious sky above. As his legs ran like the wind, he grinned. The feeling of freedom that came from running filled his soul. Big wiry haired wolf hounds barked at him as he skirted the guards at the fortress gates. He crossed the court-yard at lightning speed. The huge metal studded oak doors of the king's halla were wide open. Darting through them, he ran as fast as he could through the halla. Coloured light streamed in through thickly glazed windows. Gleaming weapons and painted shields hung on the walls. Warriors and well dressed courtiers wandered through the room, greeting friends and flirting with the ladies. Some just sat at tables eating a meal provided by the castle kitchen wenches and serving girls. Recognising his king, he fell to his knees and slid the last few lengths halting right in front of the dais.

Sat nonchalantly on a chair, his feet resting on a footstool, the king's dark haired brother, Blacarri eyed the lad with amusement.

Bending his head respectfully, Ketil stuttered, "King Anlaf, your Majesty." Although hardly winded, he could hear his own voice tremble. Glancing up to see if he had been heard, his keen eyes took in everything. The king was dressed richly in fine leather trousers and boots. His pure white open necked tunic was pulled in at his athletic waist by his wide black leather sword belt. A long crimson cape was secured by ruby clasps to his wide muscular shoulders. It hung to his knees. The King's shoulder length blonde hair was half tied back with a thin strap of leather. To him, the king's blue eyed expression looked determined and enduring.

Anlaf stood resting his hands on the huge table. Small frown lines marred his ruggedly handsome clean shaven face. He barely looked up from the scroll document. The featureless lad in front of him looked uninteresting in his faded dull garments. Impatiently, "What is it lad?"

He bent his head, his voice shook, "Majesty, a purple sailed ship is sailing towards Wood Quay." As he watched the king stride out of the hallway, followed by several of his armed guard, he muttered, "Only royalty travel under a purple sail."

Watching him thoughtfully with pale grey eyes, Blacarri drawled, "That is correct lad. Do you know who is aboard the ship?"

Looking up as the man reached for a plain gold crown that had been left carelessly on the arm of the throne, he half smiled, "No Milord Black Arailt, I did not recognise the vessel. The ship has not visited Ath Cliath before or I would remember it."

His black battle leathers fitted tight against his hard muscular body. The metal of his sword pommel and thick silver arm bands shimmered. Surprised that the lad addressed him formally, he eyed him with interest, "Have we met before?"

The lookout smiled, barely containing his nervous excitement, "No Milord, but I have seen you many times with your brother the king. You are the next in line to the throne and the greatest warrior of Ath Cliath!"

He smiled at the lad's enthusiastic reply, "What's your name lad?"

His hazel eyes twinkled, "I am Ketil, Milord."

"You are not a sailor. Who told you royalty travel under a purple sail?"

"I heard it in a tavern once. I'm good at remembering things I hear and see." He looked almost apologetic.

A muscle flickered in Blacarri's jaw. The lad was a few years older than his eldest son but he had hardly any muscle mass. Deciding to test the lad's memory, he asked, "That is a very useful skill. How many men just left with the king?"

Pure concentration glazed his eyes, "Six men followed him immediately. The warrior with the scars, I do not know his name, was eating at that table. He wore wrist guards decorated with flying eagles. He followed them too."

Surprised at his detailed reply, Blacarri nodded, "The warrior with the scars is Jarl Barrick."

Ketil eyed him, "I remember, I heard his friend's call him Scarface."

"Where did you hear that?"

Apologetically, "In a tavern."

His pale grey glinted, "Good." Blacarri took off a small silver wrist band. Throwing it to the lad, he smiled, "Well done Ketil, here's a reward for your trouble."

Catching the silver band, he gawped at it in wonder, "For me?" it was the most expensive object that he had ever possessed. Stumbling to his feet he barely mumbled, "Milord, thank you."

"I always pay well for good information." Blacarri lowered his voice, "I need an intelligent, discreet man who remembers what he hears. I am looking to employ an aide. Come to my antechamber tomorrow morning. I may have more gainful employment than lookout duties for you."

Blinking quickly, Ketil tried a curt bow. It felt a little ungainly, "Yes Milord." The silver wrist band was far too big for his wrist but it fitted his thin arm well.

Impatient to catch up his brother, Blacarri wafted his hand signalling for the lad to leave.

Hardly able to stop smiling, Ketil turned and strode out of the halla. As soon as he stepped outside, he broke into a fast run back to Wood Quay. He did not want to miss a royal ship dock.

Striding into the kingshalla, smacking horse dust from his battle leathers with his large hands, Ragnal looked around the court. Only a few serving wenches and a couple of older nobles remained, curiously, "Where is everybody?"

Blacarri's eyes flashed with excitement, "A purple sailed ship has arrived at Wood Quay. Anlaf has just left to meet it. Stay here and tell the servants to be ready to receive royal ambassadors. Have the best wine ready and tell the cooks to prepare delicacies."

Watching his brother stride out of the halla, Ragnal raised a blonde eyebrow at the remaining few courtiers and serving girls. Flexing his broad muscular shoulders, shaking his head, he mumbled, "Prepare delicacies! I think he thinks I'm his sister!"

Sashaying her hips as she walked up to him, one of the more confident serving girls smiled prettily, "Prince Ragnal," she cast her green eyes at him, her long red hair fell vibrantly down her back, "I can take care of that if you wish, Milord?"

He looked relieved, "Thank you, Helga."

She thought that she felt his eyes on her as she went into the kitchens. Smiling, she looked back hopefully but he had already turned and walked off. A little put out, she frowned as she walked up to the head cook, "A royal ship has docked. The king wants a feast of delicacies preparing now."

The kitchen suddenly became noisy with panic.

The round faced head cook spoke with authority, "Quiet!"

The servants, cooks and serving wenches immediately obeyed him.

"King Anlaf may rule the court but I am king in this kitchen! We do not have time to prepare suckling pig or pottage. We will have oysters, crayfish, smoked herring and roe. Get that salt bread out of the bread oven before it burns!" Concentrating intently, he began issuing orders to get the food preparation started.

3.2

The sailors on the purple sailed ship bustled about stowing their oars.

On the wooden quayside, King Anlaf Guthrithsson and the small army of his elite men arrived on horseback to meet the vessel. The shimmering waters of the vast wide River Liffy lapped against the wooden quay. Gulls and swans floated on the gleaming river water, close to the dock, hoping for scraps from the fishermen.

Riding his mount skilfully through the streets with twenty of his own men at arms, Blacarri caught them up. Ordering his men to dismount by the quay, he rode his horse onto the wooden dock and agilely dismounted, "Scarface, can you take my horse?"

Stepping forward, Scarface muttered gruffly as he took the horse bridle and patted the horse's neck to settle him, "Sure can."

"Thanks." Blacarri's black leather boots thudded on the wooden planks of the quay as he strode up to his brother. Grinning, he looked over to the ship. The purple sail was already furled.

Anlaf looked perplexed, "Do we know who it is yet, Blacarri?"

"No, but I'm sure when the ship has finished docking we will find out." Mockingly, "Shame you forgot your gold headband."

"Thor's hammer!" He swore loudly, "I have no idea who the visitor could be. No messengers or envoys have come to my court since last autumn. A royal ship arrives and I forget my crown! How will that look?"

Grinning as he pulled the golden headband from his black cloak, "I spotted it slung on the arm of your throne and thought you might need it."

Smiling with relief, Anlaf put the headband on. It sat well on his blonde head, "How does it look?"

He shrugged his muscular shoulders, "Well, you're still ugly but the crown looks good!"

Amused, Anlaf chuckled.

Looking at the ship, Blacarri rolled his eyes, "How long does it take to stow a few oars?"

"Be patient brother."

A short while later, as seagulls landed ungainly on the dock screeching over a few scraps of fish, Blacarri watched his brother agitatedly pace along the wooden jetty. Turning, he looked behind him at the retinue of king's men sat on horses. Fully armed and dressed in black battle leathers, they looked darkly menacing. Behind them, he noticed a small crowd of inquisitive boys dressed in rags. With their bare dirty feet dangling they sat on barrels covered with old fishing nets. In the shadowy background, he recognised Ketil's face watching them. He must have run like the wind back from the fortress.

Hearing orders being shouted onboard the docked ship, they all turned to see who had arrived.

Suddenly, two large red haired sailors slid a long wide wooden bridge from the ship to the jetty.

All of the men on the quayside waited in anticipation.

A moment later a solitary slim silhouette appeared. A woman dressed in a long flowing emerald silk gown stepped alone from the ship on to the top of the bridge. The sunset lit up the sky golden and shimmering behind her.

"A woman? Who is she?" Anlaf turned in surprise looking at his brother questioningly.

Having no idea who this maid was, Blacarri shrugged his shoulders as he watched her appreciatively.

Gracefully, she walked down the bridge to the jetty. Her

long curling strawberry blonde hair hung down her back. Her golden headband signified that she was of royal blood.

Blacarri glanced back at the men behind him. Each of their faces wore the same mesmerised look.

Even Ketil was lost in awe. His mouth agape, he barely breathed.

Anlaf stood captivated by the young woman's beauty as she slowly walked towards him.

Her fascinating proud topaz gaze never left his until she sank into low and elegant curtsy before him.

Anlaf took her hand, "I am amazed that a woman of such beauty is not escorted." His instinct told him to treat her with great respect. Gently, he bent low to kiss her ringed hand as he raised her from her graceful curtsy, "You are the most beautiful visitor to ever grace my land. Who are you?"

Self-assured confidence of royalty hinted in her voice, "I am Princess Maelmare, eldest daughter of Constantine of Alba. I bring you a message from my father the king."

"You, a Princess of Alba," He raised a blonde eyebrow in surprise, "have been sent as your father's ambassador?"

"Yes. My father's message is of immense importance and..." for the briefest of moments her voice faltered. Her eyelashes fluttered as she hesitated. Despite her show of confidence, in reality, she felt incredibly frightened and vulnerable. She breathed a soft breath of anxiety through her pretty full lips. Then, drawing on her royal upbringing, she stoically raised her chin and continued regally, "And affects both our kingdoms greatly, your Majesty."

He was intrigued by her. For all of her bravado walking into his kingdom alone, he noticed a slight tremor of fear in her voice as she spoke. He smiled gently and held on to her small delicate pale hand a moment longer than was necessary. His deep blue eyes softened as he looked into her unusual coloured topaz eyes, "Welcome Princess, while you are in my domain you have my protection."

"Thank you." The weather had not been favourable for her

journey. High winds had forced them to harbour in a small fishing port. It had taken a few days of travelling for her to reach Ath Cliath and she was tired. The ship had been far from comfortable. This was the first time in her sixteen years that she had ever felt truly afraid. As daughter of a king, she had always lived securely in the protection of her father but now she walked alone into another man's kingdom. A soft anxious breath escaped her lips again.

He smiled, "My Lady, it would do me great honour if you would join me tomorrow for a feast in celebration of your arrival to my court. I would imagine, that a woman of your refinement, is not used to the rigours of the sea. May I offer you and your servants rest, food and lodging in my fortress tonight?"

Surprised by his gallantry, she blinked. Her ladies had warned her that Norsemen were ruthless and brutal, warily, "My Lord, you honour me with your kindness. However, I am extremely tired and would like to rest. My ship serves my needs well so I will stay here tonight."

Smiling indulgently at her caution, he bent low to her ear whispering deeply, "This river is full of pirates and slave ships."

She raised her chin, "I command an army of thirty elite warriors of Alba."

He grinned at her bravado. Looking up at the ship, he saw at least twenty fully armed and battle clad men watching him intently. Most of them had varying shades of auburn hair. At the head of the small army, a young dark haired woman eyed him fiercely."

"And, I have my maid of honour to attend me. I will hold my court here on my ship."

Flicking his eyes to his brother with amusement, Anlaf grinned.

Still holding on to the horse bridle, Scarface glanced at Blacarri, he whispered gruffly, "If the Vikings of Ath Cliath don't seize her tonight then the Irish pirates will!"

Grinning, his teeth white against his tanned face, Blacarri

chuckled.

His blue eyes sparkling, Anlaf looked down at her courteously, "You and your retinue will not be safe here Princess. I would prefer it if you stay in my fortress tonight. I will also place a guard around your vessel."

Assertively, "No thank you, I will..."

Raising his eyebrows, Anlaf interrupted her, sternly to his brother, "Blacarri, extend our warm welcome to my Lady's guards but do not let them leave this ship. And, bring her maid." Scooping her up into his strong arms, he strode over to his horse. "My Lady, you will reside at my fortress."

Blacarri chuckled with the rest of the men as they watched her struggle against him. Turning to them, he consciously deepened his voice, "The king is not a patient man when his mind was made up."

She gasped as he swung her up onto the saddle of his horse as if she were a child.

A moment later, Anlaf mounted his horse behind her and placed a muscular arm around her waist. Taking the bridle with his free hand, he grinned.

Her eyes sparkled angrily, "Sir! You are over familiar with my person!"

Chuckling, he held her tighter, "I apologise my Lady." Leaning in close to her slim white neck, he whispered huskily against her ear, "Next time I will ask permission." He did not see her alarmed look as he dug his heels into the flanks of his horse. The stallion spurred into a gallop back towards the fortress. Two of his guards followed him.

The princess barely heard her maid of honour scream "No!"

Lifting her mulberry skirt, the maid ran down the jetty to the dock, followed by several of the Alban warriors.

They drew their weapons as they ran.

Quickly drawing their swords, Blacarri's guardsmen braced themselves.

Ketil and the street boys jumped back off the barrels in alarm.

Grabbing the maid and pulling her to him, his strong muscular arm tight about her small waist, Blacarri shouted to the Alban warriors, "King Constantine's daughter and this maid will bring you death if they remain on this ship at night! Surely every pirate and slaver within ten leagues of here will bear down on your small vessel," he deepened his voice ominously, "for such rare and beautiful royal prizes!"

His hazel eyes glinting anxiously, Ketil was almost ready to run. If a full skirmish broke out he did not want to get caught up in it, especially with these hardened warriors.

The Albans stood in their tracks, their weapons drawn, they eyed Blacarri agitatedly.

The woman struggling in his arms gazed over her shoulder, she screamed, "Stop them! They are taking the princess!"

Confidently, Blacarri eyed them. He raised his voice loudly formal, "I am King Black Arailt of Mann, Colonsay and Norse Gailgedhail. My brother, King Anlaf of Ath Cliath, will not allow the daughter of King Constantine to be harmed in his kingdom. She will stay in the safety of our fortress tonight. If you leave this ship, we will consider it an act of war." His grey eyes flashed warningly, "Stay here. My guards will protect your ship. The princess will be brought to you unharmed tomorrow."

The tallest Alban warrior took a step closer. He frowned. He knew they had no choice but to obey him, loudly he ordered, "Fallback men!" Eyeing the dark haired Viking aggressively, he added loudly, "If anything happens to his eldest daughter, King Constantine will rip out your brother's heart with his bare hands!"

The dark haired maid looked at her guardsmen in total disbelief. Her mouth fell open as she realised they would not fight the heathens. She started struggling and kicking out. She would fight them all the way to hell and back to save the princess!

The ride to the fortress was a frightening blur for Princess

Maelmare.

As soon as they arrived at the king's halla, Anlaf dismounted. Placing his hands around her tiny waist he gently lowered her to the ground.

Angrily slapping his hand away she faced him, "My father will hear of your impertinence!"

Confidently, he softly drawled, "Good, your father will be grateful that I did not leave you on the quay. I can assure you, my Lady, that by nightfall, you would have been abducted by pirates. By the time the sun arose tomorrow, you would be halfway to the slave halls of Constantinople."

Blinking with surprise, "No pirate would dare to touch me," haughtily she lifted her chin, "I am a Princess of Alba."

"Indeed you are a Princess of Alba and worth a fortune as a hostage. Even more, I wager, as a beautiful slave." Mockingly, "My Lady, I am amazed you made it here at all."

A look of real fear crossed her face. Involuntarily, she trembled as she realised he was right.

His blue eyes twinkled as his gaze softened, "You are much safer here Princess. I keep a full guard inside the fortress. You and your retinue will be shown every courtesy. Please allow me to escort you into my halla." Holding out his arm, he smiled gently, "Come, we will take wine whilst we watch the sun set and wait for your maid to disembark from your ship."

Suddenly feeling very alone, her lip trembled.

Watching her reaction, he gently looked into her beautiful topaz coloured eyes, "I promise you will be safe."

Summoning every ounce of bravery from the core of her being, placing her arm delicately on his, she took in a deep breath. As he led her through the doors to the great hall, she looked up at the great apex beamed ceiling. To her, the hall seemed vast. It was already well lit by hundreds of creamy white beeswax candles and great iron torches. Shimmering weapons and painted shields hung on the walls, as if waiting to be grabbed for battle.

Word had got round that a royal vessel had docked at the

quay. Men and women filled the room. Most of the men wore battle leathers and carried weapons. Nudging each other, they quickly bowed as she passed them.

Leaning confidently against the wall, Ragnal eyed her curiously as she passed.

Watching her thoughtfully as well, Prince Olaf and Jarl Canute, stood close to the dais.

Leading her to the dais, Anlaf turned to his court. Still holding her arm, he announced loudly, "I present, Princess Maelmare of Alba."

Murmurs of interest filled the court.

Gallantly, he added, "The princess has my protection, as do her retinue." Turning her to the slightly smaller throne next to his, he smiled, "Pray be seated. You must be thirsty. I have some very good wine from Europe."

Hearing him from the kitchen doorway, Helga immediately grabbed one of the better silver decanters and filled it with the king's best wine from a large open barrel. Taking two of the more delicate silver goblets, she placed them on a tray and walked confidently towards the dais.

"Thank you, your Majesty." Sitting down gracefully, Maelmare gazed out to the room full of warriors and ladies. Realising that they were assessing her, she lifted her chin confidently and eyed them back with her unflinching topaz gaze.

Noticing her fearlessly proud performance, a smile twitched at his lips. He sat down on the larger throne.

Inquisitively, Helga's green eyes flashed a glance at the princess as she curtseyed and offered her a full goblet of wine. To her, the princess looked incredibly elegant in her green gown.

Anlaf smiled, "Try it."

She barely noticed the serving wench. Taking the wine, she took a small delicate sip of the deeply dark crimson liquid. It really was very good. Hearing a commotion, her gaze turned to the open halla doors.

As Helga finished serving the king, a woman's voice cried out angrily, "Unhand me you heathen!"

Maelmare proudly masked her relief as her young dark haired maid of honour was brought to her.

His deep blue eyes sparkling, Anlaf grinned. Half dragged into the vast room by his brother, the maid struggled valiantly all the way.

Some of his men followed them into the halla. They could not stop laughing as she lashed out.

The warrior with the scars stood well back and chuckled as the maid tried desperately to kick out at anyone who was near her.

Alarmed, Blacarri threw a look of warning to his brother as he held on to the wrists of the struggling woman. She writhed and thrashed so much, the long sleeves on her mulberry gown ripped at her shoulders. He announced loudly, "May I present, Lady Muldivana."

Anlaf could not stop his grin deepening, she looked furious.

"Unhand me you heathen!" Angrily, she kicked the black haired Viking in the shin.

The pain was intense. Taken by surprise, Blacarri foolishly let go of one of her hands.

Incensed, she suddenly lunged at him hitting him with a mighty, and resoundingly loud, slap across his face.

With the pretence of bravery, smiling at his chuckling men, he rubbed the angry red mark stating slowly, "Ouch!"

Wrenching her other hand from his grasp, she rounded on him clenching her fist she hit the other side of his face with some force.

"Ouch!" Taking a long step back, his pale grey eyes glinted with alarm. A trickle of blood ran from his lip. As she took another purposeful step towards him, with both of her fists clenched, he backed off even further, "Get away from me you hell cat!"

Furious but free, she lifted her mulberry brocade gown above her slim ankles and dainty leather boots. Her ruby red underskirt flashed ominously as she marched straight over to Anlaf. Her dark hazel coloured eyes sparkled with indignation,

"This is outrageous!"

Sat on his large wooden throne, Anlaf looked taken aback. As she came closer, he quickly rose to his feet. He smiled with uneasy amusement at his brother.

Raising his dark eyebrows, Blacarri grinned back at him, "My Lady Muldivana please let me introduce my brother, King Anlaf." Relieved that the young woman had turned her attention to his brother, he stood back, feeling full of amused trepidation, waiting to see what she would do next.

Maelmare watched fascinated. Muldivana was at least a foot shorter than both the well-built King and his brother. But as the pretty brown haired woman unleashed the full force of her rage upon them, it was obvious that it was them who felt intimidated. Seeing the king's apprehension, she barely hid her smile.

Alarmed, Anlaf chuckled idiotically.

Even Helga barely suppressed giggle.

Marching up to him, Muldivana scolded loudly, "I will not have my Lady treated in this manner! You may be King of this dreadful heathen land but you will treat my Lady with respect, as her status befits her!"

It was not the first time that Maelmare had seen grown men in fear of her formidable maid. Muldivana was very petite and graceful but when provoked she had a fearsome temper. She almost felt sorry for the king, softly, "Lady Muldivana you forget yourself." She asserted with quiet dignified force, "As you can see, I am quite safe."

She marched over to her mistress, "Forget myself! Forget myself! I thought you should be killed or worse when he carried you off on that horse! How dare they treat a Princess of Alba this way? Your father would wage war on these heathens for less!"

She kept her voice deliberately steady and commanding, "Lady Muldivana control yourself." The princess fixed the twenty year old maiden with a warning silencing stare.

Breathing deeply, it took every ounce of effort for her to restrain her temper.

The princess turned gracefully back to the blonde haired king who was looking extremely entertained, as did the rest of the men in the room, "Your Grace, I am very tired and I wish to retire. May I be shown to my quarters?"

"Certainly," eyeing Muldivana with a wicked mischievous glint in his eye, "you will stay in my rooms."

The strain of the journey and the terrible anxiety she had felt as she had watched her charge abducted by the Norse king, and the stress of being at the mercy of these men, suddenly erupted from her core, "That will not do!" She almost exploded with rage, "My Lady's reputation must be protected! I insist that she does not sleep with you!"

Anlaf lifted his chiselled chin in exaggerated shock at her suggestion.

Watching them, Blacarri chuckled. His white teeth gleamed against his tanned face.

Anlaf continued feigning appalled shock, "I would not dream of defiling a princess's reputation. I was about to add that I would vacate my rooms for you and the princess."

Muldivana gazed at him astounded for a moment. Then her face reddened in embarrassment.

Even Maelmare, could not mask the smile twitching at her lips.

As the two ladies were escorted from the room by a male servant, Canute looked thoughtfully at Olaf. Could this be an opportunity to raise Olaf's fortunes?

Olaf's eyes glittered with ambition as his gaze followed the Alban princess.

A short time later the two ladies walked alone around the king's bed chamber in surprised awe. The floor was covered in rich soft furs. Curtains of breathtaking red brocade were draped back from stained glass windows. Tables were bedecked in gold and silver plates, goblets and candelabras. His vast collection of weapons and armour hung on the walls.

Even his large mahogany four post bed was beautifully dressed with the red brocade. Two maids had just finished dressing the bed with clean sheets. They quickly fluffed up the large duck feather pillows and bobbed curtseys as they left the room carrying baskets of bed linen.

Thoughtfully the king had arranged for female slaves to fill two large baths with steaming hot water.

Eyeing the opulence with astonishment, Lady Muldivana whispered to the princess, "I was not expecting this richness from the heathen king."

The loud knock on the chamber door startled them.

Taking in a deep over stressed breath, she lowered her voice, "Princess, shall I open the door?"

Resolutely lifting her chin, Maelmare nodded.

Grabbing one of the king's long knives and hiding it behind her back she glared at the door. Taking another deep breath, Muldivana scowled as she opened it.

A large ruddy round faced man bowed. His apron over his lightweight leggings and thin mulberry coloured tunic was clean. Deeply, "I am the palace head cook Milady. Food and wine Milady."

The food looked and smelt good. Immediately relaxing, she stood back, "How kind. Please bring it in."

A plain faced plump serving woman followed him in carrying a platter of hot food. Her blue eyes glinted with excitement. She stood still, a little overawed. Wisps of her blonde hair fell loosely from her cap.

Muldivana wondered if she was a little dim.

The cook looked irritated, "Kari! Stop staring at the ladies!"

Regaining her wits, smiling inanely, Kari moved to the table.

Behind her, a smile twitched at Helga's lips, as she followed carrying a silver flagon of wine.

Looking at the maids, Muldivana thought that their everyday dresses and leather boots were dull but the women were clearly clean, well fed and healthy.

Placing the wine on the table, Helga confidently bobbed a curtsey to her.

Feeling a little foolish to be holding the long knife behind her back, Muldivana quickly placed it on a nearby table.

A beautiful woman, dressed in a pure white gown, entered the room. Her long perfumed, white blonde, hair hung straight and loose down her slim back, almost trailing to the floor.

Surprised, Maelmare noticed the woman wore a slave armlet made of gold.

The cook bowed and the two kitchen servants bobbed clumsy curtseys to her and the slave, as they left the room, leaving the door open.

Quietly watching her, Maelmare thought she must be high ranking. It was strange that servants showed so much respect to a slave.

The slave woman stated confidently, "Come."

Fourteen pretty women walked into the room each carrying a silk gown in their arms.

The elegant slave motioned for the women to give the gowns to the princess and the lady.

Captivated by them, Lady Muldivana picked up each gown and studied the garments. She sighed with awe as she marvelled at the intricate stitch work.

Sweeping back her long white blonde hair, she stated eloquently, "I hope that Princess Maelmare and Lady Muldivana enjoy wearing these gowns. They are a present from the king." Her long flawless white skinned arm swept to her side and her tapering fingers appeared to extend softly and naturally, as she sank into charming curtsey. Rising with poise, she turned to leave the room.

Surprised by the slave's obvious genteel nobility, Maelmare spoke with the authority of a princess, "Wait."

Turning back to her, the lovely slave bowed her head submissively.

Looking over her with interest curiosity prickled, "You wear a slave bracelet yet the servants treated you very respectfully.

Who are you?"

"I am the slave called Driffa, my Lady." She spoke softly but did not make eye contact.

"Look at me."

Slowly, dutifully tilting her head up, Driffa looked directly into the princess's bright topaz eyes.

"Your eyes are the palest blue that I have ever seen and your hair is the whitest. Driffa, what an unusual name, what does it mean?"

"My name means 'drift of pure white snow' my Lady."

Looking at her gleaming white hair, Maelmare smiled gently, "I see why you were given that name. Pray thank your master for the dresses. They are very beautiful."

"My Lady, my master did not give you the dresses. The dresses are a gift from King Anlaf."

"The king is not your master?" She looked surprised, "I assumed that you were the king's property."

"No my Lady, my master is the king's designated heir, his brother Prince Black Arailt Guthrithsson."

Muldivana frowned, "He was that hateful heathen who dragged me here."

Maelmare looked curious, "I see. Why then, are you in the king's apartments?"

"The king requested my presence to serve you my Lady." Serenely, "I am admired for my gentleness. The king thought that a lady of your grace and elegance would appreciate this."

"Thank you Driffa. You are a slave now but I sense that you are of noble blood. Am I right?"

"Yes my Lady."

Intrigued, "Who was your father?"

"I was born a Princess of Sweden. My father was King Bjorn Eriksson. I was captured by raiders when I was twelve years old and sold to Black Arailt's wife, Queen Tasha. She kept me as a hand maid to her children."

"I have been told that the king's brother is also free to wed."

"Yes, that is true, Queen Tasha died after giving birth to her third child."

Maelmare frowned as she gazed at the woman who had once been a princess but was now a slave, "You must be very disillusioned by how your life turned out."

A small smile played on Driffa's lips, "My Lady," She spoke gently, "as a princess I would have been married, against my will, to any noble or prince who would bring my father's land bounty or protection. I am content. I love Queen Tasha's children and I am respected in my master's house. I am under his protection."

Her topaz eyes widened for a moment as Driffa's words resonated with her. She asked too quickly, "Does the king's brother use you as his wife?"

She blinked in surprise at the princess' blunt question, "No my Lady. Black Arailt does not rape. He has had mistresses since his wife died, but none last for very long."

A look of fear passed over her lovely face, Maelmare's voice trembled, "Does the king rape?"

Driffa held Maelmare's gaze, gently, "No my Lady, King Anlaf does not rape. He too has had many willing mistresses."

Used to court intrigue, Maelmare asked impassively, "Who is his current mistress?"

"No one at court but I believe he is a regular visitor to a tavern girl on Fish Street."

"Is he in love with her?"

Thoughtfully, "If the king was in love, he would house her at court. No, I do not think he is in love."

She decided to ask one more question, "Is the king kind?"

Driffa nodded, "Yes, the king is kind to his friends." She added candidly to the Alban princess, "However, he is a brutal warrior and ruthless to his enemies."

Maelmare smiled at her honesty, "You may return tomorrow to help me dress."

"Thank you my Lady." She curtseyed and left the room.

"Well," Muldivana stated bluntly as she closed the door and turned the large key, "at least this heathen king has some knowledge of refinement. I was surprised at the bath but sending the dresses and a maid to help you! I thought I should faint I was that flabbergasted!"

Maelmare nodded rather surprised herself, "Indeed, it was all very thoughtful of the king. What do you think of him?"

She did not hesitate, "He is handsome and has kingly manners but I will never forgive him for dragging you off on that horse. I thought I would die from the shock of it."

"Yes, me too." Suddenly remembering the sensuous feel of his warm breath against her neck, she tingled as she ran her tapering fingers over her skin just under her ear. Looking away trying to hide her flush she walked to the food table, "It has been a very exhilarating day. I am going to eat, take a bath and then I will sleep the night through."

Turning to the large bed, Muldivana ran her hand over the luxurious soft red brocade bedspread, tentatively, "Do you think that we will be safe here tonight Princess?"

"Yes we will be safe. Of that I have no doubt."

She watched the princess pour herself a goblet of wine, "Really, what makes you so sure?"

Lifting her chin with self-assured confidence, Maelmare gazed at her, "I am sure because we are under King Anlaf's protection."

"Well, I do not think I shall sleep a wink this night!"

A short time later, both dressed in their pure white chemises, they fell asleep in the large bed. Not even Muldivana's soft melodious snoring could wake the princess.

In his small dark chamber, Olaf's deep blue eyes glinted. Eyeing Canute, he scowled, "What are they doing here?"

Calmly, Canute stoked the fire, "I don't know but this could be a real chance for you."

He looked sullen as he brushed back his blonde hair.

Bluntly, "Olaf, I thought that you would have to marry one of the Irish princesses to further our ambitions but this is far more fortuitous."

His eyes widened as he shook his head, "Why do I have to marry? I will take my kingdom back by force!"

Tired and grouchy, Canute almost growled, "And how do you expect to pay an army?"

Alarmed, Olaf eyed him warily, "I don't know."

He shook his greying head, breathing deeply, "You need support! You are poor! Your only chance is to wed a rich princess!" He rarely raised his voice to his charge. He immediately regretted it, "I am sorry my prince, I grow old and tired."

Olaf's blue eyes looked young and bright, "I hate him!"

"Who?"

"Anlaf!"

Canute looked surprised, "Why do you hate the king? He has protected you."

He snarled, "He has everything that should be mine!"

Taking in a deep breath, Canute frowned, "Your day will come Olaf. Get some rest and think about courting the Alban princess. She will have a fortune in dowry." Standing up, he strode to the adjoining door between their rooms, "If you marry her, you will have the King of Alba's support and her personal guard. Then we can plan how you will take back Northumbria."

3.3

Scone, Alba

Many thousands of stars glittered in the vast night sky, the moon was almost full. River waves lapped against the wooden jetty. In the distance an owl hooted eerily. Waiting on his ship, Archbishop Wulfstan eyed the heavens haughtily, his black eyes glinting. It had been a dangerous journey and uncomfortable in the extreme but necessary to meet the King of Alba. He imagined the man who had sat on the throne of Alba for decades now as old, plump and conceited. Only an ageing, overconfident ruler would plan to overthrow High King Athelstan. A huffy breath escaped from his lips. Shaking his head, he wondered to himself, why was he here? Of course the answer screamed at him in his head. Constantine's plan could work. If all of the Kings of Britain stood together against King Athelstan, they could actually overthrow him. But Constantine needed the Norse, and so did he. Pulling up his dark green cape hood to cover his head, he glanced sideways at his men. Blowing contemptuously through his thin lips his black eyes flashed. He felt irritated beyond words. Travelling incognito, he had commanded his men at arms to remove his heraldic colours. The ship looked stark with the sail furled up against the rigging. Most of his men sat on chests or barrels. Dressed in their battle leathers, they silently looked towards the distant lights on the higher ground. The Palace of Scone was well lit tonight.

One of his men stood up, his voice deep, "Your Grace, riders are approaching."

His jet black eyes slanted as he looked over the side of

the ship. He saw two well-armed, muscular warriors riding towards his ship. One held a blazing torch. They wore long hooded cloaks over their battle leathers. Slowing their horses they waited by a copse of trees.

Tedium tinged his tone, "Wait here. I will go to the palace alone." Walking confidently down the draw bridge to the jetty, he strode along the wooden planks until his boots felt the soft brush of long grass. His cloak billowed behind him exposing the shimmer of his long sword. Striding up to the fully armed warriors, he ordered aloofly, "Take me to your king. He is expecting me."

Sat on his white stallion, Constantine eyed Cellach from under his cape hood. Silently, they turned their mounts, walking into the copse of trees.

Glad of the moonlight, he followed them until they stopped.

Deciding that they were far enough away from the jetty not to be seen by the men on the ship, turning his horse, Constantine nodded to Cellach.

The heat from the torch was irritatingly close to his face but Cellach did not flinch, "You are in the presence of his Majesty, King Constantine of Alba."

Removing his hood, Constantine lifted his chin. His topaz eyes eerily reflected the orange, red flame of the torch.

His dark eyebrows momentarily lifted in surprise as he looked up at the warrior king. He was the exact opposite of what he had been expecting. Constantine was in his forties but he was still chiselled, muscular and obviously physically powerful. Suddenly bowing theatrically, Wulfstan attempted a sort of a smile. It did not come easily. It was more like a grimace, "Your Majesty, I am overwhelmed by your cunning disguise."

Eyeing him indifferently, Constantine shrugged his huge muscular shoulders, "It does me no good to meet you publicly, Archbishop. Your reputation as a treacherous spy precedes you."

A twinge of a snarl formed on his upper lip at the open

insult, coldly, "Famous men have always been at the whim of slanderous rivals. My allegiance is always to Northumbria, Majesty."

Holding his bridle, his thumb stroked across the soft leather strap as he watched the archbishop's heated reaction.

Still bristling from the insult, his black eyes hardened, "You of course appreciate this Majesty. I understand that your allegiance is so strong for Alba, that you have sent your virgin daughter as your envoy to the Norse king's court." He bated, "Norsemen have a reputation for rape."

His fist, squeezing about the bridle leather, was the only outward sign that Constantine was furious. Sending his own daughter to Ath Cliath had been the hardest thing that he had ever done. She had cried in his arms and begged him not to send her away. He had tried to tell himself that he had no choice. It was his duty as King to put Alba first. His kingdom had to be protected above all else. Since the humiliation of that hated procession through England, his vendetta against Athelstan had become overwhelming. He suddenly realised that it consumed him enough for him to sacrifice his eldest daughter. His knuckles turned white as he felt riddled with guilt.

Experienced at noticing such small details, Wulfstan's black eyes glinted shrewdly as he eyed the king. He drawled insolently, "How many times do you think he has mounted her already?"

Rage shot through Constantine's being like a blast of furnace heat. His topaz eyes flashed. Explosively reaching forward with his immensely strong sword arm, grasping the Archbishop's throat with one huge hand, he lifted him off the ground. His horse flinched and neighed at the unexpected weight.

Suddenly unable to breath, Wulfstan's mouth gaped open and his black eyes bulged. Frantically grasping at the king's hands his green cape hood fell back from his face. His black leather boots kicked about wildly trying to reach the ground.

Carefully controlling his skittish white horse with his

knees, Constantine felt the first judder of shock go through the archbishop's body.

Raising his two pale auburn eyebrows, Cellach shook his head. His topaz eyes glittered, mirroring the flame torch, "We need him Da."

Looking pitilessly into the archbishop's bulging eyes as he laboured each word, "Watch your tongue your Grace or I will cut it out myself!" Suddenly letting go of him, Constantine watched the archbishop fall backwards to a heap on the ground.

Raising himself up with one arm, gasping in huge mouthfuls of air, Wulfstan felt his bruised neck. Raggedly coughing, small droplets of spittle flew from his mouth. He felt as if his windpipe had all but closed, rashly, "I am a man of God! May He strike you down for this sacrilegious abuse?" His black eyes looked up to the heavens waiting.

Nothing happened.

Lifting his chin regally, Constantine's topaz eyes flashed impatiently, "Your Grace, you are well aware, that I invited you here, to find out if Northumbria will join my coalition against King Athelstan?"

Gasping in another choked breath, his top lip snarled as he glared at the king. He really wanted to refuse out of principle for this insult to his person! He gulped as he hesitated. "Northumbria wishes to be rid of the English king!" He croaked loudly, "However, we will only pledge our allegiance to your alliance, if I can choose the new King of Northumbria!"

Calmly, "And who might that be?"

Standing unsteadily to his feet, Wulfstan eyed Constantine fiercely, "Northumbria's loyalty is with the Norse! I will have a Viking king!" Taking in another rasping breath, he growled, "Northumbria will only join your alliance if the Norse King of Ath Cliath does!"

Calmly, Cellach grinned, "We will send word of King Anlaf's decision in due course."

Turning their horses they cantered off towards the palace.

A smile played on Cellach's lips as he eyed his father, "I thought you were going to murder him."

Flicking his bridal against his horse's flank, he snarled, "I very nearly did. That man should be grateful to be leaving my kingdom alive!"

Cellach added thoughtfully, "Maelmare will be okay Da."

His topaz eyes flashed with guilt but Constantine said nothing.

Watching them ride off, the torch flame disappearing behind trees, Wulfstan's top lip snarled as he looked up to the glittering heavens, "Just one bolt of lightning to knock him down to hell! Is that too much to ask for?" Shaking his head in disgust, he turned back to his ship. Striding along the jetty, he growled forcefully to his men, "Set sail! We leave for Jorvic!"

3.4

Ath Cliath
The Next Evening

Music filled the torch lit kings halla and nobles congregated for the feast, held in Princess Maelmare's honour.

At the far end of the room on the raised dais, illuminated by four elaborate silver candelabras, the richly decorated top table stood out. Behind the table a huge colourful tapestry hung to the floor, creating a walk way behind for servants and sheltering the nobles from cold drafts. Seated on his high backed throne, King Anlaf looked happily entertained. Dressed in black leather trousers, boots and a golden silk shirt, he smiled. His muscular body turned slightly towards the princess beside him.

Maelmare had thoughtfully chosen one of the dresses from the king, a cobalt blue silk gown trimmed with golden thread. She smiled back at him. Her long strawberry blonde hair shimmered with golden ribbons intricately interlaced through her locks.

On either side of King Anlaf and Princess Maelmare, richly dressed high ranking nobles sat conversing happily.

Down each side of the halla, long tables were filled with well-dressed and boisterous lesser ranked nobles and ladies of the court.

Stood back in the shadows, Ketil watched as serving girls circled the room, carrying large decorated silver jugs filled with wine or mead. He had never seen so many clean women before, he felt a little overawed. The women ensured that no goblet or drinking horn was empty for long. He turned his head as a ripple of applause filled the room.

The head cook strode into the halla as if he were the king himself.

Following him, four strong male servants carried in a huge silver platter. On top of the platter sat a magnificent cooked swan. The white feathered wings had been arranged dramatically flared, as if the swan was about to fly. The swan's slim white feathered neck and head was erect as if the bird was alive.

Gasps of awe filled the room, then open applause from the nobles.

Ketil's mouth fell open and his eyes glinted in surprise at the sight of it. He had never seen anything like it.

The head cook clapped his hands loudly twice.

Four more servants carefully carried in a whole roasted steaming hot porker. A gleaming cold green apple sat in the hog's mouth. All around the outside of the tray the soft flesh of cooked apples steamed. The sweet aroma of cooked apple and pork filled the room. Many a mouth watered.

Under the proud watchful eye of the head cook, more servants entered serving venison, lamb, chickens and an array of cooked steaming hot root vegetables. They walked slowly around the tables serving the food.

A lad, wearing a grubby hooded cape over his threadbare tunic and breaches, led a blind shabbily dressed man into the room.

The blind man tapped the tiled floor with his stick as he walked.

Surprisingly eloquent, the lad announced loudly, his accent deeply Walensis, "The greatest songster in the known world is here today to entertain your Majesty." He pulled a small harp from his cloak.

Inclining his head, Anlaf smiled wryly. They did not look like they could entertain a tavern, never mind his court of Ath Cliath. Loudly back, as he wafted his hand, "Pray, entertain us."

As the lad strummed a beautiful melody on his sweet

sounding harp, the blind man began to sing a deeply moving song in his native Celtic language. The deep resonance of his incredible voice filled the hall with resounding echo.

His blonde eyebrows lifted in surprise as Anlaf listened intently.

Muldivana sat a few seats down from the princess. She looked very pretty in her new pale lilac velvet dress. Her shining dark hair was beautifully dressed with interlacing matching thin threads of ribbon. She sat transfixed by the incredible powerful exquisiteness of the blind man's song.

Scarface sat to her left and watched her from the corner of his eye. His badly scarred face looked unfathomable. His hair was cut so short that it was difficult to say what colour it was, maybe the same colour as his pale brown leather trousers and boots. His blue open necked silk shirt accentuated the darkness of his brown eyes. His sword belt shone with a huge silver buckle in the shape of an eagle.

Finishing his song, the blind man bowed as applause filled the room.

Grinning, the lad bowed as well.

Rising from his throne, clapping loudly, Anlaf threw a small bag of coins towards the young musician, "Well done, pray tarry at my court a while longer. Avail yourselves of the kitchens and hospitium."

Deftly catching the money bag, the lad elaborately bowed, "My thanks Majesty." Smiling happily, he led the blind man away through the finely carved doorway towards the kitchens. He chuckled, "Well done Da, we're guaranteed at least a month of meals and lodgings."

Four resident musicians nodded respectfully to them as they entered the halla from the kitchen doorway. They confidently walked to the centre of the room carrying their long flutes. Used to playing at the castle, they played a succession of the king's favourite melodies.

The room rumbled with conversation, as the men and women in the room half listened to the background music.

Feeling his eyes upon her, Muldivana turned proudly to the man with the scars. "From the closeness of your seat to the king, sir, you are either a close relation or are held in high regard?"

Raising a sardonic eyebrow at her abrupt question, Scarface did not answer.

Looking at him it was obvious that he had once been incredibly handsome but his face had been badly cut and disfigured in battle, "Are you a noble sir?"

Muscles flexed in his jaw, his voice deeply gruff, "Most young ladies and children are frightened by my scars. They do not normally talk to me," he added almost as an afterthought, "my Lady."

Subconsciously, she sucked her bottom full lip as she looked him over. Slowly letting her lip go, she smiled, "I have seen plenty of scars worse than yours at the court of Alba. You do not frighten me." Intrigued, she boldly introduced herself, "I am Muldivana MacDoir, MacAedh, McAlpin," she faltered, "widow to Heth McNatchan," raising her chin, her voice strong again, "sister to Murdock, Thane of Lochaber and niece of King Constantine II of Alba."

He half smiled at her long introduction, "I am honoured my Lady." Eyeing her thoughtfully Scarface decided to introduce himself formally, his voice rumbled low, "I am Jarl Barrick MacIvarr of the Clan Ivarr."

His nobility was obvious but his short reply had given her no clue to his lineage, "You sit close to the king my Lord, what is your relationship to him?"

Smiling, appreciating her directness, "We are not so distant cousins, my Lady."

Liking his smile, she smiled back, "How interesting, please tell me more of your heritage."

Thoughtfully, "My great, great grandfather was Ragnar Lodbrook. Have you heard of him?"

"He is still very famous in the court of Alba."

"My great grandfather was his youngest son, Ivar Benlaus."

She nodded, "He is still renowned in Alba as a good law maker."

"He was already King of Ath Cliath when he and another famous Viking called Olaf the White, conquered Northumbria. My grandfather was the second son of King Ivar Benlaus. His name was Barrith."

Gazing at him, she listened intently.

"He eventually became King of Ath Cliath. When my father was born to King Barrith, he was named Ivar after his grandfather. He eventually inherited Jorvic and Northumbria as his kingdom." Scarface looked thoughtful for a moment, "I never met my father. He died in a great battle before I was born."

"I am sorry." Looking into his dark eyes, she felt strangely at ease with him, "What happened to your mother?"

"After I was born a second suitable marriage was arranged. My mother was still young. She was married to Jarl Olaf, a grandson of Olaf the White. Olaf was the Jarl of Skappa."

Her dark shapely eyebrow lifted quizzically.

"Skappa is one of the many islands of Orkney. My mother refused to leave without me, so my step-father adopted me as his son."

She looked impressed, "Your step father's pedigree is as notable your own father's my Lord."

Nodding, "Jarl Olaf cared for me as if I was his blood son, as is the custom of the Norse people. When I reached the age of seven I was sent to Ath Cliath to be fostered with a close relative. That relative was King Guthrith, Anlaf's father." Glancing up the table he added, "I grew up with King Guthrith's sons. We learnt to fight together. We are brothers of the shield wall."

Thoughtfully, "That is a good expression my Lord Barrick. It must have been hard to be separated from your family so young. Do you regret that your mother was not made Queen of Jorvic? You would have been king."

His dark eyes rested on her as he shrugged his muscular shoulders indifferently, "I enjoy my life as it is my Lady. Kingship is hard on a man." He paused to contemplate, "However, if

I had been born to assume a throne, I would have done it well."

Looking into his confident eyes, she smiled. She felt very sure that he would have made a very noble king.

Watching them with mischievous interest, Blacarri called out, "Jarl Barrick, could you stop flirting with the lovely lady long enough to pass me the salt?"

Reaching for the plain silver bowl full of salt, Scarface smiled at her as he stretched a muscular arm close to her, "Excuse me, my Lady."

Flushing slightly at the closeness of his face, she felt her heart almost skip a beat.

Feeling his own pulse quicken, Scarface looked into her eyes.

Her eyelashes fluttered slightly.

His eyes held hers. Watching her subconsciously suck in her bottom lip then let it go slowly, he smiled. The feeling of attraction pulsed through his body. Slowly taking the salt, he passed it up the table to the dark haired man, jovially gruff, "Are you jealous Blacarri?"

He grinned, his teeth white against his tanned face. Sitting back comfortably against the high back of his chair, the black silk of his tunic shirt fell open at the neck, exposing fine dark tufts of black chest hair. His black leather breeches fitted his muscular thighs like a second skin. The fine quality boots on his feet gleamed from the light of the blazing torches behind him. Blacarri's pale grey eyes held hers for a moment, "Yes I am."

Immediately recognising the handsome dark haired man a smile twitched at her lips. He was the one whom she had slapped across the face only yesterday. Lifting her chin proudly, Muldivana eyed him as she turned to Jarl Barrick expectantly.

He felt the muscles in his jaw tighten for a moment with annoyance. His friend had a formidable reputation for winning the hearts of the ladies of the court.

Noticing his friend's scowl, Blacarri smiled, mischievously

formal, "Come now, Jarl Barrick, you cannot keep this beauty to yourself all night."

Throwing Blacarri a warning frown, he introduced her, "My Lady Muldivana MacDoir, MacAedh, McAlpin, widow to Heth McNatchan, sister of the Thane of Lochaber and niece to Constantine II of Alba." Taking a breath, "May I formally introduce my good friend, the King of the Isle of Man, Colonsay and King of Norse Gailgedhael, Prince Black Arailt Guthrithsson of the Clan Ivarr, Tosiac and designated heir to the throne of Ath Cliath."

His pale grey eyes twinkling mischievously, Blacarri smiled and looked deeply into her eyes, "My friends call me Blacarri."

Realising immediately that he was flirting with her, Muldivana lifted her chin imperiously.

Behind Lord Blacarri, still standing unnoticed in the shadows, Ketil watched and listened. His new dull brown leather trousers, boots and plain brown tunic made him look older. No one bothered him. He obviously was not a slave or a servant. His new employer had tasked him to listen to courtly gossip and relay anything of interest to him.

Smiling, Lady Muldivana looked a picture of innocence, "I met you yesterday. I am afraid I may have slapped you. Please forgive me. I was very perplexed by my Lady's abduction."

Blacarri stroked his jaw remembering the stinging slaps, "My Lady, your reaction was understandable."

Raising an eyebrow, Barrick drawled sardonically, "It would not be the first time that Blacarri has been slapped by a lady."

She felt a giggle bubble up from her core.

Before Blacarri could say another word, smiling at her enchanting laugh, Barrick skilfully moved on to the very young and delicately beautiful blonde haired girl who sat next to him, "And this is Blacarri's eldest child, Lady Gytha, Princess of the Isle of Man."

Slightly built and quite pretty, Lady Gytha looked about ten years old. Her royal blue dress was extremely rich and obviously expensive. Smiling, she nodded gracefully to Muldivana,

"I am pleased to make your acquaintance, my Lady."

Sat next to her, dressed in an exquisite pale mulberry gown, Driffa smiled proudly. Her charge had remembered her manners well.

Muldivana smiled at the child, "You have your father's eyes Lady Gytha."

Blacarri looked indulgently at his daughter, adding warmly, "And her mother's beauty."

The girl smiled prettily at her father's compliment. Contented and happy, she took the smallest piece of meat on to the end of her two pronged fork and ate it delicately.

Barrick continued as he looked friendly into Driffa's pale eyes, "May I introduce Lady Driffa. She is the royal nursemaid to Blacarri's children and a trusted friend to us."

Driffa smiled, "My Lady."

Smiling back at her, Muldivana nodded. It was extremely clear how highly the men in this room respected Driffa. It was very unusual for a slave to be held in such high regard. Spending time with Driffa today, she had realised just how noble, graceful and elegant she was. She had already decided to treat Driffa as an equal, "Good evening, Princess Driffa. We had a wonderful time with you today. We hope to see you again tomorrow."

It had been a lovely change for her too, "I would be delighted my Lady."

A muscle flickered in Barrick's jaw. Most of the men here felt deep protection for Driffa. Her beauty made her a target for unscrupulous men. Over the years, Driffa had proven her deep affection to Blacarri's children and her loyalty to the clan. He looked at Lady Muldivana admiring the way she adopted Driffa as a peer. "Next to Lady Driffa is my good friend, Jarl Ragnal Guthrithsson. He is Blacarri and Anlaf's younger brother."

Yellow haired and bear like with big blue smiling eyes, Ragnal had just bitten off a large bite of meat from a huge cooked leg of lamb. Still chewing, he turned to her nodding affably.

Muldivana nodded to him respectfully, "I am honoured Jarl

Ragnal."

Turning to his left, Barrick introduced an older, white haired man, "May I introduce Jarl Canute, Protector of Olaf Sihtricsson, late of Jorvic."

The young flaxen haired man sat to the other side of Jarl Canute looked up sharply. His wide blue eyes flashed angrily, "I am," he stressed, "Prince Olaf Sihtricsson, late of Jorvic."

Softly menacing, Barrick eyed him back, "I too could call myself a Prince of Jorvic. My line is closer to King Ivar the Law-maker than yours Olaf."

His mouth pursed. Olaf often felt disrespected by the nobles of the court. Had they forgotten that he had once been Jorvic's king? He was about to remind him but he held back. They had often teased him as a child because he had lost his kingdom after just a few days. Belligerently, "Are you saying your line is closer than the king's? I will speak to him of your treachery."

Laughing sarcastically, his eyes never left Olaf's, gruffly, "Anlaf is well aware of my true loyalty to him. However, en-lighten him to your thoughts if you wish."

Olaf's lip snarled.

Blinking, Muldivana raised her chin. This altercation felt very awkward. Replying with trained courtly political formal-ity, "Jarl Canute, Prince Olaf, I am honoured and pleased to make your acquaintance."

Grateful for her interceding, Jarl Canute nodded, "My Lady."

Prince Olaf smiled. His young face was suddenly very hand-some, "My Lady, your beauty brightens our court."

Surprised at his sudden charm, she smiled back.

His eyes glinting with aggression, Barrick lowered his voice to her ear, gruffly, "The lad grows more quarrelsome every day. He lost his kingdom, fortune and family when he was very young. All he has is his title."

Her eyes softened as she looked at him. Very gently she whispered back, "Then we should use his title Jarl Barrick, if it is all that he has left."

A muscle flexed in his strong jaw. He suddenly realised that

Olaf was only defending his birthright. Feeling his anger subsiding, a little guilt filtered through into his heart. The muscle in his jaw flexed again, "You are right my Lady." His eyes lingered on her thoughtfully, "You are kind." He turned to the two red haired men further to his left.

Her eyes followed his. They looked so alike it was obvious that they were brothers.

"May I introduce my cousin Erland Einarsson and his younger brother Arnkell of Orkney?"

Arnkell chuckled, "Younger my Lady, but I think you will agree, better looking?"

"The only person in the room who would agree with that," countered Erland, "is the blind minstrel!"

Giggling, she turned back to Jarl Barrick. Taking in a deep breath, she whispered, "Are they the brothers of King Thorfin Skullsplitter of Orkney?"

He nodded, "Yes my Lady, they are."

Excitedly, "Have you met him?"

"Met who my Lady?"

"Skullsplitter," she felt genuinely thrilled, "he is a living legend at the court of Alba."

"Why?"

"It is rumoured that he has cleaved the heads, clean in two, of every man that has ever challenged his reign!"

"That is true my Lady. I was witness to one such cleaving."

Blacarri called out again, "Scarface, my friend, could you pass that plate of chicken along?" He managed a gleaming white flirtatious smile towards Lady Muldivana.

Without thinking, Muldivana asked, "Why does he call you Scarface?"

Picking up the plate of chicken with one strong hand, the muscles on his tanned forearm rippled. Barrick raised his scarred eyebrow sardonically.

Blinking, suddenly seeing his scars again, she blushed with fluster, "Oh, Jarl Barrick, Scarface is your nickname. I'm so sorry. I just did not think." She added desperately, "You have such nice eyes. One does not see your scars."

Looking blankly at her, he watched her blush deepen.

Listening intently, a smile twitched at Ketil's lips.

Taking a large sip of the fragrant smelling red wine, she asked hurriedly, "How were you, err, injured?"

Looking at her pretty flushed face as he passed the plate up the table, Scarface felt his gaze soften for a moment. Thoughtfully, he watched her for a few seconds longer before he replied, "I was injured in battle when I was fifteen years old." Looking at his friends he continued, "All of us were sent by King Guthrith, Anlaf's father, to a warrior school on the Island of the Clouds. We had been there for two months training, when we were attacked by an invading band of Irish pirates. We all fought them, students and masters. I got cut up pretty bad. I was sure that I was done for but I was saved by a warrior culdee."

She nodded, "In Alba, healers are also known as culdees."

His eyes looked distant for a moment as the memory played out in his mind, "He was a Celt and one of the tallest men that I ever met. He was a true warrior and a master of two sword fighting." Taking a deep sip of his wine, "He was on pilgrimage, travelling to the sacred Celtic shrines of Britain, honing his skills as a warrior. He came to the Island of Clouds because he had heard of my Master, Thord the Blade's, skill with the sword. He wished to study the techniques of long sword fighting. Even though he had no interest in the battle, he fought alongside us."

Softly, "It is strange that he was a warrior and a healer."

Her statement brought him back to the room. "Yes, in the battle I was surrounded by four men. I killed them. But I was so badly wounded that my sword was placed back in my hand, so that when I died I would meet my Gods in Valhalla."

She gasped.

"The warrior culdee cleaned my wounds and sewed me up." He chuckled, "He sewed my face up like a purse. I was lucky, he stopped the bleeding. He treated me with herbs and a seaweed poultice. I had no fever and I survived. While I was recovering, Master Thord asked the warrior healer to fight each of the older pupils in turn. I was weak from loss of blood and could only watch. I have never seen anything like it, before or since. The man's skill with two swords was amazing. He fought at least fifty apprentices, each more skilled than the last. He did not injure any of them, not even a scratch. He disarmed them all." He took another deep sip of wine, thoughtfully, "Last of all he fought Master Thord. Their contest lasted for what seemed like an age. As we watched none of us could believe the skill and techniques that we were witnessing. They were two true masters in combat."

Looking around the room, she asked curiously, "Where is the Celt? Is he still with you?"

"No my Lady, he left when I was well enough to fight again. He said that his home was calling him."

"Tell me Jarl Barrick," her hazel eyes gazed up at him, completely fascinated by his story, "who won the contest between your Master and the Celt."

Ketil's eyes glinted as he listened avidly.

Scarface took a slow sip of his wine as he looked deeply into her eyes, "The Celt won."

3.5

A stream of dancers, minstrels and jugglers entertained the court as the nobles dined.   Ketil noticed as he listened in the shadows that King Anlaf had a way of making all men and women feel at ease in his company. Watching the princess a look of awe passed over Ketil's features. She was the most beautiful woman that he had ever seen.

Helga swayed her hips as she walked past him. Her red hair and prominent breasts caught the attention of many a man in the hall. Barely seeing the new court aide, her green eyes glanced provocatively towards the king as she refilled his wine goblet.

Ketil smiled. King Anlaf only had eyes for the princess. Ignored and huffy the serving wench wandered off.

Gazing into her lovely topaz eyes, Anlaf smiled, "Princess Maelmare, it is time for you to tell me why you are here."

Taking in a deep breath, she nodded, "My father has entrusted me with a message, King Anlaf. He has asked that you travel back with me, to my home in Scone, so that my father can speak to you in person. My father wants to discuss an alliance between our kingdoms."

His blue eyes glinted.

"It is no secret that you covet your lost Kingdom of Northumbria."

That statement surprised him but he looked impassively back at her.

She confidently lifted her chin, "My father has a plan. He wants to form a great alliance between the Sub-kingdoms of Britain," she paused briefly, "against King Athelstan."

This alliance interested him on many levels. "Which of the sub-kings have already pledged their allegiance to this alliance?"

She carefully skirted the question, "You will understand my Lord, that to protect Alba's security, my father has not divulged this information to a mere woman."

He countered, "Yet he sends you, a mere woman, as his emissary."

Lifting her chin, she held his eyes, "If you join the alliance and if we triumph, my father will give you Northumbria."

Eyeing her indifferently, he shrugged his muscular shoulders, "With the greatest of respect Princess, I do not need your father, or the forces of Alba, to conquer any kingdom. I can take Northumbria on my own."

Her voice suddenly trembled with anxiety, "Of course my Lord, my father knows this." She hesitated, trying to regain the strength in her voice, "In addition my Lord, if you accept this alliance, to celebrate our kingdom's allegiance to each other, my father will offer a princess of his realm in marriage to you."

Surprised, he sat up straighter in his chair. Feeling his heart double beating in his chest, Anlaf leaned forward. His voice deepened as his eyes looked into hers, "Who does your father offer in marriage to me?"

She could not control the tremble in her hands so she placed them in her lap. Lowering her eyes, "I am offered Majesty."

Taking a jug of wine from a passing maid's tray, Ketil moved unseen back to Blacarri. As he poured a fresh goblet of wine for his new employer, he whispered quickly to Blacarri's ear, "Milord, the King of Alba has offered your brother the hand of the princess and the Kingdom of Northumbria. This is in exchange for an alliance with all of the Sub-kingdoms of Britain, against the English."

Blacarri's pale grey eyes glinted with surprise. His young spy had already impressed him. He looked thoughtfully at his brother and the princess. He could tell that Anlaf was very taken with her. His body was turned towards her and he had barely taken his eyes off of her all evening.

Smiling, Anlaf took her hand and kissed it as he gazed deeply into her eyes, "Your father was wise to send you as his ambassador. He probably guessed that once I had seen your beauty, it would be difficult to resist his offer."

Feeling her own breath catch in her throat, she looked anxiously down at her lap.

He noticed the slight tremble in her hands. Gently, "Do not be frightened of me Maelmare."

Flushing, she nodded. Proud of her heritage, she had tried hard to maintain her stoic demeanour but now her future was becoming very real to her. Not only was she being offered to a man that she had only met yesterday, her life would be far away from her family. Her thoughts filled her with apprehension. Only his kindness stopped her from running to her ship.

"Wait here. I will discuss your father's proposal with my brother." Standing up he ordered abruptly, "Blacarri, come with me."

He did not hesitate. He quickly wiped his hands on an ornately embroidered azure blue napkin. Rising from his high backed chair, he followed his brother.

Watching them intently, Canute nudged Olaf.

As his cousins strode away, Olaf quickly rose to his feet. Approaching Maelmare, he sharply signalled the musicians to change the music. Charmingly, "My Lady, may I have this dance?"

In the shadows, Ketil raised an eyebrow as he watched them discreetly.

"I am greatly in need of diversion, my Lord." Seeing how close this nobleman sat to the king she agreed graciously, "It would be my pleasure." Smiling she placed her delicate hand in his as she rose to her feet. She glided to the dance floor her blue gown shimmering as she walked.

Ketil's sharp ears heard again how the refined princess said 'my lord'. He decided at that moment that he would never say 'milord' again. Whilst Lord Black Arailt trusted him to work at the palace fortress, he would do everything he could to better himself.

Tutored in all courtly arts from a young age, Olaf gallantly guided the princess to the dance floor.

Canute's eyes glowed with satisfaction. It was not often that a princess of such high status came to this realm. What an opportunity for his charge!

The music started and the pair danced.

Gazing intently at the princess, he courteously asked her many questions about her journey, her family, and her life at home. Soon, Olaf he had a very good idea of her sheltered life, her high morals and her grace.

The musicians in the gallery looked down when the dance ended.

Gallantly holding on to her hands, he begged her for another dance. Her eyes and lovely smile told him she was charmed. The music started and they danced again. Feeling more confident, Olaf decided to make his move, "I myself am a Prince of the Clan Ivarr. My father was Sihtric, King of Jorvic. I was in fact King of Jorvic myself for a few days after his death. I was very young though and I was exiled by the English. But I hope to regain my father's kingdom again and become King of Jorvic."

A fleeting look of alarm passed over her features. Carefully guarding her expression, she replied cautiously, "Then you will be very rich indeed, for he who rules Jorvic rules Northumbria."

Smiling, he eyed her intently, "Thank you my Lady. Do you think it would please your father to have a daughter of Alba married to the King of Northumbria?" Feeling her body stiffen, Olaf looked surprised. He blurted, "You are a beautiful woman and I feel a deep love growing for you."

Hiding her alarm, Maelmare looked away, "My Lord, this is the first conversation that we have had. I hardly think that enough time has passed for you to fall in love."

Forcing a look of overstated disappointment across his face,

"From the first moment I saw you I swear my heart was captured."

Looking away from him cynically, she countered, "Really my Lord. Do you think that you are the first man that has attempted to flatter me for my fortune?"

He began to feel flustered, "Princess, I would ask you to wed me."

Dryly, "I am well aware that it is my position in society that attracts noble men."

This was not going at all to plan, desperately, "I can assure you my Lady that it is your obvious beauty that I worship."

Used to fending off men, she stated piously, "Sir, I am a very religious woman. I hope to enter a convent shortly." Looking away uncomfortably, as Prince Olaf continued to try to convince her, she wished that the music would end so that she could graciously leave the floor.

Watching them from the shadows, Ketil thought he caught a glimpse of discomfort in her expression but she quickly hid it with a polite smile.

Anlaf's small well lit antechamber was filled with curiosities. There were beautiful shells next to tiny patterned glass beads. A large carved ivory chess set sat with all its pieces in place, ready to play. The small blazing fire in the grate cast shadows across the faces of two ancient female Roman marble statues. Their expressions appeared to move almost life like with the changing light and shade. Large pieces of topaz glistened in the candlelight. Insects, frozen in time, could clearly be seen in them. Ignoring the intricately carved wooden chairs, Anlaf spoke quietly so only Blacarri could hear, "The princess has confided that King Constantine is building a great alliance, between all of the Sub-kingdoms of Britain, against the English. If I join this alliance I am offered Northumbria, and the hand of a princess of his realm."

Smiling proudly at his brother, Blacarri pale grey eyes glinted, "This is excellent news. An alliance through marriage with Alba can only be good for the Clan Ivarr."

Grinning, Anlaf's teeth looked white against his tanned face, "My greatest ambition has always been to regain Northumbria. It would be a fantastic achievement for my reign. Constantine requests I travel with Maelmare, to his palace at Scone, to discuss marriage terms and the dowry."

Blacarri frowned, "Constantine has two daughters and there are many lower status Princesses of Alba." He already knew the answer but he steered the conversation, "Who does he offer to you?"

Anlaf looked delighted, "Maelmare, his eldest daughter, is offered."

"So that is why he sent her. She is indeed a beauty and is surely a magnificent match for you. But this may be a ruse to lure you to Alba. Once you are in his domain, he may give you a princess of lesser status and lesser beauty, who you would feel obliged to accept in the circumstances." Blacarri frowned, warning, "This could be very embarrassing."

Forcefully, "Maelmare is a rare woman of high morals. I should know." His blonde eyebrow lifted, "I have tried to toy with her since she arrived and she has refused all of my advances. She told me she wants to enter a convent." He chuckled, "She is far too beautiful for that life. I tell you brother," his blue eyes glinted, "I want this woman."

Blacarri lifted his chin, "Advantageous marriages secure thrones and the acquisition of land quicker than any war. An alliance and a marriage to the House of Alba would indeed be a great stroke of good fortune. Maelmare is a considerable prize."

Anlaf looked perplexed, "What should I do brother?"

Unhesitatingly, "Accept King Constantine's offer," Blacarri paused, "but forgo the dowry. You do not need it Anlaf. Take Maelmare, this week in marriage, here in Ath Cliath. She cannot refuse a marriage contract if her claim to be promised to you is true."

Anlaf half smiled thoughtfully, this could work.

"Then travel later on honeymoon to Alba, to discuss this

intriguing alliance." Blacarri's brow furrowed, "But bear in mind brother, it is the Bishops of Northumbria who elect Northumbrian kings, not King Constantine."

Anlaf's smile deepened, "You're right of course. However, married to the King of Alba's eldest daughter, increases my standing with the bishops, and brings me ever closer to my ultimate goal." He almost growled, "I want Northumbria back for the Clan Ivarr."

Blacarri nonchalantly raised a thoughtful eyebrow, he had always agreed with his father that cousin Olaf should be offered Northumbria. But that was not his decision. He ignored the comment, "One thing at a time Anlaf. If she does marry you, take gifts to your new father in law. There will be little the King of Alba can do after you are wed," he chuckled, "other than give you marriage gifts, of equal wealth, to match the dowry."

"Yes, once I have taken Maelmare in marriage, there will be little her father can do to claim her back. If Maelmare agrees to this, we will announce our betrothal tomorrow, and we will wed on the full moon."

Emerging from the annex, a confident smile played on Anlaf's mouth. Seeing Olaf dancing with Maelmare, he frowned. Growling menacingly, one hand moved subconsciously to his sword pommel. He strode purposefully to the dance floor.

Blacarri barely acknowledged Ketil as he walked back to his seat.

Watching from the shadows, Ketil thought he saw the apprehension in Prince Olaf's eyes.

Looking over Princess Maelmare's shoulder, Olaf took in a deep breath as the king approached. Alarmed by Anlaf's expression, he stopped dancing and released her hand.

Relieved, she turned towards the king and sank into a deep curtsey.

Glowering threateningly at Olaf as he strode up to them, Anlaf flicked his blonde head to the side dismissing him.

Blinking uneasily, Olaf gulped as he backed away quickly. Frowning with humiliation, he bowed his head as he moved back to Canute.

Seeing the capitulation in his charges body language, Canute quickly stood and rasped gruffly as Olaf reached him, "The court is watching, control yourself! Do not show submission!"

Suddenly gathering himself, his deep blue eyes flashing with determination, Olaf stood tall and clapped loudly for the princess, as she rose elegantly from her curtsey. Smiling handsomely, he bowed deeply to her. Rising up, standing tall, he clapped his hands towards her effusively. By ignoring the king, he managed to express only gallant deference to the princess.

Observing the subtle change in Prince Olaf's performance, even Ketil mentally questioned his first thoughts. Prince Olaf, unquestionably, was not submissive to the king.

Convincingly, Canute also started clapping his hands loudly.

Suddenly all of the court stood up. The nobles respectfully clapped and cheered her.

Her mouth opened with surprise. Prince Olaf's obvious open and public admiration for her person left her no option but to acknowledge his esteem. Curtseying to him formally, she inclined her head respectfully.

As applause filled the kingshalla, many of the courtiers eyed Prince Olaf with renewed interest. He no longer had the fluffy stubble of youth on his face. His body was tall and thick with muscle. Many suddenly remembered his father had been a king. Yes, there was something about this man. Was it his noble presence, or the keen look of ambition in his young eyes?

Satisfied, Canute lifted his chin protectively. His boy had done well.

Delighted by his court's obvious admiration for the princess, taking her delicate hand in his, Anlaf bowed and kissed it. As he stood tall, still holding her hand, only he saw the look of relief pass over her face. It pleased him.

Gazing up into his eyes, she whispered breathlessly, "Thank

you my Lord."

Anlaf felt her hand squeeze his. He suddenly realised that he felt immensely protective of her. He leaned in close to her little ear, "Did my cousin offend you my Lady?"

Her voice was over dramatically tinged with barely hidden tedium, she whispered, "He bored me Majesty."

Amused, feeling his mood suddenly soften, he chuckled, "My court adores you." Looking into her lovely topaz eyes, he added possessively, "my Lady."

She smiled. The way he said 'my Lady' sounded like an endearment. Elegantly, she slowly curtseyed to him again.

Watching them, still feigning a broad grin, Olaf's eyes hardened with jealousy.

As the applause died down, Anlaf escorted the princess to her throne.

Sitting down again, Canute eyed him. Gruffly, he whispered, "You did well to pull that off."

Frowning with disappointment, Olaf stared at his plate of food. It no longer interested him. He hissed, "Little good it did me!"

Confidently, Canute murmured, "You impressed many a jarl in this room. Look at them watching you."

Looking around the room, Olaf noticed two or three lesser ranking young nobles nod to him respectfully. Surprised, he inclined his head to each of them.

Eyeing Prince Olaf with interest, Helga swayed her hips provocatively as she walked up to him with the wine jug. Gazing her green eyes sideways at him, she let her alluring eyelashes flutter, "Wine milord?"

Looking into her pretty almond shaped eyes, he felt instant attraction. He nodded, his blonde eyebrows lifting with surprise as she continued to gaze at him.

Well aware of her ample assets, she bent forward as she filled his wine goblet, giving him an enticing glance of her cleavage.

For a moment his heart pumped with carnal desire. Sucking

in a deep breath, Olaf exhaled slowly. As she moved away, his gaze followed her.

A knowing smile played on her full lips as she sashayed off to the next table, already being served by Kari.

With a jealous glint in her dreary blue eyes, Kari quipped, "Surely, he is a little young for you Helga."

Looking at the older woman, Helga smiled, "I cannot help it Kari, if men find me attractive."

Pensively, Kari eyed Helga's slim body and vibrant red haired looks. Looking down at herself, she felt plump. Her light flaxen hair was dull against her pale skin. Now in her thirties, her back was rounding and her once pretty neck was flaccid. Smoothing down her skirt over her rotund midriff, Kari enviously watched Helga sway her hips to the next table.

Olaf's eyes also followed Helga.

Getting affably drunk on sweet honey mead, Ragnal chuckled, "Lock up your daughters' men! My cousin is obviously in need of a wench!"

Good-naturedly the men on the table laughed. Arnkel was the loudest joking, "Thor's hammer! With the look on his face I'm going to lock up me mother!"

Erland spat out some of his ale as he burst out laughing.

Usually left on the fringes of the warriors repartee, grinning at the amiable banter, Olaf laughed along with them.

Breathing in deeply a smile played on Canute's lips. Olaf had done well this night. The nobles were now seeing him as a man. So what if the lad fancied a dalliance with a serving girl. That would serve their cause to further impress the jarls.

Ketil's keen eyes picked out at least six nobles looking towards Prince Olaf. He mentally noted their names for his report.

As the king sat down next to Maelmare, she looked up at him expectantly.

Leaning in towards her, Anlaf whispered softly to her ear, "This match is agreeable to me. I will send word to your father that we will wed within the week."

She tingled, as his soft warm breath caressed her neck, "But the terms my Lord, my dowry must be agreed. This accord will take time."

He looked directly into her eyes, carefully watching her reaction, "For you Princess, I will forgo a dowry. We will travel to Alba together as King and Queen of all of the Norse of Britain and Ireland. Do you agree Maelmare? Will you marry me within the week?"

Blinking in surprise, she hesitated for a moment, "If you forgo my dowry," she breathed softly thoughtful, "then there will be no legal reason to delay our marriage." Carefully thinking, "I own property in my own right, will that remain mine?"

A smile flickered on his sensuous lips, "Yes Maelmare, I will have no claim over your lands."

She eyed him intelligently, "Will you confirm that in a contract?"

A breath of laughter bubbled up from his core, his eyes twinkling with respect, "Yes I will."

"My father has already agreed to our match." Thoughtfully looking up at him, "You are the only man that I have ever met, who has not been interested in my dowry or lands, more than me." Gazing into his eyes, a rare feeling of trust passed through her, "I agree to marry you here in Ath Cliath," suddenly careful again she added quickly, "subject to the signing of an agreed written contract."

A broad grin lit up his handsome face, "Then it is settled, I will have my clerk draw up the contract tomorrow."

Looking into his eyes, "And, I will have my clerk appraise the document tomorrow." She smiled, "If everything is in order we will have an accord."

Listening carefully in the shadows, Ketil's eyes glinted with wonder. All of his life, he had lived on the brink of starvation and destitution. Overnight that had changed. He felt deeply that this woman, this beautiful princess, had brought him luck and changed his fortune.

Much later that night, in the privacy of the king's chambers, the two ladies of Alba sat on the vast bed brushing out their hair. Maelmare fluttered her long eyelashes thoughtfully, "Two marriage offers in one night, what do you think of that?"

Muldivana sighed, "It is not so incredible Princess. You are a very beautiful woman."

"Prince Olaf only wanted my dowry. He is handsome though and he dances well. He hopes to become King of Northumbria again."

"Jorvic and Northumbria are rich with traders. If he regains his father's kingdom, he will be a powerful man indeed."

"His overtures felt false to me."

Muldivana smiled indulgently, "Your father, the king, often says that you are very astute for a princess."

She smiled, "My father warned me to be wary of ambitious men."

"Your King of the Norse is very different Princess. Your dowry is a fortune of land and silver, yet he has forgone it for you."

Thoughtfully, "He insisted on walking me to my bedchamber tonight. Just as I was about to retire, he tried to kiss me on the lips. He told me that now that we are engaged to be married it is permissible. I had to slap him hard on the face to stop him."

Muldivana giggled, "What did he do?"

"He thought it very funny. I told him that I would change my mind about marrying him and enter a nunnery." A smile played on her lips, "He said if I did that, he would abduct me and marry me anyway."

Muldivana's dark eyebrows lifted with concern, "He is a heathen."

"He is quite handsome though." Maelmare's smile deepened. Flushing, she added, "I did not expect to like him."

"I have to admit my Lady, I did not like him one little bit, when I first met him. I thought him to be a rogue." Grudgingly, "He can be quite the refined gentleman though, when he puts his mind to it."

Dropping her ornately carved comb on to the rich brocade bed cover, Maelmare lowered her voice, "I most definitely would not describe King Anlaf as a gentleman, too much leather, sweat and overtures for that."

Muldivana's eyes widened with refined alarm.

Her topaz eyes shone, "I have never met such a heathen but somehow," she paused, "I feel that I can trust him."

Sat on the vast bed slowly brushing her shimmering dark hair, Muldivana looked thoughtful.

Watching her for a moment, Maelmare asked softly, "What think you of Lord Barrick?"

Surprised by Maelmare's direct question, she looked up, "How did you know I was thinking of him?"

Smiling knowingly, "You talked with him all evening. Does he interest you?"

Sadly, "Since my husband died I have felt dead in that way."

Gently, Maelmare sighed, "But you are so young. You are too young to be alone. It is natural to like other men."

Frowning, "I know. I do not feel guilty," she paused thoughtfully, "just surprise."

She looked intrigued, "Why surprise?"

Muldivana sucked on her soft full lower lip, "Maelmare, when I look at Lord Barrick my body tingles and I feel such wanting as never before."

The princess looked little shocked, "Lady Muldivana!"

Inside a disused ramshackle stable close to the edge of the castle ramparts, Olaf chuckled with delight. The red headed serving wench pushed her soft hands against his tanned muscular chest and shoved him back on to the straw. The coarse bedding prickled his bare back and arms but he barely felt it, "What is your name?"

Where the slate roof had crumbled, moonlight streamed through.

"I am called Helga, Milord." Smiling, she confidently lifted her skirt with both of her hands to show her long shapely legs. Climbing onto his lap, she sat astride him. She knew herself well. She was a woman who had found out early that she loved the pleasure of a man's body. Desire, sensuality and ultimately sexual climax, was something that she craved. Pulling off her short tunic top garment, her tongue flickered over her lips. Moonlight travelled over her bare breasts as she leant forward. Her nipples were already hard with desire.

Gazing up at her, Olaf's eyes glinted with passion. Awkwardly, he grasped at her breast squeezing it hard.

Feeling pleasure and pain at the same time she gasped, it was not a sensation she enjoyed. Realising he was inexperienced, Helga smiled gently as she pulled his hand away. Softly, "Am I your first?"

A little ashamed, he blustered, "Err no." His eyes darted to the side. "I have slept with at least ten women."

A giggle of disbelief welled up but she suppressed it. Her green eyes twinkled with amusement, "You will not be the first lad that I have taught how to pleasure a woman." Softly enticing, she rubbed her hands over his chest lingering on his nipples. As she leaned in closer to kiss him, she whispered huskily, "I always wanted to be a lord's mistress."

3.6

One week later

Clothed formally in brown leathers, waiting in the shadows, Ketil looked up. Princess Maelmare of Alba stood before the great doors of the king's halla.

Dressed in cloth of flowing gold, she looked radiant. Looking down at the material, smoothing out her skirt, she knew she had never looked lovelier. Smiling as she waited, feeling beautiful in her truly ornate gown, her long strawberry blonde hair softly curled around her shoulders. A sheer gossamer gold veil, held in place by her gold headband, fell trailing to the floor behind her. Pure happiness shone in her eyes.

A little pink in the face, Muldivana fussed over her princess's gown, arranging it just so. Her own gown was a simpler cut and made of shimmering white material threaded with silver.

Barely noticing her, Ketil felt wonder as he watched the princess. To him Princess Maelmare was pure beauty, untouchable celestial, like a Valkyrie. A trumpet signalled it was time. It drew him from her radiance to reality, "Serene Majesty, it is time."

Looking up at him, Maelmare smiled, "Thank you Ketil."

Blinking shyly, he mumbled, "You know my name, my Lady?"

"Of course I do. Lord Black Arailt informed me that you are his trusted man. He advised me that you would let me know when it is time to leave today, so that I would not be late."

Ketil suddenly grinned as pride filled him. Lord Black Arailt had called him his trusted man. Confidence filled him as he bowed his head.

Curtseying elegantly, Muldivana smiled as she backed away, "My Lady, you are ready."

Feeling incredibly calm, Maelmare nodded to Ketil.

Slowly opening the huge doors, Ketil blinked as sunlight filled the halla. He watched the princess lift her chin and stand with luminous regal poise. His mouth opened as he sighed in awe of her.

Feeling true pride in her princess, Muldivana lifted her chin too. To her, Maelmare looked with every inch of her being Alban royalty.

Anlaf stood impatiently waiting. Wearing dark brown leather breaches and boots, his tunic and cloak made of cloth of gold shimmered in the sunlight. His most impressive gold crown glimmered on his handsome blonde head. He turned to see Maelmare. Smiling broadly, he knew without doubt that this woman was right for him. To him she glowed, goldenly ethereal, like a deity. She was his match, his wife and tonight, touchable.

Smiling happily, she gracefully walked out into the courtyard.

Nobles and ladies cheered, startling the castle doves. They took flight loudly flapping their wings.

The beautiful day shone with azure blue skies. Only a slight breeze fluttered the colourful flags. The waft of wind, caught the light gauze of her golden veil, carrying the body of it into the air, like gossamer fairy wings. Her gold headband kept the shimmering veil from floating up to the cloudless sky.

Striding towards her, Anlaf took her hand. He smiled, "A present for you my love." Opening his hand, he held a beautiful gold bird brooch in the shape of a stork. He looked into her eyes watching her smile. Gently, "For the Norse, the stork represents commitment to each other and our future family."

Maelmare felt her heart beat a little faster with joy, "It is beautiful my Lord. I wish to wear it today."

He gently pinned the brooch to her gown, "There, it looks

perfect." He turned to his men, "Blacarri, please help the Princess with her horse."

Stepping forward, wearing black leather breaches and boots, his deep blue tunic complimented his translucent grey eyes. Dressed formally, his black silk cloak, trimmed with dark otter fur, was fastened to his muscular shoulders by two gold topaz jewelled brooches. "My Lady," Blacarri looked into Princess Maelmare's eyes, "you look lovely. The people of Ath Cliath will adore you." Taking her hand, he gently led her to a white pony.

Walking to his horse, Anlaf grinned as the crowds cheered him. Strongly mounting the white stallion, he adjusted the bridle straps.

Smiling, Maelmare looked up at him, "Lord Black Arailt, thank you for giving me Ketil today. He has been so attentive. Lady Muldivana and I have wanted for nothing. Please will you pass our thanks on to him?"

He grinned with satisfaction, "May I call you Sister?"

Her lashes fluttered happily, "Of course, if I can call you Brother."

Bending low, he kissed her hand. Rising to his full height, he smiled as he checked her saddle and bridle.

Looking up at him, "I hope that I will serve your people well as their Queen."

Bowing respectfully, "My Lady, you are a Princess of Alba. You are also beautiful and kind. I have no doubt that you will be a good queen to our people." Watching her step towards her mount, he carefully assisted on to her side saddled pony.

Following the princess out of the castle into the courtyard, Muldivana turned to her mount.

Waiting for her, Scarface stood patiently holding the decorative reigns, "My Lady Muldivana, you look beautiful."

His deep gruff voice sent shivers of pleasure down her spine. She flushed, "Thank you Lord Barrick."

"Here, let me help you." In one movement, his powerful muscular arms lifted her by her small waist, onto her side saddled brown pony.

Feeling his strong tanned hands around her midriff, she felt her own breath catch in her throat. Looking away quickly, she carefully arranged her skirt, "Thank you my Lord."

Looking up at her, Scarface smiled, his teeth as white as his silk shirt, his deep voice rumbling, "My Lady, pray excuse me one moment, I see young Prince Olaf is using Jarl Canute's old horse again." He winked at her mischievously, "Watch this."

She gripped her soft leather bridle confidently. Turning her horse, she watched him stride over to Prince Olaf and Jarl Canute.

Checking the saddle was buckled correctly, Canute stood next to his old horse. Grabbing a large handful of straw from a bale, he rubbed the yellow fibres together so that it was not too sharp or coarse. Some of the straw floated away on the light breeze. Brushing his horse down with the straw, he did not notice Scarface approaching.

Preparing to mount the ageing stallion, Olaf checked over the reins and saddle. They looked shabby but serviceable.

"Good morrow, Prince Olaf." Scarface smiled friendly as he walked up to them. Respectfully nodding to Canute, "Good morrow Jarl Canute, I hope this day finds you both well my Lords."

Looking up, Olaf's eyes filled with dull dejection, "Good morrow Scarface."

Looking over Canute's horse, Scarface ran his fingers through the animal's matted coat. It smelt musty. Patting him, he watched yard dust float into the air. Looking at Olaf, he half smiled, "I hear from Jarl Canute, that your old horse died a month ago."

Canute's powerful arm muscles bulged as he took the bridle. His horse gently snorted as he sniffed Canute's pockets for apples.

Resolute sadness filled Olaf's voice, "She was old. Canute has lent me his horse today." Trying to muster the humour of youth, his smile did not quite reach his eyes. He patted the horse, "I will be lucky if this old boy reaches the temple."

Chuckling, Canute stroked his horse, "He will get you there Olaf."

The smile twitching at Scarface's lips reached his twinkling eyes, "Just over four years ago, my stallion fathered six foals to my stabled mares, in one year. The foals are all excellent steeds." Raising his voice, he turned to a young lad hovering near by, "Page, bring the presents!"

A young lad, dressed in brown linen, led over two dark brown stallions. The sleek horses looked splendid, dressed in their new leather saddles and decorated bridles.

Impressed, Olaf looked over the horses, "Beautiful, they are a good wedding present, Scarface. King Anlaf and Queen Maelmare will be happy."

The smile playing around Scarface's lips deepened, "Oh, these are not for Anlaf." He paused for effect, "Prince Olaf and Jarl Canute, may I present each of you a horse, as a mark of my deep respect."

Blinking in surprise, not quite believing him, Olaf stuttered, "You're giving me a stallion?"

Canute felt his own jaw drop in surprise, and it took a lot to surprise him these days.

Scarface grinned at Canute's unusually inane expression, "Yes, Prince Olaf, he is yours. Anlaf says you are both welcome to freely use the royal stables and fodder. He has arranged it with the Master of the king's horse."

He blinked again, "He is really mine?"

"Yes cousin." Smiling, enjoying himself immensely, "Blacarri had the saddles and gear made for them as a present to you both. And, King Anlaf asked me to give you both a purse, as a mark of his deep respect." Unfastening two coin purses from his belt, he handed them one each. They jangled heavy with silver, "He said it is a gift to each of you for your continued support."

Taking the purse, Olaf looked stunned. Suddenly full of the excitement of youth, he lunged at Scarface hugging him, "He is mine! Thank you! Thank you! This is the best day of my life!" Before Scarface had a chance to respond, Olaf agilely hooked his foot into the stirrup and swung up into the nearest stallion's saddle.

The stallion whinnied with excitement and shook his beautiful mane.

Patting the sleek soft neck of his horse, Olaf ordered, "Page, take this old horse back to the stables. Canute, you will be riding your new young stallion to the king's wedding today." Chuckling, his young eyes sparkled excitedly.

The young page immediately led the old horse away.

As his twinkling old blue eyes gazed in wonder at his beautiful new horse, Canute shook his head in disbelief. Finding his voice, he stuttered, "Page take good care of him."

The page turned back and bowed, "Yes Milord."

As the page led his faithful old horse away, Canute's eyes turned back to them, "Thank you, Lord Barrick."

Inclining his head respectfully, "You are both very welcome. I will see you both later at the feast. You can let me know how they ride." Feeling full of self-satisfaction, he strode back to Muldivana.

Smiling at him as he returned to her, "That was very generous of you Lord Barrick."

Shrugging his shoulders, "It occurred to me the lad is in need of family." His brown eyes gazed at her genuinely hopeful, his voice gruff, "May I carry your colours and escort you today my Lady?"

Smiling happily at his overture, she blushed, "My Lord, you may." She gently untied a long piece of white silver threaded gauze from her sleeve and tied it to his muscular arm. It sparkled in the sunlight.

Scarface bowed looking very pleased with himself. Turning away, he walked off, gruffly calling for his page to bring his own sleek brown stallion, almost identical to the ones he had just given to young Olaf and Jarl Canute.

"My Lady Muldivana, you look stunningly beautiful."

Turning her horse, she smiled indulgently, "My Lord Black Arailt, thank you for your compliment. I fear they will be few and far between this day with the princess looking so lovely." She noticed him mischievously darting a sidewise glance to Lord Barrick.

Eyeing her roguishly, he smiled, "My Lady, pray call me Blacarri. May I carry your colours today?"

Nearby, Ketil watched his employer with amusement.

Muldivana sighed, looking at him like he was a naughty child, sternly, "You have just watched me give my colours to Lord Barrick. It would be very unseemly for me to give my colours to another gentleman on the same day."

Running his hand slowly through her horse's mane, he deepened his voice, "But I am no gentleman, my Lady."

Ketil grinned.

Feeling exasperation rising up from her core, she impatiently moved her pony so that her horses flank pushed him away. Barely masking her agitation, she stated with feigned tedium, "Indeed you are not!" Flicking her reins with irritation, she walked her pony off closer to the princess.

Chuckling to himself as he watched her go, his pale grey eyes sparkled. He enjoyed vexing her. It amused him to prickle her temper.

Watching them, Scarface looked like thunder. It took only three strides for him to reach his cousin. Staring threateningly hard into Blacarri's amused eyes, growling low so only he could hear, "You may be my cousin but if you make a pass at her again I will kill you!"

Alarmed, Ketil raised his pale eyebrows.

A look of true astonishment passed over Blacarri's face, deep laughter bubbled up from his core, "Scarface, I was just flirting with her."

His voice rasped, "You watched me ask for her colours publicly! You saw me state my intentions!"

"Intentions," Looking genuinely confused he shook his head, "what intentions?"

Growling menacingly Scarface gritted his teeth, "My intention to ask for her hand!"

Astonished, "You asked for her colours Barrick, not her hand." Grinning, he placed his large tanned hand on his friend's shoulder, "Now that you have made your 'intentions' clear, I will respectfully withdraw." Smiling, "When are you planning on asking her?"

"Soon!"

Exaggerating a surprised look at the venom in Scarface's voice, he suppressed a chuckle, his voice even, "Well don't sound so happy about it."

Scarface frowned, gruffly, "I'm not happy about it!" He gulped in a deep breath, softly to himself, "Marriage is the last thing I want, but she..." his voice trailed off as he shook his head.

Watching his friend's confusion, Blacarri chuckled, "If you are lost to her charms Barrick, you may as well give in early. It will be less painful in the end. I am sorry for causing you offence." Holding out his tanned hand, sincerely, "You are my friend, next to my brothers, I hold you closest in my trust."

Taking his hand, Barrick pulled him into a bear hug, "Women are more trouble than they are worth."

Smiling, Blacarri shook his head, "Not when you find the right one Barrick, not when you find the right one." Looking over Scarface's shoulder to the wedding party, "Come on, they are about to open the gates. We need to get ready." Grinning, he turned to his horse and mounted up.

Looking over his own young grey stallion, Ketil smiled as he stuck his foot through the stirrup and mounted him. It was almost two weeks since he had been taken into King Blacarri's employment. He now had good lodgings at the fortress, a new horse, a fine saddle, two sets of new clothes and a silver arm bracelet. Not to mention a free lesson each day in horse riding. He had to admit that horse riding had not come easy to him but he was at least now able to direct his horse the right way. A little ungainly, he managed to get his horse to follow his employer's horse.

Moments later, the grand royal procession left the castle on horseback. They would have two wedding ceremonies. One at Thor's Temple and then another at the Christian abbey close to the castle.

Riding side by side, Anlaf and Maelmare, waved, smiling happily to the cheering crowds.

Their people threw flower petals and waved flags. Young mothers lifted their babies high, wishing Goddess Freya grant the royal couple a fertile union.

Only Prince Olaf looked even happier than the wedding couple. Grinning, he felt euphoric. Sat on his new mount, he waved at the cheering crowds. Flower petals of every colour floated on the air, landing on his shoulders and in his shoulder length white blonde hair. The silver, jangling heavily in the purse at his waist belt, felt full of promise of good fortune to come.

Late that night, Anlaf walked alone into his candlelit bed chamber just as Muldivana left the room.

Curtseying low to him, Muldivana closed the door behind her. She would sleep in a smaller room further down the corridor from now on.

Maelmare waited by the huge bed. Wearing a sheer gossamer night gown that barely hid her nakedness, she trembled.

His heart beating fast, he slipped his silk golden shirt over his handsome blonde head. Lifting a handful of her cascading strawberry blonde hair to his face, his tanned arm muscles rippled in the candlelight. Smelling the sweet perfume on her hair, he whispered, "You are beautiful my Queen."

Feeling breathless, she looked at him with her large topaz eyes.

Candlelight painted shadows on his muscular shoulders down to the tight flat muscles of his stomach. His breath caught in his throat. Through the sheer material of her gown, he could see the outline of her pink tipped breasts. Gently taking the shoulder ribbons of her gown into his two hands, he pulled the bows undone.

Feeling the gossamer robe slip from her shoulders to the floor, she trembled again, breathing softly through her parted lips.

Candlelight caressed her pale skin showing him her lovely lithe young body. Taking her into his arms, he kissed her mouth passionately.

Her eyes closed, Maelmare let the sensation of desire travel tantalizingly through her body, as he lifted her onto his bed.

Close to the ramparts, in the old stables, Olaf chuckled as he pulled Helga, naked onto the bed of straw. They had met here every night since the banquet and made love, slept, then made love again. He was going to tell her about the horses and the bag of silver but that would be later. Right now, he just wanted her body beneath him. Parting her lovely long legs, he ran his hands over her breasts as he mounted her.

3.7

Four weeks later

Sat in a comfortable chair, examining his favourite whetstone for flaws, Anlaf looked up as his door guard announced loudly, "Jarl Arnkell and Jarl Erland of Orkney, to see the king."

Striding into the room, they both bowed curtly.

Sitting up straighter, Anlaf smiled, "What news have you my friends?"

Arnkell scratched his short bearded chin, "We have to leave for the Orkneys."

Erland nodded, soberly, "Our brother, Jarl Skullsplitter, has sent for us. The exiled Norwegian king, Erik Bloodaxe has been welcomed to Orkney, initially as an ally. He now uses one of the islands as his base for raids. Erik has a large following of Vikings."

Arnkell inclined his head, candidly, "Bloodaxe and his wife, the sorceress Gunhilde, are becoming an increasing threat to our brother's leadership. Erik craves power and our brother senses his rivalry."

Erland eyed Anlaf, "We have to leave tomorrow with our ships and men. Bloodaxe needs to see just how much support Skullsplitter has from his family and people."

Understanding completely, Anlaf nodded, "May Odin and Thor protect you on your journey. Pray send my compliments to your brother."

Bowing, the two brothers strode out of the room.

Anlaf could still hear their footsteps when his door guard announced, "Prince Olaf Sihtricsson, late of Jorvic, to see the king."

Olaf strode into the private antechamber.

A smile twitched at Anlaf's lips, Blacarri had warned him to expect Olaf soon. Apparently, the lad had taken a mistress, "How are you Olaf."

Puffing up his chest, Olaf barely inclined his head as he lifted his chin. He was sure that Anlaf would refuse his request. He haughtily ignored his cousin's question, "I would like your permission to house my mistress, Helga, in my chamber."

Anlaf felt the smooth sides of the whetstone, "If I let you take Helga into your bedchamber, you will be announcing formally, that she is your mistress. That comes with certain responsibilities, Olaf. Are you prepared to support her?"

Olaf shrugged his shoulders. The palace provided them with everything they needed to survive. It was his other needs that he wanted to gratify. Sex with Helga was a hunger for him now. A quick tumble in the stables did nothing to appease his burning bodily need for her. He wanted to be able to take her whenever he wanted, and that meant having her close, "Yes I am."

"Are you prepared to support any children born to you?"

He grinned, swaggering, "Of course."

Looking up at Olaf, Anlaf felt he needed to spell out his concerns, "As a formal mistress to a prince of my court, Helga will have certain privileges. She will be able to eat at my table. She will be close to my queen. Helga will need to conduct herself," he paused to ensure his cousin understood his meaning, "appropriately."

His blue eyes glinted, "I will speak to her, your Majesty. I will have Canute teach her the ways of a lady."

A smile twitched at Anlaf's lips as he thoughtfully pondered, Helga would be a very amenable distraction for Olaf. He nodded, "You may move Helga to your chamber. The queen and I would be happy for you both to dine with us tonight."

Blinking with surprise, Olaf grinned, "My thanks Majesty." Thinking the king may change his mind, he turned abruptly and he left the room, practically bumping into Scarface in the hallway.

Slightly bewildered, Anlaf shook his head.

The door guard announced loudly, "Jarl Barrick of Orkney to see the king."

Looking up as he entered the room, Anlaf smiled, "Why the formality, Scarface?"

As usual, Scarface came straight to the point, his voice gruff, "King Anlaf, I wish to ask formally, for your permission, to request the hand of Lady Muldivana of Lochaber, in marriage."

Eyeing him thoughtfully, "My wife has advised me of your interest in the lady." A small frown furrowed his brow, "I have been expecting this. Are you sure Barrick?" Pensively, "Lady Muldivana is a lovely young woman but although she is of noble blood she has only a small dowry."

"Yes, I am sure."

"She has no lands or fortune, Barrick."

Scarface looked sombre. His friend only used his given name when he was deadly serious, "I want her for my wife. I am not poor. My holdings on Man and Skappa will sustain us."

Anlaf persisted, "She has been married before, she is young and healthy, yet she bore no children. This is not a good match for you Barrick."

Scarface shrugged his huge muscular shoulders, "Muldivana's husband was away at war."

Shaking his head, Anlaf looked unconvinced, "Take her for your mistress and marry an heiress with childbearing hips. That would be the smart thing to do."

"Anlaf," He frowned at his friend, "Muldivana is a lady."

"The lady has a fearsome temper. You saw her when she arrived at court, she was as mad as a berserker. Blacarri said she nearly slapped his face off." He shook his head, chuckling at the memory. Serious again, "Why her?"

Thoughtfully, his gaze softened again, "We like the same things. She is easy to talk to." Gruffly, "She does not see my scars." He paused for a moment, "I want to take care of her."

Anlaf felt himself conceding, "Barrick, you sound in love."

Forcefully, "I do not want her to leave me when you take Queen Maelmare back to Alba."

"Does Lady Muldivana agree to your suit?"

He looked sheepish, "Err, I have not plucked up the courage to ask her yet."

Chuckling, Anlaf grinned, "You need to get moving, Scarface. I am sure that Blacarri is interested in her."

Gruffly, "I warned him off!"

Raising his eyebrows amused, "Well you still need to ask her."

"I know. King Anlaf, do I have your permission?"

Standing up tall, Anlaf smiled, "I can tell that your mind is made up. I will agree this match. I know that my wife will be pleased to retain the lady. I will send word to Muldivana's brother, advising them of your interest and that I agree to this match." Smiling, "I will also petition Maelmare's uncle on your behalf. I hardly think that King Constantine will refuse a request from me at this time."

Grinning, he bowed, "My thanks my King."

"So, when are you going to ask her?"

"I am meeting her later." Scarface looked a little embarrassed, "Err, tonight is a full moon. I want to ask her in the castle gardens." Gruffly, "I think it will be romantic." He looked perplexed, "Women like that sort of thing, don't they?"

Amused, "Yes they do." Suddenly feeling the excitement of the occasion, "I will have double torches placed around the grounds and the walls."

Wandering into the antechamber, dressed prettily in her dark emerald green gown, Maelmare looked at them quizzically.

Anlaf grinned, "Scarface is going to ask for Lady Muldivana's hand tonight."

Her topaz eyes lit up with excitement, "How wonderful."

Scarface's eyebrows rose up quizzically, "Do you think I should have flowers?"

Smiling with anticipation, she nodded, "Women love

flowers. I will have the maids pick them from Ivarrs Green."
Thoughtfully, "Music, we need music."

Suddenly remembering the blind man and lad, Scarface smiled, "She loves to hear the blind man sing."

"I will have him there too and the lad with the harp."

That evening, there was quite a lot of excitement in the kitchens, as word got round, that Helga was seated on the top table next to Prince Olaf.

Her jealous eyes flashing, Kari quipped spitefully, "Well Helga always had an eye for the men!"

The head cook glanced at her impatiently, "Watch your tongue Kari! Take the sweetmeats out to the king's table."

She mumbled under her breath, "She will be lucky if I don't spit in her food!"

The head cook rounded on her angrily, picking up a knife, "You defile my food woman and it will be the very last thing you do!"

Alarmed, Kari paled. She pouted sulkily, "I didn't mean it!" Picking up the tray of sweetmeats, she hurried out of the kitchen. She barely looked at Helga as she placed the tray in front of her.

Dressed very finely in a new ochre coloured dress, Helga's green eyes flashed with the thrill of it all. Olaf had already made love to her twice in his large soft bed. Her new grand chamber was a far cry from the kitchen floor. Only last evening it was her serving food at these tables. She did not notice Kari's flushed angry face. She only saw the queen smile and nod to her. She instinctively knew that she was being welcomed into the palace inner circle. She almost trembled with delight.

Much later that night, gazing out from an arrow slit in the tower, Anlaf held Maelmare's hand warmly. They watched Scarface, lead Muldivana by the hand, into the torch lit castle gardens.

Her topaz eyes twinkled, softly, "Husband, it is just so beautiful."

Muldivana gasped with pleasure as she stepped onto sweet heady smelling meadow flowers. Looking up, she smiled. The full moon looked huge and silver white against the dark starlit sky. Lit by many torches, suspended on the wrought iron pendants hanging from the walls, the turreted tower and castle keep looked ethereally golden. Her ears almost tingled, as the minstrel sang a beautiful melody alongside a harp. She recognised the blind man's incredible voice and smiled with wonder as his song filled the air.

Maelmare gripped Anlaf's hand tighter, as she watched Scarface kneel down onto one knee.

Anlaf smiled, looking down at his wife, he felt deeply happy and in love.

Silhouetted against dark skies and the full moon, Muldivana's slim figure stood motionless.

A shuddering breath escaped from Maelmare's lips when she saw Muldivana nod her head.

Scarface suddenly stood and lifted Muldivana into the air, swinging her around. Then tenderly, just as the blind man reached a beautifully tantalizing higher note, he lowered her until her feet touched the ground. Bending his head, until his lips met hers, he kissed her passionately.

Part 4

Alliance

4.1

The sound of lire music, and the soft eyrie melody of a young slave girl's Orcadian island song, filled the court. Normally, she would be working in the kitchens but she had been noticed singing sweetly as she scrubbed dishes. This evening, she had been taken to the main hall and told to sing her island songs. Wide eyed and scruffy, she did as she was told. As she sang her gentle ballad, a page boy wandered by carrying a silver tray at an angle. She caught a glimpse of her own reflection. Her blonde hair was un-brushed and fluffy. Her little face was dirty with soot. Her dress looked old and worn. Tears filled her eyes as she remembered a time before she was a slave, a time when her mother had shown her how to look at her face in a pale of water. She remembered she looked different then, in that time of love and laughter. Her clothes had been new and freshly washed. Her eyes had been happy. It was her mother who had taught her to sing her songs, and her father had listened to them in the evenings. No, she could not think of him now, she loved him too much for that. Blinking to banish the tears she concentrated on the room. The main hall was dressed with beautiful tapestries. Many gigantic black iron chandeliers hung from the ceiling rafters, each laden with hundreds of lit beeswax candles. Wall torches and table candelabras also illuminated the huge chamber. Ignoring her, noble men and warriors laughed loudly together, drinking ale or dark red wine from shimmering silver goblets. They all wore battle leather breeches. Wide leather sword belts held their silk tunics in place. The ladies of the court stood together talking softly. They dressed in richly coloured velvet gowns and wore their finest jewellery. Working in the kitchens and tidying bed chambers, she had not seen the king before. He looked intimidatingly powerful, as he sat upon a throne, on a raised dais at the far end of the vast room.

Seated on his huge carved mahogany throne, Constantine confidently surveyed his court. Dressed in brown leather breeches and boots, the silk of his purple tunic glimmered in the candle light. He slowly sipped fine imported red wine from a golden goblet. Barely feeling the heavy gold chain around his neck and the golden crown of Alba on his head, his topaz eyes flashed with excitement. This was one of the most important days of his life. He looked impatiently at the six empty thrones to his left and the two to his right. Tonight, he needed to convince the most powerful men in Britain to join him. A dreary monotone voice interrupted his thoughts.

"Lord King, may I approach?"

Barely concealing a look of dislike, Constantine fixed his cold gaze on the archbishop, "You may Archbishop Wulfstan." Seeing the remarkably tall auburn haired man with the archbishop, he curiously eyed the man, "I have met you before. Where was it?"

Dressed as usual in black battle leathers and his long green cloak, the archbishop approached the dais. For one fleeting moment, his black eyes flashed menacingly, as he remembered their last meeting. A snarl pulled at his upper lip, before he carefully controlled himself. He bowed, reverently clasping his hands together. Taking in a shallow breath, tedium tinged his voice, "May I introduce Jarl Ragenhare of Cenheardsburgh." He carefully watched the king's reaction as he drawled, "Grand Master of Morrigu."

Wearing full battle leathers and his two swords hanging from his belt, Ragenhare bowed respectfully towards the king, "You passed through my brother-in-law's Burgh two years ago

Majesty and stayed the night."

"Ahh I remember that night well. You are a master of two sword fighting." Mischievously to Wulfstan, "You have need of a bodyguard, your Grace?"

Smiling, Ragenhare cast a sideways glance at the archbishop. His Grace would hate any remark that would infer that he could not protect himself.

Drawing in a breath, the snarl briefly lifted one side of his upper lip again. The comment prickled. Wulfstan forced his eyes to gaze tolerantly cold. A consummate politician, he ignored the remark. Instead, he inclined his head and bowed, his long lank hair fell irritatingly forward into his eyes.

Looking back at the tall warrior, "Why do you travel with Archbishop Wulfstan?"

Eyeing him steadily, "Your Majesty, his Grace recently sent for me to accompany him on his journey to your kingdom. His Grace is aware that I met King Anlaf of Ath Cliath many years ago. He hopes that I can help to secure an interview with the Norse king."

Appreciating the man's honesty, Constantine smiled, "You are welcome pagan, to my court."

It felt right to bow, "You are gracious, Majesty."

Constantine looked thoughtful, "I remember your dance with the swords. It was most impressive."

Ragenhare smiled, "Thank you, Majesty."

"I wish to see this dance again. It is a wonder to the eyes."

"I am at your command, Majesty."

Raising his voice so that it carried to his court, Constantine grinned, "We have never had the pleasure, of a Master of Morrigu, at our Court before, Lord Ragenhare. You are most welcome."

Close to the dais, Ruardri and Cellach looked up with interest as they recognised him.

"Tomorrow then, Lord Ragenhare, we will watch your sword dance. I may ask you to practice your martial art with some of my best warriors."

Raising his head, Wulfstan ordered monotonously, "You may leave us, Lord Ragenhare."

Bowing again to the king, he backed away. Turning, he almost bumped into a tall muscular young man.

His bright topaz eyes flashed with excitement, as he confidently introduced himself again, "I have met you before my Lord, I am Prince Cellach. Welcome to our court Lord Ragenhare." He grinned eagerly.

Looking over the young man, he recognised him, "I am honoured Prince Cellach."

Smiling indulgently, Cellach motioned to the lad next to him, "May I introduce my younger brother, Prince Indulf?"

He looked about eight or nine years old, with the same confident topaz coloured eyes, as his elder brother and father. Ragenhare smiled, "I am honoured Prince Indulf."

Feeling a little awed to be meeting a true Master of Morrigu, Indulf grinned inanely.

Cellach turned to Ruardri, "And you may remember my good friend, Ruardri of Moray."

"I am honoured, Lord Ruardri."

"It is us who are honoured, my lord. Masters of Morrigu have legendary status at our court."

Barely able to contain himself, Indulf gushed, "May we practice with you tomorrow Master? Can you could teach us some secret sword skills?"

Smiling cheekily, Ruardri looked at Ragenhare expectantly. He had wanted to ask the very same question.

Blinking hopefully, looking like an older version of his young brother, Cellach grinned as well.

Ragenhare chuckled, "I will meet you all tomorrow."

"Excellent," Cellach's topaz eyes sparkled with anticipation, "I will send my page to bring you to our martial arena in the morning."

Feeling tired from his journey, Ragenhare moved on, "Please excuse me my Lords, I need to get some food and ale before I retire."

Wulfstan did not notice Ragenhare pass him. His voice sounded dreary, "May I speak plainly great King?"

Eyeing him with obvious dislike, Constantine nodded.

"As soon as I heard, of your eldest daughter's marriage, to the Viking King of Ath Cliath, I was intrigued."

Steadily, "Intrigued your Grace, why?"

"Your Majesty," carefully choosing his words, "My spies have advised me that King Anlaf is a great leader." He paused, "I knew that you would only give your eldest daughter to a man that you thought most highly of."

Fixing his intelligent glinting topaz eyes on Wulfstan, he looked derisively at him, "No doubt your spies keep you well informed Archbishop, as do mine."

His black eyes narrowed, coldly curious. He lowered his voice, "Majesty, what do your spies tell you?"

Unflinching, Constantine locked eyes with him, "I am told that you sent messengers to Norway, asking for one of King Harald Fairhair's sons to be sent to you, so that you could measure him for the kingship of Northumbria."

Alarm hinted on his features before he sniffed in a deep breath of aversion. He whispered contemptuously, "That was a few years ago my Lord and unfortunately, Fairhair's sons were too busy fighting each other for Norway! There are now only two of his sons surviving." He huffed out a blow through his pursed lips, "King Haakon the Good now rules Norway and his older exiled brother, Erik Bloodaxe, now casts his covetous eyes on the Orkney Isles. Indeed, you are well informed Majesty." Calculatingly, "I have command of the two great armies of Northumbria. I wish to offer my services to your great alliance," he paused theatrically, "for a price."

Watching him, Constantine's eyes glinted intelligently, "What is your price?"

"My price is your leave to seek an interview, with your son-in-law, Anlaf Guthrithsson."

"Why do you seek an interview with my son-in-law?"

Holding the king's gaze, he faintly inclined his head, "I may offer him the Kingdom of Jorvic and Northumbria."

Constantine suddenly laughed loudly, "My son-in-law protecting my borders from the English, what could be better? We appear to have an accord."

The two thick oak doors that hung on ornate black iron hinges swung open, creaking noisily.

The deep booming voice of the door guard quietened the crowd as he announced loudly, "King Owain of Strathclyde."

Looking up expectantly, Constantine waved his hand to the side dismissively, "We will talk later Archbishop."

Annoyed at being dismissed so abruptly, Wulfstan scowled as he backed away.

As the giant of a man strode towards the dais, nobles and ladies stepped to the side, forming a walkway.

King Owain's huge muscular shoulders and craggy featured face stood higher than most of the men in the room. A gold head band sat on his light brown haired head. Dressed in black battle leathers, he stopped for a moment at the steps of the dais. Lifting his chin he did not bow.

"You are very welcome here, King Owain." Constantine swept his hand towards the thrones.

Nodding, already briefed on where he should sit, he climbed the three steps of the dais and took his throne.

The door guard boomed, "The Celtic Kings of Wallensis approach." He paused as four impressive looking dark haired, muscular men strode into the room. He noticed the four kings were at least a foot shorter than most of the men in the room.

They looked around the room, their dark brown eyes glinting challengingly.

The door guard noticed each of them wore a gold headband and jet black battle leathers. Lifting his chin, he announced them clearly, "King Idwal Foel, King Twdyrr, King Wurgeat and King Hywel Dda."

Fully armed, striding forward, they made an impressive sight.

As they approached him, Constantine's topaz eyes glinted,

excitement tingled in the air.

None of them bowed, they were his equal.

"Welcome to my domain." Constantine swept his hand towards the thrones.

They each took their pre-arranged seat.

The doors creaked opened again. The door guard announced loudly, "King Suibne of the many Western Isles."

Confidently striding into the room, Suibne's blue eyes looked intensely penetrating. His golden headband glimmered on top of his long white blonde hair. Wearing a blue silk shirt, exactly the same colour of his twinkling blue eyes, many a lady eyed him alluringly. Black leather breeches and boots covered his thick muscular legs. He strode up to the dais. A wide black leather sword belt was buckled at his midriff.

Smiling, Constantine nodded, "Welcome my friend."

He bounded up the steps of the dais, "You look well Constantine." Pushing his long sword to the side, he took his seat on the throne furthest away from Constantine. Any other king would have taken that as an insult but not him, he had no need of others opinions. He knew that he was a great personal friend of King Constantine. He looked around the room. The room heaved with well-dressed nobles. He too felt the excitement of the occasion. Anticipation filled the room.

Suddenly, the heavy doors creaked open again. Looking over the two tall men stood in the doorway, the guard looked impressed. Both men possessed similar strong aquiline facial features and tall athletic, muscular bodies. Dressed in black leather breeches and boots, they each carried an ornate pommel long sword, suspended in scabbards, from their wide black leather belts. The belts, buckled over their luxurious silk tunics, accentuated their muscular midriffs. The door guard boomed, "King Anlaf of all the Norse of Britain and Ireland and, King Black Arailt of Colonsay, Mann and Norse Gailgedhael."

Standing up, King Constantine clapped his hands loudly.

Ragenhare's green eyes glinted with curiosity as he turned to see them. It had been ten years since he had first met them on the Isle of Clouds. They both looked taller, older, and indomitable.

The music silenced and the slave girl awkwardly stopped singing mid note.

Intrigued as to why the music had ceased, everyone in the court stopped talking. Turning to look at the two tall men, the hush hung uncomfortably in the air.

Behind her father and uncle, Gytha stood waiting silently. Looking very young and delicately beautiful, her pale grey eyes glistened. Encircled protectively by Prince Olaf, Jarl Canute, Jarl Barrick, and her father's aide Ketil, she looked unruffled.

Feeling full of pent up jealousy, Olaf's deep blue eyes glinted resentfully. Adjusting his sword, he flexed his muscular shoulders and flicked back his shoulder length hair. Bitterness coursed through his veins with every beat of his heart.

Casting a slow deliberate glance around the room, Anlaf and Blacarri looked at each other and nodded. Their eyes shone, self-assuredly, as they strode towards the raised dais where the kings waited.

A murmur of awe and respect went through the court.

Wearing the golden headband of Alban Galwensis, Mailcoluim MacDovenald stepped back, as the two broad shouldered men walked towards him.

His seventeen year old son stood rooted to the spot as he watched the two warriors approaching.

Quickly pulling his son out of their path, Mailcoluim whispered gruffly, "Duff watch yourself boy. Keep your wits about you."

"Who are they Da?" His young gaze followed the very young beautiful blonde lady, as she glided towards him in a gown the colour of dark purple heather.

"They are the great grandsons of one of the greatest and wisest warlords to have ever lived. They are the great grandsons of Ivar Benlaus Ragnarsson. He was the first king of all the Norsemen of Ireland and Britain." Following his son's gaze, he added, "The young lady that you are staring at, is the eldest daughter of King Black Arailt. Her name is Gytha. A beauty don't you think?"

His young eyes glinted, "Aye Da," his voice softened to a whisper, "a beauty."

Malcolm whispered, "Both of those men have hard earned reputations as aggressive warriors."

Watching them, Duff blinked in surprise, as many famous warriors of the court, bowed their heads respectfully as the two men passed them.

"The young blonde man is Prince Olaf Curan Sihtricsson, the old King of Jorvic's son. He has no kingdom now. My informants advise me to watch him with interest, he is an ambitious man. The old one must be Jarl Canute. The one with the scars is Jarl Barrick Ivarrsson of Orkney. He is married to Lady Muldivana MacDoir, you will meet him later." He paused, "I do not know the other smaller man." Dismissively, "He cannot be important."

Reaching the dais, a smile played on Blacarri lips, as he looked at all of the kings. He could not believe it, Constantine had actually managed it. Most of the Kings of Britain were assembled in this halla. Lifting his chin, he held back respectfully as Anlaf climbed the steps to the raised platform alone.

Pulling Anlaf into a fearsome bear hug, Constantine grinned, "Welcome Anlaf, welcome."

He winced under the force of his father-in-law's enthusiastic reception, "It is good to see you so well."

"How is my girl?" Exuberantly, "I heard with joy that she gave birth to another son."

"Maelmare is understandably tired from her confinement. I could not allow her to come to see you this time. She was so disappointed she cried for days. I nearly gave in but I knew that her health could not take it. It was too soon after the birth. I could not risk it."

Constantine's topaz eyes shone, "I miss her greatly. I could never resist her tears. She was so spoilt. It is good that you do not give into her too easily. The journey would have been too hard on her. How is my young grandson Guthrith Camman? Is he growing into a fine bonny prince?"

"Guthrith is healthy. He is already talking." His deep blue eyes glistened with pride, "Our new baby boy is strong and well too. We have named him Sihtric Cam"

Concern flickered in his eyes, "Are they protected whilst you are away?"

"My brother, Ragnal, is protecting Ath Cliath while I am here." Smiling, "I also left Lady Muldivana with them. She will keep Maelmare well rested."

His eyebrows rose up, "God help the Irish if they attack. Lady Muldivana could see them off herself. My niece has a formidable temper."

Chuckling, Anlaf winked, "Don't tell anyone but she scares the hell out of me!"

Suddenly remembering his other guests, Constantine boomed a formal introduction to the court, "King Anlaf of Ath Cliath, High King of all the Norsemen of Ireland and Britain, you are welcome in my court!"

Moving to the seat of honour to the right of Constantine, "You have not yet met my brother King Black Arailt. He watched over my kingdom last time I was here. May I introduce him to your court?"

"You may."

Raising his voice, Anlaf turned to the room, "May I introduce my brother, Black Arailt Guthrithsson of the Clan Ivarr. Great sea warrior and ring giver, King of the Isle of Man, King of Norse Gailgedhael, King of the Isle of Colonsay, Tánaiste heir apparent of Ath Cliath."

Introducing a potential contender for the throne of Ath Cliath in this way, shouted the brother's allegiance to each other. Murmurs of admiration echoed throughout the gathering nobility.

Climbing the three steps on to the dais, stood tall, Blacarri eyed the King of Alba as an equal.

Constantine had successfully relied on his base instincts all of his life. As he looked directly into this man's light grey translucent eyes, he intuitively summed him up as confident, strong and resilient. His voice deep, "Your reputation as a great warrior precedes you King Black Arailt."

Lifting his chin proudly, he held the king's eyes, "King Constantine, your brilliance as a warrior and noble king precede you. As father in-law to my brother, you are my family. Please call me Blacarri."

Liking the man's directness, he smiled, "I have placed a throne for you to the right of your brothers. You will both sit to my right," pausing for effect, "a place normally reserved for my sons."

"You honour us."

Declaring in a booming voice, loud enough for every man in the room to hear, he announced, "King Black Arrie, you are welcome to my court."

Not a man to miss an opportunity to introduce his daughter to nobility, a smile twitched at Blacarri's lips, "Thank you. May I present my daughter, Princess Gytha of the Isle of Man?"

Jovially, "Of course you may. My court is always pleased to greet a new lady to our kingdom."

Smiling warmly, Blacarri motioned Gytha to come on to the dais.

Lifting her skirt, moving gracefully up the three steps, she felt her young heart beating fast. Sinking into a deep elegant curtsy before King Constantine, her exquisite silk dress rustled around her. Her long blonde hair trailed silkily down her back.

"I say this sincerely, Black Arrie," he cast an indiscreet lustful eye over her slim body, firmly budding breasts and pretty elfin face, "your daughter is a beauty and ripe for marriage. How old is she?"

Leaning forward, fondly taking her hand, Blacarri raised her slowly from her curtsy, "Thirteen years of age."

"Is she betrothed?"

Shaking his head, "No, she is too young."

"Come now, she is the perfect age for marriage!" Beaming at

her, Constantine asked loudly, "How do you find my court, my Lady?"

Smiling demurely, "Your Majesty's court is very rich indeed. I am very taken with the brocade in my apartment and my bed is the most comfortable that I have ever slept upon."

Appreciatively, he eyed her, "Beautiful, such gentleness." His voice boomed, "You are a lovely addition to my court my dear. I hope that you enjoy your stay." Gallantly, "Whilst you are in my domain you have my protection."

She curtseyed, "Thank you Majesty."

"My daughter, Princess Bethoc, is about the same age as you." Beckoning her to him, "Bethoc come here my dear."

Dressed in a pale yellow gown trimmed with gold, Bethoc passed her goblet of wine to her female attendant, "Thank you, Shona."

Inclining her head, Shona smiled. Her dark hair was interlaced back from her pretty face, showing off her incredibly unusual eyes. One eye was the most vibrant blue and the other was tawny brown. Both of her eyes had a dark ring around the iris, making them stand out attractively even more.

Looking at her, Bethoc smiled. She had picked Shona from at least ten other slave girls to be her attendant and companion. She had chosen her because of her beautiful eyes. Gracefully, she lifted her skirt revealing slim white ankles and delicately embroidered shoes. Climbing the three steps, she went immediately to her father, curtseying low and elegantly.

Watching her, Blacarri thought how alike in looks she was to her sister Maelmare. Her features had the same shaped vibrant topaz eyes and strawberry blonde hair.

"Princess Gytha," Constantine smiled, "I present my daughter, Princess Bethoc." Watching the two ladies curtsy to each other, he smiled, "Bethoc make the lady welcome at our court."

"Of course father." Immediately linking her arm in Gytha's, she led her down the steps of the dais. Smiling friendly, "Come with me my Lady. I will introduce you to some of our lords." Confidently, she walked towards a group of young men.

Her attendant, as always, followed a few paces behind her princess.

Smiling indulgently, Anlaf watched a young expensively dressed man, almost drag his father into their path for a formal introduction, "My niece is all grown up and already turning heads."

Watching the youngsters as he sat down, Constantine leaned forward. Thoughtfully, "Now that would be a good match, Black Arrie. Young, Duff MacMailcoluim is royal heir to the Kingdom of Strathclyde and Galwensis. You know of course his father, King Mailcoluim of all Galwensis, my elected Tanist heir."

Lifting his chin as he sat down, Blacaire's eyes glinted steely grey. Holding Constantine's gaze, he controlled his voice. Steadily, "I know Mailcoluim is King of Alban Galwensis, for I am King of the Norse region."

He chuckled mischievously, "Just my little joke Black Arrie, just my little joke."

A smile twitched at Blacarri's lips. He knew that his metal had just been tested. He thoughtfully watched King Mailcoluim, gallantly introducing his son to Gytha, "You are right of course, it would be a good match. But is he good enough for my daughter?"

Seriously, "King Mailcoluim is my cousin and Tanist heir to the throne of Alba. Duff is Mailcoluim's eldest son from his first marriage. As a Tosiac Prince, Duff will likely inherit the throne of Alba, after my eldest son follows Mailcoluim as king."

Nodding, Anlaf watched them, "I understand the tanistic law of the House of Alpin is similar to the Norse."

Constantine's topaz eyes glinting, he turned to him, "Everyone in this room knows, in this violent age, a king is more likely to die young by the sword, than in our beds in old age."

Blacarri shrugged his muscular shoulders. Completely indifferent to the thought, "We warriors know our fate."

Looking at his brother, Anlaf smiled, "Our people need protection. A fully grown king's brother or cousin is a better option to inherit kingship, rather than a king's son who is still a child."

He nodded in agreement, "Land and people must be protected. For the Norse, there is no better death than in battle, with a sword in our hand, for we meet our Gods in Valhalla."

A smile twitched at Constantine's lips, "I love a bit of match making. As king, I have become quite the authority of my courtier's lineages." His eyes twinkled, "Duff's mother was Gruach MacGiric, a Tosiac Princess of Alban Galwensis. After his first wife died, Mailcoluim wed Sybilla, the daughter of King Suibne of the Isles. Sybilla is young and has given Mailcoluim two more sons, Cinaed and Coluim," he added dismissively, "both are too young for betrothal." Constantine eyed Blacarri carefully, "I understand you married King Suibne's sister Tasha?"

A frown fleeted across his handsome features, but he did not have time to reply as King Mailcoluim bounded on to the dais.

Turning to him, Constantine's voice boomed, "King Mailcoluim of Alban Galwensis, welcome."

His pale eyes glittering, Blacarri turned to him, "King Mailcoluim, I hope you liked the stud bull that I sent you as a present last month?" He had done that purposely to ease the tension of their meeting. He had even asked his Norse Gailgedhail clan leaders to ease off on their cattle raids in Alban Galwensis.

Enjoying the politics and obvious rivalry of their meeting, Mailcoluim inclined his head, "King Black Arailt of Norse Gailgedhael, it is good to meet you at last. The bull is much appreciated, especially by the cows."

Chuckling, "I am glad that he has been of service."

"I will send you the first calf from my special herd."

"You are too generous."

Smiling, Mailcoluim took his seat next to Constantine.

Grinning broadly, Constantine barely suppressed a chuckle, "King Anlaf and King Black Arrie, may I introduce you to King Mailcoluim's brother, the unmistakable, Owain, King of Strathclyde!"

Blacarri blinked twice. Owain had to be the tallest man that he had ever met and he was built like an ox.

Constantine leaned towards Anlaf, as he whispered advice, "Whatever you do, never agree to an arm wrestle with King Owain. He will rip your arm off!" Chuckling, he turned to the Welsh kings, "May I introduce the great warrior Kings of Wallensis, King Idwal Foel, King Twdyrr, King Wurgeat and King Hywel Dda."

Anlaf and Blacarri nodded to each man.

Looking formidably strong, with distinctly dark features, they each acknowledged the Vikings.

His topaz eyes sparkling jovially, Constantine smiled, "Of course Arri, it will be good for you to see your brother in law, King Suibne of the many Isles."

He had always got on well with Suibne. He considered him to be a friend, "It is good to see you, Suibne."

Suibne grinned, "Good to see you too. We will talk later."

As the kings settled down, looking around the room, only Blacarri noticed Ketil blending into the shadows. Thoughtfully, he conceded that the lad was now his best spy. Feeling the hairs on the back of his neck suddenly rise, he instinctively looked round. His pale grey eyes intuitively met his cousin's deep blue eyes.

For a moment, Olaf glared at him. his eyes hard and full of jealousy.

Steely eyeing him back, unflinchingly controlling his surprise, Blacarri lifted his chin.

Gaining control of his belligerent emotions, Olaf turned away dejectedly.

Watching him for a moment longer, frowning with suspicion and unease, Blacarri felt a sense of foreboding descend into his chest. He knew that Olaf's ambitions for kingship were clawing at his soul. That made him dangerous. A muscle flexed in his jawline. Turning back to the other kings, he concentrated on polite conversation.

Stood in the crowd, Scarface drank deeply from a large silver goblet of wine, as he listened to the young slave girl sing an eerie ballad. Her lovely song reminded him of his home in Orkney.

Olaf pushed past him.

Irritated, Scarface swung round. Gruffly, "You nearly spilt my wine, Olaf."

Frowning, he sucked in a deep breath, "My apologies cousin. It is difficult to get through the crowd."

Surprised at the immediate apology a smile twitched at his lips, "No problem lad. I have never seen so many people in one place either. Are you okay?"

Hanging his head, Olaf's deep blue eyes looked dejected, "It should be me up there Scarface. I am King Sihtric's eldest son. I should be King of." He hesitated as he took in a deep breath and controlled himself, "I should be King of Jorvic. I am a prince. I should be rich. All I have is the stallion that you gave me."

Feeling sorry for the lad, Scarface placed his arm on Olaf's shoulder, his voice low and grave, "Olaf, the Gods move in mysterious ways. By all accounts you should actually be dead. Your life is not so bad is it?"

He blinked in surprise, "Why do you say I should be dead."

"If King Guthrith had not rescued you, then King Athelstan would have killed you."

"I know my uncle saved my life." His blue eyes glinted with sincerity, "I was always respectful and grateful to him."

"You are lucky lad."

"I must be," his head dropped again, "I just don't feel lucky."

"The Gods must have a future plan for you. Never give up hope and always be thankful for what you have." Thoughtfully, "You should have brought Helga with you. She would put a smile back on your face."

Petulantly, "She bores me." It was true. They had been together for over two years. He had once thought that he had deep feelings for her but that had waned lately. Now he found her lowly status an embarrassment. She had not even born him a child, which frustrated him. Some of the noblemen had laughingly questioned his virility. His eyes hardened moodily.

Surprised by Olaf's open betrayal of Helga, Scarface raised his eyebrows. Shrugging his shoulders, he looked past Olaf. A flash of surprise swept over his face as his eyes rested on the tall man dressed in battle leathers, "It can't be? His hair is whiter now. Is it him?" The crowd of nobles parted slightly. Seeing the man's two sword hilts, Scarface grinned. Immediately handing his wine to Olaf, he patted his shoulder, "Here, have this wine. It will make you feel better." Grinning with anticipation, he strolled off.

As Scarface disappeared into the crowd, Olaf lifted the goblet of wine to his mouth and gulped it back in one go.

Spotting a small curtained hallway being used by the slaves, Ragenhare looked determined as he headed towards it. Slowly making his way through the throng of courtiers, he suddenly felt a strong grip on his arm. Turning around, he blinked in surprise, "Well lad, you're still alive then?"

Scarface grinned, "Master, it's good to see you again."

Remembering how close this man had come to death, Ragenhare looked over him, "The scars aren't too bad."

"My wife doesn't mind them."

"Well now, married as well."

"It has been many years since the battle on the Isle of Clouds. I am surprised to see you again." Feeling curious, "What are you doing here in Alba?"

"I travel in the retinue of Archbishop Wulfstan. He is hoping that my presence will secure him an interview with King Anlaf."

Scarface smiled, "I will arrange your meeting with King Anlaf. Leave that to me Master, it is the least that I can do."

"Thank you lad."

Jovially, "Come drink with me, Ragenhare. We have much to talk about. Let's get a flagon of ale. You can tell me what you have been doing for the last ten years."

Two warriors bustled past him. He shook his head, "Sorry

lad, I am tired. I will find you tomorrow. It is good to see you though."

Scarface looked disappointed as he watched Ragenhare stride off towards the curtained hallway. Turning back to the dais, curiosity filled him as he looked up at the kings. They were all in deep discussion.

4.2

His fist clenched, Constantine spoke seriously, "That is why I have asked you here. Combined, our armies can defeat the English King."

Nodding in agreement, Blacarri looked at him, "I concur. To beat the English we must rise up as one army. There can be no rebel amongst us. The only way we can secure victory is to be one great military force."

Looking calm and confident, Anlaf stretched out his muscular legs, "Constantine, you have the backing of the Norse."

The other kings murmured their support.

Calmly, Blacarri eyed Constantine, he knew that there was one last stumbling block, "But who will lead us? Who will take control of our combined armies? We must nominate a High King and pledge our allegiance to him."

Constantine leaned forward, "A brave question, Blacarri" His topaz eyes sparkled with intensity, "But of course you are right. There can only be one leader amongst us. Who will that be?"

King Mailcoluim spoke, "Indeed, it is a difficult question. However, it must be asked." Bluntly, "I personally would not follow King Black Arailt. That would bring shame on me."

Blacarri chuckled, "I would say the same of you."

Mailcoluim smiled. They both understood each other's position.

Blonde haired Suibne, also eyed Blacarri, "My friend, you understand that I cannot follow you either. That may cause problems for my sons in the future, when a new King of the Isles is elected. If the nobles remember that I followed the father of my sister's sons, they may use that reason to vote against my offspring, in favour of yours."

Blacarri grinned, "Again, I would say the same of you."

Dark haired, Hywel Dda shook his head, "I could not follow another Welsh King."

Wurgeat, Twdyrr and Idwal Foel murmured in agreement, the four corners of Walensis were almost always at war with each other.

Looking around at the kings before him, Blacarri spoke strongly, "This is a very difficult situation. If we cannot agree on a nominated High King then this alliance is dead." His voice even, "I have followed my brother, King Anlaf, into battle many times. He is a great general and warlord. I nominate King Anlaf as High King."

Suibne had no problem backing the Anlaf, "I second the nomination."

King Owain spoke quietly with the Welsh kings. Looking up, he smiled, his voice resonated deeply, "Anlaf, you have the allegiance of the Welsh and Strathclyde."

Mailcoluim looked thoughtfully at the King of Alba. What would he say? Would he follow his own son-in-law, or would he nominate himself as high king?

Constantine lifted his chin, his topaz eyes hardened for a moment. It was in his blood to lead. He knew though if he stood against Anlaf now, just as all the sub-kingdoms were in agreement, he could wreck the alliance. He knew what he had to do, "Anlaf, you are like a son to me. It is difficult for a father to hand over power to a son." He felt resigned, "Eventually it has to be done for the good of the kingdom. You have my allegiance, King Anlaf."

Blacarri hid a look of relief.

His face serious, King Mailcoluim spoke, "King Anlaf, you have my allegiance."

His blue eyes glinting, Anlaf nodded, "I accept your nomination as High King of our Alliance." He grinned, "Great kings, we have come a long way this night. Our descendants will tell the story of our victory over the English king, for centuries to come." A smile played on his lips. Turning to his brother, "Tell the story of the time our great grandfather performed the rite of Blood Eagle on his enemies."

In the background, Blacarri could hear the haunting melody of the slave girl's song. He nodded, his voice low and deep, "Less than one hundred years ago our great, great grandfather, Ragnar Lodbrook, was captured by King Aelle of Northumbria. King Aelle killed Ragnar by throwing him into a snake pit. When Ragnar's youngest son, Ivar, found out about his father's murder, he swore revenge. One month later, Ivar captured Aelle and he performed the rite of Blood Eagle on the king. Years later," Blacarri softly continued, "Ivar used this gruesome rite again to sacrifice another to Odin. He was the last King of the East Angles, the last of the line of the royal line of Wuffingas. His ancestors were buried in long ships in the sands of Sutton Hoo. His name was King Edmund. This king was taken to a holy hill, where he was offered to the great Norse God Odin. King Edmund was forced to lie on his stomach. His arms were held out stretched like a man on a crucifix. Ivar took his knife and sliced the skin off of the screaming King's back. Then Ivar plunged his hands through the King's living flesh, cracking Edmund's ribs apart."

As huge as he was, King Owain visibly cringed.

"King Edmund was still screaming, as part of his air filled lungs were cut away from his dying body, then spread out. As his lungs filled with air, they looked like blood red eagle wings, fluttering in flight. It took a long time before the king gasped his last bloody breath." He smiled at his fascinated audience, "Only seven years ago, in June of 930AD, the Christians martyred King Edmund and canonised him. They had his body unearthed and moved from Sutton Hoo, to the newly named town of Bury St Edmunds." Looking into the eyes of each man before him, he finished his story with a flourish. Pulling a beautifully made dagger from the scabbard at his waist, he roared, "When we capture King Athelstan, the sons of the Clan

Ivarr will sacrifice him to Odin, using the rite of Blood Eagle." Forcefully, "Let them make a saint of him!"

The kings cheered, relishing the thought of Athelstan's death.

Hearing them, Wulfstan looked up curiously. Part of him had doubted that the kings could ever form an agreement. His black eyes glinted. He knew that he was now a step closer to a Norse king in Northumbria.

Turning to a slave, Constantine ordered, "Fetch the sacred Celtic drinking horns of the Ancient Irish Kings." Enthusiastically, "Let us drink a blood treaty to our alliance."

Sat on small chairs, Duff, Bethoc and Gytha watched the kings. They had been fascinated by Blacarri's story.

Duff whispered, so Gytha could hear, "Alban royal lineage is traceable back over many centuries. Our ancestors were originally pagan Kings of Ireland, who in the fifth century AD, invaded the Pict kingdom of Kintyre under King Fergus Mor. Centuries of battles followed. Hoping to cease the war between the two kingdoms, our great grandfather Alpin, married a highborn Pict Princess. Their son, Kenneth MacAlpin, also married a Pict Princess called Toshiac. She was the sister of the then King of the Isles, Godfrey MacFergussa. His direct descendant is King Suibne.

Gytha smiled, "I too am a direct descendant of Godfrey MacFergussa. King Suibne is my blood uncle."

"I know Princess." He looked into her lovely pale grey eyes, "We must be very distant cousins. King Kenneth was the first King of Alba and the Picts. He united our country." He paused, "Well, all except for Galwensis. The Picts kept control of Galwensis, until the Norse came and invaded."

Smiling, she corrected him, "My ancestors did not invade. They married Pict princesses as well."

Inclining his head, a smile twitched respectfully at his lips.

Taking another full goblet of wine from a passing faceless slave, Olaf sneered, as he watched Gytha talking to the Alban prince.

Feeling his eyes on her, Gytha looked uncomfortable. At their last embarrassing encounter, less than a month ago, he had asked her to marry him. She had, of course, refused him.

Olaf remembered the humiliating scene as well. Now look at her, he thought, making cow eyes at the Alban. He barely hissed under his breath, "Slut!"

"Make way!"

Turning around too quickly, Olaf spilled his red wine.

Still watching Olaf with a frown, Gytha thought he looked a little drunk.

Two noblemen passed him, carrying a huge silver tray with nine large drinking horns. They walked carefully through the crowd of courtiers.

Watching Prince Olaf, angrily shake crimson droplets of wine from his boot, Duff continued softly, "Fergus Mor originally had twelve of those great drinking vessels. They are decorated so finely with silver filigree animals, it is rumoured that fairies made them."

Her mouth opened in wonder.

"They are so fine you can see the deep red wine carried in each horn. Over the centuries three of the drinking horns have been lost. The nine that are left are considered to be sacred and are only used in exceptionally special circumstances." He breathed deeply, "The kings must have an accord."

Gytha and Duff watched, as each of the nine kings took one of the drinking horns and held it high.

Anlaf stood and spoke solemnly, "This wine represents the blood of your gods and the blood of your ancestors. Drink this blood and commit to a lifelong blood treaty of loyalty, friendship and peace between the Kings of Alba, the Norse, the Kings of Galwensis, Strathclyde and Walensis, and the kings of the Isles and of Man."

Each one of them raised their drinking horn to their lips and drank. They each believed above all else in the honour of their word.

Drinking deeply, Anlaf continued, "A true bond of loyalty is forged this night for our coalition. We will never be enemies again in our lifetime." Toasting loudly, so that the whole court could hear, he raised his drinking horn, "The plans are laid. Armies of men are promised. Fleets of ships and weapons are pledged. Each of us agrees. No more tribute will be paid to Athelstan. Let the English King roar his discontent." His voice boomed out, "We are at war!"

A great cheer filled the hall. Wulfstan almost smiled but his grimace looked like a snarl.

Constantine stood up and bellowed, "Ladies of my court leave now!"

Duff turned to Gytha, his eyes serious, "You need to leave now."

Her eyes widened as she realised with anxiety what was about to happen. Standing up, she nearly bumped into Princess Bethoc.

Quietly standing, Anlaf looked behind him towards a small side door. He knew that it led to the guest quarters on the upper floors. Turning to Constantine, he flexed his shoulders confidently, "Father-in-law, I have no appetite for a slave wenching. I am off to my bed."

His topaz eyes flashed with amusement, "Ha, my daughter has tamed you Anlaf!"

"Indeed she has." Turning to his brother, Anlaf lowered his voice, "I am leaving. The Albans still practice slave wenching." Turning, he strode out of the halla, surprised to be following King Owain and King Suibne.

Suibne looked back, he shook his head, "I have no stomach for slave wenching. It's archaic and obscene."

"I agree. My grandfather banned it at the court of Ath Cliath decades ago."

Alarmed for his daughter, Blacarri stood up and searched the room. His trained eyes immediately found Ketil. Close by were Bethoc and Gytha.

Seeing his employer stand up, Ketil looked directly at him from across the hall.

Locking eyes with him, Blacaire signalled for him to get Gytha out of the room.

He quickly made his way to the ladies. Bowing low, "Princess Gytha, your father has asked me to escort you to your room."

She looked relieved, "Thank you Ketil."

Ketil bowed slightly to Princess Bethoc, "Princess Bethoc, may I escort you too?"

Taking Shona's arm, Bethoc barely saw him. Haughtily, "You may."

A look of relief passed over Blacarri's face as he watched Ketil guide Gytha and Bethoc towards the door.

Wulfstan crossed himself feigning pious godliness. In truth there was nothing that he would have liked more, than to brawl over a pretty wench. However, he left the room with a sanctimonious glance back at the dais.

Most of the women, wearing richly coloured dresses, had already left the hall along with most of their husbands.

Just as Ketil reached the massive doorway, a tall red haired man suddenly lunged at them, forcefully grabbing at Bethoc's slave. Watching them Blacarri frowned.

Shona screamed.

Furious, Princess Bethoc slapped the jarl's hand away, "How dare you touch my property!"

Moving forward, Ketil stood between the women and the man. He eyed the warrior menacingly.

Still watching them, Blacarri spoke to himself softly, "This is bad. Ketil can barely lift a sword never mind fight." With his hand on the pommel of his sword, he took a step towards them.

Eyeing the Norwegian with the full extent of her regal topaz eyes, Bethoc glared at him, "Step aside or my father, King Constantine, will have your head!"

Suddenly realising who she was, he grinned sinisterly as he backed off.

Bethoc pulled her slave out of the room with a protective

arm around the young girls back.

Gulping with relief, Ketil led Lady Gytha from the room. His first duty was always to protect her. He would see her safely to her apartment and he would sleep outside her door to guard her.

Still watching from the dais, Blacarri shook his head, "I need to train him to fight."

Constantine laughed, putting his arm around Blacarri's shoulder, "A good girl is my Bethoc, she dotes on that slave girl."

Pensively, "Who is the red haired warrior?"

"He calls himself Jarl Kalf but he is no jarl. He is a Norwegian mercenary. My spies say he has no land or fortune, so he fights for the highest pay he can get."

"Is my daughter safe tonight?"

Chuckling, "I can tell that you are a good father Arri. Do not worry. Lady Gytha will sleep safely in her rooms tonight." As the last of the ladies left the room, Constantine roared, "Men! Left in this room are the most beautiful slaves of Alba!" Several of the women ran screaming and cowered in the corners of the room but most stood rigid, resigned to their fate. "I give you permission to take any slave girl that you want for one night!"

A moment of surprised silence hung heavily in the room. There were far more men than women in the room. Suddenly, the room exploded into uproar. Men attacked each other to get at the screaming women.

Moving quickly, Cellach grabbed a pretty wench by her hand. She did not resist.

Launching himself off the dais, Constantine wrestled his son to the floor, "The day I lose a woman to you son, will be the day I give up my throne."

Laughing, bleeding from his nose, he held up his hands, "I give up Da. It will be a few more years before I can beat you."

As Cellach went after one of the other girls, Constantine claimed the pretty slave for himself. Laughing they left the room together.

Calmly walking through the brawling men, Scarface picked up a huge skin of wine and slung it over his broad shoulder. Heading towards the huge door, he grumbled to himself, "Muldivana, what have you done to me?" A fist seemed to come from nowhere. The blow hit him in the side of his face. It was irritatingly painful. He swung around and eyed his assailant fiercely. A huge dark auburn haired warrior stood with four of his men. One of them held a frightened slave girl by her long blonde tousled hair. He recognised her as the young girl who had sung the Orcadian melodies earlier. He frowned, she was still a child. Tears were streaming down her pale face.

The leader chuckled menacingly as he blocked the path to the door. His accent was Alban, "Hand over the wine skin, Viking. We are going to have our own private feast with this little wench."

Clenching his fist, Scarface glanced at the girl. Her tear stained face still had the roundness of youth. She was about eleven years old. Her dull brown dress was frayed with wear at her ankles. He shook his head, gruffly, "She is too young."

"Mind your own business, Viking!"

Scarface raised one sardonic eyebrow as he dropped the wine skin to the floor.

To the five men before him, he looked cool and unperturbed. He was most likely a veteran fighter. More than one of them gulped.

Eyeing the huge Alban with contempt, Scarface unexpectedly jabbed a left handed punch into his cheek, followed by a stinging upper-cutting right punch into his jaw.

Knocked off balance, the Alban reeled backwards and fell limply to the floor.

For a moment, the other Alban's took in apprehensive breaths.

Then, thinking that there were still four of them, the nearest of the Albans suddenly attacked.

Instinctively lowering his upper body to counter balance, Scarface retracted his knee and thrust his foot upwards, striking the man in the face.

Blood spurting from his nose, the second man lost consciousness and sank to the floor.

From the corner of his eye, Scarface picked out the next man quickly approaching him from behind. Balanced on one leg, rapidly retracting his leg, he lifted his knee to his chest. Suddenly thrusting his leg backwards, his upper body counter balanced him as his foot struck his attacker in the chest with stinging force.

The man flew backwards through the air, landing in a crippling heap onto the nearest table. The old table splintered under his weight. Crashing through it, he landed heavily on the tiled floor.

Immediately retracting his leg, Scarface pivoted to face the last two attackers. He moved like lightening, striking a right cross punch into the jaw of the nearest man, swiftly followed by a left hook into the jaw of the second man. In unison they both fell unconscious to the floor.

Stood in stunned silence, the girl blinked at him with wide blue eyes. Her blond hair fell untidily around her thin shoulders.

Eyeing her, he flicked his head towards the doorway. He growled, "Leave now child!"

Her feet rooted her to the spot. Shocked and scared, she stared at him.

Slowly picking up the wine skin, he surveyed the five men. Grumbling as he made his way to the door, "Not a true fighter among them!" Walking past her, he ignored her.

A tremor of shock went through her thin body. Instinctively, she silently followed him.

Realising she was following him down the cold hallway, Scarface stopped and turned round to her, "What do you want? I said leave me."

She stopped. Looking up at the tall man with her wide blue eyes, she trembled. Every instinct in her body told her she would be safe with him.

Eyeing her impatiently, he ordered gruffly, "Leave."

Wringing her hands, she mumbled, "I have no where to go that is safe."

Impatiently, "Go to the kitchens."

She shook her head, "The cooks and the scullery boys wait for slave girls. They..." Her voice trailed off.

Taking in a deep breath, he frowned as he eyed her sullenly. She was so young, so vulnerable.

Her bottom lip trembled, "Please help me."

A muscle clenched in his jaw irritably. He knew what would happen to her if he left her here. Gruffly, "Okay you can stay with me, so long as you keep quiet and don't bother me." Abruptly, he turned away and strode into his chamber room.

She followed him into the dimly lit room, the door closed softly behind her. As her eyes adjusted to the light they widened when she saw the mess. Plates of half eaten food and goblets of half-drunk mead were everywhere. She sniffed the air and frowned. The room stank of sweat and maggoty rotting food. His weapons and shields were slung on the floor. Blankets from the huge bed lay in a heap on the floor on the other side of the room.

Ignoring her, he picked up a goblet and threw its amber contents onto the platter of mangled chicken.

Not moving, she watched him. He strode over to the bed. Undoing his sword belt, he dropped it onto the floor.

He glanced at her as he poured himself a drink from the wine skin. He drank it down in one swig. She had not moved. Dropping both the wine skin and the goblet onto the floor, he strode over to the corner of the room where he had placed a large pot. Turning his back to her, he urinated into the pot.

Her nose twitched as the smell of urine filled the room.

When he was finished, Scarface sat on the bed fully clothed. Ignoring her, he lay down and turned over to face the wall. Taking in a deep breath, he closed his eyes. His mind cleared as he breathed out and relaxed.

Unsure of what to do, she stared at him for a moment. Eyeing the blankets close to the door she walked over to them.

He snored loudly.

Looking back at him, she realised he was already asleep. Looking around the room again, she blew a soft breath of relief through her lips, tonight she would be safe. Climbing into the nest of blankets, she pulled them over herself. They were not like the smelly coarse blankets that she felt lucky to have in the kitchens. These blankets were softer and smelt of heather. He had obviously not used them.

He snored again.

Smiling, she closed her eyes and fell into a deep sleep.

Looking around the halla, Blacarri grinned, fascinated by the commotion. Men were brawling, throwing each other across tables. Some wrestling men were so engrossed in their fight, that they did not see the women that they were fighting over, run away out of the room. Ducking a tankard that flew past his head, he chuckled at two men, as they fell off a table in a tussling heap on to the floor. Gazing around, he watched a pretty dark haired slave crawl under a table trying to hide. Jarl Kalf went after her. His men followed him. One grabbed at her, ripping her white dress from her shoulder, almost exposing her white skinned breast. Blacarri frowned when Jarl Kalf grabbed the slave's dark hair, pulling hard. She screamed, terrified, as Kalf dragged her out from under the table by her hair. Watching the third man bend over her and punch her just below her mouth, Blacarri growled angrily. Striding over to them, he smashed his fist into the nearest man's face knocking him out.

Letting her go, the other two men raised their fists.

His pale grey eyes hard and unflinching, he crushed a right cross punch into the leaders face.

He fell back, blood gushing from his nose. His mouth gaped as he gasped for air.

The third man had no time to move. Blacarri thumped a left hook punch into his jaw.

Staggering to his feet, Jarl Kalf launched himself at Blacarri, growling fiercely.

Engrossed in his fight, Blacarri did not notice Olaf crawl out from the legs of a mass of fighting men.

Staggering to his feet, swaying drunkenly, Olaf looked around. He spotted the dark haired slave woman lying on the floor. Grabbing at her, he roughly took hold of her arms pulling her to her feet.

Half unconscious she swooned.

Dragging her towards the door, Olaf slurred petulantly into her ear, "It will serve him right. It should have been me sat next to Constantine. Am I not the son of the King of Jorvic?" Angrily, "My father was the eldest son of our grandfather. I should have been first to enter the hall. Even Ath Cliath, by rights, should be mine!"

Smashing his fist into Jarl Kalf's face, Blacarri grinned. The red haired Norwegian fell heavily to the floor. This time he did not get up. Turning towards the slave woman every muscle in his strong athletic body felt taut from the fight. Seeing Olaf roughly drag her towards the door, he growled loudly, "Olaf!"

Jumping almost out of his skin, Olaf felt the colour drain from his face. All of his pent up anger turned to drunken sickening fear. Sheepishly, he turned round.

"Thank you for your help cousin! It is obvious that you have never understood the honour of the Clan Ivarr."

The slave girl whimpered as she tried to pull away.

Olaf slurred, "Keep still you bitch!" He swung her round roughly. Barely able to stand himself, he tried to hold up her dead weight.

He strode menacingly towards him, "She is hurt Olaf, let her go."

"No, she's mine!"

"We are guests here Olaf, let her go."

His eyes darting round the room, he stumbled drunkenly. He barely managed to keep his balance, petulantly, "I caught her. She is mine."

Eyeing him calmly confident, "I'll fight you for her then."

He smiled, "You know you are no match against me, especially when you are this drunk."

Hesitating, Olaf's deep blue eyes suddenly widened betraying fear.

Taking a stride towards him, Blacarri clenched his fists.

Suddenly releasing the young woman, Olaf pushed her limp body into Blacarri's strong arms, "Take the bitch, she's just a slave!" Backing off, he slurred, "I will get myself another!"

Gently cradling her body, Blacarri lifted her into his arms. With a menacing glance at his cousin, he carried her off towards the doorway.

Olaf's eyes quickly darted around the room. Suddenly, he felt the red heat of embarrassment and shame on his face. The room was in uproar with men fighting and women screaming. Feeling relieved that no one had witnessed his defeat, he felt the hot slow crawl of humiliation running in his stomach. He turned furiously away and headed to his quarters.

Entering his chamber, Olaf angrily took a large silver wine goblet from the table and threw it against the wall.

Asleep, fully clothed in his reasonably comfortable bed, Canute jolted awake. Instinctively drawing his dagger, he blinked in alarm.

Surprised to see him in the room, Olaf tried to control his slurring, "I am sorry old friend, I had no idea that you had already retired for the evening. I thought that you were still in the kingshalla, wenching."

Sheathing his dagger, he stretched his back, "Olaf, are you drunk? You stink of wine! You nearly made my heart give out. I thought that we were being attacked."

Mischievous as ever with his old protector, "I am surprised at your age you can still move as quickly as that."

"You always were a cheeky lad!" Rubbing his hands together, "Thor's hammer it is cold in here. What's the matter with you? You look as angry as a bear chewing a honey bee."

Not wishing to discuss his embarrassing stand-off with his

cousin, Olaf walked over to the huge fireplace. Picking up two small logs, hunkering down, he placed them carefully onto the diminishing fire, "Jorvik is lost to the English unless we win the coming war. If we do win, Anlaf will likely be given Jorvic. His upper lip snarled, "Jorvic should be mine."

Thoughtfully, Canut nodded, "I see your dilemma."

Blowing gently on the glowing embers, Olaf watched a small flame burst alight around the logs. The wood crackled as the flames took hold. Smoke drifted up the chimney.

"Olaf, I will speak plainly. The only way that you will ever get Jorvic back is if you kill the King of Jorvic, or align yourself with him. To have any hope of doing either, you need more support. Clearly, at the present, you are too weak."

Olaf looked up at Canute, "I have no fortune. How can I get more support?"

Feeling exasperated, "Use your wits boy!" His eyes glinted sharply, "Think about it. How can you increase your holdings?"

He frowned thoughtfully, "I am still a Prince. You have said before, if I was married to a king's daughter, my power and fortune would increase with her marriage dowry." Dejectedly, he hung his head, "I have tried this already and have been refused. I asked Constantine's eldest daughter for her hand but she married Anlaf within a week."

"Try again."

Rolling his eyes, "I have! A few weeks ago I asked Gytha to marry me and she refused me as well. In any case, Blacarri would never have agreed. He hates me!"

Reclining back, pulling his blanket high around his neck for warmth, Canute eyed him, "Your cousins do not hate you, Olaf. They sense you covet their kingdoms. You threaten them. Would you give your eldest daughter, your highest prize, to an orphaned prince with no land or fortune?"

Holding his hands in front of the fire, feeling it's life force of warmth travel through him, Olaf sighed, "No, of course not."

"Think strategically Olaf. King Constantine has more than one daughter."

"Of course," He almost whispered, "Constantine has another daughter. If I married Princess Bethoc, her father would have to support me. Constantine is more powerful than Anlaf. Yes that's it." He raised his voice forcefully, "I need Constantine's backing. I will gain land and fortune from the dowry." He smiled, "Men and armies come with the land. Who knows, if we win the war with the English, Constantine may insist that I have Jorvic!" His eyes flashed coldly, "I need to rid myself of Helga!"

Sleepily from his blankets, "Court the princess respectfully, slowly at first Olaf. Take your time to become her friend. Winning her trust is the first battle, her love will soon follow."

More relaxed now, Olaf looked over at his protector, as Canute tried to cover his fully clothed body with the thin blankets. He could see Canute's years were starting to show on his wrinkled face.

Canute shivered, "Thor's hammer! It's damned cold in this country!"

Smiling, Olaf took a thick fur from his own bed and very tenderly draped it over his old protector. He whispered, "This will keep you warm old friend."

Immediately feeling the warmth from the fur, Canute mumbled sleepily, "You always were a good boy Olaf. You will be a king again soon."

Turning back to the blazing fire, for the briefest of moments, his last memory of the burning city of Jorvic filled his mind. His deep blue eyes reflected the flames, "Yes, I will rule again."

4.3

Gytha was asleep in her vast bed when the door of her enormous room suddenly opened with a huge bang. Bolting to the corner of her bed, she screamed, pulling her sheets and blankets up to her shoulders.

Blacarri strode into the room carrying the limp body of a young woman in his arms, "It's me Gytha. Help me."

In the hallway, Ketil woke up to the commotion of a door bang and Gytha shrieking. Half asleep, he stumbled to his feet. Struggling to pull his sword from its scabbard, he instinctively launched himself into the room, yelling at the top of his voice. His half shut eyes darted about the room. Long rich brocade curtains draped at the large windows. The walls were hung with full length tapestries. The main focal point of the room was the massive four poster bed, dressed in luxurious brocade. Realising that Princess Gytha was looking at him with wide astonished eyes, he looked taken aback as he realised, he was still bawling at the top of his voice, "Yaaaaaaa!"

Annoyed, Blacarri faced him, "Ketil! Stop screaming like a girl and get me a drink."

Awkwardly, his yell trailed off to a dazed squeak. He had not even managed to unsheathe his sword. Feeling ever so fed up, he took a deep breath and muttered bitterly to himself, "This is the worse night of my life!" Looking around the room, he spotted a small wine table. Wandering over to it, he poured two goblets of wine. Huffily lifting the first one to his own lips, he gulped it down. He had never done anything so disrespectful before but he had reached the end of his tether.

Relief almost took Gytha's breath away, "Da, you scared the

life out of me!"

"I'm sorry Gytha. I know I frightened you but this girl is injured." Placing her on to the bed, he gently pushed her soft dark hair away from her face.

Glad that she had left the room lit, Gytha threw back the bedclothes. She scrambled across the bed trying not to get caught up in the long silky layers of her pure white night shift.

Walking up to his employer with a goblet of wine, Ketil spotted Lady Gytha's housecoat on a chair. Lowering his eyes respectfully, he passed it to her with his free hand.

Gratefully, she pulled on the robe. It was thicker and more warming than most of her dresses. Looking down at the still form of the young woman, she whispered, "Her face is so bruised."

The woman whimpered again as her eyes slowly opened.

"Who did this?" A little relieved that she was regaining consciousness, Gytha soothed, "Its okay you are safe now. Don't move."

Big tears began to trickle down the slaves face as her body started to shake.

Watching her, Blacarri realised that she was probably only a couple of years older than Gytha. "Poor little thing," he spoke gently, "no one will hurt you here. You are safe now."

Touching the girl's hand, Gytha smiled, "What is your name?"

Whimpering, she answered, "Gwen, my Lady."

Blacarri gently pulled the blankets over her, "Your face is bruising badly. Gytha get a pillow."

Gytha scrambled back to the top of her bed. Quickly passing a pillow to her father, "Da, will she be okay?"

Placing the plump duck feather pillow under the girls shoulders, "Maybe, maybe not. She remembers her name which is good." Turning back to Gwen, "Do you remember where you come from and what you are doing here?"

She looked up at him, "Yes Milord. I came from Ireland. I was a nun."

He shook his head, "You have a Welsh name."

"My mother was Welsh. Vikings raided my priory a year ago. I was captured and sold here, to King Constantine. I am his slave now." She suddenly began to cry again, "Milord, I need to get my baby. I need to feed her but she is in the slave rooms. I must go to her."

Gytha watched her father. He was so gentle with the slave girl, so considerate.

Blacarri shook his head, "You are not going anywhere tonight. Where," he laboured, "exactly, is your baby?"

The slave mumbled directions to the slave quarters adding, "My baby has my dark hair and the King's eyes. Ask for a woman called Hilde, she is minding her."

Ketil stood proud, "Shall I fetch the child, my Lord?"

"No. You have barely kept out of trouble tonight." Calmly, "Stay here and try to protect the women. I will fetch her child." He turned back to Ketil as he strode to the door, "Put a chair up against your door! Open it to no one but me."

As Jarl Blacarri left the room, Ketil dragged a chair up to the door and he sat on it, shaking his head, he mumbled again, "This is the worst night of my life!"

A short time later they heard a loud knock.

"It's me Ketil, open the door."

Standing up quickly, Ketil moved the chair to the side and pulled back the door.

Blacarri confidently strode in to the chamber, carrying the infant wrapped in a swaddling blanket. Gently, he passed the baby to Gwen, "She is still fast asleep."

Relief almost banished the pain that she was in, "Thank you Milord." She carefully took her child from his arms.

Gytha smiled, "Gwen can stay here with me tonight, and if she is well enough, she can help me dress in the morning."

Blacarri's pale grey eyes glinted in agreement, "Gwen you will stay with my daughter, Lady Gytha. If you feel unwell or sick, tell her immediately." Turning to Gytha, he ordered, "If she is ill fetch me straight away. I will sleep outside your door tonight."

Looking around the vast shadowy room, Gytha grabbed her father's arm, softly, "I am a bit frightened."

"I am just outside and now you have Gwen to keep you company." Kissing her on the forehead, he walked to the door, "I will be just the other side of this door."

"If you sleep outside we will be fine. Will you be okay out there?"

He chuckled, "Of course."

"Wait Da," She ran to a huge wardrobe on the other side of the room. Swinging the doors open, she pulled out blankets and three pillows, "These will keep you warm."

"You are a good girl, Gytha." Taking the bedding, he left the room.

Bowing to her, Ketil followed his lord, closing the door behind him.

The wooden floor boards of the upper levels of the castle creaked as they hunkered down.

Shaking his head, Blacarri sighed. For all of his bravado with his daughter, he already knew that it would be a long and uncomfortable night. He passed a blanket and a pillow to Ketil.

Gratefully, Ketil tried to get comfortable.

Blacarri eyes him with amusement, "I saw you stare down the Norwegian, Ketil. You did well."

He smiled at the compliment.

"It is time for you to start martial training."

Ketil looked surprised, "Martial training?"

"Yes, tomorrow you will begin. Now get some sleep."

"Yes Lord."

The next morning, Blacarri woke sleepily to the sound of his daughter and the slave girl's laughter coming through the door.

Ketil was snoring loudly. Dry crusted dribble had stuck to his face in the night.

Shaking his head, Blacarri gingerly stood up, he tried to stretch but everything hurt. Knocking on the door, he waited for his daughter's permission to enter her room.

Just a few doors down the hallway, opening his eyes, Scarface looked up and blinked. His room gleamed. All of the platters and goblets were piled in a basket by the door. His weapons and shields were stacked carefully in the corner of the room. The room even smelt better. He did not know it but the girl had managed to empty the stinking chamber pot out of the window. She stood silently folding the blankets in a neat pile. His voice sounded hoarse, "Do you have duties in the castle?"

Skittishly, she jumped at the sound of his voice, "I clean chambers and work in the kitchens, Milord."

He eyed her dull clothes, they were barely rags. Her blonde hair looked unbrushed and fluffy, like soft swan under feathers. Not sure what to say, he asked gently, "Do you like it?"

She cast her eyes down, "Some of the men wait for me to come into their chambers. They hurt me."

He frowned angrily, he could never stomach rape. His eyes flickered to her as he got up and walked over to his sword belt. He deftly buckled the belt to his waist. Without looking at her, he opened the door, "What is your name?"

Looking up at him, she lifted her chin proudly, "My name is Audna Kaerlsdottir."

"Where are you from?"

"I was born on Skappa."

His eyes glinted as he looked back at her, "You are from the Orkney Islands?"

She nodded, "My father was a land owner."

"I too own land in the Orkneys. I thought I recognised your songs." He looked at her curiously, "How did you get here?"

Dropping her head, she looked sadly at the blanket, "My mother died a year ago. My father re-married a woman from another island." She looked at him, "I did not like her. Two months ago my father broke his leg. The bone stuck out from his skin and he," her voice faltered as tears filled her eyes, "he died from the wound. The day we buried him, my step-mother sold me." Her eyes were full of suffering as her words poured out wretchedly, "She sold me into slavery and took my father's farm. She told the slavers that I was thirteen years old, so that they would hurt me." She looked up at him forlornly, "I turned eleven years in March. The slavers took me to Caithness and I was sold on to King Constantine's man. He said, I was not pretty enough to be one of the king's favourites. He said, the king needed girls to work in the kitchens and the chambers."

Scarface looked at her thoughtfully. She looked pretty enough to him. He wondered if Constantine's man was trying to protect her. He felt the same, "You can stay here today and finish this room." He strode out of the room banging the door shut.

Blinking in surprise, she gazed at the closed door.

4.4

Rubbing his aching back, Blacarri strode up to the wooden stairwell leading to the royal enclosure. The raised royal gallery, overlooking the martial arena, was full of colourfully dressed nobles. Built on high ground the arena looked like a brown mud scar in a verdant green field. Lower down the valley, past huge copses of trees, he caught a glimpse of the sparkling River Tay. He could not see them from here but many ships were moored at the Kings Quay, including his. A crowd of people sat in the circle stalls. Brightening up the gathering, groups of prettily dressed young ladies sat under velvet awnings.

His eyes down cast, Ketil followed his employer. Unlike Lord Black Arailt, he had slept extremely well. He was used to sleeping on hard floors. Very refreshed, he sprinted up the steps.

Blacarri held back when he saw Scarface talking to King Constantine. They looked like they were bartering.

Stood facing the king, Scarface shook his head grimacing, "Three silver pieces is too much. The slave Audna is just a service slave. I will give you two pieces of silver for her."

Sat casually on his throne, King Constantine eyed him mischievously, "I want three pieces Jarl Barrick. The slave is hard working." In truth, he had no idea who Audna was. She was just a faceless slave, who serviced chamber rooms and worked in the kitchens. He loved to bargain and he sensed the jarl could be pushed.

Irritated, he rolled his eyes and growled. He knew the king would not budge on the price. Scowling, he opened a pouch hanging from his sword belt and put another silver piece on the table next to the other two coins, "Okay, three pieces of silver for her." He held out his hand, "Do we have an accord?"

Taking the silver pieces, he shook Scarface's hand, "Yes, the slave is yours." Dropping the silver into his own purse, he chuckled as Scarface strode off with an annoyed grimace evident on his face.

Barely noticed, Ketil hung back. His eyes took in everything from the breeze fluttering the flags of Alba, to Lady Gytha chatting happily with Duff MacMailcoluim. His intelligent eyes watched as Prince Olaf gallantly escorted Princess Bethoc to her seat. Surprisingly, the princess motioned for Prince Olaf to sit beside her. Ketil inclined his head as he watched them, they barely took their eyes off of each other.

Blacarri strode up to King Constantine.

His topaz eyes glinted, loudly, "Ahh, welcome Blacarri. Did you enjoy your night? The slave girls of Alba are the best in Britain, don't you agree?" Mischief twinkled in his eyes.

The muscles in Blacarri's jaw flexed, last night had been most uncomfortable. Forcing a smile, he squeezed the bag of silver coins hanging from his belt, "I wish to purchase the slave girl Gwen and her child of course."

Ketil's eyes glinted as he looked out to the arena. In the distance, starlings soared in ever increasing swirling flocks, creating the most amazing eddying shadows in the sky. The resonant sound of drums brought his attention back to the arena. Four tall men dressed in leather breaches and white tunics stood behind four huge drums. Each of the men had varying shades of long auburn hair, half tied back from their faces. Lifting their muscular arms, they beat their drums quickly in booming synchronization. The sound filled the show ground.

Wearing his brown leather battle gear and his two swords at his belt, Ragenhare walked tall into the arena. Looking up at the raised royal gallery, he bowed low.

His topaz eyes full of excitement, Constantine grinned. Deeply, "Wait one moment Arrie." Standing up, he held up his hands to silence the drummers and the crowd. Feeling the anticipation from the crowd, his voice boomed out, "Welcome Lord Ragenhare, Master of Morrigu."

An expectant murmur travelled through the audience.

His intelligent eyes glinting, Ketil looked at the man in the arena.

Turning to watch the familiar warrior, Blacarri smiled, "Scarface told me he was here."

Sitting back down, Constantine waited.

Silence filled the air.

With long drum sticks in each hand, the drummers began to thud a slow booming beat in the background.

Ragenhare slowly and deliberately began the dance of the swords, expertly controlling each of the martial moves.

The crowd watched in silent awe, as the warrior gradually moved from one stance into another.

Constantine leaned forward, fascinated as Ragenhare stretched and balanced.

Respectfully, Blacarri watched as Ragenhare moved into each position.

After showing the crowd about twenty stances, Ragenhare suddenly unsheathed both of his weapons.

The young ladies gasped.

The drummers immediately upped the tempo of their beating to an exciting crescendo.

Using superb skill, his swords shimmering in the sun as Ragenhare performed each thrust, each high arching leap, each powerful acrobatic lunge.

Even Ketil gasped, as the warrior performed dazzling sets of moves in quick succession.

Finally, Ragenhare threw his swords high into the air.

The drummers lifted their drumsticks above their heads. Their climax was silence.

The swords fell, pommels first, Ragenhare caught them expertly.

After a moment of shocked silence, the crowd erupted into deafening cheering.

Constantine stood to his feet, clapping enthusiastically.

Ragenhare bowed to the crowd, then he turned to Prince Indulf, beckoning him into the arena. Walking over to his gear, he found two sets of wooden practice swords.

Young Prince Indulf, flustered as he grabbed his shield and helmet from his page boy. Still quite short in height but already thickset and muscular, he strode onto the field trying to look like a warrior.

As the crowd continued to cheer, Constantine turned back to Blacarri. Looking at him gravely, he shook his head as he picked up their conversation, "No Arrie, the slave Gwen still pleases me. I have no wish to sell her."

Seriously, "You understand that I do not purchase the woman for myself. My daughter has asked me to purchase the slave from you, as she needs a personal dress maid. She will be well taken care of, as will her child."

In the arena, Ragenhare began taking Indulf through a few easy parries and deflections.

Constantine frowned, "My spies informed me of last night's events. My property was damaged. They say that you spent the night on my hallway floor." Coldly, "One of my spies advises me that Prince Olaf struck my slave."

Raising a surprised eyebrow, "Your Majesty, I can vouch for my cousin. He was very drunk but he did not strike the girl. I saw the man who did and I will be happy to point him out."

Constantine shook his head thoughtfully, "That will not be necessary. Two servants saw the incident from the doorway. They said Jarl Kalf and his men attacked Gwen violently. The servants said, you knocked the men unconscious. Is that true?"

Impassively, "Yes it is true."

The crowd cheered as Indulf made a series of attacking strikes. Grinning, Ragenhare parried them all easily.

Watching them spar, Cellach and Ruardri loosened up and put on their helmets and protective gear.

Constantine eyed Blacarri, "Jarl Kalf and his men have been removed from my court." He paused, "I blame myself. I should have made arrangements for Gwen to leave my halla before the fight. I was distracted. You will understand, my friend, Gwen's baby is my child. I cannot sell them."

"I do understand. I also have children born of concubines. You love them no less."

"We are both men of the world, Arrie."

The muscles in his jaw flexed, "Gytha will be disappointed."

Jovially, "How about this? Whilst Gytha is in my domain, she may use Gwen as a personal maid."

Blacarri knew, that to pursue the issue would be an embarrassing waste of time. Constantine had not even given the bag of silver a second look. No, he would not sell the slave. Bowing his head, he smiled, "That is very generous of you. I thank you on behalf of my daughter." He picked up his silver. Changing the subject, "May I watch the practice?"

"Of course, pray be seated."

He had no idea that immediately withdrawing, had impressed the mighty King of Alba, more than any increase in offer, no matter how high. Watching him stride to a seat, Constantine whispered to himself, "You are of the same mould as your brother Anlaf. You impress me."

Striding to the nearby drinks table, Ketil picked up a silver jug and poured sweet honey mead into a goblet. Placing the silver goblet onto a small silver tray, he carried it expertly to his employer. Respectfully bowing, "Mead, my Lord?"

Taking the drink, Blacarri watched young Indulf deflect several blows with his two practice swords.

Anlaf walked up chuckling, "I heard you spent the night on the hallway floor."

Rubbing his back, he grimaced as he lowered his voice, "Worst night of my life."

Grinning as he strode past his brother, Anlaf took his seat next to Constantine.

Still looking aggrieved, Scarface approached bowing low in front of Anlaf. His voice rumbled, "Majesty, may I introduce Archbishop Wulfstan?"

Surprised that Scarface addressed him so formally, he eyed him quizzically, "Of course," one eyebrow rose up sardonically, "Jarl Barrick."

Bowing elaborately, Wulfstan's green cape billowed up revealing black battle leathers, almost as black as his shoulder length limp hair. His sword and dagger hung from his belt. He deigned to attempt an elaborate half bow, both hands swirling in circular movements to his side. His voice sounded flat and condescending, "Majesty."

Eyeing the archbishop's sword, Anlaf felt surprise. All of his instincts cried out that this was a man to be wary of. Thoughtfully, his voice even, "Our campaign depends on Northumbrian opposition to English rule, Archbishop. Your support is crucial to our strategy."

Scarface took a seat next to Blacarri.

Ketil offered Lord Barrick a goblet of mead on a silver tray.

He took it and swigged it back. He still could not believe that he had paid three silver pieces for the girl, it stung. He mumbled gruffly to himself, "Three siver pieces!" Exhaling deliberately, he turned his attention to watching Lord Ragenhare demonstrate combination attacks with two swords to Prince Indulf. He drawled to Blacarri, "The lad is pretty good."

Blacarri nodded politely. He was trying to hear what the archbishop was saying.

"Majesty, I am a staunch northerner and as chief of the Northumbrian Witan I am," Wulfstan's voice drawled drearily as the faceless servant offered him mead, "powerful and," he wafted his hand irritably dismissing the servant, "influential."

Moving on, Ketil offered a goblet to King Anlaf.

Barely noticing Ketil, Anlaf took the drink, "I understand you have pledged two armies to our alliance."

The Archbishop's eyes sparkled with dark intelligence, "Yes Majesty."

Watching his reaction, "You will place them under my leadership?"

"Yes Majesty." Wulfstan's eyes flickered to Constantine. He

still could not quite believe that the powerful King of Alba had deferred to his son-in-law's leadership. Looking back at King Anlaf, he droned, "I have been authorised by the Northumbrian Witan, to pledge our armies to your cause and," pausing for effect, "when you triumph King Anlaf, we would ask you to consider becoming King of Jorvic and Northumbria."

Anlaf answered carefully, "As soon as our plans are consolidated we will invade."

Constantine looked fiercely at the archbishop, "Your Grace, you have also met with Prince Olaf Curan Sihtricsson this morning. Did you offer him the Kingdom of Northumbria too?"

Raising a surprised eyebrow, Wulfstan's enigmatic gaze fell condescendingly on King Constantine. His voice tinged with tedium, "Your Majesty, I did meet with Prince Olaf this morning. I was intrigued. Indeed, I do not deny that he was a contender for our support. He was for a short time Jorvic's king after all."

Anlaf's eyes hardened, "Archbishop, what did you think to my cousin?"

Disdainfully, "I found him wanting, Majesty."

Anlaf's smile did not reach his eyes, "Your Grace, I favour men well who show me loyalty." Harshly, "If you betray me, I will find you and I will rip out your guts and," clenching his fist, he leaned forward threateningly, "I will set fire to your entrails in front of your eyes."

Unnoticed, Ketil backed away with the tray, surprised at the venom in King Anlaf's voice.

His eyebrows rising, Constantine looked astonished at his son in law's blatant cold blooded threat to a man of the cloth.

Archbishop Wulfstan felt alarm course through his body. Even he, a man used to the changing loyalties of politics, knew better than to ignore the warning.

Much later, Scarface entered his chamber room carrying a

brown leather package.

Audna sat in a chair by the fire, concentrating as she sewed up his damaged tunics. She looked up and smiled, she had enjoyed her day safely tucked away in his room.

Striding to the table he dropped the package onto it. Unbuckling his sword belt he threw it on to the floor.

Putting down her sewing she immediately got up. Picking up the sword and belt, she placed it in the corner of the room next to three knives, an axe and his shield.

Thoughtfully watching her, he opened a leather bag at his waist. Taking out a silver torque slave bracelet he ordered brusquely, "Come here."

Her eyes widened for a moment. Walking up to him, she looked up at him with wide worried eyes as he took her thin arm in his big warm hand.

He pressed the silver bracelet around her arm. Gruffly, "I bought you from King Constantine today. You belong to me now. This slave bracelet identifies you as my property."

Surprised, she blinked.

Loudly he added, "You were expensive!"

Forlornly, she lowered her head. Her soft fluffy blonde hair fell forwards. She trembled and her voice shook, "I am very sorry, Milord."

A little remorseful he eyed her. Deliberately softening his voice, "That is okay The king said that you are hard working, so he wanted more silver for you."

A little surprised, she cheered up at the compliment.

Taking the package, he undid the leather straps. Inside was a pale heather coloured wool shawl. The shawl was wrapped around a pale green dress. There was also a soft cream chemise, under garments and a pair of soft leather tan coloured boots. Taking the clothes out of the shawl, he handed them to her. Gruffly, "Here are new clothes for you. Put them on now."

Thinking he expected her to undress in front of him, she sucked in a fearful breath. Slowly resignation descended over her. Her eyes glazed over as she undid the shoulder straps to her dress.

Turning away, he walked up to the fire place. Crouching down he picked up the thick metal poker and stoked the fire. Flames slowly caught and warmed the room. He had always been fascinated by fiery sparks, as they drifted up black sooted chimneys.

Feeling the warmth fill the room, she blinked warily as she looked over to him. Surprised, she realised that he was not watching her. Relief surged through her.

The burning wood crackled and smoked as he watched the flames lick higher.

She turned away and went behind the free standing wooden dressing panel. While he watched the flames, she quickly stripped off her old clothes. Pulling on the undergarment and the chemise, then the dress over her head she looked down surprised, they were exactly the right length. Grabbing the boots she dragged them on. They fitted as well. Peeking out from the panel she took a breath, "I am dressed."

Turning around, he watched her step out from behind the panel. He looked over her, "The dress seems a little baggy." He strode over to a leather bag and pulled out a wide belt. It had a good silver buckle. Walking back over to her, he held the belt at her midriff. He took the knife from the scabbard at his waist and cut a length of leather from the belt. Taking a metal dowel and a hammer from a small bag of tools, he loudly punched three new holes in the leather for the buckle. "Here does this fit?"

Taking the belt, she wrapped it around her waist and buckled it, "It fits well."

"You are thin. When did you last eat?"

"Yesterday, I think."

He passed her the lilac shawl, "Wear this shawl. It will keep you warm."

She draped the shawl around her thin shoulders, it immediately fell off.

Shaking his head, he opened the leather bag at his waist. He pulled out a small silver round brooch. Handing it to her, he ordered gruffly, "You may use this to pin your shawl. Do not lose it. It is worth more than you."

She eyed him warily for a moment. The silver brooch shone in the firelight. Her hands shook as she pinned the silver brooch to her shawl. Unsure what to say she cast her eyes down, "Thank you Master."

"Call me Jarl Barrick! Now go fetch us some food from the kitchens. We need to fatten you up!" Watching her pensively walk slowly to the doorway he added, "If any man bothers you, show them the bracelet and say you are under Jarl Barrick's protection."

Her eyes widened as she opened the door. Fear filled her as she left the room. For a moment, she pushed herself up against the wall of the hall, not daring to move.

Many men passed her and a few eyed her leeringly but as soon as they saw the Norse slave bracelet they backed off.

Slowly she set off. No man bothered her as she walked the halls to the kitchen. Not even the cooks or the scullery boys troubled her, as she helped herself to a fat chicken off of the spit. Grabbing a carrying basket, she put the steaming chicken into it, along with several large apples, a huge loaf of bread and a skin of wine. She could barely carry the basket but she did not care. Her new clothes and boots felt warm. For the first time since her step mother had sold her, she felt safe again.

45

Two weeks later, Ketil met with Jarl Blacarri privately, in a small field close to the martial arena. The leaves in the trees around the field rustled as gentle breeze blew through the verdant canopies. Red squirrels ran up the tree trunks and cavorted through the branches, before disappearing into the foliage.

Holding his shield protectively in front of his torso, Ketil lifted his wooden sword uneasily, "My Lord, I have my daily report."

Lunging forward, Blacarri struck Ketil's sword so forcefully the sound disturbed a small flock of wood pigeons pecking at the ground. They took to fight, loudly flapping their wings. Ignoring the birds, he grunted, "Good, keep it concise and factual."

Parrying the blow, he recoiled and backed off, "Three ladies of King Constantine's court are still ill with spreading sores. No others have been affected, not even those close to them. The court physician believes them to be getting better."

"Make sure Princess Gytha does not go anywhere near them."

Warily stepping closer, "Jarl Barrick is keeping a female child slave in his room."

Impatiently, "Yes I know this. The girl tidies his room."

Raising his eyebrow as he edged closer, "He is considering adopting her as his daughter."

Blinking in surprise, Blacarri frowned, "What?"

Shrugging his shoulders, Ketil's hazel eyes glinted as he backed off again, "He said his wife believes she is barren but craves a child."

A little disconcerted that his friend had told this private information to Ketil before him, he demanded, "Did he tell you this or did you hear it from servants?"

Circling his employer cautiously, "My chamber is next to his. He has invited me in a few times, to play board games, and to take wine." He shrugged his shoulders, "I was surprised to see the child, so I asked him."

Impatiently eyeing Ketil, "He invited you!" Irritably, "It is to be expected I suppose. I treat you so well, you are starting to look like a nobleman."

Grinning, Ketil inclined his head, dryly, "I am indeed most fortunate, my Lord."

Surprised at Ketil's drollness, Blacarri's pale grey eyes twinkled with suppressed amusement. He tried to sound annoyed, "Are you going to attack me or dance around all day!"

Grudgingly, he frowned, "Ealdorman Ragenhare has left the service of the archbishop." Suddenly, he lunged forward and struck Blacarri's wooden sword strongly.

Raising a black eyebrow, Blacarri parried the blow, encouragingly, "Well done."

Smiling, Ketil added, "He is already travelling back to Northumbria. My source advised me, that he overheard Ealdorman Ragenhare saying his work here is done."

"I am not surprised that he has gone home so soon." He attacked with several fast strikes against Ketil's sword, "Wulfstan is a most irritating man."

Overwhelmed, Ketil fell backwards landing on his backside.

Grinning, Blacarri swung his replica sword swishing it through the air, "Stop lazing about Ketil, get up!"

Brushing the dust off of his new battle leathers, he got to his feet. Continuing his report evenly, "I often notice Prince Olaf Curan Sihtricsson talking to…" he paused as Blacarri lunged again hitting his sword. Deflecting a second blow with his shield, he sucked in air as he quickly backed off, "King Constantine's second daughter, Princess Bethoc."

Blacarri lifted his chin. This was interesting, "Really, go on."

Sensing his lord's distraction, Ketil suddenly attacked hitting Blacarri's sword with several heavy blows. Feeling the power of his blows, he growled excitedly as swung in another mighty strike.

Taken aback, Blacarri sucked in a deep breath as he was forced to defend. Suddenly swinging round, side stepping him, he slapped his sword against Ketil's buttocks as he hurtled past.

Stumbling face first into the dust, feeling stinging pain across his backside, Ketil roared at the top of his voice, "Ouch!"

In the distance a dog howled loudly, followed by several more barks from around the fortress.

Chuckling deeply, Blacarri spoke encouragingly, "Well done, you are improving. Get up."

Standing to his feet, Ketil bent forward as he spat the grit in his mouth out onto the ground. He coughed and grunted hoarsely as he continued his report, "Deciding to make a few enquiries, I concluded that Prince Olaf is actively courting the princess." He coughed and spat vociferously again.

Blacarri eyed Ketil impatiently, "What else?"

Frowning, "The servants talk in the kitchens. One of the servants was in the royal anti chamber this morning. He heard King Constantine refuse a marriage offer from Prince Olaf to Princess Bethoc." Pausing, he hesitated.

The memory of Olaf's jealous glare filtered into Blacarri's mind, he frowned, "Go on Ketil."

Looking unsure, "Lord Blacarri, I wish to make it clear, I have no serious evidence of this, only servant's gossip. The servants were told to leave the room by the princess, so it is unclear as to the outcome." He paused as a drably dressed man ran up to them.

Keeping his eyes low, the servant bowed, "My Lord Black Arailt.

Blacarri turned to him impatiently, "What is it man?"

"King Anlaf requests your presence, immediately, my Lord."

Throwing his practice sword to the ground, motioning Ketil to follow him, Blacarri strode from the field. As he passed the servant, he ordered, "Take that back to my chamber!"

Looking at his wooden sword unsure where to leave it, Ketil suddenly nonchalantly threw it behind him as he walked off past the palace servant.

Eyeing him submissively, the servant bowed deeply to Ketil.

Surprised, he blinked guiltily as he hastily followed Lord Blacarri. Class ranks were strictly enforceable in their society. Glancing backwards, he saw the servant run to pick up both of the practice swords. Picking up his pace, he jogged after his employer.

The dark mahogany panelling in the winding hallway was eerily lit by shafts of light from open doors. Light streamed from Anlaf's open antechamber door.

Walking in unannounced, Blacarri eyed Anlaf curiously, "You sent for me?"

Closing the door, Ketil hung back quietly in the shadows.

"Olaf Sihtricsson is on his way. He has requested an immediate audience."

Lowering his voice, Blacarri leaned forward, "I have just found out that the servants have overheard Olaf, ask for Princess Bethoc's hand in marriage."

Surprise passed fleetingly over Anlaf's face, "How do you find this sort of thing out so quickly?"

Lifting a dark eyebrow, Blacarri looked enigmatic.

A sharp knock at the door interrupted them.

Instantly, Blacarri moved to Anlaf's right shoulder. Facing the door, he nodded to Ketil.

Bowing slightly, Ketil's hazel eyes glinted curiously as he opened the door.

Puffing up his chest, Olaf strutted into the room. Striding up to a respectful distance from the throne, he bowed low. He could barely contain himself. His deep blue eyes sparkled with excitement.

As ever, Anlaf looked composed, "Welcome cousin. You asked for an audience?"

Imperiously, "Constantine has offered his daughter, Princess Bethoc to me," he paused for effect, "in marriage."

Anlaf looked indifferent.

He had expected a reaction, at least surprise, but his cousin eyed him with the self-assured confidence of a man who already knew. Olaf flushed. The silence was becoming embarrassingly long. Hiding his disappointment, he continued, "As you are my King, I ask your permission to accept the betrothal."

Smiling sardonically, Blacarri bent forward whispering in his brother's ear, "My informants have told me that Constantine refused Olaf. I expect Bethoc pleaded a love match and her doting father gave in."

Rubbing his top lip with his forefinger, Anlaf hid his smirk.

Olaf did not notice.

Quietly unobserved, Ketil moved discreetly to the antechamber behind the drab curtain.

Watching Olaf with expressionless steely grey eyes, Blacarri could not resist taunting loudly, "Perhaps this marriage will be the making of you Olaf. A pretty young Princess of Alba is a good match for you. Maybe she will take your mind off your lost Kingdom of Jorvik, or my brother's Kingdom of Ath Cliath."

Blinking uncomfortably, Olaf feigned a look of surprise, "I do not know what you mean cousin."

"Really," he asked pointedly, "do you deny that over the years you have tried to acquire support to claim Ath Cliath for yourself?"

A fleeting look of concern passed over Olaf's face.

Eyeing him, Blacarri stated bluntly, "Because your father was the eldest son of our grandfather, you think you have a better claim to the throne."

Nodding, Anlaf sighed, "If only your father had not died when you were a boy Olaf. You would not now be prowling around my throne."

Feeling himself reddening, hating his betraying emotions, Olaf's upper lip snarled.

Raising his voice, Anlaf persisted, "You are a man now. You are hungry for power and kingship. You forget that if you had not claimed the protection of the Clan Ivarr as a child, you would be dead."

Nodding, Blacarri added sarcastically, "You have managed to draw some support from the younger ruffians at our court but not enough to be a serious threat."

Blinking uncomfortably, Olaf raised his chin, petulantly, "Your father always supported my claim to Jorvic. He said I was like a son to him."

Flicking his eyes to his brother, Anlaf inclined his head remembering his father's fondness for Olaf.

"King Anlaf, I do not deny trying to raise a small army to support my claim to Jorvic."

Anlaf nodded, "Indeed Olaf, you have never made secret of your intent to regain your father's kingdom."

Feeling resentment rising, Olaf clenched his fists uncontrollably, "Northumbria was my kingdom too and my birth right!"

Raising his chin menacingly, Blacarri baited, "But what lengths will you go to Olaf, to regain Jorvic?"

Olaf suddenly snarled, "I will do what it takes Blacarri!"

"What? You would throw yourself at any fortune in a silk skirt that comes your way?" Mocking him, "You are turned down by the elder Princess of Alba but accepted by the younger."

Olaf reddened immediately. His blue eyes flashed with humiliation.

His face impassive, Anlaf eyed him, "My wife informed me of your marriage offer Olaf."

He stuttered, "At the time of my offer I had no idea of your interest. I removed myself from the pursuit as soon as I heard of your betrothal."

Blacarri smiled mockingly, "As I said Olaf, refused by the

elder, accepted by the younger."

Anger coursed through Olaf's veins so loudly, he could hear his own heart beating rapidly. He jerked his head up, "Tell me Blacarri! Is it true that you married your heiress wife for the Kingdom of the Isle of Man?" Rounding on Anlaf accusingly, "And you Anlaf, it is well known that Maelmare's promised dowry was immense!"

Smiling coolly, Anlaf placed his hand on the pommel of his sword.

For a moment, Blacarri's eyes blazed with fury. His fists clenched. Coldly, "You have a point cousin on both counts, but Anlaf did not take Maelmare's dowry and I," he took a menacing step towards Olaf, "I loved my wife."

From behind the antechamber curtain, Ketil suddenly appeared wearing an apron over his leathers. Noisily coughing to distract them, he expertly carried a silver jug and three silver goblets on an ornate silver tray. Loudly, he asked, "Wine Milords?"

The three nobles stonily ignored Ketil as he poured red wine into the goblets.

Feeling the tension in the room, he bumbled about, "Wine Milord?"

Breaking the silence, Olaf looked at Blacarri, "I know you loved Tasha, as I love Bethoc."

Glowering, Blacarri did not answer. This upstart had no idea what true love was.

"Wine Milord?" Handing Lord Blacarri a goblet of wine, Ketil frowned warningly.

His pale eyes glittered angrily. Scowling at Ketil for his impudence, he felt the muscle in his jaw twitch. Clenching his fist, he forced control over himself. He had come close to really losing his temper publicly. Taking a deep breath, he sipped his wine.

Anlaf watched Olaf with an unfathomable expression. He barely noticed Blacarri's servant pass him a goblet of wine. He was fully aware of Blacarri's concerns about Olaf, and he had good reason to share them.

"Wine Milord?"

Ignoring the servant, Anlaf asked loudly, "Bethoc's dowry, what is it?"

Olaf puffed his wide chest out in pride. He smiled suddenly cheerful again, "A fortune of silver, several score of cattle and over three score of horses. One stallion is a beast and a half!" He paused, his eyes glistening with self-importance, "The princess brings with her several villages under her ownership in Alba. Her personal guard is a veritable army of over sixty men. But the best part of the dowry is a drakkar warship." Pausing, he smiled with satisfaction, "You should see her Anlaf, sleek, beautiful." His eyes glazed full of youthful eagerness, "She skims through the waves. I have named her Dolphin Queen."

Ketil passed Blacarri with the tray and empty wine jug. He whispered brazenly just in earshot of Blacarri, "Prince Olaf seems keener on his new ship and stallion than his wife to be."

Regaining his humour, he felt his eyebrows lift in surprise at Ketil's impertinence. He was unable to prevent a hint of a smile passing across his handsome face.

Confidently, Ketil raised his eyebrows too. A cheeky half smile played on his lips.

Blacarri motioned, with amused eyes, for him to leave.

Disappearing behind the curtain, Ketil stood still and quiet so that he could hear them.

"And," Olaf hesitated as he smiled with open gratification, his handsome face lit up with pleasure, "the beautiful island Kingdom of Iona, which I will rule with Bethoc as my Queen."

Smiling, Anlaf felt the warmth of genuine indulgent enjoyment at the lad's good luck, "It would seem that you have made your fortune and gained yourself a kingdom."

Nodding, Olaf looked incredulous, "Iona is a sacred holy island. The island is the final resting place for many of the sovereigns of Alba. I will one day be buried there," he paused with self-satisfaction, "with the greatest Kings of Alba."

His eyebrows rising, Anlaf considered this great honour,

"Constantine must value you greatly as a man, and already see you as a son."

Looking at his cousin, he felt a little surprised at the compliment. Accepting it for what it was he smiled broadly, "Thank you cousin."

"Bethoc is a lovely woman. My wife always talks very fondly of her. You have done well Olaf. You are a young man still, yet you have gained a kingdom and a lovely princess as wife."

He looked back at him, genuinely, "Perhaps for the first time since my father's death I feel confident of my destiny."

Looking at the lad with surprise, Blacarri spoke candidly, "I sometimes forget what you have suffered. Orphaned as a child and ripped from the only home that you knew."

Frowning, Anlaf inclined his head, "A prince without a kingdom."

Olaf turned to Anlaf, "My kingdom is Jorvic! Every night, my last memory of my home, the red glow of Jorvic, burns into my thoughts and my dreams. I want to be her king again."

Thoughtfully, Anlaf looked back at him but said nothing.

A frown passed over Olaf's handsome features, "Your father, King Guthrith, promised me Jorvic."

The curtain moved. Ketil appeared with the refilled wine jug, "Wine from the vineyards of Rome my Lords." In truth he did not have the faintest idea where the wine had come from. Placing the wine flagon on the table, he bowed as he disappeared back behind the curtain.

Blacarri conceded softly, "Our father always favoured you Olaf. Well done for securing this marriage cousin. You have made our father proud. I wish you good fortune."

"My thanks Blacarri." He looked up earnestly, "Cousin, when I was young we were friends. I know that we have not recently seen eye to eye. I blame myself. The older I get the more I want Jorvic back. I feel so much," he searched for the word, "anger."

Shrugging his muscular shoulders as he strode over to the wine pitcher, Blacarri re-filled his goblet, "We change as we grow up." Offering the wine, he re-filled their goblets too.

Having drunk his wine quickly, Olaf smiled, "I hope that we can put our differences behind us?"

Behind the curtain, Ketil poured himself a goblet of wine. Sitting down on a high four legged stool, he listened.

Nodding, Blacarri raised his cup, "Of course cousin, I will drink to that."

Smiling, Anlaf lifted his goblet of wine, "I will agree to this marriage but what of Helga?"

Olaf's eyes hardened, "What of her?" He snapped, "She can go back to sleeping in the kitchens."

Surprised by his cousin's outright dismissal of his long term mistress, Anlaf glanced at Blacarri.

Ignoring the comment, Blacarri raised his glass, "Take wine with us cousin and tell us of your plans for your Kingdom of Iona."

Raising his goblet, he took a large gulp of wine. His young eyes glistened with excitement, "I have plans for a fortress on Iona where my army will train." Dragging up a high backed chair he sat down close to Anlaf.

With one strong arm, Blacarri lifted a heavy wooden chair closer and sat down as well.

Taking out a rolled up hide skin map from his boot, Olaf unravelled it.

Anlaf and Blacarri poured over the map fascinated. Someone had painted, quite roughly, the outline of the island. Cobalt blue ink indicated waves around the island.

His deep blue eyes glinting, Olaf pointed to an area on the map, "This is a beautiful natural harbour. I will base a fleet of warships here."

Smiling warmly, Anlaf offered, "I will give you a ship from my personal fleet as a wedding present. I will give Wave Traveller. She is a good vessel, very hardy."

Blinking in surprise, Olaf sucked in a deep breath.

Grinning, Blacarri looked up at him, "I was wondering what to give you as a wedding present." Deciding quickly, "I will give you one of my ships too. Sea Horse is a beauty, only three years old. She is fast and easy to handle. I bet she would give Dolphin Queen and Wave Traveller a thrashing in a race."

Astonished, Olaf shook his head, "Thank you, thank you both." He chuckled, "I cannot believe it. I will have three ships to my fleet."

"That will be enough to carry one hundred and fifty men." Blacarri looked back at the map, curiously painted with a scythe, "What is this area?"

"It is farmland. I have only seen the island on the map but I'm confident I can cultivate the land."

Thoughtfully raising his dark eyebrows, Blacarri noticed the crudely cross shaped building, "I have heard that Christian culdees live on the island?"

Nodding, Olaf pointed to the building drawn on the map. He took a gulp of his wine, "This is the area where they live. Bethoc talks well of her Christian faith. I admit I am intrigued. I have already decided to meet with the monks of Iona and explain that I intend to protect them."

Genuinely impressed, Anlaf looked up at him, "Your benevolence to the monks is wise Olaf."

Warming with praise and wine, "I tried to learn from your father and from you, cousins." He smiled, "Of course Jarl Canute will be well taken care of as well. I have already given him a goodly portion of the island and some stock to fill it."

Smiling Anlaf advised, "You do well to remember your old friend Olaf. Jarl Canute gave up much of his life to protect you. He grows old now and will benefit from your kindness."

"He tells me he wants to rest now and settle down. He has a wench in mind to take as his wife."

"He is taking a wife, that old dog!" Anlaf laughed.

Olaf chuckled, "Canute has been respectfully courting a fishmonger's daughter for six months. She is willing to wed but her father refused Canute's offer of marriage."

Nodding knowingly, Blacarri looked up, is pale grey eyes sparkled translucently, "I am informed that the fishmonger said 'no' because Jarl Canute no longer has property in Northumbria. Perhaps Canute's acquisition of land on Iona will change the old fishmonger's mind."

Smiling thoughtfully, Olaf looked at his map, "Yes, a farmstead for his daughter and a small protected bay with good fishing may well be enough to change the old fishmonger's mind. If not, I am sure that Canute will abduct her!"

They all burst out laughing.

Grinning, picking up his goblet of wine, Blacarri took a drink, "I hear that the old fishmonger wants to retire, and leave his son the shop but he does not want to lose his daughter. In any case the old man only has his shop. He has nowhere else to go. Perhaps Jarl Canute should offer to take the ladies father with them, to your kingdom Olaf."

"Of course," Olaf blinked, "I could give the old fishmonger a small portion of land by the sea, and arrange for a small homestead to be built, close by to Canute's farmstead." Smiling, "I will give him a few cows, sheep and chickens. I could build him a fish smoke house and a brewery. He would be self-sufficient, a man of means."

Pushing back his dark hair from his chiselled face, Blacarri looked pensive, "Will that be enough to convince the old fishmonger?"

"I will personally request that he move to Iona." Olaf lifted his chin imperiously, "I will tell the old fishmonger that I require his skills in my kingdom." Smiling, "It is true in a way. No one fillets a fish as well as him."

Anlaf smiled, "Excellent idea Olaf, well done."

Blacarri smiled into his goblet of wine.

Much later, slightly drunk, Olaf bowed low and left the room slurring, "Cousins, I must leave you now. The princess is expecting me and I am already late."

Turning to his brother, Blacarri looked serious, "We did the right thing, calling him out over his ambitions for your kingdom. Now, he will think twice about trying to raise an army against you."

"Let us give him a chance Blacarri." Anlaf felt affable, "Now that he has his own kingdom and wife, he may settle down."

"I don't know what it is but I do not trust him." Frowning, he shook his head, "He is cunning. But as you say, he lost much as a child, hardship like that changes you."

"Our father always saw the good in him and I see it too."

Blacarri's pale eyes glinted, "Do you remember the first time we met him? He was only five years old."

"He was just a child but he was King of Jorvic. He knew it too."

"Just for a few days but he has never forgotten."

Thoughtfully brushing back his unruly blonde hair from his eyes, "Our father always told him that Jorvic would be his again."

Blacarri smiled, "This change of fortune may make a man of him. The old man may have been right, perhaps he will regain Jorvic."

Anlaf's eyes glinted, piercingly blue, "I want Jorvic for myself!"

Looking at his brother, he felt no surprise, "Really?"

Coolly, "Why do you think I agreed to Olaf's marriage? If he is King of Iona the blow will be softer."

Raising an eyebrow, Blacarri's jaw flexed pensively, "Da always said, we must give Jorvic back to Olaf. He said it will be the only thing that will satisfy him, and stop him from fighting us for Ath Cliath. The richer Olaf gets the better chance he has of securing Jorvic and Northumbria."

Shaking his head, Anlaf smiled, "True, but leaders do not need a fortune to secure thrones. Men follow leaders. If Olaf cannot become king on his own, then men do not instinctively follow him." Smiling confidently, he swallowed a big gulp of wine. Then he frowned, "I feel for Helga. Did you notice how Olaf has discarded her without a second thought?"

"Olaf would not be the first man to turn a mistress on to the streets." He looked at the floor, "It does not sit well with me though."

"I will speak to Maelmare when we get home. Perhaps there is something we can do."

Blacarri decided to change the subject, his face serious, "May I speak to you about Gytha?"

"Yes of course, is there a problem?"

"No Anlaf, its good news." He smiled broadly, "Duff MacMailcoluim has asked me for Gytha's hand in marriage. He says he has Constantine's consent. I have agreed, on the understanding that you give your permission."

He shook his head, "Little Gytha getting married, she is too young."

Seriously, "She is thirteen years old now and beautiful. You cannot be surprised."

"It makes me feel so old." Anlaf chuckled, "Of course you have my permission. What a match Blacarri, what a match. Duff is a strong contender for the throne of Alba. Of course I agree."

Frowning, he felt true sadness at leaving her here, "I will miss her though. They wish to wed whilst we are here, so that I can give her away."

Suddenly serious, his deep blue eyes flashed, "What is her bride-price? I cannot agree to her taking the Isle of Man or Gailgedhael. I hope that you understand brother?"

"Anlaf, I am not yet rich enough to give any of my land away." He grinned with amusement, "Not even Colonsay. Gytha's bride-price is five warships from my personal fleet, and she will keep her mother's jewellery. It is a considerable fortune."

"Why five warships?"

"Apparently, Mailcoluim is trying to increase the fleet of Alba for the coming war. He shrugged his shoulders, "He wanted ships."

Anlaf smiled, "Still a very rich dowry, worthy of a Princess of the Clan Ivarr. I will also give a drakkar for her wedding present."

"Thank you Anlaf, Gytha will be very happy." Chuckling,

"You will not believe it. When Constantine agreed to the match, he made the mistake of asking Gytha publicly what she wanted for a wedding present. She asked only for his favourite slave girl Gwen as hand maiden and her baby of course."

"What, the slave girl that he refused to sell to you? What did he say?"

Grinning, "Well, he had no option other than to agree. He did order that as he is the father of the slave's child, they must live at his palace."

Anlaf frowned, "What did Duff say? As her husband he will decide where they reside."

Smiling, "Duff had the intellect to consult his father. Fortunately, Mailcoluim approved of Duff and Gytha residing at the palace. Mailcoluim has his eye on the crown of Alba. He sees living with King Constantine as informal training for his son. It will be good for Gytha too, safer."

He smiled, "Constantine must be feeling out done by your daughter.

"He must be kicking himself. I offered to pay a huge bag of silver to buy the slave for Gytha. Now she has her as a present." A chuckle bubbled up from his core.

Behind the curtain, Ketil smiled as he sipped wine from an elegant goblet.

4.6

A few days later, in the long hall of Scone Castle, the whole of Constantine's court gathered.

Archbishop Wulfstan, dressed in his long green cape and mitre, presided over the joint wedding of Gytha Blakarsdottir to Duff MacMailcoluim, and of Bethoc Ingen Constantine to Olaf Curan Sihtricsson.

Stood in front of the archbishop with their husbands to be, both ladies looked stunningly lovely in their white flowing gowns.

Gytha wore her mother's ornately designed silver tiara studded with amber flecks.

Bethoc wore an equally lovely diadem headdress crowning her flowing auburn hair.

His facial expression was abject tedium, as Wulfstan eyed the two young couples jadedly. His voice sounded drearily monotonous as he finished the ceremony, "I now pronounce you man and wife. You may kiss your bride."

Colourfully robed courtiers and nobles clapped and cheered. Ladies threw freshly picked petals into the air.

As petals fell around them, Olaf gently bent his head and softly kissed his wife's lips, whispering so only she could hear, "My beautiful Queen of Iona, I love you."

As Duff kissed Gytha, he whispered gently, "God bless you dear, for loving me."

The next day, most of Constantine's Court made their way to the sparkling river Tay. All manner of shipping vessels moored along King's Quay. Some large cargo barges carried goods for trading. Other smaller vessels carried barrels of fresh sea fish and crabs. Gulls circled these ships, noisily harassing the sailors. The most impressive vessels were the Viking fleet of dragon headed drakkars. Their black sleek hulls and dark dragon headed prows, made the other ships look stout and ungainly.

Sullenly, Archbishop Wulfstan boarded his ship, his green cape billowing about him. Confident that the foundations of the coalition had been formed, he felt impatient to leave. Striding up to a tall ruggedly weathered man, his black eyes glinted as he ordered sharply, "Commander set course for Jorvic."

Bowing respectfully, he yelled deeply, "Make ready for oars!"

Thirty of Wulfstan's men bustled into position.

The commander ordered loudly, "Raise oars!"

The men clumsily lifted their oars so the blades stood vertically high.

Raising his hands to his mouth, he shouted "Lower oars!"

Thirty men lowered their oar blades too quickly, heavily splashing into the river.

Many of the Viking sailors on the Norse drakkars struggled to contain their laughter, as they watched the archbishop get a face full of river water.

Glaring at his bumbling crew, Wulfstan berated loudly, "For God's sake! You are an embarrassment!"

Pursing his lips, the commander shook his head. The archbishop had not let him choose his own crew. There was barely a good sailor amongst them. But his Grace had wanted good fighters, not good sailors. Shrugging his shoulders he took the helm oar.

As Wulfstan's vessel pulled away from the quay, Anlaf's party prepared to board their ships. Many were eager to get back to Ath Cliath.

Audna's eyes sparkled with excitement. Her fluffy blonde hair blowing in the sea breeze, she followed Scarface around like a faithful hound.

Wearing an impressive black bear fur cape over his black

leathers, he wiped his hand across his brow. Breathing out deeply to cool himself, he frowned, wishing he had packed the long cape instead of wearing it. The double layer of fur over his shoulders felt stiflingly hot.

Several fishermen pushed past him, carrying big baskets full of fish that smelt of the sea.

Perspiration beaded on his head. Suddenly, he lifted the cape from his shoulders, gruffly, "Audna, carry this."

Looking up at him, she blinked with alarm. Quickly holding out her thin arms, she braced herself as he dropped the cape. Crumbling under the weight of the fur, her knees buckled and she fell to the ground.

Chuckling fondly, Scarface helped her back up to her feet.

Trying to hold up the cape, Audna giggled as he steadied her, "I need more warning before you chuck it at me." Taking in a deep breath, her blue eyes twinkled boldly, "You nearly killed me."

Amused by her growing confidence, "You are getting so cheeky, I forget how little you are." Taking the cape off of her, he slung it over his broad shoulder, "I will carry it. Come on let us get you on board. Here, hold my hand or I will lose you."

Smiling with the faith that she was safe with him, she held on to his large warm hand as he led her towards the ship.

On the wharf, Blacarri held onto his daughter's small pale hand as he spoke forcibly to Duff, explaining precisely what his punishment would be if he failed to make Gytha happy.

Gytha looked mortified.

His eyes twinkling with amusement, Ketil watched her as she raised her eyebrows up to the sky wishing her father would stop.

Duff visibly paled as he listened intently to his father-in-law, nodding his head dutifully.

Unaware that he was having a fatherly tirade, Blacarri frowned, "And I will gut you with a blunt knife and feed you to my dogs if a hair on her head is ever harmed."

Sighing deeply, Gytha interjected quickly, "I am going to be fine. There is no need to give him your 'I will hunt you down' speech."

Ketil chuckled softly as his employer ignored his daughter and carried on his paternal outburst. Looking around at the bustling noisy dock, Ketil could see that most of the royal court of Alba had come to see them off.

Under a colourful golden canopy, King Constantine sat on a grand throne. The newly wedded King Olaf and Queen Bethoc of Iona chatted cheerfully at his side.

Stood close to her mistress with her hands clasped together, Shona kept her eyes downcast. Anxiously she waited to board the drakkar. Born into slavery she had lived at King Constantine's court all her life. She did not want to leave the only home she had ever known but she had no choice.

Striding over to the royal pavilion, Anlaf smiled warmly, "King Olaf, you must delay your arrival at Iona for a few days and come and spend your honeymoon at Ath Cliath. It will be a good opportunity for you to secure your affairs there." He chuckled, "You can collect your wedding presents."

Bethoc clapped her hands ecstatically, "I am so happy at the thought of seeing Maelmare and the babies."

Looking handsome, dressed in new expensive clothes, Olaf grinned, "How could I deny my wife anything when she smiles like that? What say you Jarl Canute of Iona?"

Canute felt impatient to get back to Ath Cliath for his own reasons. He bowed low to Bethoc, "I agree with you my King. How could any man deny that smile? My Queen, go where you will, I am sure our king will follow."

Laughing, Constantine boomed, "Well said Jarl Canute!"

She giggled. She already felt a great fondness for the old Jarl who always showed her so much respect.

Smiling, Olaf easily agreed to the request, "Cousin, we will make ready our drakkar and leave three days after you."

"Excellent, that will give Maelmare a few days to prepare. I will arrange a procession for you through the streets of Ath Cliath. I hope that you enjoy the rest of your stay here. Fare ye well, cousin."

Feeling the power of youth and fortune at his feet, Olaf watched his cousin say goodbye to Bethoc and Constantine.

Turning to Olaf, quickly checking that he could not be over-heard, Canute whispered, "Well done Olaf. The first part of your plan has succeeded. You have your fortune and a king-dom."

As Anlaf walked off towards his ship Olaf's eyes narrowed and hardened. A fleeting snarl played on his lips, he hissed bitterly, "But I have not secured Jorvic!" Watching Anlaf stride strongly up the gangplank, he scowled, "If he intended to give me back Jorvic he would have said so by now!"

Canute frowned thoughtfully as the crew on Anlaf's drak-kar quickly withdrew the gangplank. He watched them skil-fully raise the oars with incredible precision. They held the oars aloft for a moment. At Anlaf's command they lowered them cleanly, with barely a froth of spray into the shimmer-ing river waters. His eyes intent, he rasped gruffly, "Think strategically Olaf. Wedding a princess has helped you win the first battle. Now, what can help you get back Jorvic and Nort-humbria?"

Glaring at Anlaf's drakkar as thirty oars pulled in perfect synchronisation away from the wharf, he muttered, "The sup-port of King Constantine."

Later that afternoon in the main hall of Scone Castle, Cellach sat close by the fire with the dogs.

One of the hounds licked his hand. Stroking the dog's dark head and silky ears, he overheard Olaf talking to his father.

"Yes, Anlaf could easily have an army ready for war this year. I do not understand his delay. Far be it from me to judge my cousin but Athelstan's reputation is great. Perhaps Anlaf and Blacarri secretly fear him."

"I cannot believe that." Constantine stated abruptly, "They both readily agreed to the alliance."

"It is easy to make sweeping statements, Majesty. As I said,

I can see no reason why they would delay. I know Anlaf wants Jorvic back in the hands of the Clan Ivarr." Shrugging his shoulders, "Perhaps he realises that he cannot adequately govern both Ath Cliath and Jorvic. The distance between the kingdoms is too great."

Looking up, Cellach's eyes filled with mistrust.

Eyeing Constantine intently, Olaf added, "Old King Guthrith always said that Anlaf would have Ath Cliath. Blacarri is King of Man and Norse Gaelgedhail. Ragnal would have Waterford and I," he paused, "King Guthrith always said that I would rule Jorvic again."

Evasively, Constantine parried, "I really think that is a decision for the Northumbrian Witan."

"Of course," he inclined his blonde head, "I felt it my duty to you to advise you of my concerns Father-in-law."

His topaz eyes glinted, "Thank you Olaf." Thoughtfully, "I appreciate your loyalty."

"I must leave now, Majesty. Your daughter is expecting me." Smiling, confident that he had seeded doubt in his Father-in-law's mind, he left the room.

Disconcerted, Constantine looked at his son, "What do you make of that son?"

Standing up, walking away from the fire, "Well Da," Cellach answered honestly "I cannot see why Olaf would lie about his country's resources, and put his friends and family in danger."

His brow furrowed, "They are his people. They took him in and gave him protection after his father died." Thoughtfully, "He might be jealous of Anlaf's position. That would explain why he would try to undermine him."

Shaking his head, Cellach clenched his fist, "There is something about the man Da. I can't put my finger on it." He abruptly shook his head, "Just a feeling."

"He still covets his lost crown of Jorvic. I agree we cannot trust him." He added pensively. "Be careful what you say in front of him and also Bethoc. Her allegiance is now with him."

"As you wish Da." A little intrigued, "Obviously Olaf wants

Jorvic for himself? Will you back him?"

"Wulfstan says the Northumbrian Witan want Anlaf as king." He shrugged, "It matters not to me. Either one of my son-in-laws will protect my borders. Meanwhile son, we will play along with Olaf's suggestion and send messengers to Anlaf. I will pressure Anlaf to get ready for war this year. My spies will inform me if Anlaf dallies in his preparation."

Thoughtfully, Cellach nodded. Flexing his immense shoulders, he stretched, "I personally think that Olaf is ambitious but weak. He shows a flaw in his character."

Constantine shrugged, "It is obvious that he married Bethoc for the power that a Princess of Alba will bring him."

Pensively running his hands through his auburn hair, his young topaz eyes glinted, "Perhaps the Isle of Iona will satisfy his aspiration for a kingdom."

Grimly, "I doubt it."

A muscle flickered in Cellach's jaw as he thought anxiously of his young sister, "Do you think Bethoc will be all right Da?"

Hardening his heart against the doubts that filled his mind, he stated forcefully, "She knows that I was against this marriage. She has made her bed, now she has to lie in it!"

Part 5

The Honeymoon

5.1

Ath Cliath,
1 June 937

Under a purple sail, King Olaf and Queen Bethoc sailed up the river Liffy. Many square sailed drakkars and knarr barges glided past them. The fast moving glinting river reflected the clear sunshine and hazy blue skies above.

Approaching Wood Quay, Olaf felt the cooling breeze through his blonde hair. Looking over the side of his ship, he saw two swans elegantly bobbing in the shimmering river waves. Alongside them large seagulls floated on the water, their black eyes glinting steely, as they waited for the fishing vessels to arrive.

Not waiting for King Olaf's order, the ship suddenly became hectic as the crew rushed to lower and stow the sail.

Olaf grinned as his drakkar glided up to the busy wharf of Ath Cliath and bumped gently against Wood Quay. Small rippling waves lapped against his ship as his men threw ropes to tie off his drakkar.

Swooping seagulls shrieked raucously as they hovered above their heads.

On the noisy quay, fishermen and their boys ignored everyone, as they concentrated on mending nets. Their wives struggled to tend to their infants and keep their noisy energetic youngsters under control.

In front of tethered knarr ships, hawkers and shop owners bartered loudly with Viking traders for goods. When they had fixed a price, the Vikings used scales and weights to measure the hacked silver payment. A stream of hawkers made their way off the wharf and up the main street towards the shops. They carried huge baskets of goods on their backs. Some of the richer shop keepers paid for strong young men, to push hand carts full of goods up the street for them.

Eyeing Olaf's ship with interest, poorly dressed street urchins watched the gangplank bridge being lowered.

Grooms from the fortress stood waiting with horses. One of the more spirited stallions stomped the wooden quay deck with his hooves.

Stood close to her mistress, Shona looked pale in her yellow dress. Under her gown her arms and breasts were deeply bruised and painful. Before they had left Alba, King Olaf had taken on several Norwegian mercenaries. Yesterday, three of them had managed to pull her behind some barrels and maul her. She had only got away because Jarl Canute and two large sailors had rescued her. Since then, she stayed very close to her mistress.

Gallantly escorting Bethoc down the bridge to the deck, Olaf led her gently to a beautiful snow white mare.

Her unusual coloured eyes downcast, Shona followed them past the leering mercenaries.

Jarl Kalf licked his lips obscenely as she passed him. He and his men chuckled at her petrified face.

Fear knotted in the pit of her stomach as she hurried past them. She felt her heart racing with panic.

Lifting his queen up into her side saddle, Olaf's strong tanned arm muscles rippled and pulled against his purple tunic. Looking up at her pretty young flushed face, he smiled. He could still not quite believe that he was the husband of the King of Alba's daughter.

Sat back straight, looking lovely in her purple silk gown, she smiled back at him fondly as she adjusted her skirts and bridle. Golden sheer cloth shimmered regally from her elaborately pointed head piece and caught in the gentle breeze. Leaning towards him she whispered, "I need a horse for Shona, my Lord. She is too delicate to walk the streets."

Shaking his head with amusement, he whispered back, "She is just a slave, my love."

Taken aback that he would deny her such a small request, unease caught her breath.

Listening carefully, Canute looked surprised too. His eyes blinked in quick succession as he realised suddenly, Olaf was not as deeply in love with Bethoc as he acted.

Lifting his chin haughtily, feeling powerful, Olaf motioned for Canute to come forward.

Inclining his head, Canute strode up to him, "Yes my King."

"Tell my Norwegian mercenaries to join the procession."

Concern glinted in his eyes. He glanced towards the seven red haired Norwegians. Fully armed and dressed in battle leathers they looked menacing. Lowering his voice, he chose his words carefully, "My King, the crew do not trust them."

Nodding, Olaf lowered his voice too, "Their leader, Jarl Kalf, spoke well when I first met him. I hired them to increase my army. However, the queen says they are harassing her maid, who is under my protection," he wide blue eyes glinted, "and that disrespects me. I intend to discharge them." Dismissively, "I think I will leave them here at Anlaf's court."

Uneasily, "How will you do that Olaf? Jarl Kalf will be insulted."

Impetuously, "I will recommend them to King Anlaf as experienced warriors for the coming war."

It was a good idea, "Good." He brusquely changed the subject, "There is only one horse left. Your queen has requested it for her injured slave. Do I have your leave to let the girl use the horse, or should I honour Jarl Kalf and reward his," he almost spat out the word derisively, "disrespect?"

Flicking his blonde head back imperiously, Olaf shrugged, "Give it to the girl."

Bowing to him curtly, Canute strode back up the gangplank. Beckoning the leader of the mercenaries to him, he waited.

His eyes slanting, Jarl Kalf swaggered up deliberately slowly. His voice tinged with sarcasm, "Yes, old man?"

For a moment the insult prickled his mood, ignoring the gibe he eyed him coldly, "Jarl Kalf, King Olaf wishes to present you to his cousin King Anlaf, High King of the Norse of Britain and Ireland."

Arrogantly, the Norwegian lifted his chin as he glanced sideways at his men to see their reaction.

They all looked impressed.

Puffing out his chest, Jarl Kalf jutted his chin out. His eyes slanted, "I am honoured."

His face unfathomable, Canute drawled, "You and your men will join the procession to the fortress." Turning away he added, "You will walk at the rear." Striding down the gang-plank, he walked up to the one small horse that was left. He took the reins and led the horse to Shona. Lifting her up strongly by her midriff, he sat her on the mare.

She submissively took the bridle and kept her eyes down-cast.

Looking up, he saw Queen Bethoc's grateful glance towards him. He bowed to her before mounting his own horse.

Already on his horse, Olaf turned his spirited stallion. He ordered loudly, "Jarl Canute, you will have the honour of leading the procession."

Inclining his head, Canute gently flicked his reins. As he walked his horse past the seven Norwegians, he haughtily ignored their leader's jealous scowl.

As they left the wharf, Olaf felt the hairs on the back of his neck prickle. Looking around quickly he saw Helga. She smiled and waved to him as if nothing had happened. Surprise jolted through him. He had not even considered that she would be here. For a moment, he wondered if anyone had told her that he had wed. She stood with some of the other castle serving girls. She was hard to miss with her brazen red hair and low cut red dress, exposing a fair amount of her cleavage. A few months ago that would have attracted him to her bed that night but today, she looked common and inferior. Compared to his wife, to him, she looked positively vulgar.

Looking plump and plain, Kari eyed her deviously. Hiding her true thoughts behind a smile, she asked carefully, "Helga, did you know that he is married now?"

She really disliked the woman. Her false smile and meddling ways irritated her even more than her half-truths and deceit. Helga decided to smile confidently, "Of course I did Kari." That much was true. Queen Maelmare herself had kindly warned her. She had explained, most gently, that she would need to vacate Olaf's chamber and make way for his bride, her sister. Taking advantage of the queen's kindness, she had burst into tears and sobbed what would become of her. The queen immediately arranged lodgings for her, above the new fortress stables. She had smiled at the irony of it all. The queen told her, she would always have work in the castle, which gave protection and food. They had walked together to the stables. The queen had been dressed in a rich emerald green gown. In her third best dress Helga had felt dowdy, but then everyone did next to elegant Queen Maelmare. She remembered her eyes widening with awe at the sight of the lodgings. Although it was unused and filthy, with dirty black spiders' webs everywhere, it was much bigger than she had expected. In fact, it was much bigger than Olaf's castle chamber room. The lodgings even had a private kitchen area, with a grate and griddle pan, so she would be warm in the winter. There was room for a bed chamber and a sitting area. Queen Maelmare had given her permission, to take the clothes and presents that Olaf had bought her over the years. She was also allowed to take his old bed and bedclothes. The queen had said that her sister, Queen Bethoc, would have a new honeymoon bed. A little hurt, Helga had not dwelt on that. Instead she set about finding furnishings. After she had made a good strong broomstick, she had pestered the head cook for a good sturdy chair from the palace kitchens. To get rid of her, he had also given her two pillows full of freshly plucked duck feathers, a bucket full of firewood, several wooden bowls of varying sizes and a good large kitchen knife. She had cleaned and swept out the apartment until it gleamed. A short time later, she heard a knock at the door. The queen's maid had been sent to her with two silver platters and two silver goblets as a gift. A page held a large silver wine flagon full of wine. The flagon lid had been lost some time ago and the top was covered with a piece of delicate white linen. The jug was worth a fortune. Still stood in front of Kari, Helga smiled at the memory.

Kari eyed her jealously. Helga's smile infuriated her. Disappointed not to get the reaction she had hoped for, she quipped, "It must be terrible to be cast aside."

Shrugging her shoulders, Helga giggled, "I can see no reason why this marriage would stop our affair." Looking up at Olaf, she had expected him to return her smile, at least acknowledge her with a wink. However, he ignored her.

Haughtily shunning Helga, he rode past her without a second glance.

Slyly, Kari tried hard not to smile openly, "Well now, he looks much taken with his pretty young wife. Do you think that she is about ten years younger than you?" When she did not answer, she eyed Helga maliciously, "Did you notice, he barely cast you a glance."

Humiliated, she stood rigid. Her cheeks felt hot with shame. Suddenly pushing past Kari, she angrily walked off. Even from a distance, she heard Kari's loud parting shot, "Look, Helga is so angry she has forgotten to sway her hips." The serving girl's laughter rang loudly in her ears.

Their slow parade through the streets, up to the castle, was a delight for Queen Bethoc. The people of Ath Cliath lined the streets and loudly cheered their welcome. During the previous three days, Maelmare had been busy arranging a wonderful reception for them. Colourful flags hung from every doorway. Children carrying big baskets giggled as they scattered petals into the air. Trumpets blew on every corner as the royal party slowly made their way up through Fish Street.

Seeing a familiar face, Olaf called, "Jarl Canute, pray stop."

Gently pulling on his bridle, his horse halted and snorted excitedly, Canute turned, "Yes Majesty."

Olaf dismounted from his horse in one lithe jump. Landing squarely on the ground, he strode over to the old fishmonger.

He looked ancient in years, his dark straggly beard hung almost to his waist against his dark leather apron. Stood in awe, tightly holding his daughter's arm, he eyed the young man.

"Good morrow fishmonger." Turning to Bethoc, he smiled, "My Queen, this is the best fishmonger in Ath Cliath."

From her horse, she caught the distinct aroma of fish on the air. She smiled at him prettily, gracefully nodding to the old man, "I have heard that your smoked herrings are the best in Britain and Ireland."

The grey haired man's chest puffed up in pride. Bowing, he smiled a toothless grin, "My wine vinegar herrings are even better. The recipe is from the Baltics." His weathered hands brushed itchy fish scales from his hairy forearms. He turned to Olaf, "Good morrow lad. I hear that you are now King of Iona, praise be to Thor."

A crowd of people murmured as they craned their necks to hear what was said.

"The Gods move in mysterious ways." His deep blue eyes glinted with amusement, "Jarl Canute, pray come here."

Surprised at the order, Canute dismounted from his horse, "Majesty?"

"Jarl Canute, I understand that you have a proposition to make. Best make it now."

"Lad you always were impatient."

Smiling cheekily, Olaf persisted, "Get on with it Canute, while we are still young enough to celebrate!"

Warily, the fishmonger held onto his daughter's hand tightly.

Taking a deep breath, he looked at the old fishmonger. Canute was completely aware that the crowd had gone silent and most would hear his proposal. Jutting out his chin, his voice deepened strongly respectful, "Sir, I come again to ask for your daughter's hand in marriage."

A few of the women in the crowd gasped.

The fishmonger shook his head, "Again Jarl Canute, with deepest respect, I say no. She is all I have in the world. You have nothing to offer her."

Olaf smiled gently, "Fishmonger, Jarl Canute gave up much for me. Now that I have a kingdom, I have rewarded him with lands and livestock."

Quickly pressing his point, Canute flexed his still muscular shoulders, "Sir, I ask that you let me wed your daughter and in return, come and live with us on the Isle of Iona."

Trembling, the old man stuttered, "No."

Interrupting impatiently, Olaf smiled, "As wedding gift, I will present you with a farmstead by the sea where there is good fishing. I will build you a cook house for smoking your herrings. You will also own cattle and chickens."

A few of the men in the crowd nudged each other, it was a fortune.

Taking the old fishmonger's arm, Olaf gently led him a few paces away from his daughter, "I need the best fishmonger in Ath Cliath to fillet my fish. It would be a great service to me, personally, if you came to Iona."

The old man looked deeply surprised. Often these days, he felt overlooked because of his age, "You say you need my services?"

Smiling, he brushed his blonde hair from his eyes, "Indeed I do. As reward for moving to Iona with me, I will of course gift the land to you. It will be transferred to you and your descendants legally by charter."

"I will have a farmstead, you say, with cattle." Shrewdly his eyes narrowed, "How many head?"

Olaf's left eyebrow raised, "Five cows, one bullock, twenty sheep, one ram and twenty chickens.

"Any cockerels?"

Both of his eyebrows rose higher, "One."

He lifted his chin thoughtfully, "Any hogs?"

Taking a deep breath, Olaf smiled indulgently, "A breading pair."

"By the sea you say?"

His wide blue eyes glinted with good humour, "Yes, by the sea. You can fish every day for the rest of your life. You will be close to your daughter and the Goddess Freya willing, your grandchildren."

The old man turned back to his blonde haired daughter, "Ethe, Do you want this man for husband?"

She looked beseechingly at her father, "Yes Da, I love him."

"And, you don't mind me coming with you?" His old eyes filled with tears as fear struck him that she might say no.

"Of course we want you to come with us Da."

Canute smiled.

The old man turned back to Olaf. A large tear fell down his wrinkled cheek, "And, you need my services you say?"

Sincerely, "Every day that I am in residence I will eat your fish. When I am not in residence the priests of my Christian priory will eat your fish."

"Well, if I am needed."

"Fishmonger, you will be doing me a great service."

Grinning a toothless smile, "Then I agree this match!"

As the crowd cheered, Canute lifted his wife to be up into his arms and swung her around, "Ethe, I am marrying you today, before he changes his mind."

Waiting at the gates of the castle, the royal retinue led by King Anlaf looked up in surprise, as the cheers of the crowds reached them.

Looking pale, Queen Maelmare smiled, "My King, it would seem that our people are well taken with my sister and King Olaf."

Anlaf nodded, feeling a little disconcerted.

Noticing, Maelmare added quickly, "They only ever cry louder for you my King."

Eventually, King Olaf and Queen Bethoc arrived at the gates of the palace and were met with a fanfare of trumpets, so loud they set the castle hounds barking.

Spotting Scarface standing next to Lady Muldivana, Olaf grinned at him.

Inclining his head, Scarface smiled back. His eyes twinkled genuinely pleased that the lad had made his fortune.

Wearing a new pale blue dress, smiling happily, Audna waved her colourful voile flag excitedly. Her hair was neatly braided into plaits.

Indulgently watching her, Muldivana giggled. Turning to her husband she took his big tanned hand in hers, "I am so glad that you bought her for me Barrick. I am already very fond of her."

Smiling, he squeezed her hand, gruffly, "I know, she grows on you." He chuckled, "She told me she was going to impress you, by working hard to be helpful, so that you would want to keep her too." He lowered his voice, "Do you think you would want to adopt her as a daughter?"

Gazing up at him astonished, Muldivana raised her eyebrows. Loudly, her Alban accent deepening with every word, "You ask me something like that here?"

He blinked uncomfortably. Realising that he should have approached her privately, he looked at his feet, gruffly, "It can wait till later."

Breathing out deeply, she lowered her voice, "You want to adopt Audna?"

Holding her gaze, he felt his heart palpitate, "Yes I do. She needs our protection."

Looking at Audna merrily waving her voile flag, Muldivana's gaze softened. Then a look of sadness passed over her face.

He squeezed her hand, "Are you okay my love?"

She gazed up at him her eyes sparkling with unspent tears, "I am so sorry. I do not think I will ever conceive."

His voice deepened, "So many of my friends have lost their wives in childbirth. I could not bear to lose you my love. I am almost glad that you have not become pregnant."

Looking up at him, she smiled with relief, "I thought I would lose you when you gave up on me ever conceiving."

Bending his head, he kissed her gently on her soft forehead, "Silly, I am never letting go of you." Breathing deeply he looked back at Audna, "We have so much to offer her. Please will you consider adopting her?"

Her face softening, she smiled, "I do not have to think about it. My answer is yes."

Relief shot through him like an arrow. Pulling her into his arms, he kissed the top of her head.

The crowd of courtiers bowed and curtseyed as their Queen and her sister walked past them.

Looking with concern at her sister's pale face and faint shadows under her eyes, Bethoc whispered, "Are you well sister?"

The briefest of frowns drifted across Maelmare's delicate features, "My boys tire me." Changing the subject quickly, she smiled, "I am so happy to see you. I have missed you so much."

Bethoc held her sisters hand tightly, "We must make the most of our few days together."

Ignoring the sudden searing pain in her stomach, Maelmare slowly exhaled a deep breath. Over the last few months the pains had been coming on more and more often, but they did not last long. Already feeling better she smiled again, "Yes we must. Let us take you to meet our boys."

Swaggering beside Anlaf and Blacarri, as they walked into the cool hallway, Olaf turned to Anlaf, "King Constantine has sent me as his ambassador. I have questions regarding the preparation for invasion. He has asked that I take back your answers."

Carefully, Anlaf countered, "I thought that you would go on to Iona after your visit with your new bride."

Imperiously, "Matters of state will always come before pleasure for a king."

Anlaf raised his eyebrows. Mentally, he questioned Olaf's true feelings for Bethoc. Putting his misgivings aside, he spoke formerly, "Come now King Olaf, we have such a short amount of time together. Queen Maelmare has planned our entertainment whilst you are here. We cannot disappoint her. This is a time to celebrate your honeymoon. Our people expect it. Your wife expects it."

Disappointment was evident on Olaf's face, he pressed, "King Constantine wants to invade by the end of the year."

"Olaf, now is not the time to talk about this."

He frowned, "Perhaps we can make time later?"

"We will see."

As they approached the dais and four thrones, Blacarri held back as the court erupted with clapping.

Stood by the wide kitchen door, Helga frowned grudgingly as Olaf took his young bride's hand and led her to her throne. She knew that he had seen her but he practically looked through her. At that moment, she realised that Olaf would never acknowledge her again.

Giggling excitedly, Kari entered the kitchen from the outside door. The other serving girls followed her in. Kari eyed Helga pitilessly. She had not finished with her yet. Walking straight over to her, she glared her with her cold blue eyes. Her voice sounded sickly-sweet, "Are you too upset to work today Helga?"

Swinging round at the sound of her voice, she felt like slapping the smirk off the heartless woman's face. Seeing Kari's callous eyes, Helga's auburn eyebrows raised as she suddenly realised what she was up to. Clearly, Kari was looking for a reason to cause trouble. If the king heard that she was not working she might lose her new home. Kari wanted her to react to her jibes and lose her temper. She wanted her to make a scene. Helga's green eyes flashed, she would not give her the pleasure. Smiling innocently, she picked up a large jug of ale. Elegantly placing her hand on her trim waist, turning her hip slightly to accentuate her lovely figure, she eyed Kari and forced a pretty smile.

Looking over Helga's slim profile, jealousy shot through Kari. Her lips pursed as she felt the tightness of her dress stretching over her own thick girth.

Smoothing down her skirt against her flat midriff, she brazenly winked at Kari, "Plenty more like him out there." Sashaying through the kitchen doors, she smiled becomingly as she served the men in the room. The only table she discreetly avoided was the table with the Norwegian mercenaries new to court. Experienced at serving warriors, her instincts told her those men were trouble. Loud and uncouth, they leered at the women and grabbed at any maid who strayed close enough. Word went round the serving girls quickly to be careful at that table.

Stood by the door, Kari scowled. Her hard blue eyes turned cold as she jealously watched the men in the room flirting and laughing with Helga.

Much later, King Anlaf strode up to her with an empty ale goblet, "How are you Helga? Kari has come to me and said that you were upset earlier."

Alarm sped through her body quickening her heart beat. She knew that she no longer had Olaf's protection. She was vulnerable. Bobbing a curtsey, she managed to muster up a forlorn smile, "Thank you Majesty, for your concern. I did shed a tear when I saw how beautiful his bride is."

He looked uneasy, "Kari said that you were angry and left the parade."

Carefully controlling herself, she feigned a look of surprise, "Majesty, I was not angry when I left the parade. I was just devastated to see him." She closed her eyes momentarily, as if holding back the tears, "I had not expected it to hurt so badly. I rushed back here so that no one would see me weep." She took a deep breath, "I do not think that I would have coped if it wasn't for your support. I have forced myself to work hard today because I am just so grateful to you and the queen."

Frowning, he nodded. He remembered that it was only weeks ago that Helga was eating at his table. Now she was cast aside. "The queen has ensured that you are not on the streets?"

"The queen's compassion and kindness has filled my heart with faith that I can," she stuttered, "get through this."

Pensively, "Kari was concerned that you would cause a scene."

Taking in a deep breath, she looked into his eyes, sincerely, "My Lord, I would never do that. I am sure Kari is just being kind." She felt the exact opposite to that. She swept her fingers across her forehead as if she was very tired, weakly, "I thought that I was working hard. Have I displeased you, Majesty?"

The muscle in his jaw flexed, "No Helga. Even my wife said that she had noticed how hard you were working tonight, compared to some of the other maids."

She looked relieved.

His eyes rested on Kari. He looked sternly at her. Every time he saw her, just like now, she was stood still and pushing food into her mouth. Eyeing the woman's rotund body he frowned. He started to think that Kari was meddling again. Maelmare had advised him that it was well known that Kari was a trouble maker. A little annoyed with himself for being taken in by her, he hid his irritation. Dismissively, "Kari was worried."

"She knows that I loved Olaf deeply." Deep inside she knew that was untrue but she fluttered her eyelashes as if blinking back tears, "I am just so grateful to have a roof over my head. I will work hard every day for you and the queen, for the rest of my life, Majesty." She looked at the empty goblet in his hand, "May I, your Majesty?"

At ease now, he smiled gently, "You may Helga, well done."

"Drinkhail Majesty."

He took a long drink, "Wassail Helga. We will miss you at our table. The queen has taken you into her protection. You can count on our support."

Relieved, she sank into a deep curtsey.

As he strode back to his guests, he glanced at Kari with disappointment. He knew that she had tried to cause trouble for Helga. It was obvious Helga was trying hard to make it through the day with some dignity.

Seeing her king look at her with displeasure, Kari quickly picked up a tray before sidling off towards the kitchens.

Shaking his head, he sat back down. Taking Maelmare's hand as she looked inquisitively at him, he whispered, "You were right my love, Kari was meddling again!"

Shaking her head, Maelmare tutted, "Poor Helga, she has been through enough." She sighed, "Such is the fate of cast-off women." Thoughtfully, "My Lord, I wish to make it clear to all that Helga is under my protection. I want to give her ownership of her apartment by Charter."

He smiled as he kissed her hand, "You are kind Maelmare."

Every time Anlaf caught sight of Helga that long evening she was working hard. Her cheeks flushed, she served ale and cleaned tables. Sat next to his wife, he looked at fair Queen Bethoc. Dressed elegantly and very pretty she giggled as Olaf whispered in her ear. Not once, Anlaf realised, had Olaf asked about Helga's welfare. He had coldly and cruelly discarded her. It was as if Helga had never existed in his life.

Much later that night, after all the tables had been cleared, Helga was the last maid to walk back into the dimly lit kitchen.

Snoring loudly, Kari was asleep in the corner. Her plump pale skinned face contorted against a linen bag of flour.

It had been two years since Helga had to sleep in the kitchens. Back then it had seemed like an adventure, until one of the scullery lads had tried to attack her. She only got away from him because she had managed to grab a red hot griddle pan. The man still carried the burn scar on his face. Thankful that she at least had a home to go to, she ignored the wretched woman. Kari had really tested her temper today.

"Hello."

She jumped in surprised. A tall good looking man smiled at her, his dark blond hair was tied back with a thin leather strap.

Sat in the shadows, at the far end of the huge table, he was eating the remains of a loaf of bread and butter.

She raised her eyebrows, "You're not a cook, what are you doing here?"

His glittering blue eyes looked over her with interest, "I am the Master of the Queen's Horse. The queen has asked me to see you home at night."

"She did?"

"Yes mistress Helga. The queen says that you are under her protection. You live in the lodgings above the stables next to my abode." He smiled as he stood up, "It is late. Are you ready?"

She blinked, "I am grateful to the queen but I am quite capable of seeing myself home."

He nodded curtly, "The queen is concerned because we have new mercenaries to our court, that have a reputation for," he paused deciding to use the queen's word, "atrocities."

She nodded cautiously, understanding his meaning perfectly. Looking up at him, she noticed his broad shoulders. She felt a stir of attraction. Then, feeling emotionally and physically exhausted, she suppressed the feelings. She looked away from him. Taking some cheese, a small loaf of bread and a small scoop of butter from the churn, she walked out of the kitchens towards the stables. As it was a dry night she did not need to hold her long skirt up from the mud. Her leather boots padded on the dry dirt. A myriad of twinkling stars lit up the clear moonlit night sky.

Following her, he said nothing as he looked at her pretty curvy figure and long red hair.

Feeling his eyes on her, she thought about sashaying her hips, but tonight she was just too tired.

When she reached the steps to her lodgings she looked back at his tanned face, "What is your name?"

A muscle flickered in his jaw, "Thorsson mistress."

She smiled, "Thank you Thorsson."

Thoughtfully, he watched her climb the steps. Surprised, by the sudden feeling of protectiveness for his new charge, he quickly added, "Lock your door tonight mistress."

Looking back at him, she nodded as she turned the key to her new home. Closing the door behind her, she locked the door and then lifted the heavy door bar into place. The beam sat on the two metal brackets either side of the door frame. Smiling, she whispered to herself, "It would take an army to break that door down." Her broomstick was exactly where she had left it by the door. Looking around her lodgings she smiled. It looked clean and new, and it was all hers. Opening up the shuttered windows she breathed in the cool night air. The moonlight lit up her lodgings showing her cot bed and rich bed linen. Smiling, as she walked over to her cooking area, she carefully placed the cheese, loaf and butter on one of the silver plates. Delicately removing the white cloth, she poured herself wine from the silver flagon. Moving to her new chair and side table with her meal, she sat down and looked out at the moon. Hearing soft bumps and noises from the room next door she smiled. It was strangely reassuring to know Thorsson was there. Sipping her wine, she closed her eyes and lent back as she wound down from her emotional day.

5.2

The three days of celebrations had passed quickly. It was with relief that Anlaf watched King Olaf and Queen Bethoc's small fleet of three ships as they set sail for Iona.

On board the slowest vessel, smiling with amusement, Canute's blue eyes lit up as he watched his father in law scurry about the vessel. The old man was so excited he kept getting in the way of the sailors.

Mindful of Canute's status, the crew acted with immense respect towards his wife's father.

Stood holding their horse bridles, watching them sail away from Wood Quay, the Norwegian mercenaries stood a short distance away. They looked menacingly at Blacarri.

Fully armed and dressed in black battle leathers, he lifted his chin and nonchalantly looked back at them with cool unflinching grey eyes.

Remembering their beating from him, they lowered their eyes first.

The gulls, floating on the updraughts, screeched loudly overhead.

As the drakkars sailed away, Anlaf felt himself take a deep stressed intake of breath. Dressed in black leather breeches, boots and a deep red silk shirt, he rubbed his tanned hands through his blonde hair.

Watching him, Blacarri frowned, "Are you okay?"

Turning to him, Anlaf rolled his eyes upwards, "Thank the Gods he has gone. I have spent the last three days, trying to avoid his questioning about my plans for the invasion. I did not discuss this with him but it is too soon. We have not had enough time to prepare. The Clan Ivarr needs to find weapons, warships and horses."

A muscle flickered in his jaw, "He tried to talk to me about the invasion this morning as well. He inferred that Constantine thinks you are delaying."

Frowning with surprise, "He undermined me to you. What did you say?"

"I pointed out it was less than a month since we formed the alliance in Alba, and you are giving the kings time to prepare for their peoples' winter stocks as well."

Smiling he nodded, "What did he say?"

Shaking his head in disgust, Blacarri raised his dark eyebrows, "He was taken aback. It was obvious he had not given winter a thought."

"Winter is always at the back of a Norse King's mind. Some reserves must be saved for this season of hardship. I can take nothing for granted. As King I must provide, not only for my men, but also the women and children."

Flexing his wide shoulders, his pale grey eyes hardened, "I don't trust him Anlaf. Is he trying to cause a rift between you and Constantine?"

"Let him try." Thoughtfully, "I need to meet with the jarls. I will hold a meeting of Thing Lawmen. Arrange it for tomorrow morning." As an afterthought, "Bring the Norwegians."

Seriously, Blacarri eyed his brother, "I don't often question your decisions Anlaf but can you tell me why you allowed those dogs to stay?" Tilting his head to one side, "I told you, they are the ones who attacked Constantine's slave woman."

"Maelmare told me they tried to rape her sister's slave too." Scowling, "Cousin Olaf practically insisted they stay as paid mercenaries for the war. I had no choice."

Gruffly, "They are trouble."

Turning away, annoyed with himself, Anlaf lifted his leg and put his black booted foot into his stirrup. Mounting his horse, he snarled, "If they become a problem eliminate them!"

Raising his dark eyebrows, his pale grey eyes glinted. He

rarely saw his brother so tense. Nodding grimly, he strode over to his horse. Hooking his foot into the stirrup, he swung himself strongly up onto his saddle.

Flicking his reins, Anlaf broke his horse into a canter and rode through the busy streets back to the fortress. Blacarri followed close behind him.

Quickly mounting their horses, the Norwegians followed a short distance behind them.

Wearing a dark green dress, Helga smiled as she swept the steps to her lodgings with her broom. For the first time in her life, she felt totally self-sufficient and she was enjoying it. Seeing the king and his brother canter into the stable yard, she respectfully bobbed a curtsy to them as they dismounted.

Their faces serious, deep in conversation, they did not notice her as they strode off towards the kingshalla.

Dressed in frayed breeches and dull dirty tunics, stable lads ran up as more horses' hooves clattered on the cobbles. Dismounting quickly, the Norwegians threw their long bridles at the stable lads.

As the lads led the horses away, Kalf scowled. He felt sick of following the king around like a dog, it was demeaning. Noticing the red headed serving wench sweeping the steps, he eyed her keenly. His face had the look of a starving dog. Her body still had the slight, nubile sleekness of a woman ten years her junior. He recognised her from the kingshalla. He had often called her over but so far she always managed to avoid serving his table. He muttered under his breath, "What a beauty, I bet she could lighten a man's mood."

Led like sheep, his men goggle eyed her too. One made crude gestures at her which made the others laugh.

Years of serving at warrior tables had hardened her to this sort of behaviour. It was daylight at the busy fortress so she did not feel in danger. She decided to ignore them.

Looking around the stables, Kalf saw no one else about. Barely more than an opportunistic villain he sauntered towards her.

Menacingly smirking, knowing what was to come, his men followed him.

Seeing them all walking towards her at once, she suddenly felt very vulnerable. Deciding to get indoors she bolted for her door.

Although a big man, Kalf was fast on his feet.

Suddenly pulled back by her hair, shocked by what was happening, she gasped fearfully. His free hand went round her waist like a vice.

Splaying his hand to touch as much of her body as possible, he reached up over her breasts to her neck.

Feeling his hands on her body, she screamed.

Inside the stables below, Thorsson heard her. Grabbing a pitchfork, he strode outside. Seeing seven hardened warriors circling Helga, he felt alarm course through his body. Recognising Jarl Kalf, he took in a deep breath as he approached them.

Gripping her neck tighter, Kalf new exactly what he was doing. He had done this many times before. When he wanted to take an unwilling woman and share her with his men, he would hurt her first, bad enough so that she thought she would die. Few women fought back after that, allowing them all to violate at will.

Absolutely petrified, she almost dropped her broom.

Looking at them calmly, Thorsson's eyes glinted, his voice loud, "I would not do that if I were you."

Swinging his head round, Kalf eyed him murderously, "Walk away, now!"

He was pressed so hard against her, she could already feel his arousal. Her green eyes wide with fear, she screamed, "No, don't leave me to him!"

Hearing the commotion, totally loyal to each other and their equestrian community, several stable lads strode up behind Thorsson. The older lads also carried pitchforks, the younger ones held whips and two had long knives. They stared at the warriors hostilely.

Kalf's men swung round. A couple of them put their hands on the hilt of their swords but they did not draw them.

Looking up at them, Thorsson stood his ground, "I would not do that if I were you."

Feeling the warmth of her body so close to his, Kalf felt deeply aroused, he growled loudly, "Walk away!"

Shrugging his broad shoulders, Thorsson eyed him, "It's up to you but I would warn you, that this woman is under the queen's protection. If you defile her, you will be disrespecting the queen. And, if you disrespect the queen you personally insult King Anlaf." His blue eyes glinted with confidence as he grinned, "The king will chop off your cock and balls, and feed them to his dogs in front of your eyes."

Alarmed, Kalf's men stepped back.

Eyeing them, Thorsson could tell straight away that they were cowards, "Leave now and I will not report this incident to the king."

Kalf's men eyed each other, not sure what to do.

Hesitating, Kalf let go of her hair and loosened his grip on her throat.

She suddenly shrieked as she pulled away from him. Gripping the staff of her broom, she twisted her body as she jabbed it into his testicles.

The pain was intense. Taken completely by surprise, Kalf stumbled backwards down the steps.

Rounding on him, her heart full of outraged fury, she screamed as she smacked him in the face with the broom head.

His feet left the ground as he missed the last two steps. Falling backwards, Kalf landed painfully on his back on the cobbles.

Descending the steps, still screeching like a banshee, she raised the broom in a high arc.

Yelling out with alarm, he just managed to turn over before she rained blow after blow on his back and head.

Blind rage and red mist engulfed her as she smashed the

broom into his body again and again, and again.

Watching her unleash her fiery temper, Thorsson felt a chuckle of amusement bubble up from his core.

Some of the stable lads started to laugh. It was infectious.

Kalf was only saved because her broom snapped in two and his men managed to drag him away from her. She hurled what was left of the broom handle after them. Red faced and breathing deeply, she finally caught her breath.

A wide grin on his handsome face, Thorsson's dark blonde eyebrows lifted, "Well mistress Helga, you really kicked the shit out of him."

Breathing deeply, everything suddenly slowed down and came back into focus. Her dark green dress billowed against her legs. She shuddered as she realised how close they had come to really hurting her. Suddenly bursting into tears, she sobbed as Thorsson took her into his arms and cradled her. Lifting her into his arms, he carried her to the steps and sat down on them as he held her. Her face against his chest, she cried for a while. She wept for losing Olaf, she wept for losing her place at court, she wept for not ever having children, but mostly, she wept because she realised her vulnerability. Alone in this world, without a man's protection, without a son's protection, she would always be in danger.

It was strange. At that moment the stable lads just seemed to adopt her. As Thorsson held her in his arms, one lad fetched a horse blanket and placed it around her shoulders. Another got her a piece of clean cloth to wipe her face. One of the younger lads brought her a beaker of honey mead.

Her voice shook as she gulped in a very shuddery snuffle, "Thank you, for helping me."

As he looked protectively down at her, a muscle in Thorsson's jawline flickered, "We take care of our own Mistress Helga. Now that you live in the stables, you are one of us."

Gazing up at him, she blinked, as deep shuddering breaths shook her and one last big glistening tear rolled down her cheek.

Looking at the tear, Thorsson had to stop himself from kissing it away.

5.3

The meeting of the Thing Lawmen

From the Thing Motte hill, the leather clad nobles of Ath Cliath could see the palisade surrounding the enclosed city. Smoke streamed out of the bake houses and the blacksmiths' shacks, drifting up to the rolling cloudy skies above.

Formalities reverently concluded, Anlaf eyed them seriously, "I meet with you, to inform you, that war with High King Athelstan is imminent."

The crowd of men looked serious as they murmured to each other.

The Norwegians looked on with irritation evident on their faces.

Jarl Kalf's eyes narrowed, flexing his shoulders he winced in pain. Just below his cheekbone he sported a dark maroon contusion. But that was nothing compared to his back. Underneath his tunic, his back and hind quarters were covered in black and purple bruises.

Ketil stood next to Blacarri. He knew exactly where the street urchins were hiding in the long grass. He could feel their eyes on him. He probably knew some of the older lads, although they would have a hard job recognising him in his expensive leathers and tunic. His hand rested casually on his new sword pommel. He looked down at his own thick arms. Now eating plenty of meat, and the dedicated martial practice regime that Blacarri had set for him, he was quickly building his body bulk in pure hard muscle. As the long grass moved unnaturally, a smile twitched at the corners of his mouth.

King Anlaf spoke loudly, "The Clan Ivarr will regain Northumbria!"

A great cheer erupted from the men. Many of their fathers and uncles had lost land and riches in Northumbria, when the English had invaded.

His voice deepened, "I would ask that each jarl gathered here today pledge men, ships and silver, to the coming war."

A mutter of discontent went through the throng of men.

Blacarri eyed Anlaf with concern.

His long yellow hair plaited back from his handsome face, Ragnal stepped forward, loudly, "I Prince Ragnal Guthrithsson would address the Thing Lawmen."

Acknowledging his youngest brother, Anlaf inclined his head, "Speak Prince Ragnal."

"King Anlaf, the Clan Ivarr no longer has Jorvic gold and silver to fill our coffers. The only way for our jarls to raise enough silver for war, is to go on a summer raid. We need to attack churches in the hope of finding gold."

Anlaf chuckled, "What better way to pay for war against the English than by stealing English gold!"

Many of the men cheered.

Holding out his immense tanned arms, Ragnal chuckled deeply, "The thought of a summer raid is exciting for our men. The winter was long and tedious!"

"I Arnkell of Orkney would address the Thing Lawmen."

Anlaf nodded, "Speak Arnkell of Orkney."

"I pledge my knarr ship to the summer raids, that goes without saying. But I would know who will lead us?"

Answering without hesitation, Anlaf looked at Arnkell, "I cannot leave my realm at present. We are visited daily by ambassadors and my wife, the queen," a fleeting look of concern passed over his features, "is still weak after the birth of our son. I have already decided that my brother, King Black Arailt will lead the raids."

Kalf's eyes hardened.

"I, Barrick of Orkney would speak."

Anlaf nodded, "Speak Jarl Barrick."

"I pledge my ships and men." His voice rumbled, "My banner will ensure safe passage through the Northern Isles."

Anlaf brushed his blonde hair back from his tanned face, "I thank you Jarl Barrick."

"I do have a concern though. A lot of the coastal priories are robbed out."

Anlaf's blue eyes glinted, "What do you suggest, Jarl Barrick?"

Scarface eyed him, "We need to go inland and take slaves."

Thoughtfully, Anlaf considered this, "It is far more dangerous to attack inland."

"I Black Arailt, King of Man, Colonsay and Norse Gailgedhael would speak."

Scarface bowed his head in deference to his friend and he took a step back.

Anlaf smiled, "Speak King Black Arailt."

Grinning, his teeth white against his handsome tanned face, "Firstly brother, it will be an honour to lead the summer raid." Turning to Scarface, "You are right Jarl Barrick, raiding inland will be more profitable, especially if we go for slaves instead of the priories. However, we can only do this with a smaller raiding party. I would say a maximum of four ships and three of them would need to be knarrs to carry the shipment."

Looking back at him, Scarface nodded, "If we limit our raids to three days we can get in and out before any serious counter attacks."

Turning to his younger brother, Blacarri eyed him, "Ragnal, I propose that we take my best drakkar to escort the knarrs."

Nodding, Ragnal spoke strongly, "Agreed."

Quickly taking charge, Blacarri added, "We will take our raiding party to the North East coast of Britain. We will sail down the East coast." Pausing, he glanced at Scarface with steely eyes, "Under cover of the night we will slip into the Humber Estuary and traverse the River Ouse until we reach the village of Richalle."

Eyeing him steadily, Anlaf nodded, "The chieftain of the village of Richalle is of Danish descent. His family has long supported the leaders of the Clan Ivarr."

Blacarri grinned, "There we can safely moor our ships and use the village as a base. We will be able to borrow horses and mount quick successive slave raids on villages."

Ketil looked around at the nobles. Many of the men were nodding.

His pale blue eyes hardening, Blacarri eyed the Norwegians. Tersely, "Jarl Kalf, you do not own a ship."

Glaring back at him, feeling immensely embarrassed that he did not have the wealth to own a drakkar, his eyes narrowed with anger.

"You can join my ship, if you pledge allegiance to me."

Disconcerted, Kalf frowned. It would look cowardly if he refused to accept. Glowering, Kalf shrugged his bruised shoulders, "I pledge my allegiance!"

Pleased that his brother was taking the Norwegians with him and feeling excitement in the air, Anlaf shouted deeply, "Who else will join my brothers on this raid?"

Every man bellowed deeply in unison, "I will join you!"

Two days later two knarrs and two sleeker drakkars sailed away from Ath Cliath. His dark hair tied back from his face, Blacarri's grey eyes glinted as the wind filled the square sails.

Sat on a barrel looking ahead, Ketil glanced around himself at the crew. They all felt the excitement of a new voyage. Only the Norwegians looked sullen and brooding. Unease filled him as he watched them huddle together whispering. It was obvious they were not loyal to the clan.

Stood on the wooden quay watching them leave, Anlaf sighed. He felt deep disappointment that he was not going too.

Next to him, Maelmare looked very pale. She watched as Muldivana and her adopted daughter Audna, excitedly wave off Jarl Barrick. Suddenly feeling sharp pain in her abdomen she flinched. Sadness filled her as part of her cried inside.

She had always been slim but even her sister had commented on how thin she had become. Deep in her soul, she knew that something was very wrong. Turning to Anlaf, she sighed, "Take me back to our castle husband. I want us to spend time with our babies."

Part 6

The Slave Raid

6.1

The Market,
Cenheardsburgh, Northumbria,
11 July 937AD

The two heavy clay tankards that he had just picked up chinked against each other. Looking up at the hot midday sun, the thick set man mopped the sweat from his large round ruddy face with a rag from his apron pocket. His brown eyes travelled the ramshackle buildings that lined the road, serving the locals as shops and homes. Eyeing the bustling market opposite his beerhalla, he grinned. It was full of noisy traders and local folk. Most would wander over to his establishment as the day passed, to drink his ale. Not many had silver, most bartered for their ale. His serving girls had accepted today a bag of grain, a bucket, and several dozen eggs. One customer offered a small beaker of sea salt, another a bale of spun wool. Market traders were the best customers, offering items from their stalls. He had taken from them today a hand whittled antler comb, a few beeswax candles and several clay pots of jam. This was the best market day of the year and it was already looking profitable. Squinting against the sunlight, he was the first to notice the band of darkly impressive looking Norsemen, cantering their fine war horses up the busy high street. Lifting their smaller children up into their arms, most people quickly got out of their way. A scruffy haired farmer, pulling a huge hand cart full of purple carrots, was slower to move to the side of the road.

Impatiently controlling his horses, Ragnal eyed the yellow and orange ochre painted beerhalla with interest. A blonde wench was serving the tables. Even from this distance she looked comely. His blue eyes glinting, a smile played on his full lips, "I'm parched, let us get a drink at that beerhalla."

Blacarri nodded, "We will have a good view of other women from there."

Their red hair tied back from their tanned faces, Erlend and Arnkel grinned at each other as they sat astride their fidgety snorting horses.

As the farmer strained to pull his cart out of a huge rut in the road, Scarface turned to Ketil, even to him his voice sounded gruff and hoarse, "I'll have died of thirst before he shifts that barrow."

Chuckling, Ketil gazed around. The market was big and noisy. He could hear caged chickens clucking and dogs barking. A small pen of herdvyke sheep bleated loudly as they huddled together. The ewes grey shaggy fleeces contrasted sharply with their black fleeced lambs. The air stank of tanning leathers and burning charcoal. Inside a makeshift smithy, the blacksmith's hammer clanged against hot metal. Two young lads manned noisy bellows, keeping the fire in the pit fiercely hot. A myriad of coloured materials, silks and voiles hung from the fabric sellers stalls. All of the time, traders shouted out their wares, as people wandered around the stalls.

As soon as the farmer had pulled his cart out of the way, they flicked their bridles breaking their horses into a trot. The six steeds' hooves pounded the ground kicking up dry dust into the air.

Still eyeing them, the landlord noticed five of the Norsemen were tall muscular men. Dressed in battle leathers and fully armed they were obviously seasoned warriors. The sixth man was also dressed in battle leathers and armed with a sword. Although he was a brawny man, he was shorter and he did not have the heavy muscle definition of the others. As he rode at the back, the landlord decided he was more likely to be a servant. They were probably travelling to Viking Jorvic. He grinned. Of course they were no threat, travelling openly in broad daylight. His dark eyes glinted when they reined in their huge horses outside his beerhalla. They were all looking at Lady Blanche. Her back was to them, but you could not miss her curvy figure and cascading blonde hair. Busy at the noisy tables she did not notice them. Picking up empty tankards she went back into the beerhalla. Pleased with himself, he grinned. Deep lines crinkled around his dark eyes. He had decided today to ask her to serve the row of tables nearest to the dry mud road. Those tables had the best view of the market and gave passing young men the best view of her.

Dismounting from his favourite grey stallion, Blacarri looked around the beerhalla. Licking his dry lips he smiled.

Seated at the tables were the weathered families from the surrounding settlement and farms. They took a curious interest in the strangers. Most of the village men were dressed in dirty brown leathers and grey wool tunics. The plain, rosy faced women wore dull brown smock dresses and aprons. Most of them were married and had their hair up and hidden under cloth bonnets. They smiled happily as their filthy urchin children ran in packs around the rustic tables. Their laughter filled the air.

The landlord's dark eyes glinted as he confidently walked up to the strangers, "Welcome gentleman, welcome." Noticing the shorter man hanging back with the horses he looked at him closer. There was something in his mannerism that confused him, he had a certain confidence. Was he a servant? Gruffly, "For a piece of silver my son's will take your horses to my guarded paddock." His forced smile did not quite reach his eyes. "The price includes a watering and a feeding of fine hay." Two of his sandy haired sons jogged up to him. His youngest craned his neck, trying to appear as tall as his older brother.

Casting a glance at the two strong lads dressed in dirty brown breeches and jerkins, Blacarri watched the eldest gently stroke his stallion's silky white mane. His stallion nuzzled the lad. Sensing the lads were competent with horses, he threw a piece of silver at the landlord, ordering deeply, "Take good care of them lads."

Catching the silver, feeling the weight of it, he grinned at his sons, "Take the gentlemen's horses to the paddock. Feed and water them well."

Pulling the bridles over the steed's heads, they confidently took three horses each and led them away towards the stables.

Pushing the piece of silver into the well-worn pouch on his belt, the landlord watched the five tallest wide shouldered Norsemen strut over to his best table. The slightly shorter man hung back as they stood menacingly over several young men. Eyeing him sharply, he felt sure now that he must be a servant.

Intimidated and red faced the farm lads knew their place. They quickly gulped the remains of their beer. Doffing their caps to the Norsemen they left.

The landlord smiled, this time his smile reached his eyes. He was not sorry to see those lads head off. Watching the five tallest Norsemen sit down, he took the rag from his apron and quickly wiped it over the table. Brusquely, "Those scruffy farmer boys have been nursing warm beer for most of the morning. Good riddance is what I say!" His brown eyes glinted. Norsemen are well known as good drinkers and they usually paid with hacked silver. This looked like it was going to be a very profitable day, he grinned, very profitable indeed. "What can I get you gentlemen, our finest ale?"

Looking up at him, his pale grey eyes cool Blacarri nodded curtly, "Yes landlord."

His eyes glinted greedily, "A piece of silver will serve as payment."

Assessing the price, Blacarri nodded, reaching into his pocket he threw a small chuck of hacked silver at the landlord.

Ginning as he caught it, he bellowed, "Lady Blanche, five tankards of ale for the fine gentlemen!"

Motioning Ketil to sit down, Blacarri glanced sharply at the landlord, "Six ales landlord."

Moving his sword to the side, swinging his muscular leg over the bench, Ketil confidently eyed the landlord as he sat down.

Noticing the man's expensive battle leathers and fine sword, the landlord realised he must be a noble, probably the youngest son of a lord. Disconcerted, he bowed his head, "My apologies Milord."

His black eyebrows rising, Blacarri muttered to Ketil, "He thinks you are a lord. I am definitely treating you too well!"

A smile played on his lips, a little tongue in cheek, "I am most fortunate Lord."

Surprised amusement glinted in Blacarri's eyes. It was strange, since he started to train Ketil to fight, he thought of him more as a friend than an employee.

The landlord bellowed again, "Make that six ales for our esteemed customers!"

A refined shout came back from the halla, "I'm just getting the chickens off the spit. Please would you get them yourself Edwin?"

Scowling in the general direction of the halla Edwin muttered to himself, "I am busy with customers! That is why I asked you to get them!" Forcing a smile back on to his face, he turned back to the men, amiably, "Where are you travelling to gentlemen?"

Grudgingly, Blacarri eyed him, "Jorvic landlord. We have business there."

Edwin summed up the Norsemen immediately. Of the six warriors sat before him it was obvious the black haired man was their leader. The hackles on the back of his neck twitched. There was something about the dark haired man that made a man wary. It wasn't the fact that he had a well-developed muscular body, or that he carried high status weapons. This man knew how to handle himself in a fight and Edwin instinctively recognised it. He had the distinct feeling that the man did not want to discuss his business but he felt he needed to entertain the men until Lady Blanche could serve them. Jovially, "Ahh, Jorvic," he vigorously buffed their table with his well-worn cloth, "the gemstone of Northumbria. Our great city is only three leagues to the East. The English King Athelstan rules it now. Even so, Norsemen such as yourselves often travel through these parts on their way to Jorvic. Many Norse merchants have settled down in our great capital, trading in furs, amber and," he paused eyeing the men cautiously, "slaves." The dark haired man looked back at him coolly, his expression inscrutable. He decided to carry on regardless, "Most Northumbrians hate the English and their great King Athelstan!" He spat on the ground with vehemence. "That bastard was born to a shepherdess they say. He has almost pushed the people of Northumbria to the brink of starvation with his ever increasing taxes! We would rather have a good strong Viking Lord to protect us."

Impatient for his ale, Blacarri scowled, "Landlord, we are thirsty."

Edwin's dark eyes blinked rapidly as he wiped the sweat off his face with his rag. If he did not get them a drink soon he was sure that they would demand their silver back, then leave and go to one of the other beerhallas. "Of course you are gentlemen. Of course you are." He yelled desperately, "Blanche, get me six ales now!"

Unused to being shouted at, she raised her voice, "If you want them any quicker get them yourself!"

He could not contain himself. He yelled loudly at the door, "You strumpet!" He winced as he said it. He rarely, if ever, raised his voice to her.

She shouted back, "Don't be calling me a strumpet when I've got a red hot poker in my hand Edwin! Or there will be more than spit roast chicken on the menu tonight!"

The farmers at the next table started to chuckle.

His voice coarsely country, one of them laughed, "Spit roasted Edwin!"

Another man half stood and crudely waggled his backside at them, "Where will Lady Blanche stick her poker?"

The Norsemen burst out laughing. They were enjoying the midday sun and the entertainment.

Pretending to laugh along, forty year old Edwin's expression almost grimaced. As far as he was concerned English, Northumbrian or Norsemen, they were all the same, potential customers and potential enemies. He would of course prefer to have them as customers. His dark eyes glinting, he took the opportunity to assess the other men. The blonde haired man was as big as a bear but he seemed affable. Two of the others had red hair and short well-kept ginger beards. Their deep blue eyes sparkled vibrantly with amusement. They were obviously brothers. The shaved headed man was horribly scarred on his face, neck and arms. Edwin tried not to stare. He must have been cut up really bad in a fight. How had he survived the terrible injuries? The man's right eyebrow was cut through by the long snaking pink scar. Somehow the scar travelled miraculously around his eye and down to his chin.

Sensing the landlord's curious eyes on him, Scarface flexed his chest and clenched his large fists. He fixed him with a challenging stare.

As their laughter quietened, feeling extremely uncomfortable, Edwin quickly lowered his eyes. Each of the muscular Vikings carried beautifully decorated gilded long swords and shorter knives hung on their sword belts. The two red headed men also carried huge axes on their backs. These weapons and their well looked after horses shouted their wealth, nobility and their warrior status. He could see that each of these big men, all in their mid to late twenties, were battle hardened warriors and they could be real trouble for a landlord if they got out of hand. They were starting to look impatient again. Thankfully, Lady Blanche suddenly appeared at the doorway of the beerhalla.

Expertly carrying three large tankards of ale in each of her hands, her soft blonde hair dropped in wispy ringlets around her lovely elfin face and shoulders.

Moving deftly, for a big man, to the door of the beerhalla, Edwin looked sheepish, "Please accept my apology, Lady Blanche."

Lifting a blonde eyebrow, she threw an annoyed glance at him.

Edwin added quickly, "The gentlemen are paying with silver."

Taking a deep breath she marched past him, "That is no reason to call me a strumpet Edwin!"

Smiling at her temper, Edwin watched the six men as they watched her. She was worth waiting for. Lady Blanche stood out from most of the women in the settlement. At only seventeen years of age one lingering glance from her deep dark blue eyes was enough to make most men yearn to have her. Her long curling blonde hair hung to her tiny waist advertising her unmarried status. The chaste cut of her woad blue gown could not hide her magnificent bosom, it only added to her allure. Her tables were always full of parties of happily drunk young men, each vying respectfully for her attention. She was happy to laugh along with his customers and toy with them a little but she refused all serious advances.

Watching her, Ragnal felt his heart miss a beat. He could barely take his eyes off her.

Setting down each of their ales, she smiled at each of the men in turn. Suddenly feeling a strong hand around her midriff, she gasped as the big yellow haired Viking pulled her onto his lap.

The other men chuckled as they gulped their ale thirstily.

Uneasily, Edwin scowled. This could get out of hand. He walked a few paces towards them, loudly, "Milord."

Ignoring the landlord, Ragnal smiled at her, "Hello my pretty."

A little flustered, she pulled against his arms, "Please let me go my Lord."

The farmers at the table close by looked uncomfortable eyeing each other uneasily.

Surprised at her aristocratic tone, Ragnal hesitated, his voice deep, "You are a lady." It was not a question. A little mischief twinkled in his eyes, "I'll let you go if you tell me why you serve the tables."

Deciding it would be quicker to tell him, she looked into his eyes flushing with embarrassment, "Sir, my parents were nobles. When they died," she paused uncomfortably, "I could not manage my land."

He eyed her kindly, "You could marry."

Looking steadily at him, she shook her head, "There were suitors but they wanted my land to be signed over to them. I refused."

A smile twitched at his lips, "So, you work as a serving girl?"

She shrugged her shoulders, "Landlord Edwin was a good friend of my father. He always gives me food for my table, so I try to help out here when I can."

Growing more apprehensive, Edwin sucked in a deep breath. Striding over towards the leader, "Sir, my girls are good girls."

As the landlord approached the large weathered wooden table, Blacarri watched him with expressionless steely grey eyes.

Edwin did not notice, he was eyeing Ragnal pointedly with annoyance.

Ragnal continued to hold her, "You need a strong man to look after you, my Lady."

Eyeing him coolly, Blacarri ordered evenly, "Let the lady go Ragnal."

Hearing the authority in his brother's tone, he immediately obeyed him.

Suddenly free from the Viking's grip, she stood quickly and walked away to another table.

Edwin felt relief but he did not show it. Gruffly to their leader, "Can I get you more ale gentlemen, something to eat perhaps?"

Casually, Blacarri threw a piece of silver to him, "Six more of your best ales Landlord."

Greed glinted in his eyes as he deftly caught the shiny lump of metal in his grubby right hand.

Watching the landlord walk away, Blacarri subconsciously noted that the landlord was right handed. Under his filthy leather apron, he carried a partially concealed long dagger on the left hand side of his hip.

Leaning forward, Ragnal glanced at Blanche as she happily served her other tables. He lowered his voice, "I've seen three other beauties trading on the market stalls. They will all fetch a good price in Birka." Grinning, he picked up his ale. He was about to drink it down but a commotion further up the dry mud road near the market gates distracted him. His blue eyes sparkled with curiosity as a large curved horned ram suddenly bolted from a small paddock. Escaping his pen, the ram charged into the market spooking a horse and female rider. The jet black horse reared up and leapt into a full gallop straight towards them.

Jumping up, Ketil shouted, "Move!"

Turning to see what had caught Ketil and Ragnal's attention, Blacarri's eyebrows rose up in alarm. A young dark haired woman almost lost control, as her huge black stallion galloped towards them at break neck speed.

Mothers' shouted frantically for their husbands and older children to pick up their youngsters and move them to safety.

Scarface, Arnkel and Erland leapt up. Grabbing their ale they got out of the way quickly.

Seeing a toddler on his own, Scarface dropped his tankard to the floor, the last of its amber contents spilled onto the dirt. He picked up the flaxen haired boy gently cradling him in his arms.

Transfixed by the awesome power and speed of the horse hurtling towards him, Ragnal froze.

The horse and rider were almost upon them. His brother's body weight trapping him, unable to move the bench backwards to escape, Blacarri braced himself. Every muscle in his hard body tensed for impact. At the last possible moment the young woman managed to rein in her mount. He watched the powerful muscular animal rear up. The stallion's leathery nostrils flared as his front legs kicked out wildly in the air. Completely in control, she expertly turned the huge shimmering black horse, pivoting on his two hind legs away from their table. Using all of his brute strength, Blacarri shoved the heavy wooden table forward and stood up to watch her. The woman's long shining dark brown hair flew up catching the breeze. Her darkly beautiful eyes seemed to sparkle with excitement. He noticed her small button nose and high cheekbones, even the small scar at the base of her graceful neck. Her dark blue gown, made of rich velvet, announced her high status.

Shifting her body forward, her horse landed his front hooves steadily to the ground. Unruffled, Rafyn gently petted her snorting horse to quieten him.

Unaware that he was leaning further and further back on the bench, Ragnal suddenly tipped backwards. Falling heavily to the dusty ground, he could not save his large tankard of ale from spilling into his face.

A young woman anxiously ran up to Scarface and took her child from his arms.

Spluttering as he sat up, Ragnal shook his soaked blonde hair in disbelief.

Smiling, his grey eyes twinkling with amusement, Blacarri helped him to his feet, "Are you okay brother?"

Gruffly, "Do I look okay?"

Eyeing her thoughtfully, Blacarri purposely strode over to her.

Looking calmly down at him from the top of her fidgety horse, she held his gaze.

Casting a deliberately slow appreciative look over her body, he smiled, "You did well to stay on him. You sit astride your horse like a warrior."

Looking directly into his eyes, she raised her left eyebrow haughtily.

Confidently holding her dark gaze with his ice grey eyes, he lifted his chin. Softly, "A warrior horse rider always leaves his stirrups long so that he has greater balance. This enables him to wield a sword or spear at full gallop." Taking hold of her bridle in his strong tanned hands, he smiled casually.

Placing her left hand on the hilt of her right sword she looked steadily back at him. An unmistakable threat tinged her voice, "Take your hands off my bridle."

Surprised by her authoritative tone, Ketil watched his lord's reaction.

Blacarri hesitated as he looked over her again. Her dress was rich velvet. Her stallion looked sleek and very expensive. Curiously, she wore a long toughened black leather wrist guard on each wrist. He noticed they were each decorated with a man's face surrounded by leaves. She carried two unusually short swords on her waist belt and a small metal buckler shield hung from the right hand side of her belt. Raising a dark eyebrow sardonically, he smiled at her and half bowed. His pale eyes glinted with attraction, "My Lady," letting the dark leather reins slowly slip through his fingers, he took a step back, "please accept my sincere apology for handling your bridle," a playful smile hinted on his lips, "without a by your leave."

She nodded dismissively.

Watching her thoughtfully, Blacarri felt intrigued. There was something different about this unusually confident woman. Something prickled his interest. Irritatingly the young woman raised her chin up haughtily and ignored him.

Mischievously, Ketil grinned. Turning to Scarface, he whispered, "My Lord Blacarri is known at the court of Ath Cliath as a charmer of the ladies." Pulling a comical expression, "He does not appear to be having the same success in this little burgh."

His brown eyes twinkling, Scarface softly chuckled, "Perhaps the ladies here are more discerning."

Ketil chuckled.

Turning to the blonde man, Rafyn smiled prettily. Her voice soft, almost soothing, "I apologise Sir. My horse bolted. I will replace your spilt ale as soon as my father gets here."

Over hearing the commotion, Edwin rushed up to them. Red faced and breathless, he looked at Blacarri not Ragnal,

"Lady Rafyn is good for the ale Viking." He gasped in a deep breath, "Her father is lord here and his brewery makes the best ale in these parts. He's promised me ten barrels today." Beads of glistening perspiration began appearing on his forehead. He wanted no trouble between the Norsemen and his lord's daughter, "While you wait I will get you each a tankard of ale," exuberantly, "on the house!" Not waiting for a reply, he looked up at Rafyn, "Milady, how far away is your father?"

Steadily, "He is driving the wagon and four from the brewery. He will be here soon." She confidently ignored the Vikings, "Father was hoping we could stay in your lodgings tonight Edwin, if you have room? My sister-in-laws' are staying in the fortress keep with their bairns." She rolled her eyes, "It will be so noisy. We only need two rooms, one room for myself and one for the men."

Looking up at her, "I've saved you and the men the two rooms above the stables. There's plenty of room in the stalls for your horses." He half bowed, "Milady, pray make your way to the stables, my sons will take care of Storm."

"Thank you Edwin." Her bridle resting delicately in her right hand, she gracefully turned the stallion. Flicking her reins, she cantered off towards the stables.

Feeling glad to get her away from the big men, Edwin frowned. There was something in the dark haired leader's eye that he did not like the look of. As he strode off to help Blanche pour the ale, he muttered to himself, "I will have to warn Lord Cenheard."

Ragnal noticed the look in his brother's steely grey eyes as well. He smiled, "You like her?" It was more a statement than a question.

Looking at him sharply, Blacarri picked up the heavy long wooden bench with one powerful muscular arm.

They all sat back down.

A smile twitched at Blacarri's lips, "She is lovely. There is something different about her. She has status."

Arnkel looked at him, "Did you notice her dress? It is made

of the most expensive velvet."

Ketil's eyes glinted, "Her horse must have been bred from the finest stock."

Inclining his head, Blacarri agreed, "Her weapons are unusual. They are made of good quality steel."

Thoughtfully, Erland glanced at him, "Her weapons must be for show of course, a mark of her rank, perhaps a custom here?"

Carrying six more tankards of ale to the table, Blanche overheard him. As she set a tankard down in front of him, she smiled, "Oh, her weapons are not for show my Lord. I've seen her fight."

Ragnal interrupted her, disdainfully stating dryly, "Her swords looked like toothpicks to me."

Shrugging her shoulders, she walked off to the next table muttering, "Men can be so arrogant."

Blacarri chuckled at Ragnal's joke.

Scarface's voice rumbled deeply, "If I were not happily married, I wouldn't mind a tumble with little Lady Rafyn."

Scowling, Blacarri deliberately kept his voice low and deep, "She is mine."

Lifting his eyebrows in surprise, Ketil eyed him, and then he flicked his gaze to Scarface to see his reaction.

Amused, Scarface grinned.

Ragnal, Arnkell and Erland looked at Blacarri in stunned silence, then laughter bubbled up from their core.

Surprised by his desire to possess the dark eyed irritating lady, Blacarri chuckled too. Shrugging his shoulders he picked up his ale.

Seeing Edwin hovering by the halla doors gulping a beer, Blacarri beckoned him over.

Looking uncomfortable, Edwin forced a smile, "What can I get you fine gentlemen, chicken or freshly baked salt bread?"

"Sit down landlord. Tell me about the woman."

"Lady Blanche?" He hesitated looking a little puzzled, "Her

father was a gentleman landowner, a great grandson of some king."

Ragnal's deep blue eyes glinted as he looked up interested.

"He was a good friend of mine. He died a few years ago leaving her and her sister orphaned. Err, she is a good girl, not a whore if that is what you want. But I do know a woman, not pretty but very accommodating, if you know what I mean? Breasts like a couple of goose feather pillows." He pursed his lips into a kiss and cupped his hands to his chest to accentuate his meaning.

Even Ketil chuckled.

"Not her." Blacarri interrupted impatiently, "Tell me about Lady Rafyn. What is her background?" Encouragingly, "She is obviously a woman of status."

Shifting uncomfortably, he gulped the dregs of his beer, "Lady Rafyn? Err' what do you want to know?" He offered, "Her father is Lord Cenheard, he is an earl."

"I see. Is she betrothed?"

He smiled, slowly understanding. More cheerily, "Ah, you are looking for a young wife, Milord?"

"I may be so minded if the right woman was available." Amenably, "She intrigues me, is she available?"

"I am very sure that she is not, as yet, betrothed." He added quickly, "Even though there has been much interest in her from the local gentry."

"Of course there has, she is lovely."

"Her father dotes on her and has promised her that he will only agree to a love match."

Surprised, "So, she will choose her own husband?"

"Yes Milord. I could perhaps arrange a meeting for you?"

The muscle in his jaw flickered, slowly, "What is her father's background?"

Feeling far more comfortable now, Edwin grinned, "Jarl Cenheard is a good man. He has done much good for our settlement. Families from local villages now travel to our market, to trade and to socialise."

"I noticed the market is fine, very fine indeed."

"Our burgh grows bigger each year. More and more permanent shops are being built around the market square. There are now four beer halls, three smithies and a potter. We have a baker of bread, a tanner and a wheel maker."

"Today is market day?"

"Yes Milord. On special market days, such as this one, traders travel here to sell their wares."

Smiling, Blanche walked over carrying six ales and placed them on the table.

Looking up at her Ragnal smiled. His teeth looked white against his handsome tanned face.

Gazing at him, she smiled prettily. He was tall and broad shouldered, his eyes seemed kind. Yes, she thought to herself, very handsome.

Not as used to strong ale, Ketil placed his tankard in front of the landlord.

Nodding cheerfully to Ketil, Edwin continued to chat as he drank with the gentlemen, "Lord Cenheard's ancestors have lived here for many generations. He can directly trace his ancestors from the Celtic Kings of Deira."

"He is royalty?"

"Well," Edwin conceded, "his blood is a bit diluted now." His dark eyes twinkled as a memory returned, "In point of fact, his most famous ancestor was Aelle, a legendary King of Deira."

Raising an eyebrow, Blacarri blinked, "I have heard of him." Looking at Ragnal pointedly, it was their great grandfather who had killed King Aelle many years ago.

Lifting his tankard, Edwin did not notice, "Lord Cenheard is a skilled leader who knows how to work the land. He breeds and trades the best horses. He even mastered the art of making steel."

"I noticed Lady Rafyn's weapons are very fine quality."

Nodding, Edwin gushed as the ale loosened his tongue, "Lord Cenheard built our fine fortress."

Blacarri smiled as he let him talk.

"It is very imposing and will be a place of refuge in times of danger. It already has a long house, just like the ones at Jorvic. The long house is now called the Judgment Halla and Lord Cenheard holds court there. The Archbishop of Jorvic, Wulfstan himself, visited here two years ago and left a monk to deliver the Christian faith. Lady Rafyn commissioned the building of the church and a fine house for the monk."

He interrupted with interest, "Is Lady Rafyn a Christian?"

"Oh no Milord, Lady Rafyn is of the old Celtic faith. Her father brought up his children to tolerate all religions."

Carefully, "Is his allegiance to the English or Norse?"

Edwin smiled, "He once made the long and perilous journey to Jorvic when he was twenty five years old. As earl, he was required to pledge his allegiance to the Viking King Sihtric."

His eyebrows rose up in surprise at the mention of his former uncle. He nodded encouragingly, "Did he pledge his allegiance?"

Edwin prattled, "Of course he did. King Sihtric got mightily drunk on Lord Cenheard's present of thirty barrels of ale. His ale is excellent and good King Sihtric, who appreciated fine ale, ordered a yearly shipment."

His pale grey eyes glinted.

"The English King Athelstan and the gentry of Jorvic, have continued to place orders for Cenheard's ale and he has become a man of means. Lord Cenheard owns most of the land in these here parts. He has over two hundred head of horse and several hundred hides of cattle and sheep."

"He is a very wealthy man indeed. Is Lady Rafyn heiress to any of this fortune?"

"No Milord." Seeing the lord's disappointed expression, he continued rapidly, "But as I said, her father dotes on her and her mother is a fine breeder of boys. You will be pleased to hear, if you are looking for a wife with a good pedigree, Lady Rafyn's mother gave birth to eight healthy sons."

Shaking his head, Blacarri pretended to be disappointed, "With eight sons there will be little chance of a dowry?"

Edwin hurriedly added, "It's well known in these parts that she doesn't need her father's fortune. Her grandfather gave her presents of an estate, including land and horses. She is an earl in her own right and a woman of means. She is wealthy enough to refuse several prestigious offers of marriage."

His eyebrows rose up, genuinely impressed, "Indeed, very interesting. Please continue, tell me a little more about her mother's background."

"Her mother is called Cyngytha. She is a woman of great standing here." Edwin added mysteriously, "She has the knowledge of the herbs."

"A culdee?"

"Yes Milord, she is a healer and a midwife."

6.2

Cenheard took his time driving his brightly painted wagon pulled by four huge dark draft horses. The horse's padded leather collar harnesses, studded with metal horse brasses, creaked as they trundled along. In the wagon seven huge barrels of ale were stacked on their sides, and on top them six more sat firmly in the grooves where the barrels met below.

Riding their mounts next to him, his sons and grandson Samwulf, slowly trotted towards the church.

Feeling the warm sun on his tanned face, Cenheard looked up to the heavens. He smiled. There was not a cloud to be seen in the deep blue sky. Nothing escaped his proud dark gaze. The lovely lush and fertile valley seemed to shine the colour of green gemstones in the glimmering sunlight. Down the dirt track, past the wide meandering silvery river, he gently encouraged his farm horses to turn. His strong tanned hands gripped the lengthy reins. Flicking them, he made clicking noises in his mouth. The huge horses slowly turned and pulled their heavy load up the road. Approaching the elaborately carved wooden church, Cenheard's dark eyes sparkled with amusement. As his wagon and four horses slowly meandered along, he watched brother Ordberht struggle to mount his loudly winging donkey. He smiled amiably, "Good morrow brother."

Just managing to climb on to the donkey's back, Ordberht hung on nervously as the animal kicked out one of his back legs, "Lucifer! You evil beast!"

Honking loudly, Lucifer shook his matted dark grey head irritably.

Looking towards his smirking sons, Cenheard grinned. It always amused him that the normally placid monk always resorted to shouting insults at his donkey, "Are you well Brother? Your donkey is giving trouble again I see."

Hanging on to the two thin reins, Ordberht lifted his eyebrows to the heavens dramatically, "He was sent to me by the devil himself to torment me!"

Chuckling, looking over the elaborately carved gargoyles on the church as he slowly passed by, "Your church looks magnificent Brother. I hear that you now have a congregation of ten."

His wide dark nostrils flaring, Lucifer suddenly bucked and spun round in a tight circle, honking ear splittingly loud.

Looking concerned, Ordberht tried to keep his balance. Shouting hopefully above the donkey's din, "I always have room for more souls, Lord Cenheard. You are always welcome." As Lucifer spun around again, his pale monk's habit rose up above his milk white knees, harshly, "Lucifer! You are the spawn of Beelzebub!"

An incensed look of madness appeared in the donkey's dark eyes. Suddenly, Lucifer charged off at full speed towards the market.

Squealing high pitched, "Ahhhhh!" Brother Ordberht hung on for dear life as he bounced rapidly and painfully on Lucifer's back.

Realising that his mouth had dropped open in astonishment at the spectacle, Cenheard looked at his boys. They all had the same dumbfounded look. A chuckle bubbled up from his core.

Little dimples appeared in Badwulf's cheeks as he burst out laughing.

Samwulf's handsome face lit up with amusement, his chuckle sounded just like his grandfather's.

Seeing Cenheard's wagon drawing in, pulled by the four huge farm horses, Edwin immediately got up from the table, "Excuse me gentlemen, my ale has arrived." Jogging over to the side of the halla, he felt his breath catch in his throat.

Smiling at Edwin's red face, Cenheard reined in his horses, "Good morrow Edwin."

Looking up at him, placing his large hand on his chest, Edwin puffed as he stopped to catch his breath, "Good morrow Lord Cenheard, my thanks for the ale."

"I have an extra three extra barrels, usual price, do you want them?"

Cheerfully his eyes lit up, "I do Milord. This is the busiest market day that I have ever known. My sons are occupied at the paddock." He rubbed his back, a little melodramatically.

His dark eyes twinkled. He knew that Edwin needed his help, "I will move the wagon to the hatch?"

Cheerfully, "I will be in the cellar." He quickly sprinted off before Lord Cenheard changed his mind.

Not noticing the six Vikings watching him and his sons, Cenheard flicked his long bridles. The four horses immediately responded to him, as he skilfully steered the heavy wagon to the left hand side of the beer halla.

Watching the dark haired Celts dismount from their fine horses, Blacarri noted every detail of their unusual height and obvious strength.

It took a huge amount of power and skill to control the four draft horses, so that they moved the wagon right outside the cellar entrance.

Striding confidently up to the lead draft horse, Samwulf held the bridle close to the mouth bit and gently patted the horse's thick neck. The horse nudged him, inquisitively sniffing for carrots.

Extremely strong and agile, Cenheard still felt in his prime. Jumping down from the wagon, he lifted an incredibly heavy full barrel of beer on to the ground. His huge arm muscles bulging, he rolled the barrel to the hatch.

Edwin heaved up a long plank of wood, carefully shaped so that it bridged the hatch opening to the cellar floor at a gentle angle. Happy with its position, he lifted the second plank into place.

Peering into the dark cellar, Cenheard called down loudly, "Are you ready Edwin?"

He braced himself, "Ready."

Heaving the barrel on to the planks, Cenheard shouted deeply, "In coming!" Letting go, he watched the barrel roll down to the straw covered floor.

Down in the cellar, Edwin skilfully caught the barrel and using the barrel's own moving weight, he rolled it to the side wall.

His eyes glinting, Blacarri watched as each one of Cenheard's sons lifted down a barrel from the wagon and rolled it to the hatch. The barrels were quickly dispatched to the cellar.

Cenheard smiled at Samwulf, "Would you take the horses and wagon to the stables for me lad. I'm parched."

His wide smile lit up his handsome face, "Course I will Pap."

Ragnal spoke quietly, as the youngest Celtic man climbed up onto the wagon and drove the team of horses off towards the landlord's stables, gruffly, "She is well protected. Some women are more trouble than they are worth."

As Edwin appeared again from the beerhalla, carrying three tankards of ale in each hand, Cenheard chuckled, he was thirsty.

Flicking his ice grey eyes to his brother, Blacarri frowned. He knew Ragnal was right.

"We are already undermanned and if one of us is killed it will seriously jeopardise the shipment to Sweden." Ragnal leaned forward, "You know I love a good fight, especially over a pretty wench, but these are serious times brother. The Clan needs gold and silver for the coming war."

Thoughtfully he stretched his arms, "You are right Ragnal. I cannot afford to fail this trip, there is too much at stake."

Carrying a tankard of ale, Rafyn carefully walked between the tables avoiding the children careering about. Her long dark hair glimmered in the sunshine.

Seeing her walking towards him, Blacarri's breath caught in

his throat and his eyes darkened a deeper shade of ice grey. Watching her through his thick dark lashes, he noticed that she carried herself proudly. Her dark blue velvet dress accentuated the curve of her full breasts and slender hips. Her wide black leather belt, fastened to her small waist, held two short swords. Smaller than he had first thought, she looked almost vulnerable as she made her way over to the six Vikings.

Reaching the old weathered wooden table, she carefully placed the large tankard of ale onto the table in front of Ragnal, "Your ale, Sir."

Blacarri watched her. Suddenly her eyes flickered to him. Holding her gaze, he felt his heart beat quicken. Enjoying the feeling of attraction flowing through his body a faint smile played on his full lips.

Feeling her own breath catch in her throat, her long dark eyelashes fluttered. Quickly lowering her eyes she turned away.

Catching her small wrist gently in his strong large tanned hand, he smiled.

She noticed the roguish twinkle in his eyes.

Charmingly, "Has anyone ever told you what beautiful eyes you have?"

Amused, Ketil looked up at them barely masking his smile.

Surprised at his open compliment, her dark brown eyes widened, her long black eye lashes fluttered as she felt her heart rate quicken.

A slow smile played across Blacarri's sensuous full mouth.

Annoyed at her body's reaction to this man, she spoke deliberately slowly, as if he was a fool, "Yes they have. Now let me go."

Chuckling, Ketil turned to see Blacarri's reaction.

Watching her, Blacarri felt his own mouth twitch with amusement. For a moment there, he thought he had seen a glimmer of interest in her eyes. He was sure he sensed mutual attraction.

Ragnal and Scarface smiled at each other across the table.

Expecting trouble from the lady's father and brothers, they kept a careful eye on the Celts.

Cenheard and his boys stood in the shade of the huge oak beamed halla. Drinking cold ale they looked relaxed. Not one of them looked in the slightest bit concerned that a stranger had taken hold of her hand. In fact, if anything, they were amused by it.

His grip still tight around her wrist, he looked up at her smiling.

Placing her free hand on the hilt of her sword she eyed him back. There was a tinge of a warning in her voice, "Let me go."

Amused by the definite threat in her voice and angry sparkle in her eyes, he smiled. She was not making this easy for him, "My Lady, may I buy you a cool drink on this lovely hot summers day?"

Haughtily, "No you may not. Let me go."

His eyebrows rising in surprise for a moment, he looked disconcerted. A handsome man of means, he was not used to rejection. Ignoring the feeling of discouragement, he looked at her appealingly, "My Lady, I would very much like to get to know you better."

"Sir, a gentleman would have asked for a formal introduction prior to holding my hand." she held his gaze, "Now let me go."

"My Lady may I assure you that I am a gentleman and...."

She interrupted disdainfully, "No you may not assure me but you may let me go!"

Disappointed, he frowned as he gently released her and watched her turn away. As she walked back to the protection of her father and brothers, he whispered softly to himself, "I will see you later, my Lady" Making up his mind, he thoughtfully flicked his eyes to Ketil. Glancing quickly towards Lady Rafyn, he signalled silently for him to follow her.

Grabbing his dull brown hooded cape without a word, Ketil got up and left the table.

His voice low and rumbling, Scarface mimicked, "Has anyone ever told you what beautiful eyes you have?" He grinned cheekily, "I think your losing your touch Arri."

Raising a sardonic eyebrow, he grinned, "Tonight we will leave Ketil to guard the camp while we capture the specials." Confidently, "I am going for her."

6.3

Walking around the canopy covered market stalls with Samwulf and her father, Rafyn stopped to marvel at the beautiful coloured silks and voiles. Trailing her fingers over the cool
glossy materials, she smiled as she lifted sheer blue voiles and
matched them to a blue silk. Filled with pottery stalls and
tanners, the market bustled with noise and colour. Men and
women on the fruit and vegetable stalls shouted out, "Turnips
and strawberries!" Other stalls sold live chickens that clucked
and pecked at the ground all day. In contrast, hooded majestic hawks and falcons perched silently haughty on their posts.
The fishmonger wore a blood stained apron over his well worn
breaches and jerkin. He yelled deeply as he gutted a carp for
a woman, "Fresh bream and eels! Get your fresh carp here!"
Fur stalls laden with colourful pelts from otters, red fox and
deer filled the air with musky smells. Wandering blacksmiths
had set up ramshackle temporary smithies. The acrid smell
of burning coals filled the air. The sound of their hammers
clanging on metal, and noisy young apprentices working the
bellows, was deafening. Wandering to the next stall, she held
up amber jewellery. to the light. As she gazed at them, fascinated by the myriad of insects frozen in them, she had no idea
that she was being followed.

Just another stranger at the market, Ketil mingled in the
crowd stopping at stalls pretending to look at the wares.

At the next stall she admired the quality of delicately carved
hair combs. She did not see the drably cloaked man following
her, pretending to look at the amber jewellery.

The local miller and his pretty plump wife's stall smelt

wonderful. She had baked herb breads and sweetmeats. Smiling happily, she offered small tasters to potential customers.

His dark eyes twinkling, Cenheard happily obliged. Taking his time tasting most of her wares, he bought a hefty chicken pasty. Then he decided he needed two large venison pies and some flat bread. He paid with a piece of silver.

The miller grinned as he packed a sturdy wicker basket full of the lord's goods.

Chuckling, Cenheard eyed Rafyn, "Don't tell your mother. She never lets me buy food."

Raising her eyebrows to Samwulf, she giggled, "I wonder why Da?"

"Here Samwulf, hold these for me."

Samwulf's handsome face lit up with a good natured smile as he felt the weight of the basket.

Enjoying himself, Cenheard moved on to the next stall tasting honey and jams before purchasing a selection. The small clay pots all went into the basket.

Samwulf's eyes widened as the basket got heavier and heavier.

Eventually taking the heavy basket off Samwulf, Cenheard grinned as they carried on.

Giving brother Ordberht's noisy cantankerous donkey a wide birth, thankfully the beast was tied with coarse rope to the sturdy wood pen, they wandered over to a small crowd of people. The Christian monk stood on a springy long plank of wood bridged across two tall mead barrels.

Shouting out at the top of his voice, his face contorted with religious zeal, Ordberht walked precariously across the thin beam trying to keep his balance, "The demons of Hell and Damnation will take those of you that do not believe in the one true God!"

Surprised at the usually placid monk's tone, Rafyn eyed Samwulf with alarm, "Whatever has come over Brother Ordberht."

Humour filled Samwulf's twinkling brown eyes as he

grinned at the spectacle.

Walking towards him, she called demurely, "Good afternoon Brother Ordberht, I hope that this day finds you well?"

Pleased to see her, Ordberht smiled, his voice abruptly calm, "Thanks be to our merciful Lord, I keep robustly healthy Lady Rafyn." Seeing a few of the townsfolk stop to listen, he suddenly re-launched into his screeching tirade, his face contorted again, "You may know him as Beelzebub!"

Warily, she eyed him sideways as she passed him.

He wailed, "You may call him Lucifer!"

His dark eyes twinkling, Cenheard comically smirked as brother Ordberht bounced up into the air.

"It matters not his name! The horned Devil will take your souls!" He laboured the word scarily, "Screaming!" He nodded dramatically, "Burning!" He vividly pointed down to the earth, "To the very depths of hell, if you do not believe in the one true God!"

Samwulf chuckled as he stopped to watch. The portly monk's weight almost threatened to snap the yielding length of wood clean in two. He sprang high and low, then high and low, as he walked ever more confidently along the plank, screeching out his tirade.

Following Lady Rafyn as she walked away with her father, Ketil ignored the monk.

Spotting Samwulf in the ever increasing crowd, Brother Ordberht strode bouncing precariously to the centre of the springing bridge. Speaking calmly, even though with each step he bounced higher up into the air, "Ahh Samwulf, I am glad to see your new interest in God and my teachings." He was completely unaware that his light summer grey habit floated up behind him exposing his white bare rear. His face suddenly grimacing with exertion, he shouted, "The burning fires of hell will lick your bones!" Holding his hands up to the summer heavens as, he screamed, "Repent, repent, repent!"

Looking around realising that Samwulf tarried behind, Rafyn hurried back to get him.

Seeing her turn back, Ketil bent his head forward so that the large hood of his dull cape covered his face. Turning naturally, he pretended to look at the fine cloth.

Gawping at the monk, Samwulf crossed his arms across his stomach chuckling.

Brother Ordberht bounced high again as he screeched, "Let Jesus save your souls!" He descended sharply amidst his floating grey apparel.

Trying to avert her eyes from the priest's bare white posterior, Rafyn gasped out loudly, "May God protect us!"

Pointing theatrically to the heavens above, Brother Ordberht yelled as the plank ascended high, then low, "Yes Lady Rafyn! May the one true God protect us all!"

Dramatically crossing himself, Samwulf managed to sputter through uncontrollable chuckling, "Amen!"

Seeing Lady Rafyn dragging off her nephew, Brother Ordberht called hopefully as he bounced high again, "Samwulf, see you at church!" Unfortunately at that moment the plank finally snapped loudly in two, throwing him inelegantly to the floor in a cloud of dust. As he landed in an inauspicious heap on the ground, Ordberht coughed into the dust.

The crowd clapped enthusiastically.

Truly pleased with himself, he grinned, "That was my best sermon yet."

Beads of perspiration glistened on his brow as the day reached its hottest. Cenheard's nose twitched, "Mmm, hog roast." Turning, he saw a huge golden porker turning on a spit over a burning fire. Every so often fat dropped from the pig onto the logs, they caught light noisily, spattering flames into the air. Hurrying over to the cook, his mouth watered, "Will you take one of my jams to fill this loaf with meat and apple sauce?"

As he turned the spit with strong muscular arms, tendrils of fire licked at the meat, eyeing the lord's wares, "I would rather have a pot of honey Lord Cenheard."

Grinning, Cenheard passed a pot of honey to him, "We have

an accord."

Ripping open the loaf, the cook obligingly cleaved off huge chunks of steaming hot meat then loaded the loaf with apple sauce, "Here's a bit more roast for you Milord."

His mouth watering, Cenheard took a huge heavenly bite.

Walking as fast as she could through the market stalls, Blanche barely noticed brother Ordberht getting to his feet. She needed to speak to Lady Rafyn privately.

Grateful of the shade from a canopy, Rafyn stopped to look at another stall. Surprised she smiled. Coluim had set himself up a makeshift stall, "Good morrow Coluim." Impressed with his ingenuity, she complimented, "Well done. I like your stall." She looked at his shop full of decorated leather wrist guards and leather strap belts. They were all excellent quality. Only one belt had a buckle though. She realised that it was just for show, so customers could see what the belt would look like with their own belt buckle. He would never be able to afford to put a buckle on each belt.

His longbow and quiver of arrows sat in an unused corner of his ramshackle shop. Looking at her with his kind blue eyes, he smiled, "Good morrow Milady, how are those cuffs I made you holding up?"

Looking down at her wrists, she smiled at the green man pattern on her wrist guards, "These are the most comfortable that you have made me yet."

Rubbing his stained brown dirty nailed fingers through his short dark hair, "They still look good."

Picking up a long wrist guard, she checked it for quality, "I like this one with the beautiful fish. The scales and fins look so life like." The hard leather cuff had that new musty leather smell. "What will you take for two of them?"

"Milady, I only have the one. This pattern takes me a while to make because I use different tanning methods to get the swimming effect."

"I understand. Samwulf, what do you think to the pattern?"

His dark eyes glinted with concentration as he looked at the fish, "The fins and tail look like they could really move."

"If I make another one, to make a pair, each fish will be slightly different Milady. You will not see another pair like them. I will need to make them especially for you because your wrists are so small."

Realising he was trying to drive up the price, she eyed him shrewdly, "They are not for me. This is the right size. What will you take for them Coluim?"

He grinned, "I will take a barrel of your father's ale."

Her eyebrows rose up, "A whole barrel!"

His smile deepened cheekily. Waiting for her to start the bartering, he hoped to get a half barrel of ale at best.

Looking at the pattern thoughtfully, she nodded, "We have an accord."

He looked surprised that she agreed so quickly, "Really."

"Yes, they will be beautiful." Passing him the wrist cuff, she smiled.

He looked delighted, "I will bring them to you when they are ready."

"Thank you Coluim, good day." Turning to her father as he approached with a half-eaten loaf of hog meat, she giggled.

He strode up to them, "This is so good."

A little breathless, Blanche caught up with them, "Lady Rafyn, may I speak with you." Curtseying, she smiled, "Lord Cenheard, Samwulf."

Smiling at her, Cenheard bowed his head, "I hope this day finds you well Lady Blanche."

Pleased that Lord Cenheard never failed to show her the respect befitting a high-born lady, she smiled happily, "I am very well, thank you my Lord."

"I am pleased to hear it. Now please excuse me, I will leave you with my daughter. I am going to check on the horses. Samwulf, are you coming with me?"

Pinching a piece of the steaming hot hog meat from his grandfather's loaf, Samwulf grinned, "Yes Pap."

Watching them walk off, amused at how alike they walked

and looked, Rafyn smiled, "Lady Blanche, you wished to speak to me."

Blanche took Rafyn's arm and led her away past the archer's stall set up with long and short bows. Many feather tipped arrows sat in their leather quivers all lined up in rows, "My sister Emma, is being courted by Earl Orm's son, the noble Gamel Braham."

A short distance behind them, Ketil noted the name and listened as he looked at a tanner's wears.

Stood at his high bench, Coluim used a hammer and dowel to punch patterns on to a piece of leather that would later be made into wrist guards. He looked up hopefully. Underneath the well worn cloak the warrior looked expensively dressed, "Are you interested in the cuffs?"

Noticing the skilful patterns of animals and mythical creatures on the wrist guards, Ketil's eyes glinted as he picked up a pair of cuffs decorated with wyverns. The wyvern's wings looked as if they would fly, "I'm just looking." Thin leather strap laces criss-crossed through dowel punched holes. He took off his old cuffs and tried on the wyvern cuffs, pulling the laces to fasten the straps. A smile twitched at his lips. He really liked the pattern and they fitted him like they were made for him.

Surprised, Rafyn looked at Blanche, "I see."

"Seventeen is a good age to marry don't you think?" Not waiting for a reply, "I believe that you know Lord Gamel well. I understand that it was Earl Orm's wish that you become betrothed to Lord Gamel, yet you refused him."

Softly, "Earl Orm and his son are good friends of our family. It was natural that a betrothal be considered by our fathers."

"But you refused?"

"Yes I did."

"May I ask why?"

"Of course, it is no secret. My father has given me leave to choose my husband."

"You did not choose Gamel?"

"No I did not."

She persisted, "Why?"

Thoughtfully, "Although I have great respect and friendship for Lord Gamel, I do not love him as a woman should love a husband. I have known Gamel all my life and he feels more like one of my brothers."

"There was no other reason?"

Honestly, "No Lady Blanche, Gamel is a good man and will make a good husband to Emma."

Looking relieved, Blanche sighed, "Thank you Lady Rafyn. May I question you further?"

She smiled, "Of course."

"Do you know much of Lord Gamel's family history?"

"Earl Orm is a noble of Danish decent. He married the only daughter of the Celtic chieftain of Folesfight. I heard it was a love match"

"Go on."

"Gamel's sister, Aldgytha, is young. She is a kind girl." Smiling, "Emma has done well. Earl Orm owns a massive portion of Northumbria, including holdings in Jorvic. My father thinks he is a shrewd man."

Blanche looked at her blankly, "Shrewd?"

Elaborating, "In this dangerous world of politics, with the Norse Kings exiled and the English Christian High King in power, it is a wonder that a Norse Earl like Earl Orm has managed to survive."

Ketil's eyes glimmered beneath his hood. Noticing the two women were moving further away, he eyed the tanner. He liked the new pair of cuffs but he did not have time to barter. Offering a piece of hacked silver from his pouch he frowned, he knew he was paying too much, brusquely, "Will you take this silver for these two cuffs?"

Gruffly, "Let me see it." Holding the silver in his hand, Coluim grinned as he felt the weight, "Yes Milord."

Tucking his old cuffs into his cloak, Ketil quickly caught up with the women by the ribbon stall.

The sun was hot, the ladies moved under the shade of the next canopy.

The ribbon stall vendor was a pretty young woman with long brown hair. She busied herself folding voiles and winding up reams of ribbon.

Shrugging her petite shoulders, Blanche sighed, "Lord Gamel has asked Emma to church and requested that she become Christian too. Emma will be baptised before her wedding."

Smiling serenely, Rafyn shrugged, "Everyone has a right to choose their faith."

"That is true. What of Lord Gamel's personal holdings?"

"Gamel is the eldest and only son that lived. He will inherit his father's estate. His sister will receive a goodly dowry share, which will include land I dare say."

"And what of his interests?"

Looking thoughtful she smiled, "He has inherited his mother's Celtic love of horses."

Blanche nodded, "I am told that he could sit a horse before he could walk."

"I have traded horses with him for breeding. He is a brilliant horseman."

"Better than you?"

Tilting her head to one side, thoughtfully, "He seems to have an instinct for matching mares to stallions, breeding the best foals for speed and fighting."

Shaking her head, Blanche frowned, "I have never understood that sport. Horse fighting is barbaric!"

"I agree. I hate it too. But the Norsemen love it so there is money to be made. Gamel is already rich from trading. Even without his father's estate, he is a rich man."

"He is rich indeed. Lord Gamel says he wants to help me to start managing my land again. He will give me a dozen of his serfs. The old empty crofts on my land are a bit dilapidated but their families can make them good. I will be able to farm and have an income. I may even marry."

Rafyn smiled.

Smiling back at her, Blanche's eyes glistened with excitement, "Did you know that Earl Orm is a member of the Witan? Only yesterday Gamel was invited to the Witenagemot for a meeting of the council. Archbishop Wulfstan himself presided."

Lifting his head, Ketil stepped closer.

"Really, why was Gamel invited?"

"You'll never believe it." Blanche gushed, "Gamel is being groomed to join the Witan."

Genuinely surprised, "The Witan is the highest council in the land. A king cannot be crowned without their approval. This is a great honour. Did he tell you anything else?"

"Well you know they are sworn to secrecy on all things but he was showing off to Emma. He told her that his father and Archbishop Wulfstan, had discussed secrets of state in front of him."

"Secrets of state?"

Blanche squeezed in another quick breath before continuing, "Emma was a bit vague but apparently there will soon be a war."

"War?"

"Yes a war. The sub-kings have refused to pay High King Athelstan's tribute again. Gamel said that King Athelstan has press ganged almost every blacksmith and leather worker in the south into making weapons and armour."

Softly, "Archbishop Wulfstan wants a Viking King back on the throne of Northumbria."

Blanche took a deeper breath. Looking around the market, she sighed, as locals bustled about and several white geese ambled by herded by a farm lad, "It will not affect us though." She looked extremely bored, "Nothing ever happens here." Quickly changing the subject again, "Lady Rafyn, I need to ask you something about Emma's health."

Listening carefully, she looked up, "What is it?"

"I am concerned for Emma. It is only natural that she will

get pregnant soon after her marriage to Gamel. Emma is a tiny thing and many women die in childbirth."

It was natural for sister to be concerned about her sibling, gently, "She is healthy Blanche."

"You have helped midwife the birth of all of your brother's babies. Your mother has taught you a good knowledge of healing herbs. Please would you midwife for Emma?"

"Lady Blanche you honour me but I am not a healer. I will ask my mother to midwife Emma."

"Rafyn, she wants you." Blanche shook her head exasperated, "I'm worried that Gamel will not agree to a midwife at all. Christian men do not hold with the old Celtic ways. He would rather follow current fashion and pay for a filthy male physician to paw all over her."

"Well," She nodded thoughtfully, "I see your point. Those men are little more than butchers. If Emma would like me to help her, I don't think that Gamel can do much about it."

Turning back to the ribbon stall, Blanche smiled charmed by the colours. To the vendor, "I want two yards of the pretty pink ribbons for my sister and two yards of these blue ones for myself. Will you take a half spit roast chicken for them?"

The pretty woman shook her head. She smiled. Her looks were marred by several missing teeth. "These ribbons are from the Baltics. I want a whole chicken and a loaf of salt bread."

Feeling the softness of the material, Blanche frowned, "Indeed the ribbons are fine but that is too much. I will give you half a chicken plus the leg and a wing from the other half."

A hard glint appeared in the vendor's eyes, she half smiled, "I have many children to feed. The ribbons are yours for the whole chicken."

Raising her blonde eyebrows, Blanche looked exasperated, "Agreed."

Taking her huge scissors the vendor cut the ribbons and folded them carefully.

Sighing, Blanche watched her, "I will fetch a chicken from the beer halla."

Passing her the ribbons, the woman inclined her head, "I prefer hot chicken. I will be passing the beer halla later, Milady. I will collect the payment then."

Huffily, "Of course and I hope you enjoy my dinner."

Her eyes twinkling the vendor chuckled, "Milady, the chicken will be gone by nightfall but you will still have the lovely ribbons."

Looking at the ribbons, Rafyn smiled, "She is right, they are lovely."

Leading her away from the stall, Blanche's giggled, "Well at least I still have my salt bread." Lowering her voice, "Will you look after my sister's ribbons? I will collect them in the morning."

"Of course."

"Lady Rafyn, I talked with the tall blonde Viking for a while. He told me that his brother, the dark haired one, thought that you were very pretty."

"Did he?" She smiled feeling pleased at the compliment, "My brothers were teasing me about him and the way that he held my hand. I thought that he had nice eyes."

Looking down, Ketil's lips twitched.

She looked at Rafyn with astonishment, "Did you? I would never have guessed. You were not very nice to him. Edwin told me that the dark haired one asked many questions about you and your availability to wed." She looked thrilled, "Apparently, he wants to court you."

Her eyebrows rising she flushed, "We have barely spoken."

Breathing deeply, Blanche smiled, "For some it only takes one glance to fall in love."

6.4

Finishing her work, Blanche blew out nearly every bees wax candle in the beer halla. Leaving one candle lit she brushed through her curly blonde hair with her delicate antler comb. A smile played on her lips as she tied her new pretty ribbons to her hair. Smoothing down her long skirt, she draped her shawl around her shoulders. Quickly blowing out the last candle, she quietly left the beer halla. The full white moon glimmered large and luminous in the night sky along with a myriad of sparkling stars.

At the edge of the market, hidden in the shadows, Ragnal watched her leave the halla. "Hello my pretty."

Feeling her body tingle with attraction, Blanche walked up to him smiling.

"I was beginning to think that you weren't coming."

"I wanted to make sure that everyone had gone home before I left, to protect my reputation."

A smile played on his lips.

Taking his strong warm hand she led him to the High Street. They passed several small hovels and make shift shelters. A little concerned that she would be seen, she pulled him into a side street, "Come this way. It's called Water Bag Way. The townsfolk only use this path to collect water."

The track was steep but easily passable. As they approached the river, the moon lit the water up with silver iridescent sparkles. It was not far to the bridge.

Listening to the sound of his horse's hooves clip clopping across the wooded bridge, he looked down at her, "Where are we going my pretty?"

Turning left, again following the bank of the river, she smiled, "This is Lady Rafyn's land. There's a place that I go to sometimes, to escape and be by myself. I thought I would share it with you. Then the next time I go there I'll remember you."

He asked gently, "What does a pretty thing like you need to escape from?"

"Life has been hard since my parents died. I had to protect and look after my sister. I have had to do things to survive."

His strong warm hand tightened gently around hers, softly reassuring, "We all have to do things to survive. It is the way of the world."

She looked up at him.

Looking down into her trusting large blue eyes, he felt his heart miss a beat.

"A suitor came to my land a year after my parents died. He offered me marriage in exchange for my estate. When I refused him, he had his men hold me down," she paused as pain filled her eyes, "while he raped me."

He took in a deep breath. Her eyes looked harrowed.

"He said no other man would want me now."

"He was a fool."

"You are the only person that I have told." Trying to shut her mind to the memories that still haunted her, she walked quietly for a while. Softly, "This is the place that I come to Ragnal."

Looking at the shallow part of the river, where the glistening water bubbled over small rocks and larger boulders, he smiled, "It is peaceful."

Pain flickered in her eyes as she stepped closer to the bank.

Taking her gently by her shoulders, he turned her back to him and hugged her, protectively wrapping her in his big arms.

Relaxing into his strong chest, she closed her eyes, just letting him hold her. For the first time since her father had died she felt completely safe.

Lifting her chin with his big hand, he looked deeply into her eyes, his body tingled with desire.

Looking up at him she knew that she wanted to kiss him. She tilted back her head.

He kissed her gently on her full parted lips. She did not pull away. Groaning his kiss deepened as he ran his fingers through her long soft hair, his hand gently stroking her back. Holding her to him, still kissing her, he moved his hand to her tiny waist. Caressing slowly up over her ribs, he hesitated, his hand just under her full breast. Raising his head, he looked into her lovely eyes, huskily, "Blanche my pretty, if you want to escape me tonight, you need to go now."

Stepping back from him, she gazed up at him, "No, I don't want to escape you Ragnal."

Breathing deeply, he pulled his tunic over his head. Soft blonde downy hair covered his chest and muscular stomach. Taking her gently by her waist he bent his head, letting his lips travel over her neck.

Feeling wonderful tingling sensations travelling from her neck through her body, she barely felt him sink to the ground taking her with him.

The meandering river sparkled silver in the darkness. The glimmering moon lit up the sheen on every leaf and blade of grass. Leaning on his arm, Ragnal looked down at her, softly stroking her dishevelled soft hair and ribbons away from her pretty face. Gently, "I have to go soon. You had better get dressed."

Standing up, she stretched, her lovely white skin glistened with perspiration in the moonlight.

He watched her mesmerized by her beauty. Shaking his head, he remembered the clan needed gold. He clenched his fist forcing his heart to harden.

Wrapping her hair up in her hand, she expertly tied it up with a ribbon. Walking naked into the river shallows, she gasped against the refreshing chill of the water. Immersing herself, she quickly washed the perspiration from her body.

Icy determination filled his eyes fortifying him for what he must do. Quickly pulling on his breeches, boots and tunic, he frowned. Striding over to his horse, he coldly checked the saddle buckles.

Moments later, she walked back and quickly pulled her dress on over her wet body.

Ignoring her, he prepared his horse bridle and stirrups.

Looking back at him, Blanche was not sure how to say goodbye. It had been so perfect. Walking over to him, she smiled happily.

With both of his strong hands around her waist, he suddenly lifted her up high, placing her on his horse's back.

As he climbed up behind her, she giggled, "Are you taking me home?"

For a moment, he squeezed his eyes shut hating himself for what he was about to do. Opening his eyes, he hardened his voice, gruffly, "No, you're coming with me." He dug in his heels and swung his horse eastward.

Giggling, she glanced back at him, "I enjoyed tonight and I would love to see you again but I have to get back before morning."

Holding her by her small waist, his eyes glazed like stone, "You're coming with me."

Slowly realising that he was deadly serious, her eyes widened. Trying to pull his arms from her waist she gasped, "What are you doing?" Beginning to panic she screamed, "Ragnal! Stop, please turn back!"

As they galloped away towards his camp for the first time he felt sick of this trade. Frowning, he forced his heart to harden. In his mind, he told himself, the Clan needed gold to go to war. The fastest way to make money in this brutal world was to deal in human lives.

"Please Ragnal, let me go please!" Desperately, "I can pay ransom. My sister is marrying an earl. He will pay my ransom!"

He knew if they tried to bargain her for ransom it could put the Clan Ivarr in great danger. He shut his ears and his mind to her pleas.

As they rode further and further away from her home, she felt sickening fear as tears streamed down her face.

6.5

Blacarri left their makeshift camp on horseback. The full moon's glowing light lit up the way back to Cenheardsburgh. Reaching the wooden bridge, his eyes glinted as he galloped up the high street. The dry packed road dirt helped muffle the sound of his horse's hooves. It did not take long to reach the market. Some traders were still sat around open fires, telling stories and drinking ale, but most had retired to their tents. Without a sound, he dismounted from his horse and casually looped the bridle to a tree branch. He could not risk his horse's hooves clattering on the cobbled stable yard. His leather boots barely made a sound on the ground as he strode across the courtyard. Looking around, his pale grey eyes looked translucent in the moonlight. The stables looked as if they had been there for many years. A huge pile of fresh hay had been heaped to the side of the stable doors. Inside, he heard a horse move. Above the stables were two rooms and a balcony. An old flowering vine, growing up the side of the stables staircase, looked twisted but sturdy. The steps creaked softly as he climbed them. Younger, thinner vine branches clambered over the balcony guardrail, heavily laden with sweet smelling flowers. Hearing loud male snores from one of the rooms, he turned to the smaller room. Creeping to the shuttered doors, he pushed against them. Locked from the inside they did not move. Glancing at the other door, he realised that he could not break this door in without raising the maid's father and brothers from their slumber. There were too many of them to fight. Frowning, he put his ear to the shutters. Hearing movement from inside the room, he quickly stepped back into the shadows.

Uncomfortably warm and still unable to sleep, Rafyn looked around her dark room above the stables. Her father and brother's snores from the next room were irritatingly loud. Sitting up on the small rickety bed, she whispered to herself half smiling, "They could all sleep through a thunder storm." Standing up, she stretched up her arms. Dressed only in a long white lace trimmed chemise, she tried to waft her flushed face with her hand but she still felt too warm. Whispering to herself, "If I open up the doors, I can get some cool air into the room." Automatically reaching for her wrist guards, she deftly fastened them to each of her small wrists. Taking her wide black leather sword belt, she slipped it around her tiny waist and fastened the large silver buckle. The belt pulled her thin chemise tight against her full breasts. Subconsciously, she adjusted both of her swords so that they lay comfortably and familiarly against her legs. Whispering to herself, "I know you told me to the keep shutter doors locked Da, but it is just too hot." Lifting up the wooden bar, she opened the two shutters wide. The coolness of the night drifted against her skin as she stepped out onto the veranda balcony.

Watching her from the shadows, Blacarri could not believe his good luck. A smile played on his lips.

She breathed deeply as a sudden cool night gust of air rustled through the nearby trees and blew gently across her face. Through her thin chemise, she felt the breeze cool her body. The ancient vine clambered twisting and gnarling up the stables to her balcony. The flowers on it smelt sweet and headily perfumed. Leaning against the guardrail, she looked up at the full moon and smiled. The Moon God's face looked so beautiful, shining big and bright in the clear night sky. The stars, carrying the souls of the ancestors, twinkled all around. The hoot of a nearby owl carried on a gust of air. A feeling of total peace swept over her, as she stood looking up at the beautiful panoramic star filled heavens. At that moment, she felt like she was the only person in the whole wide world.

But she was not alone. His steely grey eyes missed nothing as she stepped out on to the veranda. Her long thin white chemise blew against her body. She was obviously naked under the nightdress. He could faintly see through the thin material her full breasts, tiny waist and curvy buttocks. His breath caught in his throat and a muscle clenched tight in his strong jaw as he watched her. The light of the full moon shone down on her, illuminating her lovely face and cleavage with a lustrous ethereal glow. Smiling, showing two rows of pearly white teeth, he slowly drew his dagger.

Stood quietly looking at the huge silvery full moon, she felt her over heated body cooling down. Suddenly alarm coursed through her. She heard the unmistakable soft steely sound of a blade being drawn behind her. Acting only on instinct moving at lightning speed, she grabbed the hilt of her left sword with her right hand. Drawing it in a single fluid protective arc, she turned to face her attacker. Seeing only the shimmer of a steel blade in the shadows, she exploded into an immediate attack. Thrusting, she rotated her wrist suddenly, sending her assailants dagger flying through the air. It flew over the veranda, clattering onto the cobbles below.

Taken completely by surprise, with the tip of a steel blade at his throat, Blacarri backed out of the shadows with his hands in the air.

Recognising him from the beer halla, she uttered sharply in surprise, "You!" Softly menacing, "You make one false move and I will kill you. Keep your hands up."

Wincing, feeling the sting of her sword and a trickle of his own warm blood travelling down his neck, he raised his hands higher. Backing up towards the guardrail he spoke softly, "I don't doubt that." Smiling appreciatively, "You are full of surprises my Lady. That was a very skilful move. Where did you learn to sword fight?"

Warily, "Never you mind." Her eyes glinted as she kept her right sword arm out stretched. With her body side on and as far away from him as possible, her body was in perfect balance, if he attacked.

Raising a dark eyebrow at her posture, he looked surprised, "Your stance is impressive my Lady. The way you control your attack position and your balance shows you have been trained well." He noted that her sparkling eyes never left his. "If you were a man I might be worried."

Watching him carefully it was easy to see he was a warrior. He probably could and would kill her with his bare hands, if he could get close enough. Softly, "I should kill you now." A familiar feeling of dread came over her.

Taking in every detail of the mixed emotions playing across her face, he wondered if he had found a chink in her armour. He decided to tease her. "What's the matter my Lady? Haven't you killed a man before?"

Without taking her fierce gaze from his mocking steely grey eyes, she stated quietly, "You would not be the first man that I have had to kill to protect my honour."

Slowly, his eyes travelled over her body, lingering on her breasts, he grinned as she demurely blushed, "So you are a virgin. I should have known." He shook his head, wondering how he was going to get out of this without hurting her. He was a seasoned warrior but she had taken him by surprise. Trained from the age of six in hand to hand combat and martial arts, he was sure that he could easily take her out with a sudden kick to her stomach. However, that went against everything he believed in. He could never strike a woman unless he was fighting for his life, and he also knew that she would probably die from the injury, days later, in agony. No, he thought as he looked into her beautiful eyes, it would be such a waste. Casually leaning back on the balcony rails with his hands in the air, he tipped his head slightly to the side. From the corner of his eye he noticed the huge hay mound below. Looking back at her, he smiled as he looked over her body again almost predatory. Huskily, "You are beautiful my Lady. I want you. I thought you felt the same. That is why I came to you tonight."

Astonished at his brazen pass at her, she blinked, "How dare you! Your impertinence is overwhelming. Don't your people believe in courtship or manners?"

With mocking charm, "What am I supposed to think when you are looking at me with your come to bed eyes?"

"What!" Raising her eyebrow sardonically, "You have a vivid imagination Viking. You are not my type."

Softly, teasing, "How do you know I am not your type when you have nothing to compare me to?" His white teeth shimmered in the moonlight as he smiled roguishly.

Waspishly, "You can't be that confident in your love making skills, or you wouldn't need the knife!"

Evenly, "Your brothers are close by. They might not take kindly to our tryst."

Her eyes widened, "Our tryst! How dare you!"

Enjoying her temper, he grinned, "You clearly invited me here with your....."

At that moment a colony of bats suddenly flew noisily out from a hole in the stable loft. The little black creatures screeched as they flew past her, their leathery wings beating against her face and hair. She gasped, dropping her guard. One of the bats tangled in her hair. She wanted to scream but at that moment another bat flew into her face. She closed her mouth and shut her eyes tightly.

In that split second, he lunged at her grabbing both her wrists, forcing her to drop her sword. Pushing her backwards, using his superior strength, he raised both her arms above her head and pressed her up against the wall of her room with his hips.

Feeling a bat still caught and tangled in her hair, she struggled against his grip.

Holding both her small wrists above her head with one strong tanned hand, with his other hand, he calmly disentangled the screeching little creature from her long dark glossy hair. Gently, he threw the bat into the air, watching it fly into the darkness silhouetted against the large shimmering white moon. Turning back to her, he slowly pushed her tangled hair away from her face. He smiled at the slow soft sigh of relief that she blew through her parted lips.

Opening her large beautiful brown eyes, looking up into his amused pale grey eyes, her eyes widened. She realised the new and more formidable danger that she was now in.

Huskily, "Well now," pressing his pelvis provocatively against hers, holding her wrists above her head with one hand and a clump of her hair with the other, "what were we saying about our tryst?" Not waiting for an answer, he gently but firmly pulled her head back with a strong grip of her hair. Seeing her upturned face, he lowered his head kissing her forcibly on her soft full mouth. He expected her to fight, perhaps try to bite him, or even freeze. Instead, unexpectedly, she slowly kissed him back opening her mouth to his softly exploring tongue. Feeling her move her pliant tongue against his, he loosened his grip on her wrists. Letting go of her hair, he ran his hand caressingly down her back. With her head tilted back, her eyes closed and mouth open, she seemed to just surrender herself to him. He had never enjoyed a kiss so much.

Protected all her life from the attentions of noblemen, and sheltered by her rank in society from local men, Rafyn had never been kissed like this. Her body tingled with pleasure. Tipping her head back, she suddenly felt a little scared by the overwhelming sensations. Pulling her mouth away from his, she whispered, "No Viking, this is wrong. You must come back tomorrow."

Intrigued, he looked down at her. Softly, "Why tomorrow?"

"So that you can ask my father if you can court me."

Lifting his head he chuckled, "I don't have time to court you."

His reply sounded disdainful. Unsure, "I am a lady. You must ask my father's permission to court me."

"Little virgin, you will be mine tonight." Lowering his mouth on hers again, he passionately bruised her lips with his kiss.

Pulling her mouth away, she gasped, "Stop," Looking up at

him with eyes full of hurt, "do not treat me like a bed woman."

Huskily, "I can feel you are willing."

"I thought you wanted to court me."

Smiling, he lowered his head again bruising her lips with his kiss.

Pushing him back, her eyes wide, she gasped, "No!"

Ignoring her plea, he lowered his head again.

Feeling almost overwhelmed by his strength and his forceful kiss, she suddenly felt defiant fury course through her body. She lifted her knee up sharply between his legs.

Suddenly feeling intense excruciating pain shooting into his groin, he broke off his kiss with a groan. The searing pain disabled him as it pushed up into the pit of his stomach.

Furious with her body's almost uncontrollable reaction to this man, she pulled her hands away from his grasp, "I will be no man's bed woman!" She suddenly shoved him backwards, with all her strength, forcefully towards the edge of the balcony. Without taking her eyes off him, she grabbed her right hand sword from the floor. In a swift fluid movement, she pulled her second sword from its scabbard. Turning her body into a right facing on guard position, she suddenly exploded into attack.

In that split second, he knew that the immense pain in his groin had completely disabled him. He had to escape her. Leaning backwards, he saw again, the large mound of hay. Tipping backwards over the edge of the balcony, he felt himself drop like a stone into the darkness. Fortunately, his sudden landing was surprisingly soft.

Both of her blades swooshed as they hit thin air. Sure that the Viking must be dead on the cobbles below, she took in a deep breath. She peered over the edge of the balcony. Seeing him lying in the huge bale of hay, unexpectedly, relief flooded through her, "Are you okay Viking? Are you hurt?"

He groaned as he looked up at her. Surprised that she was not calling for help, he took his time, allowing himself to slowly recover. He grunted, "I don't think I'll be able father any more children." Holding his groin with both hands, he struggled to his feet.

It had not occurred to her till now that he could be married and already have children. Waspishly, "That's probably a good thing. I feel sorry for your wife!"

He flinched with barely hidden sorrow, "My wife died many years ago."

She immediately felt contrite.

"I am free." He felt unsure why he wanted her to know that. Taking in a breath, "You are a surprising woman my Lady. I should not have been so rough. I apologise for any offence. I wish that I had time to get to know you better but I have business in Jorvic."

Hurt filled her eyes, "So, you never intended to court me?"

A muscle in his jaw flickered, "No my Lady. As I said, I thought you were willing."

Her cheeks flushed with mortification. Her eyes hardened, "I will never be your lady." Dismissing him haughtily, "You may leave me now." Turning away, she went back into her room and put the bar across the doors.

Below in the courtyard, irritated by her blunt dismissal, he jutted out his chin as he mounted his horse.

Cantering back into camp empty handed felt embarrassing but at least the others had been successful. The women looked shocked and terrified but he could see they were exceptionally beautiful. They would be well taken care of on the trip. No one would touch them, these women were special. They would make more gold from these four women than from the whole of the rest of their shipment.

Already mounted on his horse, Ragnal looked angry.

Blanche sat in front of him. She looked dishevelled, with her pretty blue ribbons hanging limply around her tear stained face.

One of his big hands held her around her waist, his other hand held his bridle. Seeing the drying blood trickle down his brother's neck, Ragnal turned his horse towards his brother, "Are you okay? What happened?"

Flatly, "The lady can fight and she's good." He looked blankly at Ragnal's surprised face.

Stood by his horse listening, Ketil smiled as he adjusted the stirrup attached to his saddle. Stretching his hands, he looked down at his new wrist guards. They felt hard at the moment but in time they would soften as they took on his skin oils. The raised wyvern pattern was very intricate and unusual. Pleased with them he ran his fingers over the pattern.

Smiling cheekily, Scarface strode up, "You were beaten by a woman." His eyes twinkled with amusement, "By the Hammer of Thor! I'd hang up my sword now if I were you."

Sticking his foot into the stirrup and swinging strongly up into his saddle, Ketil chuckled.

"She took me by surprise." His excuse sounded lame even to his own ears, growling, "I'd like to see you fight her, Scarface. I lost a good dagger."

Realising who they were talking about, Blanche looked up, her voice shook, "You went after Lady Rafyn too? What do you want with us?"

Turning to her, Blacarri's eyes hardened, coldly, "You are going to Sweden to be sold at the slave market."

Ragnal suddenly felt protective of her. It surprised him. He frowned, "Don't scare her."

Raising his head looking directly at him, Blacarri looked serious, "You know it is better to explain to them their fate at the start. Most realise that it is useless, even fatal to resist." Lifting his chin, eyeing her, "The few that do resist suffer."

As she began to weep again, Ragnal began to deeply regret capturing her. He spoke gently, "Be quiet my pretty. I will take care of you till we get to Sweden." As he spoke, he gently stroked her blonde hair and a mangled blue ribbon away from her face.

Blacarri watched him a little surprised. Like him, he thought Ragnal was indifferent to this way of making money.

It was necessary for their Clan's survival. The mental and physical suffering of their captives meant nothing to them. He looked away dismissively.

Blanche suddenly slapped Ragnal's hand away from her hair. Furiously, "Don't touch me you pig!" Turning angrily to his dark haired brother, "I'm glad the Sorceress cut you. I hope you die from the wound!"

Deeply superstitious as all Norsemen are, they looked at each other in silent surprise.

Scarface broke the silence, gruffly, "Why do you call Lady Rafyn a sorceress?"

Lifting her chin angrily, "She comes from a long line of culdees and healers. Before she was born, her mother exchanged a healing spell with a Norse sorceress, for a lucky name to give to her baby. The sorceress told her mother, if your child is born a girl she must be named Rafyn, after Odin's favourite bird. The raven is the symbol of the shaman and she too will be a great sorceress." Blanche took a deep breath, "When she was born of a girl, her mother did not want to bring bad luck on to the baby, so she was named Rafyn." Looking at them, she held their gazes. Her story was almost true. She knew that she was stretching the truth. She thought Lady Rafyn was a good midwife, but sorceress, no.

"Her story must be true." Scarface looked at Ragnal, "She used the Norse word for raven." Shaking his head, "Lady Rafyn is too young to be a sorceress."

She recklessly continued, "If you do not let me go, the sorceress will curse you!"

Dismissively, Blacarri laughed, "She is making up her story. She is trying to scare us into letting her go."

Exhausted now, Blanche lowered her head, quietly, "Lady Rafyn is favoured by many Gods. She has also been gifted by our war Goddess Morrigu." Turning back to Blacarri, confidently, "You cannot deny that she is skilled with the sword."

Unimpressed, he eyed her, "It is not unknown for a Norse maiden to carry weapons and a shield. In fact, many Norse women are exceptionally skilled at fighting with the long knife. It is our custom that fathers to teach our daughters to protect themselves."

She countered carefully, "Your own God Odin protects Lady Rafyn. He will be angry." She watched the uncomfortable looks of her captors, desperately, "If you take me, you will be cursed."

Scarface blew a long uneasy sigh through his lips, "Arrie, are you sure we should take her?"

No one noticed Ragnal's fleeting look of hope that he could leave her behind.

Looking back in the direction of the market, Blacarri's horse read his subconscious body signals and tried to turn around. As he controlled the skittish animal, he felt an almost uncontrollable urge to go back and get the dark eyed wench. He had been caught totally off guard by the way that she had disarmed him. He could still taste her lips. Frowning, disconcerted by the memory, he coldly ignored his own mixed feelings. Angrily, he muttered as he looked at Blanche, "She is worth too much to us at the market. We take her."

6.6

Richalle to Birka
August 937AD

The sun was just beginning to rise, as the band of men and their four captives rode into the village called Richalle, on the banks of the river Ouse.

Forced to ride for half the night, Blanche felt sick with fear. She could clearly see several thatched huts and a long hall, with a huge winged dragon decoration on the apex of the roof. It was the sight of the three huge knarr cargo ships and a ninety foot long drakkar longship, that made her blood run cold with fear. Moored on the banks of the river, the ships bobbed in the tranquil water.

Dismounting from his horse, Blacarri ordered, "The four specials are to be kept separate from the other slaves. Ketil stay here and guard them. I will go and pay Jarl Ricderc for his hospitium."

Nodding, Ketil swung his muscular leg over his saddle and jumped strongly down.

Watching him, Blacarri added bluntly, "Bind their wrists with cloth before you tie them to the posts. I do not want their skin marked with rope burn."

The man who had tied them to the post had been gentle and respectful. Sat on the ground, her wrists bound to the post, Blanche looked at the other three pretty women.

They looked back at her with the same wide eyed fear.

Not recognising them, she whispered, "You are not from my village."

The youngest, her dark long hair fell around her slim shoulders, whispered back, "We are market travellers. Where are they taking us?"

Fearfully, Blanche watched as over two hundred bedraggled women marched in a line to the wharf. Most were crying. A few were injured, their faces swollen and bruised. All of them had a look of all consuming wide eyed terror.

Stood close to the four women, Ketil avoided their pleading eyes. Hearing raised voices he swung round.

Walking up to him, Scarface eyed him warningly, his voice gruff, "During the night, against Blacarri's orders, several of the slaves have been raped by the Norwegians."

Looking past Scarface's broad shoulders, Ketil watched Blacarri square up to Kalf. Shaking his head, "Those mercenaries are trouble."

Looking disgusted, he nodded, "Two of the women fought back. They have been badly beaten and mauled." Shaking his head, "I don't think they can travel. I am not even sure that they will live."

Confronting the Norwegian leader, Blacarri sucked in a deep angry breath, "Kalf! I gave express orders not to touch the women!"

Glancing back seeing his men close by, Kalf's dark blue eyes glinted contemptuously, "I misunderstood your orders."

His muscles taut, Blacarri clenched his fists, "Misunderstand me again and I will kill you!"

Kalf sneered as he slowly inclined his head, "My apologies Lord."

Short of men, Blacarri decided to ignore the evil glint of insolence in the Norwegian's eyes. Knowing he needed to be careful with this man, he instantly decided to separate him from his men. Pointing at the Norwegians individually, "You two, you will sail on Ragnal's knarr. You two will sail on Scarface's knarr. You two will sail on Arnkell's knarr!" Swinging back round to their leader, he stated even more menacingly, "Kalf, you will sail with me on my drakkar!"

Barely hiding his contempt, Kalf nodded. His eyes narrowed. He realised immediately that King Blacarri was purposely splitting up his men for the journey. Turning away, he knew better than to argue the point.

Watching the Norwegian saunter off towards his men, Blacarri ordered deeply, "Load the ships!" Swinging round to a tall blonde man, he frowned, "Jarl Ricderc, here is your payment. It is good to do business with you again."

Eyeing him seriously, Ricderc flexed his broad shoulders, "My wife is displeased. The screams of the women raped last night disturbed her greatly."

He exhaled deeply, "I left strict orders that the women were not to be touched. The Norwegians disobeyed me. Please give my deepest regret to your wife."

Eyeing him back steadily, "They are insolent! Do not return here with them. They are not welcome on my land."

A muscle flickered in his jaw line. Blacarri knew that it must have been really bad last night for Jarl Ricderc to order that. He nodded curtly, "Two of the women they raped are unlikely to survive. May I leave them here?"

Ricderc growled angrily, "Leaving them here could bring danger to my people!"

The door of the halla opened softly. Ricderc's tall pretty wife looked at Blacarri. She had been listening, "The women's only chance is to be left here. They will not survive a sea voyage. Bring them into my halla. I will take care of them."

Glancing at Ricderc's wife quickly, Blacarri nodded with relief. Her long curling dark blonde hair was tied in a loose plait. It hung over the front of her shoulder almost to her thigh. Her mulberry dyed gown accentuated her long slim figure, "My thanks my Lady."

Taking the purse of silver irritably, Ricderc strode back into his halla.

Turning back to the ships, Blacarri watched the two hundred female slaves being boarded on to the three knarrs. Most of them were crying. Some were obviously injured. He frowned. Walking back to where the four specials were tied up, he ordered Ketil impatiently, "Load the four specials into my drakkar. They are too valuable a cargo to risk with the other women."

"Wait!" Ragnal strode up, "I have arranged for Erland to command my ship." His eyes flickered protectively towards Blanche, "I will sail with you brother."

Watching Ragnal with glacier grey eyes, Blacarri hesitated. Quickly evaluating the change of plans he shrugged his shoulders. His voice even, "Of course."

Gently cutting her rope bonds with his knife, Ragnal led Blanche on to the ship.

Stepping up on to the high sides of the drakkar, fretfully looking back, she could see into one of the cargo ships. In the centre of the ship there was a square pit. In the pit over two score of pitifully dirty women sat crying. One of the women looked up. Blanche gasped, the woman's face was bruised and her lips were swollen and crusted with dry blood. Blanche gazed at her for a moment in wide eyed horror.

Lifting Blanche down onto the deck of the drakkar, Ragnal kept her close to him as he stowed his shield to the side of the ship.

Watching her come aboard, Karl grinned leeringly as his eyes travelled her body. Puffing up his chest intimidatingly, he strode up to her, "Now you're a pretty wench."

Eyeing him warily, she felt her body shake suddenly with stress and fear.

Ragnal eyed Kalf hostilely.

Keeping her eyes low, she visibly paled.

His eyes glittering with lust, Kalf grabbed at her body ripping the arm of her dress.

She gasped out a scream.

Suddenly, Ragnal pulled her behind him.

Glancing up to Ragnal, she realised he was easily as tall and as muscular as the Norwegian.

His powerful shoulders flexed as he shoved Kalf back against the hull of the ship, he snarled, "Touch her again Kalf and I will feed you to the fish!"

For a moment furious anger glinted in Kalf's eyes. His upper lip snarled and his eyes narrowed. His hand fleetingly touched his knife hilt. Then his eyes flickered to Blacarri.

Watching the Norwegian, Blacarri's hand went decisively to the pommel of his sword.

Ragnal's eyes glinted murderously as his fist clenched.

Kalf knew he was outnumbered. Fighting to control himself, lowering his eyes warily, he tried to cover his uneasiness with a smirk. Backing away, he looked at the men on the ship. Catching Ketil's eye, he grinned with bravado.

Watching him stonily, Ketil did not smile back. Instead, he too gripped his sword pommel.

Feeling insulted but not as confident without his men, Kalf throatily coughed up a mouthful of spittle and noisily spat it over the side of the ship.

Blanche felt sick at the sound of it.

Taking her hand, Ragnal guided her over the large triangle of deck at the stern of the ship.

A grizzled suntanned man leaned against the helm oar and watched Jarl Ragnal lead the beautiful woman down the steps, into a space under the deck.

The other three women were already there. When they saw Ragnal, they cowered together close to the furs.

"Keep quiet my pretty and don't get in the way of the men." Gently, Ragnal stroked her tangled dirty hair back from her face, "There are furs to keep the chill off at night."

Stood ridged, she said nothing. Her eyes gazed into space.

Concerned, he looked over her for a moment longer. She did not move. A muscle flicked in his jaw. Every part of is being wanted to carry her off this ship and ride away with her but he knew he had to give her up for the clan. As he went back up the steps to the deck, he frowned dejectedly.

Taking command of his drakkar, Blacarri yelled out orders, "Raise oars! Push away!"

The oarsmen, in synchronisation, lifted their oars vertically.

Excited, Ketil grinned, the warship suddenly felt alive.

Checking that each of the ships were ready, Blacarri yelled deeply, "Hook oars!"

His men deftly lowered and placed their oars into the oar hooks next to them. The oar blades plopped into the river, splashing up glistening droplets of water.

As Ketil looked towards the other ships, his eyes glinted. The sight of the painted dragon figure heads, at the prow of each ship, gave them the appearance of huge sea serpents.

Blacarri ordered loudly, "Row!"

A younger man picked up his drum and beat it slowly with his hands as the ship pulled away.

Striding up to the grizzled man now steering the helm oar, Blacarri demanded, "Navigator, did you make a sacrifice to the Gods for a safe voyage?"

His tanned face crinkled with deep wrinkles as he smiled, "Yes Lord. The Shaman read the entrails. The Gods favour us."

To the rhythm of a drum beat, they rowed down the river Ouse away from Richalle.

The sun was setting in the west when they reached the Humber Estuary. The prevailing wind boded well. Stowing their oars, the men on each ship, skilfully raised their bright red sails. The wind billowed and swelled the square sails. The drakkar and the three knarr ships seemed to take on a life of their own. They suddenly sped through the white surf, out towards the darkening horizon.

Below deck, Blanche gradually adjusted to the rocking motion of the ship. The sound of waves hitting the prow and the strange creaking sounds became familiar. Exhausted, she slept.

6.7

Slavic, Birka

The winds favoured them and the days at sea had passed quickly. Stood alone at the side of the ship, looking out to sea, Blanche could see they were heading towards a large island. Many ships sailed to and from the huge crescent shaped man made harbour.

Watching her looking out towards the island, her eyes worryingly glazed, Ragnal walked over and stood next to her, "It is called Birka Island."

She did not respond, her limp blond hair looked dirty. She had not washed since their night by the river.

His voice was gentle, "We are going to the natural harbour over there. It's smaller than the main harbour."

Looking away from him, she could see an area coming into view covered in large colourful canopied tents.

"This place is called Slavic, the place of the market." He continued, "Here a man can trade or buy just about anything. Leather, fine furs, luxurious silks imported from the orient. Even brocade from Byzantium."

Her glazed eyes gazed away from him.

Watching his brother with expressionless glacier eyes, Blacarri strode up to him. "We need to get moving." He ordered, "Ragnal, prepare to dock."

Nodding to his brother, Ragnal shouted deeply, "Stow the sail!" Looking back at her, he gently placed a strong large hand around her waist and lifted her off of her feet. Carrying her to the steps and down to the lower deck, his blue eyes held hers.

For a moment, she looked up at him and her heart missed a

beat.

Looking down at her a muscle flickered in his jaw, his voice deeply gentle, "Blanche."

She looked away, her eyes glazing again.

Up on deck, Blacarri call out impatiently, "Ragnal, prepare to dock!"

Perplexed, Ragnal shook his head. Irritably, he turned and strode up the steps. Back up on deck he shouted orders, "Raise oars!"

The crew immediately moved their sea chests into place.

The navigator steered the helm oar.

Next to him a younger man beat a drum.

With a great grunt from the men, the eighteen foot long oars were lifted vertically erect.

Ragnal yelled, "Lower oars!"

At the same moment, the men lowered their oar blades into the frothing sea.

He ordered deeply, "Hook oars!" Each man expertly placed his oar into the oar hooks. Synchronised by the beating of the drum, the men rowed towards the harbour.

Below deck, Blanche's eyes glistened with unspent tears. She felt the ship thud against the wooden quay. Then the strange but familiar feeling of fearful stillness engulfed her. She could not run. She could not hide. She could not fight. As had happened so many times on this voyage, she sank into her own mind, blocking out everything. Her wide blue eyes glazed as she stared into space.

Only Ketil noticed Kalf quietly leave the ship.

As soon as the three knarrs docked, Kalf and his men strode off towards the market, leaving the work to the rest of the men.

A little later Blacarri, Scarface and Ketil went ashore to make arrangements for the sale of the cargo. They soon returned cheerfully smiling.

Striding up to his brother, Blacarri spoke quietly, "While I take the slaves to auction, I want you and Scarface to take the four specials to that wooden long house." He pointed to the huge building, "I have made arrangements for them to bathe and change clothes." Grinning, his white teeth shone against his golden tanned face, "Each of them will sell quicker with clean bodies and a new dress. Make sure you take sixteen men to guard them." Turning to Ketil, he ordered, "Ketil, stay here with ten men and guard my ship." He strode off to the knarrs moored alongside his drakkar, ordering loudly, "Unload the ships."

From the ship, Ragnal watched as all of the women, except the four specials, were marched off. Surrounded by his clans' men as guards, the women's' faces looked gaunt as they made a pitiful procession to the auction tent. It had never affected him before. This time his eyes closed. He knew what fate awaited Blanche. He already felt bereft.

When the last of the bedraggled women had left the ships, Scarface turned to him, "Ragnal, shall I fetch them up?"

He barely heard his own voice, "Yes."

As he went down the steps, Scarface did not waste time. He quickly roped the women together and led them up on deck.

Their heads bent submissively, Blanche and the other three women did as they were told. The man with the scars led them off the ship, down a wide gangplank, on to a wooden jetty. Then they were led through a few tent lined streets to a long house.

Ragnal was already there. He stood by the long house door. He noticed Blanche's eyes. They were completely glazed. She did not seem to see him. He tried to sound indifferent, "The women in this halla will get you ready. Do as they bid you. We will wait here."

Inside the halla, the room was split up by wattle and daub walls, creating smaller chambers. In the first room were metal baths filled with warmed clean water. Specially trained slave women stripped the four women and bathed them. Ordered to get out of the baths, different slaves dried their naked bodies with soft material by an open fire pit. Then, they were clothed in very thin chemises. They were led to a second room, also warmed by a fire pit. There, they sat on stools while other slave women combed out and dried their long hair. A small amount of perfume was stroked gently through their tresses, before being plaited elaborately with ribbons made of cloth of gold.

Ordered to dress by the women, Blanche put on a pale gold coloured gown. It clung to her slim body.

An older woman, her face still very young looking, strode in from a small antechamber. Her long, thick blonde hair was elaborately plaited high, in a swirling thick arrangement, on top of her head. Her woad blue gown looked elegant on her slim figure. Her long necked, haughty demeanour showed that she was obviously in charge of the long halla slaves.

The slaves all curtseyed to her.

Ignoring them, she looked over the four women with her intense confident cobalt blue eyes. She spoke clearly, "I am a true craft woman, an artist of beauty, if you will. I was my master's favourite bed slave. Of course, he had loved me and he eventually freed me. He even bequeathed to me, by charter, this long house." Her eyes fell on Blanche, "He continued to visit me often," her voice hardened, "for his need of brutal, domineering sex." Her lips pursed, "It is true. He never really let me go."

Blanche gazed into space.

"After he died, for a short time, I actually felt his loss." Thoughtfully, "Or was it the loss of his protection?" She shrugged her shoulders, "Anyway, life goes on. I have carved out a very lucrative little niche on this island. I offer something nobody else had thought of, a beauty halla." Looking at Blanche's tiny waist, she smiled, "I have the perfect adornment for you, my dear." Moving to a small chest, she took out a heavy dark gold coloured brocade belt. Walking up to her, she tied it around Blanche's midriff so that it accentuated her hips, "Perfection!" She looked at the beautiful woman's glazed eyes. She lowered her voice, "I have seen your affliction many times before, my dear. I call it hiding in the mind." She took in a deep breath, "I myself have never succumbed to it. Instead, I endured every rape from him, every bruise and every cut." Her mouth moved closer to Blanche's ear, she whispered, "Until I found a way to kill him."

Blanche's eyes flickered to the woman, for the briefest of moments, before her eyes glazed over again.

Still whispering, "I know you can hear me." Softly, "I buried him myself under this floor, almost where we are standing." She smiled as she raised her chin confidently. Looking up, she saw that the other three women were ready. She turned to her slaves, "Excellent work my dears'."

Her slaves curtseyed as they smiled back.

Her cobalt blue eyes flashing, she led the four women out from the halla to the Vikings.

Barely noticing the other three women, Ragnal only saw Blanche. Golden ribbons plaited thinly through her hair, swept back her naturally curling blonde hair from her lovely face.

Scarface paid the owner of the halla well with a bag of silver.

Smiling, she turned elegantly and went back into her beauty halla.

A small guard of their best clan men surrounded the four women.

Scarface eyed Ragnal curiously. He seemed unusually un-focussed. Impatient, he ordered gruffly, "Let's go!" Taking the lead, he marched them off towards a huge tent in the middle of the market.

Ragnal followed.

As they reached the entrance of the tent, the bawdy shouts from inside broke through her trance like state. Fear welled up inside her. Turning to him, she pleaded, "Ragnal."

He gazed back at her. He wanted to carry her off and save her but his feet rooted him to the spot.

The guards pushed her forwards.

The shouts of many men all around her drowned out his reply.

The men in the tent were almost uncontrollable. As they tried to get a better view of the four beautiful women, fights broke out all around them. Mauling dirty hands tried to come through the barricade of circular shields.

The clan guards beat them back roughly.

Her body began to shake uncontrollably. In one last weak moment, she looked back at Ragnal again, and then she was climbing. It was only three or four steps up on to the stage but it was enough to take her away from the stinking crowd of men.

Stepping forward, Blacarri stood between the women and the crowd. Slowly, he led each of the four women to a sea chest. Turning round to the crowd, he watched as several men entered the tent. Opening up his huge arms he addressed them loudly, "Welcome gentlemen, to the greatest market in the known world!"

Many of the men in the tent cheered.

As he had watched her climb shakily up onto the stage platform, Ragnal lowered his head unable to believe what he was doing. When she had looked back at him and he saw her vulnerability, he felt like his heart was breaking. Knowing that he had to do this for his clan he shook his head. Desperately turning away, he left the tent, heading for the nearest beer halla. He needed to get drunk, very, very, drunk.

As the crowd settled down, Blacarri walked up to each one of the women in turn, "Stand on the box."

Blanche watched trembling as the other three specials obediently stood on the chests.

Striding up to her he held her arm lightly for support as she unsteadily stood on the sturdy sea chest. When they were ready, Blacarri opened his arms exuberantly, swinging round to face the crowd. Feeling the excitement in the air, he shouted theatrically, "Have you ever seen such beauties?" His voice deep, "We have saved the best till last!"

A great bawdy roar filled the tent.

Lifting his chin grinning, "Now which of you lucky men will have one of these soft skinned damsels in your bed tonight?"

Another cheer went up from the crowd. A few drunken scuffles broke out again.

Striding along the stage, "Who will be the first man to make me an offer?"

Dressed in bright red billowing trousers tucked into black leather boots and a stark white tunic laced up at the neck, a dark eyed man strode into the tent. His boots had exotic curling high pointed toes, and criss-crossing golden laces, strapping them to his shins. Thinly plaited threads of his long curling black hair, shone with several studs of gold. His short dark beard was held, just under his chin, with a single gold stud the size of a finger nail. Walking confidently up to the front of the stage, his wide black sword belt accentuated his muscular, lean torso. The luxurious red cloak draped flamboyantly around his broad shoulders, hung almost to his knees. Even the short growth of black sideburn, on his suntanned face, accentuated his chiselled handsome good looks. His accent deeply Baltic, he shouted, "Black Arailt Guthrithsson, I will give you five silver pieces for the blonde!"

Shocked to hear a voice from his past, Blacarri swung round, "It is good to see you again Gilli." Walking over to Blanche, he lifted a strand of her long blonde hair to his nose. He smelt the sweet perfume, frowning over-dramatically, "But you insult me! If you think I would accept that pitiful offer for this comely wench."

A roar of laughter went up from the crowd.

Wearing pure white silk breeches and a huge emerald green silk coat, a fat merchant lay on three purple cushions. Eyeing Blanche with small beady glinting eyes, he sipped red wine from a silver goblet, "I'll double his offer to ten."

Gilli looked disdainfully over to the huge merchant. They had long been rivals on this island. The merchant had a reputation for quickly finding high paying buyers for his merchandise. Irritated, he shrugging his broad shoulders, "Fifteen."

The traders in the crowd nudged each other. The bidding was moving at pace for the beauty.

Smiling, Blacarri confidently paced the stage. This was going much better than he had expected. It had been well worth the extra expense of dressing up the women.

The merchant looked at Gilli, his eyes narrowing. He often competed with the Russian for high quality slaves. The competitive feeling was mutual. Turning back to Blanche with piercing hungry little eyes, he shouted pompously, "Twenty! And I may just keep her for myself!"

Many of the men looked immediately to Gilli to see his reaction. They were not disappointed. Gilli's expression of immense disdain did not change, "Twenty one."

Unhesitating the merchant called haughtily, "Twenty two"

All heads turned to Gilli.

He drawled, "Twenty three"

The crowd turned to the merchant.

"Twenty four."

Looking bored, Gilli shrugged his shoulders, "Twenty five."

Blacarri looked at his old friend in surprise. This was a small fortune. Rumours had travelled to the court of Ath Cliath, that Gilli the Russ, had made his fortune trading furs and Baltic amber. It seemed that the rumours were true.

Pausing for a moment the fat merchant looked stubborn. Eyeing Gilli with contempt, "Thirty."

A murmur went through the crowd, what would Gilli do now?

The stage was usually out of bounds for the customers but nobody stopped Gilli, as he walked slowly up on to the stage over to Blanche's pedestal.

With expressionless steely blue eyes, Blacarri watched him approach her.

Hands on his hips, he strutted around her looking over her body. Stopping in front of her, he turned to Blacarri, "Her breasts are magnificent."

Humiliation coursed through her.

He smiled, "Indeed they are."

"Has anyone touched her?"

Raising a sardonic eyebrow, "You know my rules are strict on my ships. Once they are captured they are not to be molested."

He looked over again as she stood in her beautiful golden gown, "Is the dress included."

"Of course."

Turning to the crowd, Gilli raised his voice so the crowd could hear, "Thirty one."

The fat merchant smiled broadly. The Russian could only have a few more silver coins. Convinced that he had won her, he was about to shout triumphantly thirty five pieces of silver but the Russian interrupted him.

Eyeing the merchant with absolute contempt, Gilli shouted, "Pieces of gold!"

Stunned, the merchant spat his red wine out over his white breeches.

Even Blacarri's jaw dropped in surprise.

A great cheer went up in the tent.

Shaking his head in defeat, the merchant fell back onto his cushions.

Gilli grinned at Blacarri. It was worth the price just to see his old friend's flabbergasted expression.

Quickly regaining his composure, he got out his scales from an old well used leather bag. Down on one knee he set the scales on the floor boards and set out his weights.

Raising his left hand, Gilli clicked his fingers loudly.

A huge bald headed tanned man, dressed similarly to Gilli, strode up. He carried a large crescent shaped steel sword on his black leather belt, and two large heavy leather bags full of precious metal. Getting down on one knee, he measured out gold from one of the bags.

Eyeing the scales, Blacarri carefully followed his strict procedure. He meticulously checked the weight of each piece of gold. Many a trader these days, tried to cheat with paying with inferior metal. He made no exceptions. Smiling as he stood up, he shook Gilli's hand. The deal was made.

Flamboyantly turning to his aide, "Jacobus, take the slave to my villa. House her in my personal harem." His Baltic pronunciation thick, he stated over-dramatically, "Guard her with your life."

Grabbing her wrist, the huge man nodded and silently escorted Blanche away.

As total desolation consumed her, her heart beating rapidly with fear, she barely whimpered, "No." Bright sunlight glared in her eyes as he led her out of the tent.

Blacarri turned back to Gilli, "I hope he is a eunuch."

Smiling confidently, "Niat, but I trust Jacobus with my life." He grinned "It is good to see you my friend. My villa is at the top of the island but I do not stay there tonight. I sold a consignment of slaves yesterday. With the silver I will pay for a shipment of amber today." He drawled annoyed, "My shipment is late! I cannot leave the market place until my amber arrives." He tutted with annoyance, "This place is full of pirates who would think nothing of stealing my goods!"

Smiling, Blacarri raised an amused eyebrow, "I leave tomorrow Gilli, on the first tide."

"So soon? Then you will be my guest tonight. I stay in my market tent. It is the largest red tent," Gilli pointed in the general direction, "towards the east, overlooking the harbour. It is most comfortable. Come tonight, I will entertain you."

"I look forward to it Gilli. I have much to tell you." Eyeing the rowdy crowd, he grinned, "I have three more slaves to sell. I will see you later." Turning back to his impatient audience, he strutted along the stage confidently. His voice boomed out, "Gentlemen, Vikings, traders and…" he looked theatrically jaded, "the rest of you pirates!"

The crowd men grinned and chuckled.

"The first of my beauties has been sold. Now who amongst you will make me an offer for one of the others?"

A tall man yelled, "Seven pieces of silver for the brunette!"

Another yelled, "Eight!"

The first man called out, "Nine!"

Grinning, Gilli left the tent.

6.8

It was late afternoon when Blacarri and Scarface left the market tent, followed by their army of clansmen. They carried the leather bags of gold and silver. On the way back they spotted Ragnal, completely drunk and slumped over a weathered table in one of the large ale tents. With his huge arms over their shoulders, they half dragged, half hauled him back to the ships. It took all of their combined strength to carry his dead weight up the gangplank onto the drakkar. Dropping him onto a pile of furs a huge loud snore blasted through Ragnal's nose.

Chuckling, Blacarri quickly turned him over on to his side. A snuffle escaped through his lips but he was much quieter.

The vast sky was turning to pale lavender as the sun began to set, reflecting every shade from purple to lilac across the shimmering sea.

Standing up, Blacarri grinned as his men jovially drew lots to see which of them would guard the ships, while the rest enjoyed the entertainment of the market brothels. After locking the bags of silver and gold in his sea chest, he stood up and stretched. The satisfaction that he had achieved his goal glinted in his eyes.

Standing away from the men, flicking his eyes sideways, Ketil signalled to Blacarri that he had some information.

Striding up to Ketil, he whispered, "What is it?"

His face serious, "Lord, the Norwegians came back to the ships while you were selling the slaves. I overheard them talking about the coming war. They said the English king is paying fortunes in silver to mercenaries who will join him."

"Go on."

"As soon as night falls, they plan to steal your drakkar and sail to England with your gold and silver. They intend to join King Athelstan's army against us."

His steely grey eyes hardened, Blacarri rasped gruffly, "Traitors! Where are they?"

Nodding his head towards an area of stacked barrels, Ketil frowned, "Over there."

They watched as Kalf dragged a struggling market wench, by her long blonde hair, behind the barrels.

Her stack of hand woven baskets fell to the dry sandy ground.

His men, watched leeringly, knowing that when Kalf was done they would get their turn on her.

Hearing her ear piercing scream, Blacarri squared up his muscular shoulders, "Ketil, Scarface, follow me!"

Her long frayed smock dress was ripped at the shoulder. Tears streamed down her face as she desperately struggled against him. She screamed again, "No!"

Still holding a tangled clump of her hair, Kalf curled up his fist and smashed it into her face.

Stunned, her scream trailed off into a whimper as she crumbled to the ground.

Standing over her, Kalf viciously kicked her slender legs apart. Grabbing her long skirt, he looked up as Blacarri approached, he sneered, "Wait your turn! I'm first!"

Eyeing Kalf coldly, he strode up to him. His voice threateningly calm, "I understand you plan to steal my ship."

Blinking in surprise, he let the coarse material of her dress slip out of his hand. Stupidly, Kalf went for his sword.

Closing his fist, half smiling at the Norwegian's fatal error, Blacarri upper punched him under his chin.

Coughing blood from his mouth, caught off guard by the immense blow, Kalf stumbled backward. Pulling his sword from its scabbard, he growled, "I'm going to kill you!"

Blacarri unsheathed his sword. Unhesitating he lunged, striking Kalf's sword away from his body and sent it singing through the air.

The look of horror froze on Kalf's face as he watched Blacarri's sword plunge into his body. Shocked, he felt no pain. Sinking to his knees, he grunted desperately, "I am dying, let me meet my Gods! Give me my sword!"

Blacarri eyed him, coldly, "No Kalf. I'll not meet you again in Valhalla!"

A look of frantic pleading passed over Kalf's face. His eyes glazed over and he fell, face down, in the dirt.

It was over so quickly. His six men, taken by surprise, stumbled to pull out their swords.

Whimpering as she came too, the market maid squinted, everything looked blurred. Sounds boomed indistinctly in her ears. Unsure of what was happening, she rolled her slim body closer to the dark shadowy barrels.

One of the Norwegians lunged at him, drawing his sword with his right hand, Ketil instinctively got in the first blow. It went straight through the man's heart. The man dropped dead in front of him. Shaken by his first kill, he barely had time to turn and parry, as a violent crushing blow came towards him from the next man. Staggering backwards, his eyes only saw the huge man, everything else around him hazed out of sight. He almost fell but instead, he careered off two huge barrels. Surprised to be upright, he ducked another blow. Pulling his knife, he skirted sideways.

An experienced fighter, the Norwegian growled as he went after him, his face contorted with rage.

Blacarri and Scarface fought back to back, against four circling Norwegians. The sound of their swords clanging rang out. Two of the mercenaries fell quickly. It did not take long to finish off the other two. Wiping their swords on the backs of the dead men, they stood watching Ketil fend off and parry blow after brutal blow.

Gripping the barrels, her deep green eyes wide and glassy, the market girl tried to stand again but her knees buckled. The bruise on her face was already turning deep red. She whimpered weakly.

Casually turning to Blacarri, raising his eyebrow as Ketil stumbled backwards again, Scarface drawled, "Shall we give him a hand?"

His pale grey eyes glinted, "No, he needs the practice."

As he swung his sword, the Norwegian smiled, his eyes narrowing sadistically. He brought his sword down with immense force.

The blow hit Ketil's knife with such power, it flew out of his hand towards Blacarri.

Blacarri sucked in a deep breath as he ducked out of the way. It just missed him. The blade stuck vibrating into a barrel behind him. Blinking, he looked at the knife and then at Scarface. He grinned, "That was close."

Raising his eyebrows again, Scarface turned back to the fight.

Breathless and tiring, Ketil grunted. He knew he had to attack.

Knowing he was more experienced, the Norwegian flourished his sword arrogantly, "It's only a matter of time before I finish you off! Are you ready to meet your Gods?" Over confident, the Norwegian glared at him murderously, leaving his arms open one moment to long.

Holding his sword with two hands, Ketil suddenly yelled deeply as he brought a crashing blow down across the Norwegians chest. He felt the smash of his sword breaking ribs, ripping through flesh. Blood spurted from the man's chest

His heart crushed, he fell to the dirt. The Norwegian only took in three more rasping breaths before he died.

Leaning over, gasping for breath, Ketil sucked in air as fast as his lungs could take it in.

Grinning, Scarface eyed Blacarri, his voice gruff, "I thought you were wasting your time training him but it is starting to pay off. Well done Arrie."

His eyes wide and shining, Ketil wheezed in a gulp of air not quite believing he was still alive.

Nodding at the compliment, Blacarri raised his eyebrows, "Thank you. I nearly gave up. He was completely useless at the start."

"You have really got to work on his stamina though."

"I know. He's breathing heavier than a whore in a brothel." Blacarri shook his head, "It's embarrassing!"

Chuckling, they walked off together, bypassing the cowering girl, towards the ships.

Affronted but unable to move, Ketil gasped in another loud deep breath. Looking around at the dead men, he saw the young woman.

She eyed him back warily, trying to focus.

He tried to smile, "Are you okay?"

She looked at the dead men, her wide green eyes shocked, her voice sounded weak, "Did he?" She paused, unable to contemplate it, "He was going to...." Tears welled up in her eyes, "Did he...?" Her voice trailed off as tears flowed down her bruised face.

Feeling his breathing getting back to normal, Ketil sucked in another lungful of air. Standing upright, he walked over to her, gently, "No, we stopped him before he took you."

Relief flooded through her mind.

"Let me help you up." Taking her arms, he pulled her to her feet. He felt her tremble.

Woozily, she gripped his muscular arm, "He hit me. I cannot stand." Looking at the dead men warily, "I don't like it here." She almost swooned again.

Looking at her for a moment, he knew he could not leave her here. Lifting her slim body into his arms, he felt her long skirt brushing against his legs, as he carried her away from the barrels towards the ships.

Seeing him carrying the wench, Blacarri strode up to him, "Is she okay?"

"No, she is stunned. She cannot stand."

Inclining his head, thoughtfully looking at her, "She will be safer on my ship till morning."

Suddenly remembering her baskets, her eyes looked desperate. Her voice sounded weak and panicky, "My baskets! They are all I have!"

Gently, Ketil looked down at her, "I will fetch them later."

"No, they will be gone. I sell them for food. I will starve without them."

Understanding immediately that this young woman lived on the knife edge of starvation, Blacarri ordered, "Take her onto my ship. I will get her baskets." He strode back to the barrels. As he picked a few baskets up, he noticed all of the Norwegians lay dead where they had fallen, all except Jarl Kalf. There was trail of blood leading away from the barrels. He had obviously played dead and at his first opportunity he had fled. A look of concern flashed across his grey eyes. Ignoring the uneasy feeling, he looked down at the rest of Kalf's men. Unbuckling each of their sword belts, Blacarri swung them over his shoulder. Taking one basket, he filled it with anything of value from them, including their amulets, silver arm bands, pouches of silver and their knives. Grabbing the rest of the girl's baskets, he walked back to his drakkar.

Ketil and the wench sat on the sea chests.

Glancing at her, Blacarri thought she looked a little better. Striding up to Scarface, he handed over to him two silver bangles, a pouch of silver and a sword.

Grinning, Scarface checked the sword for quality.

Opening up his sea chest, taking most of the Norwegians' silver and knives, Blacarri put them into it. Then, he threw three of their swords into a larger casket. Turning to Ketil, he placed two of the finer swords, four knives, six heavy silver bracelets and a purse of silver in front of him. He grinned, "You won your fight. Here are your spoils."

Ketil's eyebrows rose up in surprise, incredulously, "This is too much."

"If it was not for your loyalty Ketil, I could have lost my drakkar and King Anlaf's fortune. You deserve a share." Casually smiling at the girl, he placed the baskets in front of her.

He looked at her kindly, "Here are your baskets." He dropped one silver arm bangle, one good dagger and a small purse of silver into a basket, "Take this as their payment for your injury."

Her mouth dropped open in wonder. It was a fortune.

Blacarri added gently, "You are free to leave whenever you feel able."

Looking up at him, she could see at a glance from his manner and the fine quality of his clothes that he was a noble. Even though it hurt to, she smiled, "Thank you Lord."

She looked a little older than Gytha. Softly, "Do you have family here?"

Quietly, "No Lord, they died."

Looking at her, Ketil asked, "Are you a slave?"

Proudly lifting her head, she eyed him bravely. The movement made her dizzy. Wincing, she touched her bruised face with her hand, "No, I am free."

Tilting his head on one side, assessing her wound, Blacarri frowned, "Where do you live?"

Her head dropped as anxiety filled her, "I look for a safe place every evening. In the day I trade baskets for an egg or a piece of bread."

Thoughtfully, Blacarri looked at Ketil, "Jarl Kalf might still be alive."

Ketil frowned.

"I think he played dead and fled as soon as he got a chance."

Ketil eyed him, "He can't get far with his wound. I drove my sword through him."

He shrugged his shoulders, "I have seen men live through worse." He glanced at Scarface.

Scarface grunted in agreement.

Looking at the woman, Blacarri looked serious, "She is safer here with you, until she recovers. I will tell the men, she is under your protection. No one will bother her. Get her some food and mead, it will help." As he strode away he called back, "I have business with Jarl Gilli. I will be back later."

Ketil took a bulky bag from a sea chest. It contained bread, cheese, a clay pot of honey and two good apples. He handed them to her, gently, "Eat."

Overwhelming relief lit up her face. She grabbed at the dry crunchy bread. Pulling off the honey pot lid, she dipped her bread into it. Her eyes glistened as she bit into her food. The sweet taste was overwhelmingly good.

He grinned, "I too have known hunger. Go easy on the cheese and honey. They are rich and too much will make you sick."

Surprised, she eyed him, "You are a Lord. How could you have known hunger?"

He blinked, then chuckled, "I am not a lord. I serve my employer."

Looking him over him, she tilted her head on to one side. His battle leathers were obviously expensive and new. Even his wrist guards were highly decorated with winged dragons, "You dress like a lord and he treated you as an equal. He even fetched my baskets while you just sat there."

Even he had not considered that. His eyes twinkled intelligently as he looked back at her, "Lord Black Arailt is my employer. I never forget that." Placing a crude pottery jug of mead and two wooden beakers next to her, he filled the beakers, "Drink." Looking down into her deep green eyes, Ketil smiled, "You did not tell me your name."

Shyly, "My name is Afrior."

His voice deepened softly, "Your name means beloved."

Her father had told her the same thing when she was young. She smiled at the memory, curiously, "How do you know that?"

Smiling, his voice gentle, "I hear things and remember."

Blacarri walked towards Gilli's large regal looking red tent. He grinned. This had been his most profitable trip yet. Even though he had given Scarface, Ketil and the girl some of the Norwegian's booty, he still had most of it, and capturing the specials had really paid off. This year, the gold and silver was for the Clan Ivarr but next year, he thought to himself, we will all come back from here very rich men.

The enormous red tent was guarded by a garrison of battle ready men. One of them demanded, "Announce yourself warrior."

Sardonically, "I am Black Arailt Guthrithsson of the Clan Ivarr, King of the Isle of Man, Prince Tanist of Ath Cliath, King of Colonsay and King of Norse Gailgedhael."

The guard's eyebrows lifted with amusement, "And I am the King of Byzantium!"

His comrades chuckled.

Raising an eyebrow, Blacarri retorted dryly, "I always imagined you taller."

Grinning, the guard eyed him as he pulled back the red canvas, "I was told to expect you. You may enter Milord."

He looked inside the tent. It was even more magnificent than the outside. Lit by many vibrant lanterns, golden silks and gossamers glimmered as they draped voluptuously from the ceiling of the tent. The floor was scattered with rich furs and large vibrant coloured cushions. Gilli looked impressive. Dressed in his large red billowing trousers and an open necked shirt made of cloth of gold, he sat on several large cushions in the centre of the room.

Next to him, a beautiful brunette slave woman, dressed only in a thin pure white smock dress looked up.

As Blacarri approached his friend, his steely grey eyes wandered appreciatively to Gilli's slave.

Lowering his head, Gilli whispered in the woman's ear.

Smiling, she slowly stood up. As she walked past the stranger, the light from the lamps shone through her sheer dress, showing the barest outline of her young slim naked body. She walked through the golden gauze drapes to the next room.

His Russian accent thick and drawling, "You like her?" He indicated with his hand that Blacarri should sit.

Sitting down comfortably against a large purple cushion, he half smiled, "My compliments, her body is lovely."

"She is my favourite." Flamboyantly clapping his hands,

several more beautiful slave girls appeared, each carrying golden trays of meat and fruit. They quickly placed the trays before their master and his guest.

Another woman with long strawberry blonde coloured hair brought out a large golden jug full of fruity red wine. Gracefully, she filled two large golden goblets.

A girl entered. She looked much younger than the others. Her body was thin and barely developed but she wore a long warm dress and shawl. She anxiously kept her eyes low. Kneeling down on the rugs, she lifted a flute to her lips. Softly, she began to play.

Lifting his goblet, Gilli drawled, "Can you believe it has been over two years since we last met? I am eager to hear news of Anlaf. I hear he married the King of Alba's eldest daughter, a beautiful prize?"

Inclining his head, Blacarri smiled, "My sister in law is a delight and our people love her. She has already given Anlaf two strong sons."

"News reached us that young Olaf Sihtricsson, has now married another daughter of Constantine's."

His grey eyes hardened slightly, "Yes, Cousin Olaf's fortunes have changed immensely. He is now King of Iona."

Curiously, "Does he own many drakkars?"

"Three."

Shrugging his shoulders, Gilli looked unimpressed, "Not many."

Raising his dark eyebrows, "At the start of this year, Olaf only had a horse. Now, he is married to a Princess of Alba and rules the Island of Iona. He is rich on wedding dowry and has an army of a hundred men."

Gilli inclined his head, "The Gods indeed favour him."

A muscle flexed in his jaw. Looking at Gilli, he changed the subject, "The Gods have favoured you my friend. Your slaves are the most beautiful that I have seen."

"Thank you." He drawled, "I try to purchase quality."

"I met with Hoskuld today. You know the man. He is King

Haakon of Norway's bodyguard. He told me that he bought a slave woman from you yesterday."

"Da, her clothes were rags but her beauty shone through."

"He showed her to me. Hoskuld had her dressed up like a princess. She is very lovely."

"Hoskuld paid seven silver pieces for her, a good price for a mute."

Chuckling deeply, his pale translucent eyes twinkled, "Hoskuld's wife may not think so."

Gilli inclined his head, "I could not get her to talk but it is obvious from the way that she carries herself, she is a woman of status."

"Yes, I thought that to. Hoskuld said she was a mute and I said, 'all the better, a woman that looks like her and cannot bore you with her chatter,'" Blacarri's voice deepened, "what a prize."

Chuckling, "Da. I should have made him pay more!" He took a drink from his goblet, seriously, "I am sure that she is not a mute though. I have seen it before. It is a rebellious streak in a slave, where they try to keep some control over their pitiful lives."

Inclining his head, he thoughtfully agreed, "Some refuse to speak, some go mad."

Gilli shook his head solemnly, "Some take their own lives."

"It is not always easy for those not born into servitude. I agree with you. I think that Hoskuld's slave woman is royalty." Seriously, "Maybe you should have ransomed her."

"Maybe I should have." He sighed thoughtfully, "She was captured in Ireland. You are right, she is obviously of noble blood, perhaps a princess of one of the provinces?"

"She reminded me of a woman I met recently." His eyes deepened to darker shade of grey as he remembered Lady Rafyn. Frowning, it annoyed him how often her image came into his thoughts and his dreams. Changing the subject quickly, he continued, "I heard King Hakon's brother, Erik, was here last year selling slaves to re-build his fortune."

Lifting his goblet Gilli drank deeply, "It is hard to believe that Erik was King of all Norway. His men call him 'Bloodaxe' now."

Blacarri looked up, "Why is this?"

His face serious, Gilli raised his dark eyebrows, "Because he killed so many of his brothers to get the throne. Erik Bloodaxe told me that his brother Haakon and the Thing men of Norway forced him out. He took his wife and children to the Orkneys." He drawled, "His wife, Princess Gunhild, is the old King Gorm of Denmark's daughter."

"I know. Erik jointly rules the Orkneys with Jarl Skullsplitter now."

Gilli smiled, "Da, some say Gunhild is a sorceress. When he is away slaving, she rules with a rod of iron."

"I heard that she is very beautiful."

"Da, she has given Bloodaxe many sons and daughters. Bloodaxe has betrothed his prettiest daughter Ragnhildis to Thorfin Skulsplitter's eldest son Arnfinn." Gilli's brow furrowed, "Bloodaxe is ambitious. He has lost Norway and now holds the Orkneys under his sway but he wants more." Warningly, "He spoke a great deal of Jorvic and Northumbria."

Frowning, Blacarri clenched his fist, "Northumbria belongs to the Clan Ivarr."

Seriously, his accent drawling, "I tell you this to warn you, Arrie. Anlaf needs to be careful of Eric Bloodaxe. He is a dangerous man."

His eyes serious, he nodded thoughtfully, "Hoskuld told me that King Haakon is making many enemies in the court of Norway, by forcing Christianity on his people. Perhaps Bloodaxe will go back to Norway."

Inclining his head doubtfully, Gilli stated bluntly, "Niat, I do not think so. Bloodaxe was tyrannical. The Norwegians are a free spirited people. They would never take him back as king." Drinking deeply from his goblet, he looked jaded, "I am bored Arrie." He ran his hand slowly through his long black hair, "I still train everyday but it is not the same as a good battle. I want to go on a raid again."

"The Clan Ivarr has joined forces with the sub-kings of Britain. We will march on King Athelstan within the year. We fight to regain Jorvic and Northumbria."

"Word has already reached this island Arrie, of your alliance. Have you heard of the Norwegian mercenaries, Egil Skalagrimsson and his brother Thorulf?"

Thoughtfully, "Egil Skalagrimsson is known in Ath Cliath as a great bard. His poems and tales have reached Anlaf's court."

"Egil Skalagrimsson is also one of the most fearless warriors, to ever be honed by Thor's hammer. He is known as the Berserker."

Raising a sardonic eyebrow, sarcastically, "Any idiot can wield a sword in frenzy. Cold skill will always overcome rage."

Smiling, Gilli nodded, "Egil and his brother were here a season ago, bragging that King Athelstan of England is willing to pay any Norwegian mercenary a fortune in silver, if they fight for him."

Frowning, "I had Norwegian mercenaries in my service. Tonight, I found out they planned to steal my drakkar and join the English bastard."

Lifting his goblet of wine to his mouth, Gilli drawled, "What are you going to do with them?"

His glacier eyes hardened, "They are already dead." Thoughtfully, "So, Athelstan is already preparing."

Gilli leaned forward excitedly as an idea occurred to him, "I will come with you, back to Britain. I will fight with you. It will be good to see Anlaf again."

Seriously, "You would be an asset to this war Gilli, but can you leave your property here unattended?"

Confidently, "Of course, my headman Jacobus will protect it. He is a formidable man."

"We leave early tomorrow, on the first tide. I cannot wait if you are late."

"Excellent!" He laboured the word in his thick Russian drawl deep, "Let us not waste any more time." He stood up and stretched his muscular arms, "Who knows when I will next have such a beautiful willing woman to make love to?" Striding to the next room, "Goodnight Arri, I will meet you at the dock tomorrow." Gilli pulled a golden cord. A large curtain dropped.

The young girl immediately stopped playing the flute. Looking frightened, she quickly stood up.

By the servant's entrance, Blacarri saw her mother's plump arms hastily beckon the girl to her.

The girl shot to the tent opening and left with her mother.

Shaking his head, Blacarri stood up and stretched, he suddenly felt very tired. As he left through the entrance, he winked at the guard as they heard the brunette laughing playfully with Gilli.

At the villa fortress, Blanche spent her first fitful night in the luxurious surroundings of Gilli's personal harem. Waking up at every sound, she expected to be called at any moment to her new master's quarters, most likely to be raped. Her nerves felt shattered. Daylight shone through the windows when the door opened. Almost sick with tiredness and fear she began to cry.

Looking over her, Jacobus felt irritated, "I am busy with the master's shipment of amber." It was not unexpected that she should look so pale, "The master has left with the Vikings who brought you here. He will not be back for many days."

Relief that the master would not be calling for her mixed with the desolation that Ragnal had left her. She sobbed softly.

More gently, "Do not upset yourself. You are safe here. The master has given me strict instructions. No one will touch you. You are under his protection." He strode over to the shutter doors and opened them on to a square enclosed garden courtyard. "You may use the garden." He opened a large chest, "There are materials and thread if you wish to sew." He motioned his hand in a swirl, "Or busy yourself in other such womanly pursuits."

Tears swept down her ashen face, she sobbed loudly.

Looking a little desperate, he added, "You may talk with the other women if you wish but you will have no contact with any man except me."

She sobbed loudly again.

Frowning, he hated to hear women crying. Awkwardly, he suddenly left the bed chamber.

Scrambling to the high window, her eyes were dazzled from the bright dawn sunshine. She could just see the natural harbour below. Even from here, she recognised the Viking's small fleet of ships. Each vessel was frothing up the waves, with their long rows of oars, as they sped away to deeper blue waters. Desperate fear overcame her, she screamed, "Ragnal! Don't leave me here!" Her cry carried away on the wind.

In no fit state to command his knar, Ragnal still slept heavily on Blacarri's drakkar deck.

Close by, Ketil stood next to Afrior, his arm gently about her waist to steady her.

The deep red bruise on her face felt painful to touch but she no longer felt dizzy. Gazing up to him, she smiled with excitement, "Thank you for taking me with you."

Looking down into her eyes tenderly, he felt immensely protective of her. It surprised him. It surprised him even more that she held his gaze. Intensely attracted to her, his hazel eyes glinted. They had talked for a long time last night. He had told her about his life at Ath Cliath. She had been fascinated by his tales. As it got darker, she had been too frightened to leave the ship. Instead, she slept next to him on the ship's deck. She had held his hand as she had drifted off to sleep and he had woken up with her arm across his chest. No one had been more surprised than him, this morning, when she had asked to travel with them back to Ath Cliath. He smiled and held her tighter.

The favourable wind rose suddenly. Grinning, Blacarri shouted, "Stow oars!"

The knarrs followed a moment later, lifting their oars in synchronisation.

Lifting his oar, Gilli smiled broadly as salty sea spray hit him in the face.

As soon as the oars were secured, Blacarri yelled, "Hoist sail!"

The wind suddenly caught in the crimson sail, the ship seemed to come alive. The drakkar sleeked through the waves at a rate of ten knots. White water thrashed at the prow enticing dolphins to play in the frothy foam.

The knarrs followed closely behind in its wake.

Watching, Gilli rush to tie off a rope, Ketil grinned. His baggy red trousers were the gaudiest he had ever seen.

Gilli's breath caught in his throat. Lifting his arms flamboyantly in the air, he suddenly shouted excitedly at Blacarri, his Russian accent thick, "This is living, my friend, this is living!"

His translucent pale grey eyes glinting, Blacarri looked past his men to the prow of his dragon headed drakkar and towards the westward horizon.

Part 7

Betrayal

7.1

Scone

Olaf's forehead furrowed as he paced outside the throne room. Wearing a fine cloth of gold tunic, over his brown leather breeches and boots, he had dressed to impress. He had been kept waiting for what seemed like an eternity. Turning to Canute, he complained loudly, "Am I not a king! To be kept waiting like a mere servant is demeaning!"

Fully aware of Olaf's impatient mood, Canute's eyes flashed with concern. His charge had never seemed to outgrow the sulky rages that had marred his childhood. Canute had put the tantrums down to the effect of traumatically losing his father. Now that Olaf was an adult, he ignored them. He eyed the dark wooden door jadedly, "My Lord, we gave no warning of our arrival. I did advise you that King Constantine was holding court for his moramers today."

His lip snarled, "My rank outweighs any clan chief!"

Suddenly the throne room door opened and several moramers noisily strolled out. They barely acknowledged Canute, but they bowed deeply to King Olaf.

Suddenly preening, Olaf inclined his head to them as he strutted past them into the throne room.

Cellach looked up as Olaf approached. Flexing his wide shoulders, he quickly rolled up a velum scroll and handed it to his clerk. Moving back to his father's side, he eyed Olaf evenly with his vibrant topaz eyes.

Sitting nonchalantly on his throne, Constantine watched Olaf confidently stride up to him. He noticed his son-in-law's ostentatious clothing, likely bought with his daughter's dowry. His topaz eyes glinted with irritation. He had to cut short his meeting with the nobles of Alba because Olaf had arrived unannounced.

Noticing his father's annoyance, Cellach raised an eyebrow.

Olaf grinned, "Father-in-law, I hope this day finds you well?"

Bluntly, "I was meeting with my moramers, King Olaf. What brings you here with such urgency?"

"I have news from Ath Cliath."

"Good, what is it?"

He blinked, this was not the reaction that he had been expecting, "Err, during my visit I pressed King Anlaf for more information, in regard to his preparation for war."

Constantine eyed him expressionlessly.

He shuffled a little uncomfortably, "Err, King Anlaf was very evasive."

Cellach eyed him coldly, "Is that it?"

Constantine's eyes glinted, "I hope that I have not dismissed my moramers for this!"

Canute shifted uncomfortably.

Feeling unappreciated and somewhat demeaned, "No father-in-law, I have had reports from a fisherman, that King Anlaf has sent his jarls on slave raids to raise money for the coming war."

Looking at his father, Cellach raised an eyebrow. They had heard this news already.

Continuing quickly, Olaf lifted his chin, "Anlaf is galvanising his forces with promises of riches. I have come here to warn you to be ready for a spring offensive."

Thoughtfully, Constantine eyed him, "My thanks King Olaf."

Feeling like he was about to be dismissed, Olaf decided to leave of his own accord. Inclining his head curtly, he span round and strode out of the room.

Surprised that Olaf left so quickly, Canute bowed a little ungainly before quickly following him out.

As the large door closed, his voice drawling, Cellach eyed his father, "Why didn't you tell him, King Anlaf has sent word to be ready by this autumn?"

He shook his head, "I did not want him to know that I have my own communication routes with Ath Cliath. Obviously mine are better!"

A wry smile played on Cellach's lips.

As he strode out of the castle heading towards the river where his drakkar was moored, Olaf scowled, "I thought he would be more grateful!"

Frowning, Canute shook his head, "I think King Constantine is more grateful than he shows Olaf. Do not forget that the pressures of kingship weigh heavily on most men."

Olaf shrugged, "I have not found it so Canute."

Deciding to dispel the lad's mood, he smiled, "You were born for kingship Olaf."

Lifting his chin confidently, Olaf grinned as he strode towards his drakkar.

7.2

Tamworth
October 937

The royal palace, surrounded by the burghs bailey settlement, had been the capital of Mercia many years ago. King Athelstan's aunt Aethelflaed, the Lady of Mercia, had rebuilt the palace keep. It stood high on the motte hill inside the deep ditched and palisade fenced fortress. In the lower level, bailey smoke seeped from the thatched roofed wattle and daub ancillary buildings and shelters.

Ignoring the arrogant soldiers, a drably dressed peasant unloaded firewood from the cart. He placed most of it into one of the shacks close to the barracks.

Several women walked by the soldiers carrying baskets of apples to a small barn. They hurried as it started to rain. Pulling their woollen shawls over their heads, their long smock dresses billowed about their legs as they scurried inside. The apples were precious. They would be prepared for storing over the winter.

Rain started to lash down stinging the peasant's face but he could not stop working. The lords needed more firewood up at the keep. Lifting up the heavy basket of firewood on to his back, he climbed the guarded wooden steps to the first level flying bridge. He knew that if they were attacked, the flying bridge could be drawn up, making it almost impossible for an enemy to scale the motte. As the cold wind buffeted rain against his body, he carried on climbing up the second set of steps until he reached the top of the motte. Chained black dogs barked at him, as he walked through the huge open gates into the high palisades protected keep. Unchallenged, he strode into the court yard of the thatched wooden palace, up to the large mahogany double doors.

A palace servant immediately strode up to him, "Go round to the kitchen entrance next time you fool!" He tutted officiously, "The king is in residence!"

That grated. Suppressing the feeling, he handed the basket of wood to the servant. His eyes downcast, he silently turned and left.

The round faced servant carried the wood into the warm great hall. Timber posts and a lattice of beams and braces held up the impressive vaulted thatched roof. At one end of the huge room a door led to the king's antechambers. On the other side of the building, two doors led to a large kitchen and an inner hallway that, in turn, led to several sleeping chambers. Glamorous ladies of the English court sat together near a smaller fireplace. They chatted quietly as they embroidered a large tapestry. Walking up to them, his head bent respectfully, the servant placed some of the new firewood in a basket close to the fire. He hoped it would dry before it was needed. None of the ladies looked at him. He knew that he was insignificant to them. He understood his place. At the other end of the hall was a dais, with a long dining table and high backed chairs, facing into the room. In the centre of the room a rectangle of fired bricks surrounded a shallow blazing fire pit. Smoke from the burning firewood drifted upwards to the roof and flowed through a small hole in the soot blackened thatch. Sat in chairs around the warmth of the crackling fire, the richly dressed Athelings gathered as usual at King Athelstan's pleasure. The servant bent his head and carried the basket of wood to the fire pit. As the rain outside fell heavily, large drips of water plummeted through the roof hole and spattered into the flames, hissing steam into the air. He could see that the fire was blazing well. He put down the basket and with a light bow, he walked back to his position by the door.

Wearing his gold crown, Athelstan sat confidently on the

large, highest backed, sturdy chair. He knew that he looked imposing. He had carefully draped a fawn coloured robe over his woad blue tunic. It hung around his muscular shoulders, held in place on one side by a heavy gold brooch. His light brown leather breaches stretched over his muscular thighs. Highest quality leather boots strapped perfectly to his feet and shins. Ever alert, he carried weapons on his sword belt and knives in his boots. His deep blue eyes glinted as the servant announced, "The Bishop of Beverley's envoy, to see the king."

The ladies and nobles looked up with interest as they watched the Bishop of Beverley's portly tonsured servant waddle into the cavernous room.

Breathing heavily, the envoy barely noticed the magnificent tapestries or the hundreds of shimmering weapons and painted shields on the wall. Shuffling past a round map table, his eyes slanted as he noticed the cardinal. Beads of perspiration glistened on his pallid brow. Dark shadows under his eyes and his sallow cheeks revealed his overburdened body was afflicted with infirmity. Bowing low towards the king, he winced. The rough rope belt, around his grey habit, pulled tight across his massive stomach. Nervously, he found it difficult to control the shake of apprehension in his voice, "King Athelstan, Eminent Majesty." Bowing again, this time, to the tall golden haired lad sat closest to the king's throne, "Crown Prince Edmund," his beady eyes took in the lad's fawn coloured battle leathers, snugly fitting to his muscular physique, "You are now of age to go into battle for your country." Casting a barely controlled furtive look towards the king, he immediately looked at the floor. It was as good as saying Prince Edmund was old enough to take the throne.

Eyeing the monk confidently, Prince Edmund smiled, "I will join my brother," he accentuated, "the king, in his next campaign."

Standing close by, Cardinal Dunstan looked impatiently at the envoy, sharply, "King Athelstan is busy with affairs of the state! What do you want?"

He bowed low, "Cardinal Dunstan, my master sends his deepest regards to you and your uncle, Archbishop Athelm of Canterbury." His eyes narrowed deviously, "My master wonders if you have taken holy orders yet?"

He eyed the priest stonily, "It is no secret. Although I am a devout Christian, I am unsure that I have the vocation for a celibate life."

Several of the Athelings frowned. They had all heard the rumours of the Cardinal's affairs, with many a court lady.

"Ahh, my master will be disappointed. He often talks of your spiritual enlightenment," barely hidden jealousy passed over his portly features, "and wise counsel to the King."

The Athelings scowled. They too were growing more resentful of the cardinal's influence at court. Even Prince Edmund stared stonily at his cousin.

Barely acknowledging the veiled compliment, Dunstan snapped curtly, "What do you want?"

Carefully relating his master's words, the envoy turned to King Athelstan, "Eminent Majesty, my master, the Bishop of Beverly, is beside himself."

Lifting his strongly chiselled chin, Athelstan looked steadily at the servant. Choosing his words carefully, he barely hid his impatience, "His Grace, the Bishop, is constantly in my thoughts. What vexes your master?"

"Majesty, massive armies under King Constantine of Alba's sway, are camped just leagues from Beverley. My master fears we will be attacked."

Leaning forward, resting his elbow on his knee, Prince Edmund clenched his right hand into a fist. His blue eyes flashed with intellect as he keenly listened.

Surprise fleeted across Athelstan's face, pensively, "Where is he camped?"

His voice effeminately whining, "It has cost me personal expense to find out my information, Majesty."

His deep blue eyes hardening, Athelstan demanded curtly, "Where exactly is Constantine?"

Talking fast, "Majesty, King Constantine's army has arrived in the Jorvic Earl's territories of Earlsness. They are camped three leagues north of Beverley."

Standing up, Athelstan strode confidently over to the map table. Giving himself time to think, he carefully plotted Constantine's army on the map with an elaborately carved king shaped chess piece.

Broodingly, Dunstan followed the king.

Turning to him, Athelstan whispered, "Excellent, now I know exactly where Constantine has based his camp, it will be easy to track his movements."

Dunstan solemnly nodded, "Yes Majesty, everything is going to your plan. The hoary traitor Constantine, is trapped."

The bishop's servant continued weakly, "I have heard that King Olaf Curan Sihtricsson, is with them."

"So Cardinal, Constantine wants the Northumbrian throne for my sister's stepson." He placed a knight shaped smaller chess piece on the map. "I always knew that he would come back one day, to challenge me for his father's throne."

Frowning, Dunstan looked up at the king, "Word reached us that Olaf had married a daughter of Constantine."

His eyebrows rose up nonchalantly, "With his son in law to protect his borders, Constantine's power will be considerable."

The envoy interrupted shakily, "The four Welsh kings and Strathclyde have joined the Alban army."

Carefully placing five smaller warrior shaped chess pieces on the map, a look of disdain passed over Athelstan's features, "An alliance between Alba and the Welsh." Scornfully, "Ha, their armies are small and of no concern."

Dunstan smiled, "The Welsh bicker between themselves. They are more likely to go to war with each other than us."

Amused, Athelstan chuckled.

Feebly the envoy's eyes looked to the ground, "My master compelled me to advise you, the four Celtic Welsh Kings, have brought a large army. They are united against you Majesty."

Edmund's young eyes flicked up to his half-brother, curious

to see any reaction.

His blue eyes glinting, Athelstan stroked his short golden beard as he eyed the envoy. His voice softly menacing, "Go on."

"Two weeks ago Majesty, a small fleet of Norse ships arrived. They are led by King Black Arailt Guthrithsson."

Placing three small replica ships in the Humber bay a puzzled look passed over Athelstan's face. He looked enquiringly at Dunstan.

The cardinal whispered, "He is the King of Man, Colonsay and Norse Gailgedhael."

A fleeting look of concern passed over Athelstan's face. He whispered incredulously, "Ahh yes Dunstan, the brother of King Anlaf Guthrithsson of the Norse?"

"King Black Arailt has command of many ships and the armies of the Gailgedhael Norse."

As he stood up, Edmund flexed his powerful arm muscles, his voice deepened, "They are ferocious fighters."

Pulling himself up to his full regal height, Athelstan's eyes glittered, "Some would say feral!" Loudly to the envoy, "King Black Arailt Guthrithsson commands a large fleet." Harshly, "You say he has come with just a few ships?"

The servant stumbled over his words, "Yes, yes, but there is more." Looking at the floor he trembled, "Forgive me Majesty, spies are expensive." He clasped his hands together weakly, "Some remuneration would ease my plight."

The cardinal snapped, "Why would a Norse Prince come here with only a few ships?"

Gawping fearfully, the envoy's eyes almost boggled, "My spies tell me that King Black Arailt does not want Northumbria for himself. Nor does he support his Cousin Olaf's claim for the crown."

Athelstan almost hissed, "What?"

Shakily, "He makes ready for the coming of his elder brother, King Anlaf of the Norse, who is also married to one of Constantine's daughters. The eldest I believe. It is King Anlaf himself who commands the main fleet. They say, even King

Suibne of the many Isles, has joined them."

Athelstan took in a deep apprehensive breath, "Alba and the Norse are a force to be reckoned with on their own. With Strathclyde, Gailgedhael, the Welsh, and King Suibne's island pirates, King Anlaf's army will be immense."

Wringing his hands warily the monk sputtered, "A reliable informant has advised my master that King Black Arailt carries an immense fortune." His greedy eyes glinted, "Enough to pay many great armies for many months." The servant could hardly look at the king in the eyes, "But most worrying of all, the Norse navy has been seen off the East coast with over a thousand ships."

Hiding his shock, Prince Edmund strode menacingly over to the map table. Eyeing is cousin aggressively, his muscular shoulder barged Dunstan aside. His eyes glinting, he stood by his brother.

Warily, Dunstan stepped away, bowing his head in submission.

Calmly, Edmund placed several small replica ships dotted along the East coast.

Watching him, Athelstan sucked in a deep breath, "The fiercest storms for ten years have battered our seas and coasts. With God's will, his navy will be wrecked."

Visibly cringing, it took all of the messenger's meagre strength to continue, "Scarborough was attacked two days ago."

Glaring at the messenger, Edmund moved the ships further down the east coast shore. He placed a blackened charred small replica of a castle on the area of the map that was Scarborough.

Cardinal Dunstan gulped in a deep breath, "How could he have made it here already?"

"King Black Arailt's ships have been attacking the southern lands on the Humber for supplies." Gulping in a shaky breath, "Reports are arriving every day, advising my master, that villages have been set on fire and looted."

Moving two ships to the southern most banks of the Humber, Edmund placed down two more charred miniature castles.

"All the men who fought back were killed and left for dead. The heathens have taken all of the winter stocks of food. There will be starvation."

Dunstan whispered, "The enemy have united and are preparing for a long winter. They too want an early spring attack."

This news filled, Athelstan with trepidation, "The Norse King's reputation is formidable. I have not been tested against this man before. It is told, that Anlaf and his brothers were trained to fight under two mythical warrior masters, on a magical island surrounded by mist and cloud."

Sensing his half-brother's foreboding, Prince Edmund turned to his cousins the Athelings. He raised his eyebrow thoughtfully. Was his half-brother showing weakness?

They all looked back at him, some expectantly, some broodingly.

Suddenly remembering that the Athelings were watching, King Athelstan laughed, stretching his arms, flexing his immense muscles, he strode over to the wine table and poured himself a goblet of wine, "I look forward to our meeting." Swinging round, his eyes gazed at each one of them glitteringly hard, "At last, a worthy opponent!"

Many of the young Athelings blinked in surprise. Observing him, like a pack of predators, they had learnt over the years to reluctantly respect him.

Following him, his head slightly bowed, Dunstan whispered, just so Athelstan could hear, "Each Atheling in this room considers the Kingdom of England should rightfully be his. But who, whom amongst them would dare to challenge you, Majesty?"

He smiled confidently as he sipped the dark red oak matured liquid.

Watching Dunstan counselling his brother, Edmund's jealous brooding eyes looked over to his lesser ranked cousins.

Golden haired and blue eyed like him, they all stared bitterly resentful at the cardinal.

Bowing his head slightly, Dunstan smiled, "You are truly, the Thunderbolt."

Casually holding the goblet of wine, he turned almost theatrically, to his waiting audience. The spicy blackberry wine aroma filled his nostrils. He ignored the annoyingly droning voice of the servant, who was now reciting his master's request for military aid. Slowly looking around at the young golden haired Athelings, he smiled as he whispered to Dunstan, "Cardinal, my spies have kept me well informed over the last four months. I have mustered and prepared my army. We are still in Mercia but it is of no matter."

Quietly, "It is so late in the campaign season. What will you do?"

Shrugging his shoulders, he looked at him, "The harvest was late this year and armies need to be fed. Everything was going to plan for a spring attack."

Nodding, "Yes, everything was going to plan," he sucked in a deep breath, "until now."

His deep blue eyes glistened intently, "With King Anlaf in our country, carrying a fortune in gold, we risk treachery from our Norwegian mercenaries. If my mercenaries change sides, England will be doomed."

Dunstan nodded thoughtfully.

"This intelligence changes everything." Suddenly Athelstan boomed, "Fetch me the Norwegian mercenaries, Egil and Thorulf Skalagrimsson."

Two soldiers obediently darted out of the hall.

Each Atheling waited with anticipation. What would their king do now?

"Prince Edmund," Athelstan walked back to the map table, "at my court you have learnt to be a respected warrior. To be king however, you need to understand the strategy of generals." He disdainfully continued to ignore the messenger, who prattled on incessantly about sufferings of the people.

Edmund inclined his head to his half-brother. The lad tried to listen intently and concentrate on the huge beautifully painted map but the whining voice of the messenger irritatingly interrupted his thoughts.

Athelstan leant on the table his fists clenched. His voice deep, he eyed his brother, "War is always fluid Edmund. We must be prepared to change our tactics. We must bend like tree branches to changing winds, even when the dangers seem immense."

He nodded grudgingly respectful, "Yes Majesty."

Suddenly the guard announced loudly, "Egil Skalagrimsson and Thorulf Skalagrimsson, mercenaries of Norway!"

Athelstan turned to the great hall's black door expectantly.

Egil and Thorulf marched into the room. They bowed their heads briefly to the king.

Looking over the two men a smile played on Athelstan's lips. They could not be more different. Thorulf, the younger of the two brothers looked perhaps in his early twenties? His body was tall and muscular. His long blonde hair was tied back from his chiselled handsome face, revealing the most vibrant blue eyes. In contrast, Egil was shorter but still taller than everyone else in the room. His hair was dark grey, wolf like. One heavily dark haired eyebrow seemed to ascend higher than the other. His dark eyes, fiercely glinting with intelligence, surveyed the room.

The dim portly servant prattled on with his unending requests.

Irritated beyond belief, Athelstan suddenly ordered loudly, "For God's sake Cardinal! Get that fool out of here before I personally cut his tongue out!"

The court ladies looked up alarmed.

Raising a dark eyebrow, Dunstan clicked his fingers at the two guards in the doorway of the hall.

They immediately marched over to the bishop's servant. He shrieked like a girl as they dragged him whimpering from the hall.

Rolling his eyes in disgust, even young Edmund looked relieved.

Smiling, Athelstan swung round amiably to the Norwegians, "Welcome."

Egil Skalagrimsson's highest eyebrow raised even higher, his eyes glinting he bowed again. In contrast to his fierce looks his voice was deep and resonant, "Great Majesty, King Athelstan the Thunderbolt, defender of the people, Emperor of this great land."

Everyone in the room felt the man's intensely deep melodic voice, travel over their skin, so that the tiny hairs on their arms stood on end.

Interest sparkled in Athelstan's deep blue eyes, "Your reputation as a poet and story teller is almost as great as your reputation as a warrior."

Confidently, Egil inclined his head, "After we have defeated the enemy Majesty, I hope that you will allow me to write a saga of your victory?"

Feeling pleased, he inclined his head. Not allowing himself to be diverted, he stated regally, "In the last two days, King Anlaf of Ath Cliath has been seen on the east coast of my land. He travels with the forces of his brother's army and the navy of the Norse Isle men. They number one thousand ships."

Smiling at his brother, Egil's face looked even more lopsided, "A vast number of men but I still like those odds."

Inclining his handsome blonde head, Thorulf chuckled.

His eyes glinting, Prince Edmund raised his head, "It would appear that King Anlaf has formed an alliance with Alba and the Welsh." He pointed to the map, "King Constantine is camped here."

Their shoulders wide and imposing, Egil and Thorulf strode menacingly over to the map table. They were obviously trying to intimidate the lad.

Eyeing them, his chin jutting out, Edmund stood his ground.

Smiling, placing his hand affectionately on Edmund's shoulder, Athelstan introduced him, "May I present my half-brother, Crown Prince Edmund."

From under his huge bushy eyebrows, Egil looked over the lad. He decided to test him, "Where is King Anlaf now?"

Bluntly, "Storms have hit our eastern coasts. I would say this slowed him down." He pushed a ship towards the Humber estuary making his decision, "He would be about here."

Impressed, Egil inclined his head respectfully, "Good, I agree. Where are we on your map?"

He pointed to the dragon shaped carved chess piece, confidently, "Mercia is here."

His dark brows furrowing, Egil stated practically, "King Anlaf wants a spring offensive."

Clenching his fist, Athelstan looked fiercely at Egil, "I need to attack him when he does not expect it." Banging his fist violently on to the map the carved pieces shuddered but did not topple, "Now is the time to strike, while Anlaf and Constantine are bedding in for the winter! When can you make your mercenaries ready?"

His voice booming, he grinned, "My mercenaries are always ready!"

As the Athelings roared battle cheers, Prince Edmund's brooding young eyes fell on the carved ship placed on the map at the entrance of the Humber.

7.3

October 937
Hessleport

Deep orange and darkly mauve rolling clouds lit up the early evening heavens. The wide Humber estuary reflected every colour on its still turbulent waters. With sails torn and shredded, Anlaf's battered fleet of drakkars and knarrs limped into sight. They looked a sorry sight but at least none were missing from the thousand ships that had left home.

Sailing out to meet the Anlaf's navy had been his idea. Blacarri half regretted it now as wind howled all around him and waves lifted his ship high then low. As his sleek dragon headed drakkar glided through the churning, frothing waves, he hung grimly on to a rope. He recognised his brother with immense relief, he shouted, "Navigator, King Anlaf's ships are close enough! Turn back to shore!"

"Yes Lord." The navigator grunted as he pulled on the main oar at the rear of the ship.

Blacarri looked up. The dark red sail billowed against the sky's stormy clouds, as the ship did a wide arching turn in the sea. From the stern of his ship, he motioned Anlaf's navy to follow him. He led them to Hessleport.

Built by the local chieftain Hessl, son of Aram, the port had a reputation for being very large and serviceable. There was no dockside. It was not needed as there were leagues of deep sand bank to moor ships. The wooden buildings in the small town looked black from the recent rain. The sand banks teamed with life. Men, women and children sat on barrels, making sails, fishnets and rope. Seagulls drifted on gusts of air screeching raucously. Fishwives crowded around baskets of freshly caught sea fish, bawling out their price barter for the catch. On higher ground, the dark wooden fortress guarded many large barns, where traders loaded and stored their shipments. Cargo ships shipped everything and anything, from slaves, jet, amber, honey, furs and wool. Some of the more heavily guarded barns even held expensive barrels of wine, reams of silks and chests of rare Swedish glass beads. Around the port, the small town was growing bigger every year. Hearth fires spewed smoke from wattle and daub hovels. Shops, smithies, brothels and taverns, serviced villagers, fishermen and sailors alike.

On his ship, Blacarri yelled deeply to his crew, "Head towards the bonfires!"

High up on the sand banks, fishermen's wives lit stone lined fires to help their men and their sons find home. On this squally afternoon, they would help an armada of drakkars make land.

Scratching his itchy unkempt dark blonde beard, Anlaf watched stoically from his drakkar, as Blacarri's crew expertly stowed the large square sail. Raising their oars high, Blacarri's men lowered them into the tempestuous ocean and rowed towards the sand bank. The dark sleek drakkar headed towards the light of the score of fires. Anlaf shouted the order, "Stow the sail!" His ship creaked and groaned. The sea, reflecting the reddening sky, looked to him like a fiery cauldron of boiling water. As soon as the sail was tied off, he yelled deeply, "Man your oars!"

His men reacted with absolute skill. Thirty oars lifted elegantly to the sky then lowered, slicing through the loudly frothing sea. Splashing through the waves in synchronization, the oars propelled the ship towards the white sandy beach.

Three ships lengths from the sand bank, Anlaf ordered loudly, "Lift oars!"

Strongly, his men lifted their oars and his shallow hulled ship soon glided up on to the gravely sand. Men moved quickly to stow their oars. Expertly throwing their ropes to the waiting men on the bank, the crew leapt onto the sand and shallows. They grunted as they dragged the ship higher up the bank. They secured the drakkar with thick ropes tied to tall, deep set posts.

The sound of the wind gusting and whistling through nearby reeds sounded wild and eerie. In the distance, reed birds warbled. Disembarking from his vessel with a jump onto the sand, Anlaf stretched. He felt small pebbles beneath his leather boots. Pushing his tanned hands, back through his blonde hair, relief coursed through his veins.

First to dock and secure his ship, Blacarri strode up, "Good to see you brother." Pulling him into a bear hug, he smiled, his teeth very white against his tanned skin.

"Good to see you, Arrie." Strong squalling winds buffeted Anlaf's body. Wearily, "Thanks be to the Gods, you look well. You did well to come out and meet us. We struggled to see land in the storm."

Another ship in his fleet made land next to Anlaf's drakkar. Some of the men jumped out of the drakkar and fell to their knees in the sand kissing the ground.

A tired chuckle escaped Anlaf's lips. The shouts of men filled the air. Grabbing a rope each, he and Blacarri helped them drag their ship higher up the beach.

His voice deep, Blacarri yelled, "Secure the ships to the posts! The estuary is tidal!"

Striding up to them, Gilli grinned as his gaudy red breaches billowed in the wind. His thick Russian accent drawled, "Welcome Anlaf. I was concerned that you would not make it. Storms have battered us here."

Standing a respectful distance away, Ketil held his horse bridle waiting for orders. His horse raised his head and whinnied impatiently. He gently stroked his horse's long dark mane to calm him. As more ships ground their hulls onto the beech, his stallion snorted excitedly. Stretching his arms, Ketil's silk shirt and silver arm bands pulled against his bulging muscles.

His face looked older, more chiselled. His newly grown dark beard was tied under his chin with a silver bead amulet, just like Gilli's gold charm. The small piece of metal was inscribed with a rune that said, 'Loyalty above all else'. His hazel eyes glinted. He watched as many more of the fleet of drakkars and knarrs, speed up on to the sand, their hulls crunching the shingle until they stopped. There were already hundreds of ships moored. He smiled. They looked like a great long line of beached black headed dragons.

Pleased surprise flashed across Anlaf's face when he saw Gilli, "My friend, it is good to see you." Pushing back his blonde hair from his face, his blue eyes looked serious, "It was the worst voyage of my life. The storm came out of nowhere." Raising his voice, "Some of the men said, 'the great God Thor is angry'. I said, 'no, the God of Thunder rides his storm chariot with us, to protect us in the coming battle.'" The wind buffeted his body again. Raising his chin assertively, his voice booming to his men, "I was right, we lost no ships!"

The men on the moored vessels cheered him.

Scarface strode up. His face looked grim, "We were told that waves higher than Ath Cliath castle could be seen from the coast. Thanks be to Thor, you made it."

Reverently gripping the miniature gold Thor's hammer pendant, hanging on a chain at his neck, Blacarri lifted it to his lips and kissed the cold metal, "Praise be to Thor."

Ragnal strode over. His voice sounded curt, "Good to see you Anlaf. You look like shit."

Raising his blonde eyebrows, his voice gruff, "Thanks." He noticed his youngest brother's face looked gaunt, it concerned him, "Brother, you look changed in some way. Are you okay?"

Sharply, "I am fine." His eyes hardened as he caught Gilli's eye. He turned abruptly back to his horse.

A little disconcerted, Gilli blinked.

Shrugging his shoulders, Anlaf turned to Blacarri, "What is up with him?"

"I don't know. He's been like it since the slave raid." He shook his head, "He's got some sort of a death wish at the moment. He wants to lead every raid. He is taking so many risks. The men have nicknamed him Berserker Bear."

Thoughtfully, Anlaf watched Ragnal mount up onto his horse. A strong gust of wind howled through the ship's riggings. The waves in the wide Humber estuary were shallower than out at sea but the ships still waiting to moor listed dangerously.

"Did the evacuation of Ath Cliath go smoothly?"

Turning back to Blacarri, his voice steady Anlaf nodded, "Yes, everyone who cannot fight has been moved to your Isle of Man. Your people have taken them in. Maelmare and the ladies of court have moved into your fortress."

"Good." Turning to two stable lads holding horses, Blacarri motioned them to bring them over.

Anlaf took the reins from the young lad. Looking over the beast, he could instantly see he was a fine stallion. Late, low sunshine, burst through the rolling angry red clouds in a rush of pale golden light. The stallions white coat shimmered. Hooking his foot into the stirrup, swinging up strongly onto the dark brown leather saddle, he smiled. It felt good to sit on a horse again, "Scarface," he ordered, "oversee the mooring of the rest of the ships. The navigators are struggling to see spaces to make land."

Gruffly, "No problem. This part of the beach is full. The waiting ships will need to sail further along. I need a horse and a torch to signal them.

Ketil signalled waiting stable lads to bring more horses. They must have been waiting behind a sand dune because they arrived instantly.

Gilli took a half burning log from a fisherman's fire pit, "Wait, I will help you."

"Thanks Gilli." Mounting his horse, Scarface rode off.

Swinging up on to horseback, Gilli cantered off, enthusiastically signalling the waiting ships with his flaming torch, to follow them down the beach.

Listening to the shouts of their navigators, the men on the ships pulled their oars strongly following him.

When he reached a gap wide enough for a ship, Gilli motioned with sharp flaming strokes and the nearest drakkar would row in and glide up on to the sand.

Crewmen from ships, that had already docked, helped them drag their ships high up on to the crunching white pebbly sands.

Mounting his horse, Blacarri turned to Scarface, "The men will sleep in the ships tonight. Food will be brought to them. Chieftain Hessl has arranged for pig roasts, apples and bread for your feast this evening." His voice deepened, "There will be a jug of ale for each man. Tell them not to leave the ships. I want them ready in case we are attacked."

Adjusting the sword at his waist, Ketil easily mounted his horse. He also had a sword in a back scabbard. The hilt could be grabbed from over his left shoulder. Two more swords hung from either side of his saddle. He wore a long knife in each boot and one on his sword belt. There were also firmly secured short knives in each of his wyvern decorated wrist guards. Confidently turning his horse, he caught Anlaf's eye, inclining his head respectfully Ketil bowed.

Recognising Blacarri's servant, Anlaf's eyebrows lifted in surprise. He carried more weapons than most warriors, "Ketil, is that you?"

Keeping his head bowed, "Yes Majesty,"

"What has my brother been feeding you? I have never seen a man go from scrawny, to this amount of muscle, so quickly."

Smiling, "I am fed well Majesty. My Lord has put me on a strict training regime. King Blacarri insisted I learn to fight for the coming war."

Surprise glinted in Anlaf's eyes, "Excellent, we need good warriors."

On his horse, Blacarri grinned, a touch of mischief twinkled in his pale grey eyes, "And, he's got himself a woman. She already carries his child."

Raising both of his blonde eyebrows with interest, Anlaf chuckled, "Ketil, follow us to the fortress."

Anlaf, Ragnal, Blacarri and Ketil cantered the short distance to the fortress.

Stable boys were waiting as they dismounted. The lads led the horses away, their hooves clip clopping on the stone cobbles.

As they strode up the hewed rock steps and through massive iron studded oak doors, Blacarri explained, "The main halla has been recently vacated by Chieftain Hessl. He is loyal to you Anlaf. You can use this fortress as long as you wish." Smiling, "I expect it will feel large and comfortable, compared to the meagre provisions on your ship."

Striding into the main hall, Anlaf looked around. The flickering flames from the vast stone lined fire pit, took the autumn evening chill off the air, and helped to light the dark oak beamed hall. Smoke from the fire seeped out of the roof through the blackened sooted thatch. Thick beeswax candles hung on metal candelabras, their flames cast shadowy light on to the faded threadbare tapestries that lined the wattle and daub walls. Straw and herbs littered the stone slabbed floor. From the clean smell of rosemary under his feet, Anlaf could tell it was freshly laid. However, his eyebrows rose up when he saw a mouse scurry across the floor and dart into a small mouse hole in the wall. Shrugging his shoulders, he strode over to the largest fleece covered chair close to the fire and he sat down. The chair was high backed with Norse designed wolf heads decorating the arm rests. He closed his eyes for a moment. The sheep pelts were thick, warm and soft. The chair felt immensely comfortable. He felt tired. Hearing a door open he opened his eyes.

Five large grey haired cooks, dressed in brown coarse linen smocks, entered the room. Between them they carried a massive tray, holding a freshly baked hog, surrounded by steaming baked apples. The pink head of the hog steamed with a huge apple in its gaping mouth. Delicious smells filled the room.

A large woman, her face not unlike the hog, carried in two jugs of honey beer. Her long brown smock dress brushed against her plump legs as she walked. She flushed pink as she put the heavy jugs on to a table. Bobbing an ungainly curtsey, she quickly left the room.

The head cook announced, "A welcome meal from Jarl Hessl, my Lord." Placing the porker on the table, the cooks carved several huge chunks of meat from the flank.

Nodding, Anlaf smiled, "Send my thanks to Jarl Hessl and tell him I will not forget his loyalty. Leave us now. We will serve ourselves." As the cooks bowed and left, he threw a hunk of the pork into his mouth. Smiling at Blacarri, he chuckled, his mouth watering, "This is so good. Ketil what are you waiting for? Get yourself a plate."

Surprised to be invited to eat with the King, Ketil hesitated for a moment.

Nodding to him, Blacarri grinned as he picked up a plate and passed it to Ketil before helping himself.

Loading up his plate with pork, Ketil sat down. Stabbing his short knife into the meat he ate it. It tasted so tender and succulent, he could not stop smiling.

"I cannot stay long." Blacarri gulped down the pork, "Some more winter provisions arrived today."

"Well done brother. I knew I could rely on you."

"I need to check the store is guarded and I want to check your ships. A few looked as though they had hull damage."

Looking up sullenly, Ragnal frowned, "I will go with you. I can help lift them for repairs." He strode off towards the door.

Grabbing one last piece of pork, Blacarri followed him, ordering, "Ketil stay here. Take some hog meat and apples for your wife. It will be good for the baby." Cold October evening air buffeted loudly through the door as he left.

Eyeing Ketil thoughtfully, Anlaf looked over him again noting his hard muscular shoulders and thighs, he looked as powerful as any noble, "You have changed much Ketil. You even have a wife now."

Putting some more meat and steamed apple on a plate, he set the plate aside, "Yes my King."

"What is her name?"

A loud knock against the huge door interrupted them.

Ketil immediately strode to the door.

Sitting upright, Anlaf nodded to Ketil.

Opening the door, he looked at the guard, "Yes? What is it?"

The craggy faced guard stood by two men dressed in long hooded capes. His voice gruff the guard stated flatly, "Archbishop Wulfstan of Jorvic and Jarl Orm of Northumbria, wish to see the king."

Eyeing the men quickly, Ketil nodded to the guard, "Wait here my Lords." Closing the door he strode closer to Anlaf, "Sire, Archbishop Wulfstan of Jorvic and Jarl Orm of Northumbria request an audience."

Anlaf sighed with tiredness, then stoic, he ordered, "Show them in Ketil. Serve them ale and wait here for my orders."

"Yes Majesty."

Opening the large mahogany door with flourish, Ketil announced loudly, "Archbishop Wulfstan of Jorvic and Jarl Orm of Northumbria to see the king."

Anlaf looked up expectantly. He watched Wulfstan approach. His long green cape billowed out behind him, revealing darkly menacing black battle leathers.

Bowing his head tedium tinged his voice, "Majesty, we are thankful that you arrived safely." His dark eyes flicked coldly assessing the king's person looking for any sign of weakness. Apart from a full beard and a malodorous whiff of unwashed travel sweat he was unchanged, "You have survived the worst storms in living memory. It is a great omen for your coming victory."

His face expressionless, he nodded, "Welcome Archbishop."

"May I present Jarl Orm of Northumbria?"

Glancing at Jarl Orm, Anlaf motioned with his right hand for Wulfstan to continue.

Ketil eyed the jarl. He looked formidable in black battle leathers and a sweeping black cape. His white blonde hair swept back from his face. Immense muscle definition throughout his body made him look younger than his forty years.

Wulfstan droned on, "Jarl Orm is an elder of the Northumbrian Witan and loyal supporter to you, Majesty."

His dark blue eyes assessing, Anlaf nodded to Jarl Orm.

Jarl Orm bowed low, "Majesty, I believe we are distantly related."

He nodded, "That is my understanding, welcome."

His eyes low, Ketil approached them expertly carrying a silver tray with goblets full of ale, "Ale, my Lords?"

Both men waved him away.

"Majesty?"

Barely acknowledging him, Anlaf shook his head.

He moved away. Placing the tray on a table, he moved back into the shadows.

Jarl Orm, his eyes as steely as his sword, spoke seriously, "May I speak frankly Majesty?"

Holding Jarl Orm's gaze, Anlaf nodded, his eyes guarded.

"For over ten years I have kept Norse fires burning in Northumbria for the day a Norse king returned to our land. There is none more than I who welcome your arrival."

"Your loyalty to me is not in question Jarl Orm."

Orm eyed him steadily, "I know you need supplies for your great army and will take these by force if necessary. If you give your word that you will only attack villages south of the Humber, I will pledge my allegiance and my army to you."

Immediately understanding the issue, Anlaf frowned, "My uncle, late King Sihtric, spoke well of you and your honest counsel. On the way here the storm hit us and I had to make landfall quickly, or I would have lost my entire navy. I ordered the sacking of your town Scarborough for food. No one was killed."

Jarl Orm nodded, "I understand that you left Scarborough bereft of their winter supplies and now they fear a winter famine. Many will die from hunger."

Frowning, "Armies need to eat."

Softly, "Indeed they do. So do farmers and their wives and children. These are my people my King. They rely on me to protect them."

Carefully considering, Anlaf nodded, "I understand. I respect your leadership. I will send supplies to Scarborough as compensation."

Jarl Orm bowed low, "My thanks Majesty."

Wulfstan cleared his throat, "King Anlaf, Chieftain Hessl is so eager to please you that he wishes to give you a present of land close by."

He smiled, "This does please me. Where is the land?"

Wulfstan flicked his black irritating lanky hair from his face. His voice droned, "A short distance north of here. There is good agricultural land and a halla surrounded by a circular fort."

Contemplating this, he eyed the archbishop thoughtfully, "Tell Chieftain Hessl, I am very pleased with this present. The acquisition of land is serious. I will re-name the town Anlafburgh." He smiled, "I may camp there tomorrow."

He raised a sardonic dark eyebrow, "Hessl is a very ambitious young man. He is thinking of the future. If the alliance wins this war and you become King of Jorvic, you will have much influence here."

Looking at the archbishop steadily, Anlaf remained impassive.

His dark eyes slanted as he looked for a reaction, "Hedging his bets, Hessl has already given your brother, King Blacarri a town. His land is less than half a day west of Hesslport. However, his land has a port, a halla and several crofts."

In the shadows, Ketil raised his eyebrows. Was the archbishop trying to goad King Anlaf?

Coolly, Anlaf watched Archbishop Wulfstan.

"It is good fertile land. Your brother has named his land Blacarscroft."

Understanding exactly what Wulfstan was doing, he remained impassive, "An excellent name for my brother's town, Archbishop."

Jutting his jaw out, Wulfstan looked disappointed. He had hoped to spark a reaction against Blacarri. There was none. He felt the need to rile King Anlaf. If he could do that, he knew that he would have power over the king. He would be able to control and even manipulate him. There was absolutely no reaction from the king. His eyes narrowing further, he decided to change the subject, "When do you intend to attack Athelstan, Majesty?"

Ignoring the question, he eyed him coldly, "Where is the Alban army camped?"

Thoughtfully enigmatic, he held his gaze, "Ten leagues north of Anlafburgh."

"Is my cousin King Olaf Sihtricsson with Constantine?"

"Yes my Lord. King Olaf commands his own force."

Turning back to Jarl Orm, "Do you have a drakkar here?"

"Yes Majesty."

"Do you, or your navigator, have a good knowledge of the Northumbrian river systems?"

"My knowledge of the Northumbrian rivers is second to none, Majesty."

"I will keep five of my drakkars here. I want you to lead the rest of my fleet tonight to Richalle. Do you know the place?"

"I am well acquainted with Richalle and with Jarl Ricderc the chieftain. He is a man of much intelligence."

Confidently, Anlaf grinned, "Jarl Ricderc has a barracks and provisions that will last till spring."

Orm nodded, "Do you wish to move your army under cover of darkness?"

"Yes."

"Very wise Majesty. There are Mercian spies everywhere. I will make ready immediately."

As Jarl Orm left, Wulfstan's eyes glinted darkly, "Majesty, many of our Northumbrian villages have pledged their support. They will see out the winter with their families and join your army in the spring."

"Thank you Archbishop. Have you arranged lodgings here?"

"Yes Majesty."

"Good, leave me now."

Bowing low, Wulfstan swept his green cape aside as he left the halla.

Anlaf lifted his goblet in the air.

Instantly, Ketil was by his side carrying a jug of honey ale. Filling the goblet, he asked respectfully, "Would you like me to see if I can acquire wine for you, Majesty? I believe King Black Arailt has some nearby."

Carefully eyeing Ketil, "So Blacarri has taken my land and my wine?"

Drawing himself up to his full height, Ketil frowned, "Majesty, Lord Black Arailt accepted a gift of land from Chieftain Hessl because it was made to him in friendship."

His voice cold, "Wulfstan inferred Blacarscroft is better than my land."

He eyed him steadily, "My King, I heard him and my instincts told me that the archbishop was baiting you."

"Blacarri has wine! Am I not the King of the Norse of Britain and Ireland? Yet I am forced to drink ale!"

"Majesty, we were not sure when you would arrive. Lord Black Arailt has managed to secure a shipment of wine which he keeps guarded for your arrival."

Angrily, "I will kill any man who undermines my power!"

Taking a deep breath, he blinked, "Black Arailt is your loyal brother, Sire."

His voice low, he glared at him, "I need a good servant Ketil. I want you to join my household."

Blinking with tension, he bowed, "Majesty, I am loyal to you my King and I am loyal to your brother." Raising himself up again to his full height, he looked at the king steadily, "Lord Black Arailt is my employer and I have no wish to leave his service."

He eyed him threateningly, "Ketil, it is very dangerous to refuse a king's wish."

He breathed deeply, "Your brother is your most loyal supporter. I would lay my life on that fact, and I have no wish to leave his service."

Humour suddenly came back into Anlaf's eyes, he grinned, "Your loyalty to my brother is reassuring Ketil. I have noticed tonight, he is placing more trust in you. I wanted to make sure of you myself."

Blinking twice more, he breathed deeply again. Relief strained his voice, "You were testing me?"

Chuckling, "I wanted to see how loyal you are to my brother." Amiably, "Fill yourself a cup of ale, it really is quite good."

Pouring himself a full goblet he gulped it back.

Amused, Anlaf watched him shakily pour another.

Taking another gulp, Ketil shook his head, "For a moment there I thought you were going to have me hanged. I may need to change my breeches!"

He chuckled. Steadily looking at him, "I trust my brother implicitly. If you had shown any disloyalty to him, I would have informed Blacarri, and he would hang you himself. Pull up a chair. I realise I know nothing about you. Tell me about yourself. What is your story?"

Relaxing, he scraped a chair across the wooden floor and sat down, "My story?"

"Yes, where were you born? How did you come to be in my brother's employment?"

Taking a mouthful of ale, he looked uncomfortable. He did not ever really talk about himself, "Err," thoughtfully, "I was born in Ath Cliath seventeen years ago. My father was killed young in battle. My mother found work salting furs." Sadness filled his eyes, "Many winters ago she died of a fever. I lived on the streets after she died, staying anywhere that gave me shelter."

"Go on."

"Err." Trying to think of something that would impress

the king, he smiled, "My mother told me that my great, great grandfather was Ketil Flatnef. I am named after him."

Anlaf's blonde eyebrows rose up, "He was a great and noble king. You are descended from royalty?"

Amused, he chuckled, "My great, great grandmother was his slave, so I am not a royal." Raising a sardonic eyebrow, "I think most of the people of Ath Cliath have some royal blood in their veins." His voice deepened, "Only the leaders of the Clan Ivarr are truly noble."

He grinned, "I was fortunate that my mother married my father. How did you stay alive after your mother died?"

Smiling proudly, he looked like a young lad again, "I am a fast runner. I worked as a lookout for the ships coming into harbour. Shop keepers paid me to let them know first when cargo was arriving."

"Ah yes, I remember. You spotted the ship that brought my Queen to me."

Smiling at the memory, sincerely, "Queen Maelmare brought me good fortune. My life has changed so much since the queen arrived. That was the day that King Black Arailt took me into his service." He chuckled, "Now I own my horse." He looked at his muscular arms, "I have many silver arm rings and many weapons." He looked happy.

Indulgently, "You have a woman now as well."

A muscle flickered in Ketil's jaw, "Yes Majesty, we are married."

"What is her name?"

"Her name is Afrior."

Chuckling knowingly, "And there is a child on the way."

His young eyes sparkled with pride and happiness, "Yes sire, she thinks that she is six weeks gone."

"Where will you live when we get home?"

"My family and I will go wherever my Lord Black Arailt travels."

The huge mahogany door to the room suddenly banged open. Blacarri strode in, "Jarl Orm has left with most of the fleet. I ordered the ships to be loaded with the hog meat and ale. At least the men will eat tonight, they are exhausted."

Quickly getting to his feet, Ketil waited for orders.

Anlaf eyed his brother, "They can take turns to sleep. I needed the ships out of sight."

Blacarri inclined his head. He knew his brother was right.

Yawning, Anlaf stretched, suddenly feeling very tired, "We barely got any sleep on the voyage."

"Your sleeping quarters are in the south wing."

"Good."

"Ketil, show my brother to his sleeping quarters then retire yourself."

Ketil nodded curtly. Grabbing the plate of pork and apples for Afrior he smiled, "Thank you Lord."

A short time later, Ketil strode into his own bedchamber carrying the plate of food. Afrior sat in the candlelight at the mahogany dressing table brushing through her long dark blond shimmering hair. Her white shift was covered loosely by her new sage green housecoat. The colour accentuated the green of her eyes. All of her bruises from her attack had disappeared. She had lost the desperate look of living on the edge of starvation. She smiled happily, "Good evening husband."

"Good evening wife." Walking up to her, he bent his head and kissed her up turned mouth tenderly, "You look beautiful."

7.4

10 November 937AD

Wulfstan's voice tinged with tedium, "It has been many days Majesty, since your arrival. How go the plans for your spring offensive?" He looked at King Anlaf, with hard assessing eyes. The king's tanned handsome face was cleanly shaved. Dressed richly in fawn coloured battle leathers and a white tunic trimmed with gold, he looked in his prime.

Looking back at Wulfstan, Anlaf barely smiled. To him the irritating man just seemed to suck the life out of the room, gruffly, "I am satisfied that we can survive the winter and..." Hearing the loud knock on the mahogany door, his voice trailed off. He nodded to Ketil.

Appearing from the shadows, Ketil went to the door and announced loudly, "The Bishop of Beverley's cleric, to see the king."

Immediately lifting the hood of his green cape to cover his head, Wulfstan eyed the portly man warily.

The cleric waddled into the room. Ungainly bowing to King Anlaf, his voice whined, "Majesty, I have most important information for your cause." Not waiting to be asked, he gushed, "The night before last, King Athelstan visited the Christian House of God at Beverley."

His lip curling, Wulfstan felt the hairs on the back of his neck rise. With every fibre of his being he felt that something was wrong.

Surprised, Anlaf sat forward.

Wulfstan's voice droned, "The old church of Beverley has been sacked many times by your ancestors, Majesty. The priests killed and virgin nuns carried off into slavery." Eyeing the cleric sharply, "The church is a ruin. Why would King Athelstan tarry there?"

Impatiently, Anlaf clenched his fist.

The cleric whined, "King Athelstan left a jewelled dagger on the altar. He swore to the church's patron saint, St John the Baptist, that if victory is his then he would rebuild the church to its former glory."

Frowning, Wulfstan demanded, "King Athelstan's army has slipped into the plains of Earlsness?"

"Yes."

"How do you know this? No one has visited that church for years."

Eyeing the man in the green cloak, the cleric could not stop a look of supreme delight passing over his face. He recognised Archbishop Wulfstan of Jorvic, in the enemies nest. Shrewdly, "I am the Bishop of Beverley's trusted aid," he added slyly, "your Grace." He felt almost overcome with his good fortune. This information would make him rich.

In the shadows, Ketil felt the tension in the room. He watched the archbishop carefully.

Wulfstan glared menacingly as he moved round the back of the tonsured man, his cloak billowed as he walked, "Why should we trust your information? What do you want?"

The cleric's eyelids narrowed deviously, "I have many expenses your Grace."

Wulfstan leaned in threateningly close, "How have you come by this information?"

Smiling confidently, "I have personally spoken to King Athelstan. My master bid me do it. Upon hearing that your fleet had been spotted off Scarborough, King Athelstan force marched his army from Mercia to Beverley. These last few days, I travelled with them."

Anlaf snarled, "You side with King Athelstan and dare to come here?"

"No, no Majesty. I only do as my master bids."

Anlaf's eyes glinted, "So, your master bid you to come here?"

"Err no. I thought you would reward good information."

Realising the man was a collaborator, out for as much gold as he could get, Anlaf had difficulty hiding his repugnance.

The cleric gushed smugly, "I had the consummate fortune your Majesty, to overhear the king order his Norwegian mercenaries to his presence. They are Egil and Thorulf Skalagrimsson. They command many men."

Grimly, Anlaf stared at the man, "I cannot abide disloyalty."

The cleric gulped. Stupidly ignoring the sense of foreboding coursing through his veins, he mumbled, "At least three hundred mercenaries." The Archbishop's voice, very close to his ear made him flinch.

Wulfstan snarled, "If you can turn against your own master, who obviously keeps you very well fed, then you could just as easily turn against our alliance for a coin or two."

Shaking his head, the cleric visibly paled, "No your Grace," he stuttered, "I am here to help you."

Glaring at him, Anlaf demanded, "Did you tell King Athelstan, where my armies are camped?"

"No, no Majesty. I would never do that!" His eyes looked away too quickly, betraying himself.

Every fibre of his being told him this man could not be trusted. Anlaf made up his mind, "You already know too much." Menacingly, "You cannot be allowed to live. It would endanger too many lives."

His eyes narrowing, Wulfstan silently unsheathed his dagger.

Barely able to comprehend the threat, the cleric stuttered, "But I am a man of God."

Wulfstan moved with lightning speed, slashing his blade through the monk's thick throat. Suddenly, blood violently sprayed out from the cleric's neck.

Blinking in surprise, Anlaf instinctively stood up pulling his dagger from its scabbard.

Shocked at the turn of events, Ketil stepped into the light.

With blood spitting from his mouth, the cleric grasped his own neck, trying to stop the fountain of blood gushing through his fingers. Gargling, he begged, "Help me! Help me!"

Breathing heavily, his hazel eyes horrified, Ketil stood rooted to the spot.

Shock suddenly hit the cleric's heart with a sudden excruciating pain. His glazing eyes slanted and his left fist clenched upwards in agony. He sank heavily to his knees. Gargling out a moan, he fell face first, thudding to the floor. He breathed no more.

Shocked silence filled the room.

Casually cleaning his blood soaked dagger on the dead man's back, Archbishop Wulfstan stepped elaborately over the body, swishing his green cape to avoid the blood. Checking the blade, he carefully replaced his knife into the scabbard hanging from his belt.

Stunned, Ketil looked down at the cleric.

Anlaf blinked, "Archbishop, you killed him."

His face indifferent, Wulfstan sneered, "God's work will be done." Raising his right hand, he piously made the sign of the cross over the man's corpse. He suddenly called out loudly, "Guards!"

Unable to speak, Ketil looked startled as two guards appeared from the doorway.

Eyeing them coldly, Wulfstan ordered theatrically, "Remove him."

Hurrying over they grabbed a foot each and quickly dragged the obese dead body away.

Rooted to the spot, Ketil watched the body as it was dragged past him, leaving a long trail of bright red blood running to the door. The dead clerics face battered into the stone steps as they heaved him, unceremoniously, out of sight.

Wulfstan poured two goblets of wine and carried one over to Anlaf. Ignoring the servant, he eyed the king. Thinking clearly, he knew that they needed to move their armies now, "Majesty, this miserable excuse for a man had no trouble finding you. What else does King Athelstan know?"

Nodding, Anlaf knew he was right. He blew a deep breath from his lips, "Spies are everywhere. They must know we are here."

Wulfstan looked irritated, "The element of surprise has been lost!"

His eyes glinted with disappointment, "Archbishop, they may know where each of my armies are."

Handing King Anlaf the wine, Wulfstan inclined his head to the side, "We need to warn the generals."

Anlaf beckoned Ketil, ordering, "Call the guard."

Loudly, "Guard!"

A tall man dressed in grey battle leathers entered bowing low. He showed no surprise to see the wide streak of blood. He stepped over it, "Majesty?"

Turning to the man, Anlaf ordered, "Send a message out to King Blacarri. Tell him to send for the Kings of the Alliance and ensure that they do not tarry. We must meet immediately for a council of war!"

"Yes Majesty." Turning the guard strode to the door.

75

The Council of War

Looking around the table from the shadows of the sparsely furnished room, Ketil's hazel eyes shone with excitement. In less than half a day King Black Arailt, Prince Ragnal, King Constantine and Prince Cellach, Ruardri of Moray, King Suibne, King Mailcoluim and Prince Duff, King Owain of Strathclyde, and the Welsh Kings, Hywel Dda, Wurgeat, Twdyrr and Idwal Foel, had arrived. They all settled into high back chairs as King Anlaf, and the Archbishop, strode in from the antechamber.

Anlaf took his seat at the head of the table.

The last to arrive, King Olaf strutted into the room wearing expensive new battle leathers and a purple cloak. He pulled up a high backed chair and glanced at the archbishop. This was his chance to impress Wulfstan, he smiled charmingly.

His black eyes hard, he did not deign to smile back. Instead he listened as King Anlaf explaining curtly the surprising turn of events.

His voice formal, "I King Black Arailt would speak."

Anlaf nodded, "Speak King Black Arailt."

"I say we move now. We know, from the spy, that King Athelstan is camped outside Beverley. If we move all our armies north west tonight to the town of Poclinton, we will have the high ground."

Over confidently, Olaf angrily interjected, "That is cowardice!" He slammed his fist on to the table beams. Many a goblet of wine wobbled. He spat out, "We have the greater force. I say attack him now, from the south!"

Flicking a sideways glance at his employer, Ketil raised one eyebrow.

Cellach and Ruardri looked at each other surprised at the outburst.

Eyeing his cousin, Blacarri slowly smiled but his pale grey eyes stayed hard, "I was speaking King Olaf and I had not finished. At the town of Poclinton there is good water and much of our reserves of food are stored there. The town is large enough to support us all, over winter if necessary."

Pushing his heavily carved wooden chair back across the floor noisily, Olaf stood up. Leaning on the table his deep blue eyes mocking, he baited, "Are you getting too old for war, Blacarri?"

Angrily, Anlaf glared at Olaf, his voice softly menacing, "If you cannot conduct yourself properly King Olaf, then leave my table. How dare you insult King Black Arailt?" Derisively, "In any case your suggestion to attack now from the south is ludicrous! Most of our army is camped in the west, at Richalle!"

Even the four dark haired Welsh Kings, looked at Olaf with disgust.

Visibly wincing, Olaf realised he had jumped in too quickly to belittle his cousin. He had not thought his plan through.

Watching him, Blacarri lent casually back in his chair sipping his wine. His eyes hard and threatening they never left Olaf. Coolly intimidating, "Please excuse my cousin generals. It is his first war."

Cellach and Ruardri sniggered, their young eyes flashing with amusement.

His grey eyes glinting, Blacarri added sarcastically, "He is so keen to blood his sword, he has forgotten where his army is."

All the men at the table burst out laughing.

Eyeing his employer with admiration, Ketil smiled.

A great booming laugh burst from Constantine.

Feeling his face turn crimson with embarrassment, Olaf glared at Blacarri threateningly.

Staring back at him, feeling completely in control, he waited for the men to quieten.

Chuckling Constantine placated, "Olaf my boy, sit down. We all know that you thirst for English blood. Listen to your cousin. King Black Arailt is a man of wisdom as well as strength."

His face red with embarrassment, Olaf huffily sat down again.

Constantine boomed, "To win a war King Olaf, you need both of your high Norse Gods skills, Thor the God of battle strength and Odin God of wisdom. Watch and learn from your cousin. He knows how to conduct himself at a Council of War."

Still angry, Anlaf stated harshly, looking directly at Olaf, "May I remind you all that this is a formal Council of War. Every man will have a chance to speak. King Black Arailt, please continue."

His hard threatening ice grey eyes stayed on Olaf for a moment longer, as he continued steadily, "As I was saying, Poclinton has the stores to support our entire armies, through the winter if necessary."

Dropping his head sullenly, Olaf listened.

Flexing the muscle in his immense forearm, Blacarri added, "It is my brother's opinion, that King Athelstan has knowledge of our current positions and possibly even the numbers of our individual forces."

Concern passed over many of their faces.

"If I were him I would divide and conquer. I believe he will split his militia, with a view to attack each of our armies separately in one day. If they manage to kill just a few of our generals, some of our armies may desert."

Suibne looked surprised, "Why not fight separately? We may win."

His voice booming, Constantine nodded, "I agree with Suibne."

Calmly, Blacarri faced them, "It is too risky to break our alliance."

Anlaf looked at his brother, "Blacarri is right." Turning to Constantine, "Father-in-law, you always said we needed to remain an alliance to win this war."

His topaz eyes glinted, "Of course you are right."

"And, it will undermine King Athelstan's leadership if he is wrong." Blacarri continued, "I recommend we send riders to Jarl Orm at Richalle, with orders to meet our armies at Poclinton tonight. Then we wait and rest before the battle." Taking in a deep breath, "King Athelstan will know that he cannot divide us. He already knows we have the superior force."

Frowning, Cellach's topaz eyes glinted, "We have no word on the size of King Athelstan's army. How do you know we have a superior force?"

Pushing his tanned hands through his long blonde hair, Suibne mumbled to himself, "We need more intelligence."

Looking up quickly, only Olaf's young ears heard him.

Confidently eyeing them, Blacarri commanded the room, "King Athelstan has been forced to use Norwegian mercenaries. This is an element that he will find difficult to control. He has been forced to do this because his army numbers are weak."

Respectfully, Cellach nodded, "I agree."

"I will send a message to offer the mercenaries gold to fight with us." Anlaf leaned back, "Without his mercenaries, King Athelstan is a dead man!"

Looking at his brother, Blacarri nodded, "While we wait at Poclinton, you can hazel a battle field of your choosing King Anlaf, ensuring that we have the high ground. If they do decide to fight now, we will be fresh and ready."

Cellach smiled, "It is a good strategy."

"Thank you." Blacarri nodded, "If his mercenaries do remain loyal to King Athelstan, he will attack within a day."

Looking quizzical, Cellach eyed him respectfully, "How do you know that?"

Self-assured, he shrugged, "His hand will be forced. He cannot risk his mercenaries changing allegiance in the future. His only chance will be a quick, decisive battle."

Archbishop Wulfstan, interjected wearisomely, "I will not

have time to summon our Northumbrian villagers. They bring up the rear in our battle formation."

Thoughtfully, Anlaf considered this, "We have the Norse Irish to form the shield wall. The Albans, Strathclyde and Welsh will form the column phalanx. The Gailgedhael men will, as always, have the honour of leading the vanguard."

Blacarri nodded confidently.

Tediously, Wulfstan drawled, "King Athelstan always uses the wedge formation as a shock tactic to break the first shield wall. He will place his mercenaries either side of his main army."

Anlaf eyed him resolutely, "I agree, your Grace. The Cumbrian militia will protect our flanks. We will win this battle!"

Blacarri inclined his head, "After the battle is over, all survivors should meet at the ships. Richalle is only three leagues south of Jorvic."

Dark haired King Twdyrr, asked curiously, "Why choose Richalle?"

"We trust them. Our ancestors have used this secret location for almost a century to moor our ships. They have barracks and store extra provisions for us. They have good lodgings for the men and horses." Smiling Blacarri added, "Ale, wine and food are also provided, for a price of course."

Anlaf nodded, "After we have defeated King Athelstan, the fleet will be made ready to leave immediately for Jorvic. I will claim my Northumbrian crown."

His fists clenching, Olaf looked up. His eyes filled with sullen jealousy. It was the first time that his cousin had admitted openly, that he wanted Jorvic for himself. His upper lip almost snarled.

Thoughtfully, Blacarri stated, "From Jorvic we will move south conquering any resistance." Confidently, "I have finished."

Anlaf smiled, "Thank you King Black Arailt. As ever your sound, level headed, military advice is much appreciated. King Olaf, you now have the floor."

Taken by surprise, Olaf did not expect to be given an opportunity to speak so soon. All of the men were looking at him. Suddenly, he felt nervous. Knowing he must offer an opinion or be regarded as indecisive he tried to think. But he had no real plan of his own. He had just wanted to belittle Blacarri. That had backfired but it was quickly getting worse. The men at the table were starting to smile with amusement at his obvious discomfort. Thinking quickly, he clutched at Suibne's words, "I think that we need more intelligence."

They all looked with surprise at him.

He stated the obvious, "We cannot trust the Bishop of Beverley's servant."

His hazel eyes glistening from the shadows, Ketil listened.

The tedium in the Archbishop's voice sounded almost sarcastic, "What do you suggest, King Olaf?"

He had everyone's attention. Knowing he had to regain their respect or any thoughts of a future Northumbrian kingdom for him would be forgotten. Full of bravado, he flicked back his blonde hair, "I suggest that I infiltrate King Athelstan's camp and find out what their actual force is."

The men in the room looked at him with impressed surprise.

Blacarri's left eyebrow raised up. He glanced sideways at Anlaf.

Anlaf's expression remained impassive, "This would be a very dangerous mission cousin. How will you get past their guard?"

Leaning forward, Olaf smiled confidently as an idea came to him, "I play the harp as good as any musician. I will disguise myself as a bard and offer to play for the king."

Wulfstan looked bemused, "So, King Olaf Sihtricsson is willing to step into the lion's den for his country!"

Eyeing him proudly, he puffed up his chest, "Archbishop, I would die for Northumbria!"

Wulfstan's black eyes glinted as they flicked towards King Anlaf to see his reaction.

Shrugging his shoulders, Anlaf decided to let him carry out his plot, "I agree with you King Olaf. We do need more intelligence. Attempt to infiltrate King Athelstan's camp and find out his numbers. Leave now and meet us at Poclinton later tonight. Let me know immediately on your return, what you have found out."

Standing up, Olaf adjusted his sword belt self-importantly. Flicking back his blonde hair he strutted from the room.

Watching him leave with slanted eyes, Wulfstan quietly stood up and followed him.

Blacarri shook his head. As the deep murmur of discussion filled the room, he got up and strode over to the table by Ketil, to pour himself a goblet of wine. His voice low, "The lad is heading for certain death."

Ketil nodded, "The archbishop just left as well. Do you want me to follow them?"

Shrugging his shoulders nonchalantly, "No, the archbishop has always hedged his bets. He will be dangling the carrot of Jorvic to the lad." Thoughtfully, "Ketil, I want you to consider sending Afrior to Richalle with the messengers tonight. It would be better for her to wait with the ships until after the battle."

A muscle tightened in Ketil's jaw. He did not want her to go but he knew it would be for the best. Richalle would be relatively safe for her and their unborn baby.

Walking hurriedly down the corridor, Archbishop Wulfstan called out wearisomely, "King Olaf, pray tarry a moment."

Surprised, he swung round smiling charmingly, "Your Grace."

His dark eyes slanting, he checked the corridor ensuring they were alone, "I must admit King Olaf, I am surprised that you are here."

His deep blue eyes blinked, "Why so eminence?"

Eyeing the lad, "I felt sure that with King Anlaf and his brothers out of Ath Cliath, you would make a bid for their throne."

Ambition intensified his gaze, he spat out, "Believe me I considered seizing Ath Cliath!" Taking a deep breath, "But this battle is my best chance, to prove to the Northumbrian Witan, that I am ready to take back my inheritance." His teeth gritted, "Jorvic will be mine again."

Moving his head slowly like a snake, Wulfstan bated, "There are other contenders."

His face hard, he hissed, "If Anlaf is killed on the battlefield, Blacarri will take Ath Cliath. Ragnal will support him. Then Jorvic will be mine!"

"So you pray for your cousin's death?"

"I pray that the throne of Jorvic is returned to me! It is my birth right!"

Inclining his head, he broodingly assessed the lad as hotheaded and reckless. Carefully choosing his words, "You are ambitious and eager like your father was. Let us first see if you return from the lion's den, before we decide if you will rule Jorvic."

"Oh, I will return Archbishop. My wife is pregnant with my first son. I vow I will take back Jorvic for him!" Turning angrily away from the archbishop, he strutted down the corridor towards the stables.

As he watched Olaf leave, his black eyes narrowed thoughtfully, he mumbled to himself, "You always seem to be in King Anlaf's or King Constantine's shadow. We will see if you can raise your face to the sun." His eyes slanted as he brushed back his lank hair, "Be careful though boy, you may get burned." He suddenly turned, his green cloak swished out behind him, as he strode back into the council of war.

7.6

Athelstan's Camp,
Beverley

The night was dark and cold. Only the army camp fires and a few flaming torches lit Olaf's path, as he strode confidently though the bustling rowdy camp. Carrying only a small harp, and dressed in his stable lad's worn out under sized clothes, he looked like a lowly bard. He had even darkened his hair with dirty cooking grease, leaving his nails filthy. Surprisingly, no one challenged him until he reached the king's tent.

The sentry, stood at the opening of the huge tent. Casually, he eyed the lad, "Who goes there?"

Flicking his cape hood off his head, Olaf bowed submissively, "Alfred, a musician to play for the king."

Gruffly, "Wait here."

Keeping his head bowed, Olaf's eyes flickered up. He watched the guard go into the tent. Feeling the warm air from the tent caress his face, his large blue eyes looked in wonder at the opulence of gold and coloured cloth in the tent. He realised that his own kingshalla, on Iona, looked more like a horse stable compared to this king's travelling marquee. He wondered what King Athelstan's palace was like. He imagined golden riches and fine tapestries.

The guard and a tall man dressed in dark grey battle leathers walked up to him.

Cardinal Dunstan looked over the unarmed lad, "What is your name?"

Bowing low, "I am called Alfred, milord."

"A good English name. Play something gentle on your harp.

The king is irritated tonight."

In the corner of the tent was a carved three legged stool. Walking over to it, Olaf sat down and began to play quiet gentle melodies. He watched and listened as King Athelstan, discussed with the Athelings his battle plan, his army numbers and even how their training was progressing. Wonder filled his eyes as he watched how the king carried himself. Athelstan did not need a crown to stand out as the king. He was imposing, dignified and had a commanding presence. He had a natural charismatic bearing. More importantly for his mission, Blacarri was right. They knew where each coalition army had been camped. They even knew the numbers of men and horses. They planned to split their forces and attack tomorrow.

Much, much later, carrying a silver coin with the image and insignia of ATHELSTAN REX, Olaf walked out of the camp. Most of the army were asleep around fires in the cold night air. Pulling his musty smelling cape closer around his shoulders, he climbed up onto his mount and rode north to Poclinton.

A few hours later, preening with supreme self-importance, Olaf reported to Anlaf, Blacarri and Archbishop Wulfstan, what he had heard, "I was so close to King Athelstan. If I had weapon I could have killed him myself."

From the shadows by the door, Ketil quietly observed them as they sat close to the crackling fire pit. King Olaf was still wearing his disguise. It surprised him how dark his hair looked greased back from his face. He could even smell the whiff of horse dung on his clothes. The king looked just like a castle servant.

Feeling curious of his rival, Anlaf asked too quickly, "What is he like?"

"King Athelstan is older than you but very strong. As tall as you I would say." Olaf motioned with his arms dramatically, "He has a massive upper body. His bearing is most," he searched for the word, "regal."

His face serious, Anlaf shrugged dismissively, "What did you find out?"

Animated by the thrill of his success his young blue eyes sparkled intensely, "Blacarri was right about everything."

Observing the lad, a muscle flickered in Wulfstan's jaw. He hated to admit it but the young king had done well.

Completely self-assured, Blacarri's pale grey eyes glinted with satisfaction as he lent back. His logical and instinctively strategic mind rarely let him down.

"They knew where Constantine and the Welsh were camped. They knew you and Blacarri were camped near the ferry point. They intend to split their forces and attack each of our armies tomorrow. The only thing they did not know about was our Norse contingent at Richalle."

His blonde eyebrows rising, Anlaf spoke quietly, "How big is King Athelstan's army?"

"There are at least one thousand English. King Athelstan boasted a few hundred mercenaries are also at his command."

Relief coursed through Anlaf's veins, "On the face of it we have the superior force, even with his mercenaries."

Leaning nearer to the fire pit to warm his hands, Olaf added, "Athelstan hopes more forces will arrive over the next few days. He spoke of several hundred more men press ganged from villages."

Frowning, Anlaf looked at Wulfstan, "This is a concern."

Tedium tinged his voice, "Majesty, it is only a matter of time before King Athelstan knows we have moved our army to Poclinton."

A smile played on his lips, "King Athelstan will know tomorrow."

Intrigued, Wulfstan's dark eyes glinted, "How?"

"King Blacarri and I left a parchment for his mercenaries, inviting them to join us at Poclinton."

Wulfstan eyed Blacarri, with an attempt at a wry smile, "Another of your strategies King Black Arailt?"

Coolly, he looked back at the archbishop shrugging his muscular shoulders before grinning.

Figuring their plan out, Olaf's mind filled with apprehension, "Then either the mercenaries will join us within the day, or Athelstan's entire force will arrive."

Determination shone in Blacarri's eyes, "If the mercenaries join us we have already won. If they do not join us, we still have the superior numbers. King Athelstan cannot risk his mercenaries changing sides. He will have no choice other than to fight now, before his reinforcements arrive."

Anlaf grinned confidently.

His eyes widening, Olaf nodded slowly, "You have complete control."

Blacarri stretched his muscular arms, "King Athelstan's forces will have already marched to our empty camps and they will need to march again to Poclinton."

Anlaf's grin deepened, "They will not be fresh for the battle."

Standing up, Archbishop Wulfstan stretched too, "An excellent and impressive strategy." He felt tired, "I suggest we get some rest." Eyeing King Olaf steadily, he decided to compliment him. Coldly, he assessed that it would keep the carrot of Jorvic dangling, "You did well King Olaf."

Nodding to him, Olaf lifted his chin the way King Athelstan had. Knowing that he had at last gained the respect of Archbishop Wulfstan, he strutted regally from the room.

Wulfstan's eyes narrowed thoughtfully as he watched him leave. Would he be a good king for Northumbria? Feeling his hackles on his neck rise, he looked up at King Anlaf's fiercely threatening stare. Bowing low, he quickly left the room.

The next day, as the sun shone at its highest zenith, Cardinal Dunstan watched, as each of King Athelstan's commanders, led their thwarted armies back into camp.

Furious that the plan had failed, King Athelstan strode angrily about his tent listening to his generals excuses.

Stood close to the tent entrance, Alfbert watched and

waited for orders.

Egil Skalagrimsson's heavy dark brows were even more furrowed than usual. His deep voice resonated through the tent, "The Norse coalition has moved all of their forces north west to Poclinton."

Athelstan demanded irritably, "How do you know this?"

Thorulf and the Athelings, watched Egil produce a role of parchment.

"This was left by King Anlaf, at Hesslport."

Surprised, Athelstan looked menacing, "What does the Norse king wish to tell me."

Egil smiled cheekily, "Nothing, Majesty." Amused, he added, "The parchment is addressed to me."

Taken aback, Athelstan threw a disenchanted look at Dunstan. Then, looking back at Egil, his deep blue eyes blazed, "What is written in the parchment?"

Steadily, "King Anlaf has asked me to join his army. In fact, he offers a fortune to any Norwegian mercenary who changes sides."

His voice coldly threatening, "What say you to this, Egil Skallagrimsson?"

Egil eyed King Athelstan, steadily, "If I wanted to change sides Majesty, I would have left by now." His eyes glinted greedily, "My mercenaries will fight for you but I expect you to better the Norse King's offer of payment."

Lifting his chin, Athelstan did not flinch, "Of course you do. I agree to the increased payment."

Confidently striding over to the fire tripod in the centre of the tent, Egil threw the parchment on to the embers. The edges of the parchment immediately blackened as the flames burst into life. His dark eyes glinted, "King Anlaf wrote that he will wait for us at the battlefield." Walking to the map table, he pointed with a thick finger, "Here at Brunnanburg."

Striding to the table, Athelstan's deep blue eyes glinted, "Brunnanburg?"

Deeply intellectual, Cardinal Dunstan recognised the area,

"This place is the shire of an ancient Celtic chief called Brundr. There is just one safe road in and out, Majesty."

His expression serious, Athelstan poured over the map, "Brunnanburg appears to be surrounded by the tidal marshes of Earlsness."

Egil looked up at the cardinal, "King Anlaf calls the battlefield Vin Moor. He says, to the east is the great woodland known to the Norse as Vin Forest."

Looking at the map, Dunstan pointed out the forest, "The local inhabitants call the forest Lund. To the west is Brunnan's beck, an ancient but much weakened river." He pointed to the long straight road on the map, "One thousand years ago a legion of Roman soldiers built a road through the heart of Brundr's land. We could use this road to march our men directly to the battlefield." His eyes shone, "This land is mystical and full of sacred healing springs. They were once dedicated to the Celtic Mother Goddess and were tended by Celtic priestesses. The Romans took the land and built small stone temples by the holy springs. They dedicated them to their goddess Diana. The local Celtic women adopted the Goddess and became her holy women. The descendants of the priestesses continue to tend the springs to this very day."

Prince Edmund spat out under his breath, "That is devil worship!"

Only Earl Ethelwine heard him. He stared warily at the cardinal.

His dark brows furrowing, Egil eyed the cardinal seriously, "How do you know this?"

"I study the history of religious sites and other religions. The Romans and their pantheon of gods have always fascinated me."

Athelstan looked taken aback. His voice hardened, "The women are misguided. They do not worship a deity, they worship a demon." He inclined his head suspiciously, "Have you visited these sites, Cardinal?"

Dunstan nodded, "Yes, Majesty. East of Brunnanburg there

is a natural spring hidden in a sanctuary of small trees and bushes." He smiled, "I once helped the women there, clear the spring of debris. It was a beautiful place. The spring still flows down a little rocky waterfall. There is an ancient temple that has fallen into decay. The local women now call the holy place, Lady's Well and the hill, Weondun."

Egil smiled as he translated, "Odin's Hill. My God will be pleased."

Edmund and Ethelwine eyed the king, watching his reaction.

King Athelstan looked perturbed. Deciding to ignore the heretical comments, he looked at the map, "King Anlaf and King Constantine are already there. They will of course take the high ground and split into their battle formation. The Norse always use a shield wall in battle."

Dunstan's eyes narrowed, "The Alban's always send in the Pict Gailgedhael as vanguard."

Egil's dark brows furrowed, "We have no choice but to approach the battle ground from the low ground. Archers and spear will have little effect until we reach higher ground."

His eyes icy in concentration, King Athelstan smiled, "I, of course, will lead the wedge formation. I will cut through the Gailgedhael ranks." Strongly, he ordered, "Egil, you will lead your mercenary vanguard taking the low ground. You will continue to decimate the Gailgedhael then protect our left flank by the river."

Egil nodded.

"Thorulf will lead my mid guard English infantry, taking the higher ground, protected on the right flank by the forest."

Thorulf nodded, his eyes glittering.

His wolf like eyebrows knitting, Egil shook his head, his voice booming, "Thorulf and I always fight together."

Excited, Thorulf smiled, his handsome face lighting up, "Egil I want this commission."

His dark eyebrow drooped over his right eye. He blinked gloomily at his younger brother, stubbornly, "No, we fight together."

Smiling, Thorulf stood tall, "Egil, I am ready. I want this commission."

Breathing out deeply his bushy eyebrows knitted. His dark eyes flashed towards the king. Bitterly disappointed, he nodded curtly.

Eyeing them regally, King Athelstan continued, "Guy of Warwick, will command the reserve infantry and protect the rear flank."

Dunstan looked up, "Sire, if Prince Edmund and Earl Ethelwine split the cavalry into two formations, we can attack both flanks."

Angrily, Prince Edmund's head jerked up as he eyed Cardinal Dunstan hostilely, "I will lead the cavalry, Cardinal! Earl Ethelwine will be under my command."

Striding up from his chair, Ethelwine sarcastically bated, "I will not take orders from a child."

"You will take orders from me for I will one day be your king!"

Ethelwine sneered, "Only a fool would say that in front of his Majesty!"

His face reddening, Edmund glanced warily at his brother.

Smirking at his cousin's embarrassment, Ethelwine scoffed, "What say you Majesty, to your brother's betrayal?"

Raising his chin, King Athelstan looked imperiously at them both for a moment. Turning to Ethelwine, forebodingly, "Crown Prince Edmund is quite right. God willing, he will be king after me."

The merest flicker of relief, that his brother had loyally defended him, swept Edmund's features before he swung round angrily to his cousin, "I am the Crown Prince!" His fists clenched, "Show me respect!"

Ethelwine provoked, "I am a prince too!"

As they continued to bicker, Athelstan looked at Dunstan frowning.

Seeing that the king was distracted, Egil looked at Thorulf, his voice low, "Brother, we always fight together."

Smiling, Thorulf leaned in towards Egil, his young handsome face excited, "Egil I am ready. I want a story to tell my wife when I get home."

He sounded so excited, Egil grinned indulgently. Placing his huge hand on Thorulf's shoulder, "I will compose our saga, Thorulf. Our battle deeds will be told throughout the ages."

Inclining his head, Dunstan whispered to King Athelstan, as Prince Edmund squared up to Earl Ethelwine, "You will not be able to control this from the thick of battle. You need to be seen and heard."

Sudden realisation hit him, that Dunstan was right. Furious, he roared angrily, "Silence!" The room uncomfortably hushed.

Ethelwine blinked guiltily.

Edmund continued to glare at Earl Ethelwine, his blue eyes glittering with anger.

Thorulf flicked his eyes warily to his brother.

From under his heavy hooded eyebrows, Egil watched the king impressively take command of the room.

His voice powerful, Athelstan eyed Earl Ethelwine, "Crown Prince Edmund commands the cavalry!" Threateningly, "If you disobey him and live," he paused for effect, "I will have your head and I will confiscate your lands."

Prince Edmund continued to eye Ethelwine hostilely

Bitterness jolted through Ethelwine's body as he looked away.

Continuing viciously, Athelstan spat out, "Sir Guy of Warwick will lead the wedge formation!"

Sat on the outskirts of the room, Sir Guy stood up. He looked tall and imposing in his black battle gear. His tawny eyes glistening, he looked momentarily taken aback. Suddenly realising the esteem bestowed on him, he bowed curtly, "You honour me, Majesty."

Eyeing Egil fiercely, King Athelstan clenched his teeth, "Egil Scallagrimsson, you will lead the mercenary vanguard taking the low ground, and Thorulf will lead my mid guard English infantry taking the higher ground."

Nodding, Egil spoke deeply, "I yield to your strategy, Sire."

Grinning with barely caged excitement, Thorulf bowed too.

"My cousin Aethelwold," he added sternly, "will command the reserve infantry and protect the rear flank."

Standing up from a chair, Aethelwold smiled and bowed, "Majesty, your will is my command."

Angrily, King Athelstan snarled, "I will command the battle field from the best view point!" Turning to his younger brother, "The cavalry will wait with me until I give the order." He eyed Ethelwine warningly, "Do not disobey my brother!"

Looking immensely jaded, Earl Ethelwine nodded curtly.

Edmund's chest expanded as he eyed his cousin stonily.

Dunstan smiled, "If Thorulf takes our archers and spear soldiers towards the mid guard on the high ground, they will split the traitor's ranks and we have a chance."

His blue eyes glinting, King Athelstan eyed each of his generals. His voice deepened as he clenched his fist, "We will grind their bones into the dirt."

Egil's melodic voice resonated around the room, "Odin's Hill is a fitting site for our great battle." He opened his immense arms, "This is an excellent omen. Our Gods will be pleased." Suddenly, he boomed out in verse:

"He, veteran of battles, Athelstan,
Bonded us like none other can,
With promise of riches great,
We sharpen our swords on whetstone weight.

Our Gods assemble on the headland,
To watch the battle they stand,
Their might and power true,
They will watch over you.

Let the raven and wolf beast,

Gather for a feast,
Not my body will they eat,
Only traitors flesh they take as meat.

Our shield wall will stand fast,
Our enemies will not last,
Anlaf and the hoary traitor will fall,
When they hear the death raven call!

The pride of my house will swell,
Breath of my praise will tell,
For years to come the story,
Of the Thunderbolt's great victory!"

The room suddenly erupted with cheering. Even Alfbert joined in.

Smiling, Athelstan took off one of his many heavy gold jewelled finger rings and he passed it to Egil.

As he took the garnet ring, Egil's features changed to wolf-like avarice.

Athelstan's intelligent deep blue eyes glinted as he noted Egil's weakness.

Part 8

The Battle of Brunnanburg

8.1

Brunnanburg
12 November 937

In the distance the tips of the trees of Vin Forest looked every shade of red to autumn amber. Every few moments, a warrior from the men of the Isles ranks, thudded his sword hilt into his shield twice and roared out a deep battle cry, "Huh!" Every Viking there bellowed, "Huh!" in synchronisation with him. The sound was deafeningly glorious.

Stood at the top of the hill, wearing black battle leathers, King Anlaf looked down at the English army. His shoulder length blonde hair caught in the cold breeze. As he adjusted the straps of his black leather wrist guards, his bare golden tanned arms rippled with powerful muscle. Unruffled, his glinting blue eyes took in everything. His united army was almost double the size of the English forces and he had the high ground. Relaxed, he smiled feeling sure of victory.

The English stood at the bottom of the hill already in battle formation. Colourful banners and flags, held high by flag bearers, caught noisily on the breeze. They flaunted the emblems of all of the powerful English houses, that had assembled to do battle this day.

To Anlaf's left, Ragnal lifted his golden Hammer of Thor amulet out from his black leather chest armour. He kissed it before tucking it back in. Checking the position of his sword and three long knives against his leather breeches, his blue eyes hardened. Calmly, he picked up his war helmet from the ground and placed it on his head.

Leaving his own blonde head bare, Anlaf felt supremely

confident in his ability as a warrior. It showed in his bearing. Casually, he adjusted the position of his sword belt. Lifting his right hand behind his head, he checked the hilt of his axe position. Leather straps secured a specially constructed axe scabbard of stiff brown leather to his back. In the scabbard the hilt of his axe rested firmly up by his right ear. Picking up his round iron bossed shield, he stood tall. In front of him all his armies stood in battle formation. Ready to charge, all their kings and jarls stood at the front of their ranks of men waiting for his orders.

His topaz eyes sparkling with excitement, King Constantine of Alba stood coolly holding a battered old round shield.

Stood close to his father, Prince Cellach flexed his immense shoulders and smiled, "I see you have brought your lucky shield Da."

Nodding curtly, he looked towards the enemy, "Aye lad, this shield has protected me in many a battle."

Chuckling at the state of it, "How many times have you fixed up the wooden struts and painted it? There cannot be much of the original shield left now Da."

Eyeing his son fiercely, "It's still my lucky shield!"

His young topaz eyes twinkling with amusement, "Aye Da, that it is."

His eyes softened as he looked at his son, "Stay close to me in the battle son."

He chuckled, "Aye Da, I've got your back."

Constantine grinned fondly as he gazed towards the battle field.

Stood next to them listening to their banter, holding the saltire cross banner of Alba, Ruardri grinned and looked back behind him. The massive, mostly auburn haired army of Alba stood menacingly defiant, as another two crashing thuds of sword on shield and the Viking battle cry, "Huh!" filled the air.

Further away agitatedly, Olaf Sihtricsson placed a brand new shimmering war helmet on his head. It was a gift from Bethoc. Trying to hide his apprehension, he looked down at his hands feeling surprised at how much they trembled. Clenching his fists, he checked his weapons again.

Stood behind their king, the men of Iona eyed him cynically. Looking at each other, they raised their eyebrows as the king fiddled about with his weapons. They were originally Princess Bethoc's personal bodyguards and were immensely loyal to her. Since her marriage to King Olaf, they were now his personal army.

One man held Olaf's colourful banner. It depicted three golden interlocked knots of Valhalla on a field of green. Leaning in to the soldier next to him, he muttered derisively under his breath, "He won't last long!"

Next to the small army of Iona, the blue painted Gailgedhael Picts, stood menacingly eyeing the English.

Blacarri stood nonchalantly relaxed at the front of his men. Like his men, his own face and muscular upper body was painted with blue woad paint. His black leather breaches and boots felt comfortable. The wide leather belt, across his flat muscular stomach, carried his long sword and four long knives. Grinning, he picked up his shield. Above his head, the Gailgedhael banner carried his colours, the silver lion rampant on a woad blue field. The banner floated on the breeze. Turning to his right, he chuckled as Ketil checked his many weapons including the two knives in each boot and the two knives in each of his wrist guards, "Ketil you look like a mercenary."

His face and torso painted blue, Ketil grinned. His teeth shone white against his blue face. He glanced to his side, past the Gailgedhael army.

Their faces serious, Archbishop Wulfstan and Jarl Orm stood close together. Their two armies merged into one. Stood bereft of their house emblems both men wore dark battle gear. Only their bearing stood them out.

King Suibne stood in front of the mostly blonde haired men of the isles. He cheerfully smiled with excitement. His banner, depicting an embroidered black Norse drakkar on a blue sea, billowed on the cold breeze. He signalled and the man next to him, who slammed the hilt of his sword into his shield twice, and another thudding deep battle bellow sounded out from the Norse ranks. He roared it too, "Huh!"

The Welsh army was a mass of slightly shorter dark haired men. Lifting on the wind, high above their heads, their red dragon on a green field banner drifted proudly. The four dark haired Welsh kings looked steadily out at the enemy.

At the bottom of the hill, sat astride his horse, King Athelstan looked up at the massive Norse army. His deep blue eyes glinted through the eye slits of his bronze crowned war helmet. His emblem, a white dragon on a blood red field, flew from many banners.

On the king's left, his face impassive, Prince Edmund sat astride his sleek brown stallion. Looking to his side, he caught the eye of Earl Ethelwine, glaring irritably at him. Lifting his chin, Prince Edmund eyed him back imperiously.

Surprised to feel so uneasy, Ethelwine dropped his eyelids quickly.

Forty of his cavalry guard behind him and his main legions in front of him, King Athelstan turned to his right and looked into the pale grey eyes of Cardinal Dunstan. It felt uncomfortable not to be stood at the head of army, almost humiliating. Agitatedly, "I always lead the wedge formation."

Strongly holding his reins, breathing deeply through his nose, Dunstan warned, "Majesty, if you lead the charge, there will be no controlling the Athelings and the mercenaries. If they do not follow your strategy you could lose this war."

His face grim, "Cousin, I trust your council but not leading my army does not sit well with me!"

"Your Majesty has selected an excellent choice of man to substitute for you. Sir Guy of Warwick, insists on leading the point of the wedge and he has used your tactic. The first ten rows of men in the wedge are all experienced young warriors. All the edges and back of the wedge are made up of hardened veterans. Conscripted farm boys and peasants fill the middle."

Athelstan's eyes glinted as he looked over to the wedge formation. He knew that his shield bearer Alfbert was one of the veterans. Gruffly, "Good. The veterans will stop the peasants from deserting when they see how bad it gets." Lowering his voice, he barely breathed, "We are massively out numbered."

Looking up at the formidable number of Norse forces, Dunstan agreed, "This has to be the largest enemy foe our land has ever seen." He took in a deep breath, "Your royal person is needed here. You must remain in full view at all times. You are the only one strong enough to keep command of this battle."

The Norseman thudded his sword hilt into his shield again, their guttural battle taunt filled the air like a clap of thunder, "Huh!"

Even from where he was, Athelstan could see the youngsters in his army shifting uncomfortably at the sound. His deep blue eyes glinted. His voice deep, he ordered steadily, "Sound the charge."

Stood close to the king holding his shield, a young shield bearer trained by Alfbert, raised his right hand to his mouth and bellowed deeply, "Sound the charge!"

Suddenly, eight footmen to his left lifted long metal war horns to their lips and blared out the battle charge.

It took all of King Athelstan's skill to keep his skittish war horse still as he watched his army advance.

Yelling battle shouts, the massive wedge formation of men marched up the hill towards the Norse.

The Norse responded resoundingly, with deafening clashes of swords against their shields, and increased the speed of their chant to an intimidating crescendo, "Huh! Huh! Huh! Huh! Huh!"

Watching the English tramping up the hill, Anlaf calmly took out a beautifully decorated golden war horn from his belt. Lifting it to his lips, he blew strongly.

Hearing the war horn blast, the Gailgedhael vanguard looked to their king.

Quickly drawing his sword, Blacarri roared deeply as adrenalin pumped through his body, "Albanich!" At the head of his men, he charged down the hill.

With a sword in each hand, even Ketil had to race to keep up with him.

The thundering bellow of their battle cries filled the air as Blacarri's army ran after them yelling, "Albanich! Albanich!"

Within moments the two armies converged with a resounding clash, as weapons met shields. Suddenly, the yells of men, fighting for their lives, filled the air.

His arm muscles pumping and his ice grey eyes focused, Blacarri slashed his sword through muscle and flesh. The ground quickly turned slippery with blood and gore.

Almost immediately, from both sides, arrows were released indiscriminately. Soaring overhead like a black cloud they suddenly dropped. Men howled as metal arrow tips ripped through their flesh.

Focused on the roar of battle, barely aware of the arrows hissing past him, Blacarri hacked his way through men.

From atop his horse, King Athelstan watched the wedge formation start to break through the Gailgedhael army. Casually to Dunstan, "You really have to admire the Gailgedhael race. They have absolutely no fear."

Coldly watching the battle, Dunstan nodded silently.

Seeing his brother's army splitting apart, Anlaf blew on his war horn twice.

King Constantine, Prince Cellach and King Olaf led the Alban and Ionan forces charging down the hill.

Still carrying the banner of Alba, Ruardri roared, "Albanich!" as he hurtled towards the battle.

Observing the battle keenly, King Athelstan drawled, "Send in the mid guard, we need to gain the high ground."

Sucking in a deep breath, the shield bearer yelled at the

trumpet blowers, "Signal the mid guard to attack!"

Hearing the trumpets blast his signal, his excitement barely controlled, Thorulf Skallagrimsson bellowed, "Thor is with us!" Storming up the hill, he hacked through any man unfortunate enough to get in his way. Their blood ran in rivulets down his face. Behind him, his men followed. They screamed out their battle cries as they fought for their lives.

The trumpets blared again, signalling Egil's low guard to join the fray. As Egil led his own men on the opposite side of the hill, his dark brows furrowed. He felt a deep sense of foreboding for his brother. But this was no place for those thoughts. That could get you killed. Suddenly several auburn haired Alban warriors hurtled towards him. Pushing his thoughts aside, he yelled out his own battle cry "Odin!" as he concentrated on his blade.

Suddenly surrounded by fighting, Olaf lashed out. All his years of training stood him in good stead. Barely winded, he cut down man after man. Growling angrily, he hit out with everything he had, his sword, his shield boss, his fist. Time seemed to stand still as he fought man after man to survive.

Watching the battle, his blue eyes glinting, King Athelstan ordered deeply, "Cavalry make ready."

The young shield bearer bellowed, "Cavalry make ready!"

Curtly turning to Ethelwine, Prince Edmund commanded, "Lord Ethelwine take the low ground as ordered!"

Ethelwine barely nodded.

Kicking his heals into his horse's flanks, Prince Edmund ordered at the top of his voice, "Charge!" His horse shrieked loudly as he bolted into full gallop towards the high ground.

Twenty riders followed him, their horse's hooves pounding into the ground.

The rest of the cavalry followed Ethelwine, racing towards the low ground.

Watching the English cavalry thunder into the fray, King Anlaf lifted his war horn to his mouth. Feeling the cold metal on his lips he blew loudly.

The four dark haired Welsh kings and their armies, bellowed war cries as they charged into the melee. The sound of clashing steel and the thud of breaking shields intensified.

Hearing King Anlaf's war horn signal them, Archbishop Wulfstan and Jarl Orm lifted their swords high yelling, "Charge!" Their armies stormed down the hill.

Anlaf bellowed deeply, "Shield wall!" His Norse warriors closed ranks with a thud in front of him as they formed a human barricade.

Surging up the hill, the English wedge formation crushed into the Norse shield wall with a resounding slam, as shields battered shields. Men roared in frustration, for a moment the wall felt impenetrable. Trained well with their short swords and knives, the English slashed through small gaps in the shield wall.

As blades pierced flesh, some of Anlaf's men shrieked with agony as they suddenly dropped. Abruptly part of the Norse shield wall crumbled.

The English rushed through yelling loudly, "Athelstan! Athelstan"

Ragnal charged like a mad bear into the fray, yelling, "Valhalla!" His long sword tore into Sir Guy of Warwick's sword arm.

Sir Guy screamed. It was the sound of devastation. He felt his arm sever at the elbow. His hand still gripped his sword as it fell to the ground. Blood sprayed from the stump of his arm. The sudden loss of blood made his knees buckle under him. In shock he fell. He tried to get up but the veterans' at the back of the ranks, including Alfbert, pushed the English peasants forward. Under the weight of their feet crushing him, Sir Guy screamed in agony. The English army pushed forward over him. He felt his ribs break and excruciatingly pierce his lungs.

His face contorted in unbearable pain as he felt his heart burst. He did not feel the foot stamp into his head, pushing his face into the blood red mud. Death was a blessed release.

Suddenly surrounded by young fighting men, Anlaf swiftly pulled his long sword from its scabbard. Some of the enemy were little more than lads but he slew them all. Their faces wild, their eyes glazed in horror, as he struck each a death blow. There was no glory or honour in these kills. All of his opponents were inferior to his skill. But he knew that if only one of them got in a lucky blow, he would be dead. There was no room for mercy. As the battle raged around him, he saw several of his Jarls fall.

His teeth clenched, drenched in the warm blood that had just sprayed out of his opponents cut throat, Gilli wildly hacked down the enemy warriors.

Further down the hill, Anlaf glimpsed Blacarri and Ketil fighting savagely encircled by English warriors.

Archbishop Wulfstan's expression was pure hate as he drove his sword into one Mercian, then another, then another.

Scarface was further away, closer to the men of Alba. His eyes glinted in concentration as a huge man charged at him. He was obviously one of the Norwegian mercenaries fighting for the English. Scarface ducked the sword blow aimed at his head.

Close to him, Prince Cellach lunged forward ramming his sword into the chest of the mercenary.

Shocked by the blow, Thorulf Skalagrimsson fell to his knees clutching his sword. His own blood gushed up through his wind pipe choking him. Burbling blood from his mouth ran down his chin and neck. His disbelieving eyes gently glazed over in death, as he slowly slumped to the ground.

Surprised to see Prince Cellach so close, Scarface shouted, "Save some for me."

Grimly, Cellach shouted back, "Our army is already less than a half its original size!" Shaking his head, he knew his voice was lost in the battle din.

Hearing only the battle cry behind him, Scarface turned and

lunged towards another warrior.

A short distance away, Earl Ethelwine's face twisted ugly with hate. Recognising Prince Cellach, he pulled his sword from its scabbard and silently dismounted from his horse.

As he looked around, he saw death and carnage. Cellach realised that there would be no glory this day. The well-equipped troops of King Athelstan's army were winning. He gasped, as he suddenly felt immense pain in his gut. Looking down, he saw the bloody tip of a sword blade protruding from his own abdomen. Shocked, he stood motionless as the sword was ferociously pulled back out of his body, and the deep scarlet stain of his own blood oozed from the wound. Turning round, already dazed from sudden loss of blood, he looked into the laughing face of Earl Ethelwine.

Grinning, brandishing his blood soaked sword, Earl Ethelwine eyed him arrogantly, "I looked for your red head, Prince Cellach." Sarcastically, "Stories will be told of how easy it was to kill you!"

Cellach's world seemed to slow in that moment. The battle din ebbed away from his mind. In his life, he had seen many battle injuries. He knew immediately, this was a death blow. He was dying. Lifting his chin proudly, he resigned himself to his fate. Slowly, he grinned, "Stories will be told of your cowardice Lord Ethelwine, for only a weakling coward would attack a man in the back."

Anger surging through Ethelwine, his eyes bulged as he charged at him.

Instinctively parrying the blow with his sword, Cellach swung his weapon in an arc with all the strength he had left. He felt his sword find flesh. It sank deep in to Ethelwine's flank.

Screaming in agony, Ethelwine grabbed at his side, as blood spurted from the deep gash above his hip. He pulled back for a moment, looking down at the crimson stain running down his thigh.

"You scream like a girl." Amused, Cellach chuckled, "Just like your wife did when I made love to her." Sinking to his knees, the light went out in his eyes and his heart stopped beating.

His face contorted with rage and pain, Ethelwine attacked Cellach's torso with a frenzy of stabbing strikes.

His eyes glazed over in death, Prince Cellach felt none of the resounding blows to his body.

Moments later, exhausted from his furious assault, Ethelwine moaned in agony. He suddenly realised, he had lost a lot of blood. The pain from his wound pierced through the red mist of his anger. Sinking onto his knees, holding his side, he looked around. His horse was still close by. His face turning ashen with the loss of blood, he used his sword to help him stand. Stumbling to his horse, he hooked his foot into the stirrup. Groaning out in pain, he mounted up. Turning his horse towards the king he rode away.

Cellach's body lay slumped in death. Deep gaping gashes open to the bone oozed out the last of his blood.

From the higher ground, Anlaf helplessly watched the death of his brother-in-law. It had happened so quickly, there was nothing he could have done. Hearing a high pitched battle cry close to him, Anlaf suddenly turned. An English lad carrying a curved farming cutting scythe ran at him. Swerving round on instinct, swinging his long sword high in an arch with both hands, Anlaf removed the boys head in one wide killing blow. The slash was so clean, the boys head flew through the air. As blood spurted out of his decapitated neck, his thin body sank to the ground. Watching the end of such a young life, for the briefest of moments, Anlaf's blue eyes glinted with regret. Hearing the hiss of a spear before he saw it, Anlaf ducked. It missed him by a Valkyries breath. Turning, he locked eyes with another Englishman. He was very different to the peasant lad. He was obviously much older, an experienced warrior of the English rear guard, placed at the back to stop the new young soldiers from running away.

Alfbert eyed the blonde Viking. Drawing his sword, he advanced.

Anlaf and the massive Englishman circled each other,

weighing each other up, as steam in the chilly November air vaporised off their battle heated bodies.

Alfbert always kept his dark silver grey hair tied back. He proudly carried deep facial and body scars from previous battles, like tributes of war. Dark, silver grey downy hair covered his thick muscular arms, down to the large fleshy fingers that held the hilt of his shimmering steel sword. His small brown eyes glinted in the sunlight. They were exactly the same colour of his leather breeches and waist coat.

Carefully observing the veteran, Anlaf could just see his gritted blackened teeth through the man's dark grisly beard. His deep blue eyes met the battle hardened brown eyes of the Englishman. Both knowing that one of them would die this day, neither flinched. They were both men of war. Flexing his muscles, Anlaf smiled to himself, at last a worthy opponent. He brandished his blood soaked sword with a flourish. Puffing up his huge chest, he nodded to the warrior.

They spoke no words. They did not need to bait each other. They both sensed that this would be a good fight. Suddenly it began. The two men lunged at each other, swords clashing heavily as they fought, parrying blows trying to gain the advantage.

Adrenaline coursed through Anlaf's body, powerfully affecting his senses.

Alfbert grunted as he smashed blow after brutal blow with his shorter sword. There was no skill in his style. He just relied on his immense strength and his wild, violent, continual attack.

Instinctively reading the warrior's body movements, Anlaf parried each attack. Forced to defend, his two hands clenched tightly around his decorated sword pommel, he felt each clanging strike. The continual savage onslaught from the Englishman astounded him. The man was immensely strong.

Eventually, Alfbert broke off his attack.

Breathing heavily, they circled each other weighing each other up.

Suddenly, Alfbert charged bellowing loudly. Sheer frustration made him careless as he savagely tried to hack at the Viking's body.

Skilfully side-stepping the hulking man, just avoiding the point of the blade, Anlaf gasped at the near miss.

Alfbert was a lot more agile than he looked. Throwing his body around, he brought his sword defensively across his body. His feet steadied firmly on the ground, bracing himself as the Viking attacked.

Using the inertia of his side step, still holding his sword in both hands, Anlaf used all of his strength to bring his sword down on to the warrior's body.

Defending himself well, Alfbert blocked the blow with his sword.

He grunted heavily as his sword met the Englishman's sword. It scraped fiercely down the length of the shimmering blade, to the hilt, making a shower of sparks fly into the air. The two sword hilts met and locked, the blades crossed. The two men battled with all of their strength trying to shove each other off balance.

Growling like an animal, spittle flying out of his black mouth, Alfbertht suddenly head butted the Viking through the V of the two locked swords.

Blood oozing from his forehead, stunned and almost knocked senseless, Anlaf dropped his sword. Staggering, he felt himself fall backwards onto the decapitated carcass of his previous opponent.

Sensing victory, Alfbert lunged at him.

Instinctively, Anlaf kicked out fiercely with both of his long muscular legs. Hearing the snap and crack of ribs as his boots made contact with the Englishman's chest, he desperately felt for his knife. It was gone.

Severely winded, stumbling backwards, Alfbert immediately coughed up frothy blood. His chest in agony, he made one last supreme effort. He slashed downwards with his long sword. The tip of his sword found flesh.

Watching the veteran stagger backwards away from him, Anlaf felt a searing pain in his left thigh. Gritting his teeth against it, in one fluid movement, he pulled his knees into his chest rocking backwards. Using all of the muscular power in his stomach, he flipped himself up on to his two feet.

His dark eyes widening, Alfbert braced himself.

Landing squarely, Anlaf reached up with both hands grabbing the hilt of his axe. Using the momentum of his landing, he expertly un-housed the axe and brought it over his right shoulder. Releasing it, he watched it fly, rotating through the air, towards the Englishman's face.

Mesmerised by the whoosh, whoosh, whoosh sound, as the axe flew towards him, Alfbert only had time to whisper his wife's name, "Elspeth." The axe blade struck him straight between his eyes, splitting his face and skull in two halves. He died in that instance, his body sinking to the ground.

Exhausted, Anlaf immediately dropped to a crouched position. His eyes darted around, expecting another opponent to take up the Englishman's attack. Quickly picking up his long sword, he looked around the battlefield. He was surprised to see that the main battle had moved a distance away from where he was. This gave him time to assess the situation. Men were still fighting. He could just see Ketil, Blacarri, Ragnal and Gilli. They were almost to the auburn leaved forested side of the gently sloping hill. Frowning with disappointment and weariness, he realised that it was over. All around him, his men lay dead. Their corpse's grotesquely distorted, brutalised with spears and arrows still jutting from their lifeless bodies. Cold realisation hit him like a punch to the stomach. The coalition had lost. He had lost.

The surviving Celts and Cumbrians were already running away from the battlefield. The blood crazed Mercian cavalry pursued them.

The Albans were still fighting. Their forces were still a few hundred men.

Grief enraged, King Constantine carried the body of Prince

Cellach. Tears streamed down his face as he looked down upon his son's battered dead body.

Olaf, Murdock and Ruardri circled Constantine, fighting off any English soldiers who approached them.

Grimacing with pain and disappointment, Anlaf stood up. He still could not believe that they had lost. Now, all that mattered was the survival of the men that were left. It was time to leave while they still could. Taking the beautifully decorated war horn from his belt, he blew the retreat.

Watching the battle, Cardinal Dunstan smiled, "The enemy are retreating, Majesty."

Through the slits of his war helmet satisfaction filled King Athelstan's deep blue eyes, "Excellent Cardinal."

"Our merciful Lord favours you again, Majesty."

Blood oozing from his wound, Lord Ethelwine crouched over his horse's neck, barely able to ride. His face was ashen with pain. He cantered up to his cousin, groaning, "Athelstan, help me!"

His eyes hard, Cardinal Dunstan ordered, "Take Lord Ethelwine to the physician!"

Two footmen ran to his assistance.

Eyeing his cousin Ethelwine coldly, Athelstan felt fleeting concern for his younger brother's safety. He turned to Dunstan, "Order the cavalry back."

Surprised, Dunstan looked at him quizzically, "Forgive me Sire. I do not understand. Surely the cavalry will rout the enemy out and finish them off."

His honey flanked stallion moved impatiently under him, "I will protect Prince Edmund, Cardinal."

"Of course Majesty, forgive me." Nodding obediently, Dunstan ordered loudly, "Sound the cavalry to fall back."

The young shield bearer ordered at the top of his voice, "Sound the cavalry to fall back!"

Eight trumpets blared out the call.

Prince Edmund and the Mercian generals, obediently

turned their mounts.

Imperiously, Athelstan drawled, "Our mercenaries will rout out the traitors."

Dunstan grinned, "Congratulations Majesty you have the victory."

His deep blue eyes glinting through the slits of his war helmet, King Athelstan nodded. Looking down at his new shield bearer, he demanded, "If any royalty are captured bring them to me alive. Order our mercenaries to rout and kill the rest."

The lad bowed, "Yes, Majesty."

"We leave for Beverley."

Anlaf watched King Athelstan's Mercian legion ride south away from the battlefield. He could just see his brother Blacarri, signalling his men to head to the autumnal forest. He frowned as a barrage of arrows flew through the air towards them. He saw Ketil fall.

Blacarri saw him fall too. Above the battle din, he yelled gutturally, "No!" He tried to turn back to reach Ketil, but Ragnal and Gilli grabbed him and dragged him away.

Anlaf gasped in a mouthful of air as deep regret filled him. He watched Ragnal and Gilli half forcibly haul Blacarri towards the forest. He felt sure he saw Scarface running towards dense thicket and the cover of Vin Forest, he whispered, "May Odin and Thor protect you." Looking up to the heavens, Anlaf asked the Gods, "Let them make it to the ships." Deciding to get his axe, he stood up. Taking a step towards the Englishman's corpse, he winced in pain, "Hammer of Thor!" Pulling back the blood soaked ripped leather of his breeches, he could see that his thigh wound was deep. White inner flesh protruded out from the deep gash but at least the blood loss was slow. Ripping a piece of clean material from the inside of his tunic, he tied it around his wound. He winced as he stemmed the flow of blood. Looking back towards the veteran's corpse, he limped over to him. Indifferently, he pulled his axe out of the Englishman's head and wiped the man's blood and brains on to the grass. Loudly to himself, "This is over." Deftly swinging the axe over his right shoulder, he re-housed it into the leather axe scabbard, "We have got to get back to the ships." Shaking his head at the prospect, "Why didn't I plan an escape?" No one, least of all himself, had expected the great alliance to lose. Grimly, he whispered, "The English always hunt down their enemies for days. I need to get moving. It won't get dark for another two hours." Making his way as quickly as he could over hundreds of mangled dead men, he slipped downhill, in blood and gore, until he got to the cover of orange tipped trees and thicket. Checking to see if he was being followed, he looked back. For a moment, he felt shock at the dreadful sight before him. The hill ran red with blood and carnage. Spears and arrows stuck out of men's bodies. Many horses had fallen, some still screamed in agony as they tried to get up. A thousand, perhaps nearer two thousand men had died this day. He was one of the lucky ones. Looking up, he could already see the dark wings of scavenging ravens, circling on air thermals above the battlefield. They had always filled him with disgust, or was it a sense of foreboding? Quickly moving away through the bushes and juniper trees, he began to smell the sweet perfume of the vegetation. He whispered, "Thanks be to Thor." No one had seen him escape the field of battle. Suddenly hearing movement, coming towards him from the thicket of bushes on his left, he ducked down. Silently, he drew his sword. Every nerve in his body alert, he waited.

The End

About The Author

Charmaine Mainwaring

My name is Charmaine Mainwaring and 'Raven' is my first novel.

I was inspired to write this story led historical fiction after first becoming fascinated by the historic Battle of Brunanburgh, which took place in 937AD. I avidly read everything I could find including Anglo Saxon Chronicles, Irish Annals and the Doomsday book.

As I continued my research lead historical characters, in the build up to the great battle, came back to life in my mind. History told of the coalition of the Sub-kings of Britain, who extraordinarily and dramatically stood together, against High King Athelstan of England.

As I began to layer my novel with the build up to the battle, detailing the rivalry, jealousy, ambition and love of the nobility, I found myself musing on the lives of the resourceful common people, who were fighting to live in these tumultuous times.

Amidst this unfolding drama, the women in my novel each have surprising resilience, strength and captivating fortitude. None more so than beautiful Celtic shield maiden, Lady Rafyn.

Some of my spare time has been spent visiting locations in my novel, researching sword fighting and martial arts. I have studied battle formations and siege warfare, as well as 10th century Viking ship navigation and harbour sites.

I have loved writing this novel and I hope you enjoy reading it. Please look out for the follow up book in this series, called;

The Raven and the Wolf

Books In This Series

Raven

An action charged, story led, historical series, set in the 10th century. Telling the tale of the dramatic fight for power between the diverse sub-kingdoms of Britain and Ireland.

Interlaced with true historical characters are fictional characters, that breathe true life into this immersive past.

Raven

It is 934AD. King Athelstan has succeeded in uniting Wessex, Mercia and Kent, calling them his England. Mounting a vicious campaign in the north and west of Britain, Athelstan becomes High King of Britain.

Increasingly weakened by heavy taxes, the sub-kings plot a great alliance against England. To succeed, they need to secure the support of the Norse Vikings of Ireland. The King of Alba must give a gift to the Norse king, so precious, it will break his heart to give it.

The Norse navy, led by King Anlaf of Ath Cliath and King Blacarri of Mann, is immense and it's warriors are formidable. However, war is expensive and the Norse need gold. To this end, King Blacarri launches a slave raid in Northumbria. There, he meets the beautiful but elusive shield-maiden, Lady Rafyn. A master of two sword fighting, she will be forced to save her honour.

It is King Anlaf, King Blacarri and their rival cousin Olaf Sihtricsson's, destiny to fight with the Great Alliance, against the English at the violent battle of Brunnanburg. Their army is massive and they have the high ground but will they succeed against High King Athelstan?

The Raven And The Wolf

In the uneasy aftermath of the great battle of Brunnanburg, defeated King Anlaf of the Norse, escapes the battlefield. As the English army hunts down any enemy survivors, Anlaf is found close to death by elegant Lady Rafyn.

King Olaf has survived and escapes with King Constantine of Alba. Will the throne of Iona be enough for Olaf's unceasing ambition to reign again in Jorvic and Northumbria?

Blacarri is torn between the guilt of betraying his dead wife and his longing for Lady Rafyn. Can he reconcile his growing love for the elusive beauty?

Proud of her heritage and status, and a formidable master of two sword fighting, Lady Rafyn will need every ounce of her fearless courage to escape him.

Printed in Great Britain
by Amazon

11080259R00234